EQUAL AFFECTIONS

ALSO BY DAVID LEAVITT

Family Dancing (stories)

The Lost Language of Cranes

EQUAL
AFFECTIONS

David Leavitt

A NOVEL

WEIDENFELD & NICOLSON

New York

Published by Weidenfeld & Nicolson, New York
A Division of Wheatland Corporation
841 Broadway
New York, New York 10003-4793

Published in Canada by General Publishing Company, Ltd.

Lines from W. H. Auden's poem "The More Loving One," © 1957 by W. H. Auden,
from W. H. Auden: Collected poems, edited by Edward Mendelson, © 1976 by
Edward Mendelson, William Meredith, and Monroe Spears, executors of the
estate of W. H. Auden, are used by permission of Random House, Inc.

Permission is granted by Alan S. Honig & Company to reprint lyrics from "Aldonza,"
words by Joe Darion, music by Mitch Leigh, copyright © 1965, Helena Music Company
and Andrew Scott, Inc.

Library of Congress Cataloging-in-Publication Data

Leavitt, David, 1961–
Equal affections.

I. Title.
PS3562.E2618E64   1989   813'.54   88-14411
ISBN   1-55584-202-X

Manufactured in the United States of America

This book is printed on acid-free paper.

Designed by Irving Perkins Associates

First Edition

1   3   5   7   9   10   8   6   4   2

For John Leavitt and Emily Leavitt

ACKNOWLEDGMENTS

I OWE a debt of gratitude to Jill Ciment, for some specific and essential suggestions; John Herman, for acute editing; Andrew Wylie, Deborah Karl, and Susan Schorr, for support beyond the call of professional duty; and especially Gary Glickman, for endurance and faith even when I was at my most unbearable.

If equal affection cannot be,
Let the more loving one be me.

—W. H. AUDEN, *"The More Loving One"*

PART ONE

T HE FIRST TIME Louise thought she was dying she called Danny and April to the side of her hospital bed and said, "Listen, kids, there's something I want to say to you both." April, who had just turned sixteen, shook out her long hair and said, "Oh, Mom, come on!" but Danny knew to stay quiet.

"No, I'm serious," Louise said. "Now I know I've done some things you haven't liked, like not letting you go to that concert, April, because it was too late, or Danny, not letting you go see *Rosemary's Baby*. But you have to understand, I had my reasons. Just remember as you get older, everyone is somebody's child, but only some people are somebody's mother." She reached to rearrange her pillow, inadvertently pulling the IV tube taut against her arm. "Oh, damn it," she said, "Nat, can you help me with this goddamned bed, I can never get it right."

From where he sat in the vinyl corner armchair, grading papers, Nat bounded up; he felt most useful when operating machinery. He cracked his fingers and began to manipulate the buttons on the bed's control panel. "A little higher," Louise said as the bed shifted and whirred. "Now a little lower."

"Mom," April said, "I know that being a mother is hard, I know that."

"Well, sometimes you've acted like you resent me, sweetheart, and I just couldn't bear it if—"

3

"But I understand! You have to make decisions which are good for us, even if we don't like them. I've always understood that." She took her mother's hand and said, "I love you, Mom," and both of them, quite suddenly, started to cry. "Well, I guess I just wanted to say I love you too, sweetheart," Louise said. "I had to get it off my chest, that's all. Danny, can you hand me a kleenex?" She blew her nose. Emotions, in her case, usually expressed themselves in a digestive or respiratory manner. She was forty-four years old.

But as it turned out, she wasn't dying. The disease was to travel along its serpentine route for nine more years, without Louise having to think again that she was dying. Illness moved into their house like an elderly aunt in a back bedroom. It lived with them; it sat at the kitchen table with them; it became ordinary.

Still, there was, from then on, for each of them, a dividing line, a before and after. Certain indestructible details bore into their long-term memories. For Louise it was the morning shower when she first felt the lump in her breast; for Nat the piece of pink notepaper on which the department secretary had written, "Call Mrs. Cooper immediately"; for April the surprising silence of the house when she got home from school that day and found no one was home. And for Danny it was when he got called away from Mr. Weston's class—they were doing American Indians—and in the school office the secretary said, "Danny, your dad called to say your mom won't be able to pick you up for your dentist's appointment, your sister's coming." April arrived at the appointed time, driving Louise's car, and Danny knew something was seriously wrong. April had had her license only two weeks; under normal circumstances she was not allowed to drive Louise's car.

"Don't get us in a crash!" Danny said as they pulled out of the school parking lot, and April said, "Will you relax? I got ninety-eight on my test, I know what I'm doing." He never understood why she chose the middle of traffic to tell him, but April was given to rash and impractical strategies. "Danny," she said, "Mommy had to go to the hospital today. You see, she found a lump in her breast, and they have to take it out, but it's probably nothing, nothing to worry about." And before he could say anything, before he could think of a question or beg for reassurance, she herself had burst into a fit of weeping so hard that her hands shook and the car veered onto the shoulder. "April, don't drive now!" Danny said. "Pull over!" "I'm fine!" April screamed. "I'm fine!"

Control would never be her strong point. A long time later, when Danny told her he was gay, her answer was, "Well, Danny, all I can say is, you'd better tell Mom and Dad tonight, because if you don't, I just know I won't be able to help telling them myself." Almost apologetically she said this, as if her actions were entirely determined by demons switching circuits in her brain. The best she could do, it seemed, was offer a little advance warning.

———

THE SECOND TIME Louise thought she was dying was altogether different. A somber, muddled moment; there were to be no pronouncements, no bedside offerings. She was sitting with Danny in the lunchroom of Neiman-Marcus, watching him eat a sandwich called the Towering Pagoda—neatly quartered stacks of toast, bacon, turkey, and water chestnut, speared with orientalized decorative toothpicks. It was the end of August. Nat was away; April was away. The last afternoons of summer sizzled toward increasingly early sunsets, each one bringing the flip of the calendar one day closer. All around them people were battling incipient end-of-season nostalgia with back-to-school shopping, new clothes, course catalogues, and white sales, but Danny and Louise, as every year, seemed somehow to have been left behind by all the activity, their feet frozen in the regretful muck, the sodden dregs of a summer passed over too quickly, not sufficiently appreciated or enjoyed. Nat always managed to get a business trip this time of year, some chatting to a corporation and a few quick fucks at the Inter-Continental Marriott Sheraton Hilton Comfort Inn. (Louise's joke.) And April too was somehow always away; even better than Nat, she had managed to disengage herself from the calendar altogether, to find a way of living and working entirely outside seasonal time clocks. So it was just Louise and Danny, as usual, at the end of August, eating at the Neiman-Marcus lunchroom together as they never had before and never would again, and Louise, for the second time in her life, thinking she was dying. This time she had known better than to share with anyone the lump, the biopsy, the barium, the upside-down

5

machine, and the phone call she would make in the morning to find out the results. Danny, slumped in his chair, bit lethargically into his Towering Pagoda, as if to say, nothing will make this time better. Around them ice clinked in the iced tea glasses of rich-looking women, there was the soothing sound of low voices discussing diets, televised infidelities, the ailments of the wives of the world's richest men.

AS IT TURNED OUT, though, she was to be spared again. "Good news!" said the doctor over the phone. Still sick, but not dying. Danny, despite protests, went to eleventh grade. Nat came home. She was fifty-three years old.

ONCE, when Danny was home visiting, he went with his mother to a knitting shop. They walked together along the sun-brightened sidewalks of California Avenue, past the Fine Arts Theatre, Round Table Pizza, La Caniche Pet Shoppe, Country Sun Natural Foods. Louise was wearing baby-blue jeans, ladies' jeans, with flowers on the hips, and a fuzzy yellow cardigan sweater. "You know, Danny," she said, "most people say being old is so tough, but as I get older, I think more and more, being old is great. You relax, you don't worry so much about things, you don't have to work so hard. And best of all, you know so much you didn't know when you were young."

"Mom," Danny said, "don't be ridiculous. You're not old."

"And the discounts! At movies, on buses. I can't tell you how much I'm enjoying the discounts."

"You don't deserve them," Danny said, and throwing his hand out hit her hard, on the forearm. Instantly a bruise bloomed—red pigment spreading fast under her skin.

"Oh, I hit you!" he said.

She shrugged. "It's nothing," she said. "Just subcutaneous bleeding."

Just! In his clumsiness he reached out to take her arm and inadvertently struck her again. "Danny!" she said. Another red welt, the size of a half-dollar, burst under the skin of her wrist. "Careful now." Neatly she tugged down her sleeve. "I'm sorry," he said. But she said, "Oh, it's nothing. I get these all the time."

They went to the knitting store. It was a dusty place, full of pattern magazines and wall nooks crammed with skeins of yarn arranged according to the color spectrum. At a big elementary school table women sat working long pink needles, drinking coffee, thumbing through magazines. She joined the circle; even though the women were strangers, they spoke together intimately, in low tones. Louise was looking for an outfit to make for a friend's soon-to-be-born grandchild—since a couple of years ago she had stopped mentioning hope for one of her own—leafing through photographs of yellow sweater jumpers, booties, elegant gray suits for little boys, hats patterned with ducks. She rolled up her sleeves, revealing two delicate, freckled forearms alarmingly patterned with dark red spirals and circles, splotches of blood, like army camouflage clothing. She was sixty-one years old.

———————

A S   A   C H I L D , Danny was shy and careful, at least where his mother was concerned. Once, when he was about six, alarmed by the photographs of cancerous lungs his teacher had shown in the antismoking slide show at school, he hid all her cigarettes. For an hour that evening she searched the house, looking under pillows and cushions, emptying trash cans, even going through the freezer. Then she noticed him watching her. "Did you do something with my cigarettes?" she said, and he stood before her, frozen.

"Tell me where they are," she said.

"It's bad to smoke."

"Tell me where the hell you put my cigarettes or you are going to get it, young man."

"It's bad to smoke."

"I'm warning you, Danny."

"In my play chest."

He followed her to his room, watched her open the chest and pull the toys out with unruly violence. "Jesus Christ," she said as she ripped the plastic off the carton of cigarettes, "don't any of your teachers give you lessons on minding your own business?" She stood hunched over, trying to light the cigarette in the hollow of her hand even as she chastised him, and he observed with some curiosity her struggles with the lighter. Finally the flame caught. She took a long, desperate puff, blew smoke toward the open window. As she smoked, she kept one arm crossed over her chest and would not look at him.

She smoked six more years, until the first surgery compelled her to quit. In the interval Danny never again touched the big red cartons Louise kept stacked in the cabinet beneath the napkin drawer, nor did he consider doing so. He had learned that afternoon what tender and desperate things his mother's needs were; that they could not be treated lightly, or cavalierly dispensed with. From then on, he knew, he would have to find more secret, undercover ways to protect her, ways that she would never recognize.

WHEN NAT COOPER was in sixth grade, in 1935, he wrote a paper called "My Family Tree Grows Nuts." "The Cooper Family Tree has few roots and many branches," his paper began, and it was true: ten daughters and two sons, born to Max and Nettie, who had come over from Lithuania. Max had to dress as a girl to escape the draft; he pretended he was his wife's sister. As for their own parents, sisters, brothers, aunts, uncles, no one seemed to know anything. Presumably they were all dead in the pogroms. Max and Nettie were a sapling, a single branch cut off and transplanted in a warmer climate. Their twelve children had forty-three children; their forty-three grandchildren had sixty more children. Very few of them were left in Boston, however, most having moved south, to Florida, or, like Nat, west.

When he was grown up, Danny liked to tell people he'd been born nowhere, in a town that might have been blown away to nothing as quickly as it had been scuffed up from nothing, a town only a year older than he was. The town was called Carrollton, California, and it was built on garbage; "bayfill" was the polite term. A few years before, there had been water there, fishes, perhaps dolphins. But the San Francisco Bay was being chemically narrowed, filled in. People slept and argued and cooked and had children on a sponge of reconstituted paper towels, kleenex, cigarette cartons, squeezed-out toothpaste tubes, dented cans. Years and years of human detritus, forged into earth. It had been Nat's idea to move there, even though, as Louise constantly reminded him, they could have easily afforded better. He liked the idea of Carrollton, the ideal of Carrollton, because it seemed like the future: biodegradable, recyclable, energy-efficient. But Carrollton's planners ran out of money; the hull of an unfinished shopping mall stood out against the multihued and pollutant horizon of the bay like an excavated dinosaur skeleton. The plumbing system broke down constantly; where there were cracks there were leaks, where there were leaks there were rats. Soon enough Louise had had enough of it, she put her foot down, and they moved Danny and April across the freeway, to the university town where Nat taught, and where the buildings had at least had a few generations to sink into the ground. Already Danny was imagining a day when, in a place far away, he'd describe this town to strangers, and the strangers would laugh.

Nat was a computer scientist. This was back in the days before the invention of the microchip, when computers were immense, ungainly things—nothing like the sleek devices of the present—and when athletic minds seemed to occupy only undernourished bodies. Nat was pale and bony, with hair the color of weak tomato soup. He didn't trim his beard, which was sometimes stuck with bits of food. He was, in his own way, a visionary, but a visionary crippled by a kind of myopia; he lived in a hive of machines, an endless corridor of technology, and seemed ignorant or confused when confronted with the goings-on of the rest of the world. ("He needs eyeglasses for his soul," Louise used to joke to her friends at the faculty wives' luncheons she hosted on occasional Tuesday afternoons.)

Still, Nat had a vision; he liked to describe to Danny and April how in twenty years the computers he worked would liberate men and women from the daily labors they now endured. "Just think," he'd tell his sister-in-law, Eleanor, who wrote a cooking column, "there'll be a day when you'll want to make something for your column and won't know what. So what'll you do? You'll punch some buttons, and lo and behold, a wonderful recipe will appear before you—along with all the ingredients, premeasured, many of them fabricated by the computer. For we'll be able to manufacture foods artificially by then. The breaking down of molecules and their re-formation in preselected forms;

even today we have some of the technology." Eleanor turned away, affronted at Nat's lack of respect for her creativity, his inability to accept her column as an expression of artistic intent. No one took Nat's fantasies of the future very seriously. She turned away from him, but years later—when the world, and particularly their region of it, really did change, and in some ways just as Nat predicted—she (and the rest of the family) were retroactively impressed, and proud of Nat, in spite of the fact that a stubborn attachment to a wrongheaded notion had long since waylaid him, leaving him sidetracked in his obscure labora-tory, while others carried the torch and changed the world forever. By then the future seemed no longer an endlessly postponed abstraction, but a present reality, a preordained age of electronic grace whose time had finally come.

———————

THE TOWN THEY LIVED IN was filled with refugees. The horrors of the urban East—the horrors they had left behind, for good—were everyone's favorite topic: broken air conditioners, stinking subways, rats in the kitchen. And there were other people, older, for whom the horrors stretched even farther east, across an ocean: old men who sat puffing cigars all day at the coffee bar, dressed in thick wool suits in spite of the heat; women with helmets of gray hair, in pale jeans and Birkenstocks, serving cookies at the Unitarian Church Disarma-ment Coalition meetings, their German accents almost undetectable, but there, in the back of the throat, behind the new language. Every adult Danny knew, growing up, craved the good karma, the endless sunshine, the clean air. And still they complained, as if under their tanned hides, inside their souls, factories were belching black smoke, and they had to let it out. "The third time I got mugged, I decided I'd had enough." "A naked woman, right there in the elevator!" And always, at the end, the familiar refrain: "Never again. Never again am I going back east."

East. In Danny's childhood the word had an incantatory quality, almost a voodoo about it. It was always "back east." No one ever referred to California as "back west." Which meant to Danny that in spite of all its terrors, that distant coast with its calmer seas was still the original, the inescapable mother culture, of which California would always be the mere rebellious child. Indeed, Louise seemed to view the East in much the same way she viewed her own dead mother, Anna— as a harrowing, exhausting, debilitating presence she had had to escape getting sucked up by.

Danny wondered if it was his destiny, from an early age, to crave that origin, that older place his parents had fled from. His father was extremely fond of pendulum theories, Danny grew up listening to pendulum theories. Therefore, it made perfect sense: The child of refugees, the child of pioneers, longs to return to the ancestral home-land, longs to go back. Anyway, he knew he didn't belong in California, among sun worshipers and Buddha worshipers. He glamorized the East, its crime and noise, grime and smokestacks. He tried to affect a New York accent. When he couldn't sleep, he pretended his bed was a plane, winging him over fields and mountains to the glittering, towered cities, the ivy-clung walls, the old, cold stone buildings with their carvings of gargoyles and monster heads. Muggings, rats, subways. Leather chairs in mildewed reading rooms. And, of course, seasons. He read books in which it snowed at Christmas. He grew furious about the fact that it never snowed at Christmas; he complained to his mother. Then one day it did snow. One day in seventeen years. Danny was eleven; he was walking to the school bus when the snowflakes started to fall. At first he couldn't believe it. He thought it was a dream. But the snow kept falling, and at the bus stop he and his friends formed it into balls, threw it into the air. They knew what to do with the snow. It was almost instinctive. All morning the snow came down outside the win-dows of Danny's classroom until the schoolyard was thinly blanketed in that still, white powder, fine as sand on a beach, but so much brighter. Again they played with it at recess; they played with it at lunch. Their shoes left muddy dents in the beach of snow. There was not really enough for a snowman, but some of them tried anyway. Then the sun came out again, and the snow started to melt. It was gone by evening.

———————

DANNY GREW UP; he went east. He followed his famous sister, April, all over the country and halted one February in New Haven. He never went back except for visits. And yet, even after he had been in and around New York almost eight years—he was twenty-seven by then, mired with his "life partner," Walter Bayles, in a morass of shared properties too extensive even to contemplate escaping—he still had trouble admitting the extent to which that original coast had become his home. Perhaps that was why he refused to trade in his California driver's license, that same license he'd been issued when he was sixteen, with that same ugly picture of his sixteen-year-old self—wild-grinned, big-nosed—staring out at him. Every four years the renewal arrived, forwarded by his mother. Every four years he thought about exchanging it and didn't exchange it. It was more than laziness; something in him refused to relinquish that single last link to his birthplace. Too many times a year he still had to zigzag across the continent to see his parents, back and forth, back and forth, until he could no longer tell which coast was his childhood and which his adulthood, which his past and which his future. After a while it was no longer back and forth; he was always traveling back, no matter which direction he was going in, carrying with him the heavy weights of attachment, throwing them down, binding himself to whatever land the plane's wheels had just touched down on.

There had been a time when the vastness of the country, the splitting of his life between the two coasts had seemed to him a metaphor for his destiny. Visiting his parents, he felt as if he were going back in time. He'd walk the wide avenues of the shopping mall and happen upon his twelve-year-old self, locking his bicycle to a streetlamp, crouched over, his fingers racing to get the combination. His real life—the apartment in New Haven, the nights he spent studying on the old Salvation Army sofa with Walter—seemed to shrink to nothing then, like the town in the musical April had starred in in high school, *Brigadoon*—a place which, once you slipped out of it, you might never have the chance to return to. But of course years had passed; he had made the journey more times than he could count. It seemed he had surpassed that spirit in himself which craved nothing more than to get out of there, that spirit which had flung him to New Haven, and cold, rainy nights in February, waiting to meet Walter when the law library closed, cold nights when, walking along the stone alleyways of the old stone campus, he breathed with gusto the moldering smell of the borrowed trench coat he was wearing, here, in this region of the world where people wore coats. That part of his youth was over. These days the winter made his bones ache. He kicked and swore at the once-beloved snow. Some days he wanted more than anything to return back west (yes, he had said it; those very words); other days the smell of warm smoke rising from subway grates renewed his old passion, as if the pendulum had ceased swinging in perfect arcs and were instead flying round and round in circles, tying itself in knots.

————

DANNY'S FANTASY: He is twelve years old, riding his bicycle to the shopping mall to read soap opera magazines. A sunny Saturday afternoon, the shopping mall quiet, full of women in tennis dresses and plump teenage girls, their stomachs bulging out of stiff jeans, who've come here in gangs to smoke. Danny is wearing shorts, a T-shirt emblazoned with the name of the university where his father teaches, tube socks, tennis shoes. His legs are brown from the sun, the hairs on them bleached white. He is locking his bicycle to a lamppost, unscrambling the combination with dirty fingers, when he feels the proximity of another body, feels warm breath against his hair. He turns around, still crouched, and a man is standing over him, a tall man in a gray leather jacket and jeans, a man who is at once a stranger and oddly, intimately familiar to him—but where from? A student of his father's? A cousin he doesn't remember? "Excuse me," the man says, "I'm sorry to bother you, I—" He puts his hands in his pockets, looks away. "Danny," he says. "Danny."

Danny's eyes suddenly fill with tears. His cheeks flush. He looks at the ground.

"I'm you," the stranger says. "I'm who you're going to become. And I've come to tell you—to reassure you—you're going to be fine, just fine."

The boy stands. Of course he sees it now, all of it—that face so familiar because it is his own, but also so strange, because he's never seen his own face before, not really, except in a mirror, and now he understands how mirrors distort, and where his legs will stretch to, and the awkward unpuzzling of his own face. Tears are welling in his eyes, and in his grown self's eyes as well, as the man bends down, leans over him, puts a hand on his shoulder. "All the things you're worried about," he says, "all the things that make you suffer—they're nothing. They're smoke. I know. And I've come so you'll know, so you won't have to suffer anymore. For you're going to be fine. You're going to leave California and head East, just like you hope. And you'll have love, Danny. I know you can't believe it now, I know everything you feel. You don't imagine anyone will ever love you, you can't conceive how anyone could love you. But someone will. You'll see."

The hand on his shoulder—larger, thickly veined, bristled with short brown hairs—is his own hand. Young Danny, crouching still by his bicycle, runs his own fingers over those long fingers, feels the warmth of the skin. One after the other he traces them, until his hand comes to rest on a slender silver ring. Slowly he strokes the ring's rounded outer edge; slowly he rotates it around the finger on which it's lodged. Under the ring is a perfect white band where the skin has not been touched by the sun.

THEY WERE Walter's hands, Danny understood later; man's hands. Bronze-colored, the skin tough and slightly dry, so that you could see the lines traced as if in white ash. Thick veins tunneling just under the surface of the skin; the nails blunt; a shiny gold Rolex slung low on the wrist, beneath the brilliant white cuff, the black sleeve.

At home Walter took off his shoes and dropped his pants almost as soon as he was in the door. The pants fell heavily and suddenly, the change and keys in his pockets made a crashing noise as they hit the ground. Then for an hour or so he wandered from room to room in black socks, boxer shorts, and suit jacket, seemingly incapable of undressing any further, biting into apples, tearing open bills and throwing the envelopes on the floor. Danny felt a strong impulse to shed the outfits of his working day as soon he was back; before he did anything else he was in a T-shirt and jeans and white socks, he was a boy again. He was usually home earlier than Walter; he didn't work as hard or as late. So when Walter stumbled through the door, Danny said hello and kissed him, he asked how his day had gone. Their suburban nights stretched out shapelessly, a series of corridors with many turns. They rarely ate formal meals, rarely ate together at all. Walter spooned reheated gourmet frozen dinners from tinfoil containers he had to balance on potholders to keep from getting his fingers burned. He walked as he ate; sometimes he sang. Danny tried to be more healthy. He made tuna melts on seven-grain bread. He vacuumed and cleaned the kitchen and ran the dishwasher. Usually at some point the VCR would switch on, but if it wasn't pornography they didn't concentrate; they entered and left, cleaned up or wrote out checks, catching snatches of whatever was on the television, asking each other who characters were, and what had happened to Joan Crawford, and what kind of creep was George Sanders playing now.

Usually by eleven-thirty a tiredness like a drug laid them out flat.

Sometimes the phone rang after midnight. Only one person ever called that late.

"Hi, it's me."

"Hi," Danny said.

"Did I wake you?"

"Well, um, I was in bed—"

"Oh, shit, I always forget—the life of a working stiff. Forgive me, Powderfoot. I live this crazy way, I go to sleep at four and get up at twelve. I forget some people are in bed before midnight."

"It's okay, it's okay—where are you?"

"Northampton. Staying with Ellie and Claire—remember them?"

"I think so—the black woman with the braids and the little blond woman?"

"Yup. The concert just ended half an hour ago. It went pretty well. Well, not exactly a huge audience, but they were enthusiastic. They seemed to like everything we played."

"So when are you arriving in the Big Apple?"

"A couple weeks, as planned. I hope you don't mind putting me up again. You don't, do you, Danny?"

"Of course not."

"And Walter doesn't mind?"

"No."

"Because I could stay with Eileen Herlihy in the East Village or else on this farm in Bucks County. But that's so far. And Eileen's apartment is small. And anyway, why would I stay with them when I could visit with my favorite baby brother?"

"April, you know you're welcome. You're always welcome."

"Good. I'm glad."

"I should be getting to sleep—"

"Oh, sure. Sorry. Forgive me. I'll hang up. Just wanted to say hi! And that I love you—"

"I love you too—"

Walter shuffled next to him. He didn't hear any of it; he slept with wax balls in his ears, a black visor pulled over his eyes. But Danny was awake again. He lay back, stretching his arms out, his hands behind his head. It was almost one o'clock.

———

APRIL WAS A SINGER of moderate fame. In the world of women's music her fame was much more than moderate, and she had made successful crossovers into the worlds of folk music and protest music as well. When they were growing up, she had a nylon-stringed guitar which she taught herself to play, and in the afternoons she sat in her room and practiced chord progressions from the Peter, Paul and Mary songbook. "Something's wrong," Nat remarked when he heard her singing. "No white girl is allowed to have a voice like that. Louise, were you fooling around with Nat King Cole behind my back?" In fact, like everyone, he was amazed by the deep voice coming out of April's slim throat. She was sixteen and Danny was seven, and she had taught him the harmony for "Leaving on a Jet Plane." While she played guitar, they sang together, and Nat, by the third chorus, had tears in his eyes. It meant a lot to him, so much that even years later, when they were home for Christmas, he still bugged them to sing "Leaving on a Jet Plane" for him. "Come on," he'd say, "you remember. Leavin' on that jet plane, don't know when I'll be back again?" "Oh, Dad," April would answer, tossing back her hair, laughing, "you're still tone-deaf." And though Danny was by that time completely tone-deaf as well, and April—well, April was famous; April was a star—they would sit down together and sing it, all the way to the end, April strumming her old nylon-stringed guitar as inexpertly as she had when she was sixteen. Nat hummed along as best he could, and smiled, transported by the music to some region of nostalgia probably reserved for fathers of grown children. Danny, on the other hand, had no room in himself for nostalgia, at least where April was concerned.

He had lived through much of her fame, in both senses. He had gone along for the ride. For two years he had watched as doors were opened to her, and loaves of seven-grain bread baked for her, and lovers procured for her in towns all over America. Most often they were smaller towns—Iowa City and Northampton and New Haven—places where rents were cheap and universities predominant; places where, in earnest, women who love other women had been for years collecting.

Danny met Walter in 1980, in a New Haven women's bar called Isadora's. They were the only two men in the bar, and both of them were tall, which was probably why they sought out each other's eyes above that crowded landscape of dancers, and why they smiled. Walter, who was at the time in his second year at Yale Law School, was in the company of seven women graduate students whose lesbianism, where not proclaimed, was at least incipient. They had invited him to come with them to the bar after April's concert, he told Danny later, while they lay huddled together in his twin bed, under blankets washed by his mother, and he had agreed to go on a lark; he'd never been to a lesbian bar before, and he wanted to see what one was like. And why had he gone to the *concert*? Danny asked. Well, Walter said, it wasn't because he was interested in women's music per se, but because he was a fan of April's earlier albums, her protest songs, which his older sister had liked to play when he was a teenager in the seventies. "This new stuff," he said, "it's okay. But it doesn't have the power, for me, of her early songs—'No More Vietnams,' say, or 'Gathering in the Fields.' I wish she'd played those. The new songs—oh, I don't know. Maybe because I'm not a woman, I can't understand them."

Of course, inevitably, he asked what Danny was doing at the concert, and Danny had to explain that he was April's brother as well as the assistant tour manager. "But I didn't see your name on the program," Walter said, after several minutes of bafflement and insistence that Danny was joking. "It was all women's names."

"Well," Danny said, "that's true," and explained that because it had been just a year since the release of April's landmark album, *Discovery*, there was a wariness among the women who worked on the tour, a feeling that the concerts had to be projects conceived by and for women alone. The inclusion of a man's name on an album cover or concert program, it had been decided, might be misperceived as a gesture toward patriarchy, putting or scaring off some women. Indeed, it was only because April *was* women's music that year that in the end he had been allowed to come along at all. She needed him. He was renamed, on the program, Danielle Powderfoot. (A joke of April's; someone had complained that Native American women were underrepresented.)

For two months that year they zigzagged across the country in a rackety Volkswagen bus: Danny, April, her three-woman band, Vickie, the stage manager, and Jennifer Cavanaugh, the sign language interpreter. They never stayed in motels, less for financial than for political reasons. Women all over the country welcomed them into their houses and fed them potluck suppers, after which they would lead them on tours of their cooperative printshops. In New Haven they were to have been given accommodation at a communal women's household on Eld Street. At least that had been the plan, until the heads of the household laid their eyes on Danny. "He can't stay here," remarked a woman with a beaky nose who appeared to be in a position of some authority. "I'm sorry, that's just the way it is."

"But wait," April said. "He's my brother, and anyway, he's gay."

They called a house meeting to decide the matter. April and Danny and the band waited in a kind of anteroom, Danny looking into his lap and trying to ignore the stares of Vickie, the stage manager—she was the most feminist of the bunch and had disapproved of his involvement from the start. He knew that somewhere across the house those serious, stern-faced women were debating. Things never came to a vote with them; they believed in consensus, which as far as Danny could tell meant arguing until one or another side got tired and gave up.

"Cheer up," Lourene, the drummer, said to comfort him, and handed Danny a piece of Bazooka bubble gum, which she was never without.

In the end the women decided that Danny could stay one night, but that after that he should try to find some other accommodations for the rest of the three-day layover.

"And I'll bet you were just hoping," Walter said, in that little narrow bed in the law students' dorm, "that you'd find a nice Yale boy with a room to share."

"I admit it," Danny said, and smiled. He was nineteen; April was twenty-eight. Up until that night he had thought he would never love anyone as much as he loved her. When she sang, he was rendered speechless with pride and pleasure and, being tone-deaf like his father, jealousy. He could not sing a note, would never be able to, and since he believed (as April believed) that there was nothing more noble or good in the world than song, no medium more powerful or lucid, he had decided that there was no reason he shouldn't be content to be April's flunky, her gofer, devoting his life to her work. As for April, she took Danny's devotion for granted. She was at her peak then—a brief span of years, as it turned out, when she could call herself a star.

Women all over the country worshiped her. In the Volkswagen bus she liked to read aloud the letters and poems they sent her. "Dear April: I'll bet you get a hundred letters like this, and are wondering why you should pay any attention to mine when there are so many, but I just want to say your record *Discovery* changed my life and that I love you and long to meet you someday. Sincerely, Jane Carmichael."

"Aww," the women in the van said. "That's sweet." And Lourene, taking the piece of cherry-colored notepaper from April's hand, added, "You know what I'd say if I got a letter like that? I'd say, 'Honey, what's your number? Lourene's coming to town.'"

April went on to the next one. "I was the woman with the red hair in Iowa City," she read. "You smiled. I sent you a note backstage. I waited two hours for you at that juice bar. What happened? Sonia." And April frowned. "Sonia," she said. "Sonia. I just don't remember a Sonia in Iowa City."

She had a lover then, a magazine editor in San Francisco who was brusque and businesslike and secretive. Her name was Fran.

Only with Fran, it seemed, could April lose control. Sometimes Danny noticed her, locked for hours in a phone booth, digging her fingers into her scalp while they fought through one enraging passion or another. Afterwards, in her dressing room, she brushed eyeliner into her lashes, combed out her hair, which was at that time cut very short, like a Dutch boy's. She wore silk pants, a shirt unbuttoned to the clavicle, a gold chain with a women's symbol dangling from it. "Do I look all right?" she said. Danny nodded. She tuned her guitar. Then she went and peered out at the vast stage rounding like a horizon to the dark clamor of the crowd. Someone signaled. She readied herself. One of Danny's jobs was to make sure everyone in the band was in position, that there were no last-minute string breaks, that Jennifer, the sign language interpreter, had the songs in the right order and was perched already on her stool. And then, finally, the familiar chant from the impatient audience: "Ap-ril, Ap-ril, Ap-ril." She blushed a little; though she should have been used to it, she still seemed bemused, perhaps even perplexed by the scale of her worship. Finally the announcer's voice: "Good evening, ladies and ladies." Laughter. Faint applause. More chanting. "Don't worry, we're not going to keep you waiting anymore." A final twitch at a string. A strand of hair brushed from her forehead. At that moment, always, Danny felt her cease to be aware of him. "And here is April Gold." A roar like nothing else, like the ocean, sounded, and he knew that he could call and call, and it would be as if he were standing halfway across the world, and she'd never hear him. April smiled, thrilled by the sound of applause. She strode out. Flowers flew onto the stage, and she raised her arms up to catch them, raised her face to the shower of petals. She was someone else now, and once she opened her mouth to sing, no one would be able to resist her.

At the bar, after the New Haven performance, April was swarmed by fans, all eager to touch her, to kiss her, to ask her to dance. There were hundreds of them, it seemed, and invisible in their maleness, Walter and Danny slipped out and went to a twenty-four-hour grocery store, where they bought chocolate chip cookies and Coca-Cola to take back to Walter's room. It was a cold night, and the old pipes knocked, making a sound like children playing with drums. Outside the little room with its diamond-shaped windows they could hear the occasional loud revels of drunken football players on their way home from parties, as well as a conversation about diaphragms being conducted by some serious-voiced young women down the hall. "Morons," Walter said, eating a chocolate chip cookie and settling himself into a tattered leather armchair. "Ingrates. Not an ounce of respect for other people's sleep." He had always been a good boy, much to his chagrin; in college, he explained, as he downed his Coca-Cola, he had wanted to be a writer, but his father had persuaded him to go to law school instead. As a result, he was full of a barely contained rage that seeped out at odd moments—a rage directed at himself, for not having followed his own instincts and become "some sort of artist," but instead having taken the cowardly path of law school. He understood, it seemed, which was the easy, unadventurous choice, and yet he had known no way of stopping himself from making it. In his oxford shirt and polished loafers he explained his self-loathing, and Danny nodded, pretending sympathy. Ironically, it was this good-boy side to Walter—the side of himself he himself despised—that Danny was falling in love with that evening, sitting across from him in that cold little room. His careful haircut, his neatly pared nails, the bleached underwear ironed and stacked on a shelf—all these things seemed to Danny the most erotic of details.

After they made love, Danny crept down dark medieval halls, looking for the bathroom, and, finding it, peed among stones, echoes, bits of hallway conversation, gargoyles, and old, old grass. All so far from that run-down house on Eld Street, where April was sleeping then, with who knew who, or how many.

———————

DANNY NEVER LEFT New Haven. The tour moved on north without him—to Middletown, Providence, finally Boston. It was midterm, and he made sure there was coffee for Walter when he got back from the library. Eventually, when it became clear he wasn't going to go home, Danny rented a small apartment and got a job serving falafel at a restaurant called Claire's Cornercopia. In the evening, after he'd finished studying, Walter would pick him up at the restaurant, and then they'd go together to the twenty-four-hour grocery store and buy more chocolate chip cookies and Coca-Cola and take them back to the apartment. Danny enrolled as a special student at Yale; the next year his transfer from Berkeley was accepted. And then, Walter's wonderful job offer; Danny's stint as a paralegal; his own acceptance at NYU Law. It all seemed far away to them now, those early days, for as is common with lawyers, they quickly grew rich, and their lives—linked together by some inevitability they were never called upon to name—changed considerably. They lived an hour from Manhattan now, in Gresham, New Jersey, the town Walter had grown up in, in a house twenty-five percent of which they actually owned. Each Wednesday night they attended the Gay Homeowners' Association meeting at the Unitarian church, and the pastor, Janice Ehrlich, asked, "Has anyone experienced any homophobia this week?" and Mady Kroger—it was always Mady Kroger—raised her hand. "This lady looked at me in the supermarket," she'd say, "and I knew she was thinking, 'What a dyke.'"

Sometimes April wrote Danny letters. "Dearest Powderfoot: We are in Iowa City. I sip orange juice at the Six-Twenty and think of you, leading your lovely suburban life. Have written a new song about Winnie Mandela which I think is pretty good. I'll be trying it out tomorrow. Remember, the tour hits the Big Apple in five weeks. Love to you—"

She never signed these letters, just as, when she called, she never announced herself. As if he wouldn't recognize, instantly, her breathy hello. She knew (and why shouldn't she?) that even through two thousand miles of telephone wire, he'd always hear her calling him: "Danny! Danny! Come sing! Daddy wants to hear us sing!"

———

APRIL WROTE A SONG that she dedicated to Walter and Danny. It was called "Living Together," and the lyrics went like this:

> After the years of the baths and the bars
> And the one-night stands in the backseats of cars
> And the nights we spent with so many different men
> It feels so good to come home to you again. . . .
>
> I'm so happy living together with you,
> There are apples on the table,
> Yes, I'm happy living together with you,
> And as long as I'm able,
> I'll take care of you. . . .
>
> Each Sunday morning through curtains of lace,
> The sun shines and draws lines of light on your face,
> We spread out the paper and lie in our bed
> And there's no place on earth I would go to instead. . . .
>
> Now the neighborhood ladies all whisper our names,
> Two young men so handsome, it seems such a shame,

One has a daughter, another a niece,
You smile and say, "Won't they give us some peace!"

I bring you aspirin when you've got the flu
And you make good omelets and great oyster stew,
And while you're at work in the city all day,
You know you'll come home to someone who will say,

I'm so happy living together with you,
All our friends join round the table,
I'm so happy living together with you,
And as long as I'm able,
I'll take care of you. . . .

The lace curtains were an invention; so was the oyster stew, and so were the neighborhood ladies, and so, for that matter, were the baths and the bars, neither Walter nor Danny having ever done more than dip his toes in the great, cold, clammy river of promiscuity. Still, when he listened to April singing that song on her live album, tears which went against his better judgment filled Danny's eyes. "Sometimes I think the most political thing a gay man or woman can do is to live openly with another gay man or woman," she said in her little introductory patter. "So I'd like to dedicate this song to my brother, Danny, and his lover, Walter, two men who took the brave step of letting the world know."

Have we? Danny wondered. They kept no secrets. The secretaries at Walter's office all knew who Danny was, and vice versa, but the wide-faced men who employed them seemed to look right through their presences in each other's lives, as if they were mere complications to each other, better left ignored. So: what it was really like, their living together. Danny and Walter are sitting in the living room on a Sunday afternoon, their pants around their ankles, having just watched *Bigger in Texas* on the VCR.

"Which of us is the man?" Walter asks casually.

Danny looks across the sofa at him. "Well," he says, "I suppose you're the man because you go to work every morning in the city."

"But you go to the city every morning too!" Walter says. "And you put in those three-pronged outlets. With your screwdrivers and wrenches and drills." He looks satisfied.

"I also do the dishes, wash the sheets, and make the beds. You take care of the garden."

"Yes. With a big hoe."

"You like boys with hairless chests and tight buttocks," Danny says, "and I like big hairy men with low swinging balls. Besides, I cook."

"You fuck *me*," Walter says.

Danny is quiet for a moment, trying to think of a retort to that seemingly definitive fact. "I stayed home all day last Monday and talked to your mother about Debbie Klinger's divorce," he says finally.

"Well, then, I guess you are the woman," Walter says. He aims the remote control at the VCR, commanding *Bigger in Texas* to rewind.

"I'd like to get that one with Brad Harden next time. What was it called? *Frat House Initiation?*"

"I think it was *Frat House Frenzy.*"

The VCR makes a thunking sound, indicating that it has finished rewinding. Walter opens the cabinet under the television and slips *Bigger in Texas* into its place in his library of pornographic videos. Danny scans the familiar titles: *Jock Itch, Boys Will Be Boys, Bigger and Bigger, Hot Oil, Grab a Hunk.* In the kitchen, something bought long ago in the gourmet deli section of King's defrosts; the sprinklers start their automatic cycle. They pull their pants up and move to opposite sides of the house, each thinking about order, contentment, each wondering whether they are sinking.

Later, when they go to bed, their bodies reach for each other instinctively in the dark; legs fold into legs, arms cross over chests in that trusted way which it seems no length of time can render ordinary. What they have given up, they have given up for the sake of settledness, and yet Danny is learning that settledness has its own complex weather. He'll be standing in the kitchen—say, he's washing dishes, his arms deep in the suds—when a prickling intimation of unease brushes up against him, lightly, like a hand on his shoulder. He lifts his gloved arms from the sink, looks around, sees only the microwave oven, the food processor, the coffeemaker, all the ordinary things shimmering in their ordinary ways. Outside the window is night. Across the house is Walter. So what is it, then, this sudden conviction that everything he imagined would stave off disaster is itself on the verge of blowing up?

Across the house is Walter. Danny envisions the hairs curling from the pale dent at the small of his back. A wave of repulsion passes swiftly through him, an astonishment that for so many years he has allowed himself such intimacy with another body. Is there any scar he hasn't fingered, any scab he hasn't scratched? He knows the dirt between Walter's toes, the food between his teeth.

He moves away from the sink, still half full of dishes, and sits down at the kitchen table. His mother, her hands bolts of fabric. What one loves can often be the most frightening. Sometimes it bears him aloft, this life, bears him higher and lighter than ever before. Then he and Walter are in a balloon, skimming the land, careering toward a cliff, waiting for that moment when suddenly the world will sink beneath them, and they will look down at the tiny details of the earth, and either they will keep flying or the balloon will fall, everything will fall. If Danny wrote a song, it's the weather he would write about: the stretches of calm, the hurricanes, how once it rained for years.

But of course he doesn't—he never will—write songs.

F OR ALMOST TWENTY YEARS now Louise had had cancer. The disease seemed to be following a haphazard progress of its own devising; it disappeared for years at a time, then emerged just when everyone seemed finally to have forgotten it. Louise mostly found the lumps when she was in the shower. Then she'd come into the kitchen, her hair wrapped in a towel, and Nat could tell from her face, could tell from how she held on to the coffeepot and breathed small breaths that in a few minutes she would be calling Dr. Sonnenberg's office. But first, a cup of coffee, slowly taken in. A deep breath. The familiar flipping of the address book, the rapid punch of telephone buttons. "Hello, Dorothy, it's Louise Cooper. Yes. Okay. I'm afraid I need to make an appointment."

Dorothy, Dr. Sonnenberg's nurse, always said something soothing then, something Nat—sitting at the kitchen table, pretending to read a cereal box—couldn't make out. "I know, I know," Louise said. "It had to happen sooner or later. I guess I was just hoping, that's all. Well, this afternoon will be fine. Yes. Just fine." She put the phone down, and Nat stood.

The waiting room was what bothered her the most, the waiting room with its fishtank and piles of old *House & Gardens*. The hours she spent there, thumbing through the magazines, watching to see if the albino catfish would ever emerge from the plastic shipwreck into which it had swum, were purgatory, she told April on the phone. It was the bubbles she concentrated on to keep sane, the bubbles rising steadily, one after the other, from the plastic diver standing amid the black glass gravel on the fishtank's floor.

Dr. Sonnenberg always smiled and embraced her in the examining room. "Well, Louise," he said, "I can't exactly say I'm happy to see you here." And then she smiled too, and they both almost laughed, Louise looking away at the window, blushing a little, like a girl whose date to the prom has just told her how beautiful she is.

But she always came out all right; she was lucky over and over again. A kind of cheerful hysteria took over then. "I just want to let you know," she'd call to tell Danny, "I'm having a little radiation, and it's working like a charm. Shrinking everything back down to size."

"Good," Danny would say, standing befuddled in the kitchen in his dress shirt and boxer shorts. "I'm glad, Mom."

"Just wanted to let you know," she'd say again.

———————

SHE WAS NOT ALONE in her illness. Doris Buxbaum's husband, Fred, for instance, just fine one day, spry as a daisy, then the next hooked up to a respirator, a tumor as large as a fist closing in on his kidneys. Nat's colleague Dale Wilson, getting along, getting by with occasional radiation: thin as a rail, but still alive. Leona from the hairdresser's, having just received the bad news, trying to open her eyes wide enough to absorb the dreadful panorama before her. Even Dr. Schoenberger, the wonderful surgeon who had saved her that first time; she never in a million years would have imagined that she would outlive Dr. Schoenberger.

It seemed to her the final twist of the knife that those who cured should also be stricken.

———————

AS FOR NAT, he endured; he did the best he could. He sat patiently with her in the waiting rooms when she needed him; he held her hand. Other times, when Danny was visiting, as he did at least every three months, he took over for Nat and went with her to the radiation center. There was a homey, almost suburban feel to the place, Louise greeting her friend Leona as casually as if they were passing in the supermarket.

Nat was having a hard time. A student had recently written on an anonymous course evaluation form that he was "an old fart." He had always thought of himself as being on the forefront of things, belonging to the future. Now the dean asked him every few weeks if he was thinking about early retirement.

What had happened was simple. He had been hopelessly sidetracked by a series of wrongheaded and visionary notions—all too arcanely theoretical for anyone outside his academic circle to understand—and, in laboring to perfect these notions, had let the true innovations of the day pass him by. Thus he had dismissed home computers as a trivial sideline; he was nowhere near the microchip, though it was being invented down the hall from him; he hadn't heard of Steven Jobs when the Macintosh was introduced. Trapped in his laboratory, he had become an old fart—an idea he didn't like, but what could he do? Knowing he was kept on only because of the ironies of tenure, his younger colleagues laughing at him behind his back, behaving cordially and eating lunch with him only because they knew he was now on the tenure committee and could have some influence on their futures. They were a far cry from his own youth. They wore Calvin Klein underwear and worked out at the gym on their lunch hours. Their futures were very brilliant. They commanded five-thousand-dollar fees for speaking engagements. Still, he accepted their flattery, their sycophantic attentions at lunch. He let them let him pick up the bill. And when it came time for the tenure committee meetings, he was generous. He voted yes more than no.

But slowly, as their power grew, these younger colleagues had taken a more condescending position. They suggested that he of all people would be best suited to teach the giant introductory undergraduate course "Applications of Computer Engineering"—nicknamed by the students Tools for Fools—because of his great knowledge, his sense of history. Previously the youngest, least experienced members of the department had taught that course, but now, it seemed, they were needed for other things. The graduate students were demanding the attentions of the young stars; *they* were the power of the department; they—not Nat—were the basis of its, and hence the university's, reputation. Indeed, no one was interested in what Nat had to say except for the woman from History of Science who was writing her dissertation on the origins of the discipline of computer science. Her name was Lillian Rubenstein-Kraft, and she was the provost's ex-wife; she had gone back for her Ph.D. after her children had left home. Each week Nat sat with her at the faculty club and told her stories about the "old days"—he was finally getting used to calling them the "old days"—and she took notes with that peculiar zeal that only historians can manage to muster. She was forty-seven, very thin and elegant-looking, with short-cropped, frosted hair and painted nails. She told him about her divorce, how ugly it had been, how Leon had hired a bastard lawyer and fought her every step of the way. "Trying to convince the judge that I'd been adulterous when he was popping every little coed who went by his office," she said. "Disgusting, if you ask me. But justice prevailed, I'm glad to say. The judge saw the truth, and granted in my favor. Mental cruelty, physical cruelty, adultery." She licked her lips with pleasure, listing his offenses, recalling how he had stood there, staring at his hands, when the judgment came down.

Her children had gone to high school with his children. Eric had had a crush on April all through their senior year, she admitted one afternoon at lunch. Now he was an attorney in Santa Barbara.

"He wouldn't get too far with her today," Nat said, and she blushed. Very little embarrassed Lillian, except when Nat alluded to his children's homosexuality. Then she never knew what to say.

Louise, of course, didn't like her, had never liked her, not even in the old days, when they had seen each other every week at faculty wives' lunches. "I have never trusted a woman with fingernails like that," she told Danny. "Not since I saw *The Women*." (She had seen it first when she was twenty, and it was still her favorite movie.)

In fact, Danny thought Lillian was a nice woman, though a little excessive in her enthusiasms, her desire to be approved of and taken seriously. She said she looked forward to completing her Ph.D. so that she could call herself Doctor. Danny remembered her younger son, Steve; he had been the star of the varsity tennis team in high school and had had beautiful, tapered legs. And now, Lillian told him, Steve was a ski pro; he lived with his wife, Cindy, in Sun Valley, Idaho. "I told him I saw you again, by the way," she said. "He says to give you a big hi."

"Tell him hi from me too," Danny said, embarrassed, wondering if Steve remembered the boy who used to stare at his legs in the warm first days of school, averting his eyes only when he heard the bell ringing for class to begin.

———————

S O M E T I M E S, when he was home in the summer, Danny followed his father around the garden, watching him crunch snails with his shoes.

"Your mother certainly was a wild one in her youth," Nat said to him once, out of the blue.

"Oh?"

"Yes, indeed. A firebrand. A real hot potato."

"How so?"

"Now, Danny, you know how Louise feels about being talked about behind her back."

"I guess I do." It was characteristic of his family to offer a secret, then retract it.

It was early August. Crickets shrieked in the warm garden; rotten guavas and persimmons littered the lawn. Through the kitchen window Danny could see his mother washing dishes, as well as the face of Dan Rather delivering the news on the little kitchen television. Nat picked up a hose and aimed it at some immense zucchini that were lounging in the vegetable garden. "It wasn't always easy for me," he said. "I realize your mother's having her hard time now, but I've had my share as well. Those first few years she made my life a living hell."

Danny listened to the water spraying against the zucchini's hard shells. The intimacy of Nat's tone embarrassed him—he wanted to run away from it—but he held fast, thinking he should hear him out.

"You've heard about Tommy Burns, I know. Unfortunately that was just the tip of the iceberg." He smiled. "Oh, well. Someday I'll tell you the whole story. Aha!" He put down his hose and aimed the flashlight anew. "So you thought you'd escaped, did you? Well, no such luck, my friend. See where he is, Danny? Right there." He spotlighted a snail in the grass, its slick body rearing from inside the fluted brown shell. "The snail carries his house on his back," Danny remembered a distant, teacherly voice telling him, and envisioned now what he had envisioned then: inside the snail shell a little bed, a light, a toilet.

"Gotcha, you bastard." Nat's shoe came down with a crack. He lifted it up again and aimed the flashlight at what remained. The snail had shattered like an egg; there were tiny bits of brown shell and a smear of what looked like snot. Strings of mucus stretched from the bottom of Nat's shoe to the grass.

"What I've told you tonight," Nat said, "please don't mention to your sister. For all I know, she'll write a song about it."

"Don't worry," Danny said. "I won't."

"Good." Once again Nat aimed the flashlight out onto the grass. "Someday I'll tell you the whole story," he said again, and Danny knew that by "someday" he meant when his mother was dead. He looked across the yard at the kitchen window. Dan Rather's tiny face was still in the television, but Louise had walked out of range.

ABOUT THEIR CHILDREN'S homosexuality Louise and Nat maintained an attitude of hopeful resignation. Their final words on the subject seemed to be: Well, there are worse things in the world. And there were worse things: Louise had friends whose children were heroin addicts, and gunrunners in Nicaragua, and—worst, unaccountably worst—friends whose children were dead, too many, it seemed, dead from car crashes, or drug overdoses, or strange cancers caused by drugs their mothers had innocently swallowed in their youth. She herself hadn't taken DES, thank God, but her sister, Eleanor, had, and now Joanne, Eleanor's daughter, was suffering the consequences: a hysterectomy at twenty-two, the difficulty of adoption, and of course the threat of cancer looming over her, as it would continue to loom over her until it was replaced by something worse or better or at least more definable, the reality of cancer, which, as Louise knew, at least carried with it a sort of reassurance of definition: You knew what you were fighting. In the long run, she recognized, she had been lucky.

She chose to ignore the articles Eleanor sent her, clipped from Sid's obscure psychology journals, knowing that it was only jealousy which made Eleanor pass them on: "The Recurrence of Homosexuality in Siblings: Nature or Nurture?" "Families with Multiple Homosexual Children: A Survey," "The Sissy-Boy and Tomboy-Girl Syndrome:

New Evidence Links Childhood Behavior to Homosexual Life-styles."
Always neat photocopies, with a note paper-clipped to the first page, a
note prefaced by a picture of a happy cook stirring a pot and the words
GOOD NEWS FROM ELEANOR FRIEDMAN'S KITCHEN. "Just thought
you'd be interested in reading this—E"; "Sid thought you might want
to take a look at this—E." But Louise had long since given up trying to
understand the complicated argot of the articles or following the elaborate graphs. She slipped them, unread, in a file marked "H" and tried to
remember the tragedies of Eleanor's own life: the cane and the brace,
and of course the daughter who would never have children and the son
she never heard from, working in a canning factory in Alaska, his mind
blown apart like a stereo speaker that has been played too loud. Eleanor's son, Markie, had killed the cat. He had put headphones on the
cat and turned the volume up full, and then he had put the cat in the
bathtub, and then he had put it in the microwave—all the result of a
bad trip, he said later, when she and Sid got home. I must remember
that, Louise always thought when the articles arrived in the mail; I
must remember how Eleanor found the cat and how she had to clean
the oven afterwards.

Anyway, Louise didn't really believe she had two homosexual children. She still didn't fully accept April's homosexuality. She remembered too vividly how in high school and college April had been so
boy-crazy, how she had fallen passionately for one boy or another up
until Joey Conway—the pinnacle of her passion. And Louise knew she
meant it; she knew. She recognized from her own youth the crazed look
in her daughter's eyes, the look that meant she would do anything for
this man, anything to continue having this man. As far as Louise could
tell, April's homosexuality was more political than anything else, a
phase she was going through, having more to do with feminism than
desire. (She chose to ignore the fact that this "phase" was now entering
its tenth year.) Danny was a different matter; with Danny there didn't
seem to be a choice. She had guessed it early on, not so much from
conventional symptoms—he didn't dress up in her clothes or play with
dolls or anything like that—but from the way he tended to resist certain
activities—sports and watching football games and working in the
garden with his father—in favor of standing in the kitchen with Louise,
just talking to her while she cooked, or sitting in his room, cutting
pictures of nature out of magazines and pasting them in a notebook he

had already filled with Magic Marker psychedelia. She smiled to think of these things afterwards; and anyway, at least he was safe now, he wasn't running around the underside of San Francisco, he was living with a responsible man in a neat house in a suburb. He was a lawyer. Successful. It could have been worse. He could have been in Alaska, working at a canning factory. He could have been dead.

Of course at first she had been angry; she had brought to bear upon him all the pent-up humiliations of her own youth. It had seemed to her on that afternoon so long ago that the world she had grown up in was infinitely less questioning, more rigid than the one her son was speaking to her from, and yet she had clung to those rigidities, understanding that their motives were to protect, to keep things stable, to keep the neighborhoods of neat houses and clean grocery stores from blowing apart altogether. "Don't you think it's selfish of you to just indulge every sexual whim you have?" she had said to him, but she meant something slightly different; she meant to ask him how he could bear to go against such a strong current as that of convention merely in order to indulge a desire, when it meant turning the world upside down, turning everything upside down. It seemed insane and also terribly brave. A bomb hovering over the neighborhood, about to drop, because this single pin, her son, had come loose. For she had grown up believing that the stability of the planet, its even orbit, required one to maintain one's own stability, one's own orbit, one's own quiet, steady attendance to the rules. She herself had been reckless, and even now, thirty years later, she was still feeling the aftershocks of that recklessness; she had irrevocably shaken the groundwork, weakened the foundation of her family. Of course she was hardly the only rebel in the world—she understood about trends—and still she believed that on some level this revelation, this news of Danny's, was the direct result of her own bad behavior, almost as if it had been transmitted through the blood.

At least that was what she believed the day Danny told them.

Within a few weeks she felt better. She remembered why she had left Boston, left her childhood, moved with Nat to California; it was precisely in order to find a freer, less rulebound world, a place where Nat could study his computers and not be frowned upon for it. And of course Danny was the child of that world, his own world, not hers. As for Nat, he was as always impregnable; he took the news in stride, seemed hardly to react to it. He had been bullied so much as a child—

bullied for nerdiness or being too smart or being too strange—that he lacked the armature of prejudice most fathers walked around in. It really hardly seemed to matter to him.

They had met one summer in their teens, when both their families had taken houses on an island called Little Nahant, just off the coast of Boston. Nat loved Louise instantly, or so he claimed; she hardly noticed him—he was nameless to her, that gawking, skinny boy with the sunken chest whose mother sometimes came over for coffee. Sometimes she waved to him on the way out to the beach, where there were better fish to fry. At sixteen he was a virgin; at sixteen she had been having an affair for two years with a forty-year-old Portuguese sailor who had only three fingers on his left hand. Of course the summer, which allowed her almost no opportunity to see Xavier, was difficult; she wrote him love letters and assuaged her loneliness in the company of Tommy Burns, the lifeguard. She loved Tommy Burns almost as much as Xavier, loved his WASPish good looks, his blond hair, his strong, chiseled face. ("Mark my words," Louise's mother had said, "the grandma was raped by a Cossack.") Tommy Burns picked her up sometimes in the early Nahant evenings, and they walked down to the shore to eat fried clam bellies. An extraordinarily intense memory for Louise: how hungry Tommy was, and how blue his eyes were, and how the grease from the clam bellies spread its grayness over the paper cone in which they were piled. He always ate half of her portion as well as his own. Afterwards, on the beach, they crawled behind the rocks to a well-worn place, and Tommy stood before her and took off his clothes. The first exhibitionist she had ever known, she realized later, but she didn't know the word yet. All she knew was that he liked to strip for her, and that by the time he was standing naked, his penis stood red and hard, nearly touching his navel. He had to be completely naked—not even his high school ring could stay on his finger—but Louise he kept fully clothed, so that he could hover and grunt over her schoolgirl's skirt and cashmere sweater, splendid in his maleness. She had to admit, she took as much pleasure in the contrast as he did; it was as if he were not a creature of this earth at all, but a god descended upon her, ravishing her through the prim clothes her mother had forced her to dress in, the very clothes her mother imagined might protect her. Afterwards, when she got home, there would be stains on the skirt, stains she sometimes touched her tongue to before she went to sleep.

She had hoped Tommy Burns might ask her to marry him. She would have willingly given Xavier up for Tommy Burns.

Then everything went topsy-turvy. Her little sister, Eleanor, contracted polio.

For weeks and weeks that hot summer they were quarantined. They could not leave the house, could not go to the beach or to the store. Only the horror of what was happening to her sister quelled Louise's rage, numbed her into a kind of complacency. She helped her mother as best she could, put aside concerns for her own health. Only at night she thought about Tommy Burns. He never called or sent messages. He was not a patient boy; probably he had found some other girl to stare at him. Many years later, when she went to a therapist for the first and only time in her life, Louise found herself talking about Eleanor and their strained, unhappy relationship, and at the same time talking about Tommy Burns and his exhibitionism. It was one of those revelatory moments so prized in therapy. "Do you think," Dr. Quinlan had said, "that you resent Eleanor now because she separated you and Tommy? And perhaps you feel guilty for that resentment—guilty because it wasn't Eleanor's fault? She was sick, and might have died, after all."

Louise had looked away. "I think," she said, "that I resent Eleanor because if she hadn't gotten sick, I never would've married Nat." And suddenly she laughed. For there, finally, there it was: the ugly bead of truth she'd come to search for.

Eleanor got sick, and Tommy disappeared. Everyone disappeared. Everyone, that is, except for Nat, the skinny boy whose mother had visited, coming by on his bicycle to shout news and gossip to her through the bathroom window. She always acted as if she couldn't care less, but then again she was also always there in the afternoon, sticking her head out the window as if she just happened to be staring at the dandelions. When Nat asked how things were or how Eleanor was feeling, she simply shrugged her shoulders and said, "Fine." She was always twisting a strand of yarn or a piece of string around her finger. "Fine," she'd say. Or: "Better today." But usually just "Fine."

When the quarantine finally ended, Nat put on a new shirt, bought flowers, and waited by the door, figuring that Louise would emerge from her entrapment full of lust and vigor and energy, that she would jump into his arms and smother him with kisses, so grateful that he alone had stuck with her, had kept in touch. But instead she headed immediately back to Boston, where Xavier, the Portuguese sailor, had just docked. Nat helped her mother clean up the sickroom.

The summer ended. They returned with their families to mainland houses. Nat and Louise dated each other when Xavier was away or she wanted to convince her own worried mother that she was seeing the right kind of boy. They didn't start having a proper love affair, in fact, until the following summer, and by that time she had returned to Little Nahant, this time without her family, to work as a waitress. Nat, in order to raise money for his tuition at Harvard, had to take a job at his cousin Sydney's garage, so several nights a week he rode his bicycle through pitch-black night along the little spit of road that connected the Nahants to the mainland, and then, in the early, early morning, with dawn just cracking, rode back.

Years later they went back.

It was the very end of April's *Discovery* tour, on which Danny had accompanied her, and they went to Boston to witness her glory. They had never been in Boston with the children before, so the afternoon before the concert, Nat, in a fit of nostalgic longing, rented a car and took his family on a drive along that legendary spit—a pencil of land just wide enough for a road, bounded by water on all sides—and Danny tried to imagine what it had felt like for his father, barreling along the flat road in utter blackness, knowing that in her little room Louise was waiting for him. The island hadn't changed much, they saw, from what Louise and Nat remembered; it was still crammed with small, brightly painted houses, and honky-tonk clam bars, and fat mothers surrounded by gaggles of children. Faithfully they drove to the address of the lemon-yellow house where Louise had been quarantined and, down the road, the lime-green house where Nat had lived and loved her. It was the very end of summer, that needy time when everything rots, and the stores fill up with notebook paper, shiny binders, pencil holders, lunchboxes. Along the sides of the roads sunburned children jumped up and down to keep the soles of their feet from getting burned. On the beaches women lay with their fists curled, desperate for last-chance tans. Louise stood on the beach, looking at the empty lifeguard stand. She was wearing a suit—a light gray skirt and matching jacket—which made her appear rather incongruous among the tanned, swimsuited children and mothers; rich; aloof. She had taken her shoes off and was rubbing her stockinged feet back and forth in the sand. She held a small, imperfect sand dollar between the heavily ringed fingers of her right hand. How strange she looked! Almost an icon, a statue, in her formal suit. The beachgoers walked around her. "Don't stare!" Danny heard a woman instruct her child, as if she already recognized in Louise herself forty years from now, coming back with that look of prior ownership and lived history, that look of someone who has been around long enough to have earned the privilege of remembering.

Danny and April and Nat stayed by the car; they waited till she was through.

Then she walked back to them, her shoes in her hand, sand in her hair. "That was the Goldbergs' house, wasn't it, Nat?" she said, pointing to a small, white, stuccoed cottage into which a little girl in flippers was just disappearing.

"Yes," Nat said. "I believe it was."

———

XAVIER, the sailor, died at sea in the Second World War. Tommy Burns went to war too, but he came back a decorated hero. His white teeth flashed across the Boston Common as he received his medal. (Louise, newly married to Nat, stood in the crowd, a scarf pulled over her hair to protect it against the rain, and clapped like crazy. He probably wouldn't have remembered her anyway. She was working in the shipyards then, welding battleships, while Nat got his degree.)

A long time later Tommy Burns became Tom Brent. He was Sheriff Bo Tucker on *The Wild Country*. Wednesday nights from eight to nine the television was reserved for Louise, until the series was canceled. Then for a while she'd see him every few weeks doing a guest spot on a cop show or sitcom. Then he disappeared for years from their television.

One afternoon in the late seventies Louise was riding the Exercycle, watching *Password*, when she started to scream. "What?" Nat cried, running in from the garden. "What's wrong?"

"It's him, Nat! It's Tommy Burns! Look!"

Well, he had come back—older now, but still handsome as ever. His hair was streaked gray. He was wearing a dark suit. He stood against a beige background, a tiny, white-shingled house cupped delicately in his hands.

Tommy Burns was the Allstate insurance man.

N O O N E C O U L D pinpoint exactly when April started singing. Danny thought he remembered, from when he was four or five, hearing her in her bedroom, strumming her little guitar in accompaniment to renditions of "Leaving on a Jet Plane," "Five Hundred Miles," "Puff the Magic Dragon." Later she performed these songs for their parents' friends after dinner parties, at the piano. "A regular Eydie Gorme!" Aunt Eleanor would say, tapping her cane against the floor. She pronounced "Gormé" without the Frenchified accent, so that it sounded like a word people might use on Mars.

They had moved a few years before to a neighborhood just off the university campus, officially called Redwood Park but affectionately known as the faculty ghetto. Every fourth Tuesday Louise hosted a tea for the department wives, and every third Wednesday Nat hosted a study break for the computer science graduate students. April and Danny usually hid in April's room during these festivities, emerging only when a sharp rap at the door demanded their appearances. Danny could hardly say which group he dreaded more. The department wives wore crisp little suits; they touched him with powdery hands and asked him how school was going. They knew too much about politeness. The graduate students didn't know enough about politeness. They didn't wash. They were vacant-eyed young men who pocketed their pens without capping them, so that their shirts were always bleeding blue at the heart. Danny did his duty, shook their slick hands, then ran back to April's room. It was a different world there. April's room had avocado-color carpeting; it had thick curtains patterned with immense, full-blown flowers and dangling with little white powder puffs. She burned incense on the desk. She had a drawer, and in it was a book called *Sexual Love* by Tamako Nagawachi, M.D., which she let Danny read all he wanted. (Danny particularly liked the chapter that described wet dreams and suggested extra-soft pajamas as a deterrent to them.) He liked to sniff the smell of April's room—a strong, female smell, which she made no effort to hide or cover. She did not believe in shaving under her arms, and she also didn't believe in deodorant, much to the chagrin of her mother, who insisted that excess underarm hair increased body odor in women—a scientific fact, she said. (April laughed at that.) She had long blond hair everywhere—on her head, under her arms, wisps of it on her legs. She made all her own dresses, mostly out of purple velvet embroidered with hearts and moons, and sometimes she wore bells around her ankles. In her room, on those occasional Tuesdays and Wednesdays when she and Danny joined together in resistance to social niceties, she liked to lie on her bed, a mirror propped in the crick of her elbow, and work the long blond hairs under her arms into tiny braids. Other afternoons, when she was feeling more industrious, she gave Danny guitar lessons. She showed him how to pick, and how to make A and D. He sat on her lap, her fingers pressing his smaller fingers down onto the frets, and while he strummed, they sang together: "Puff the Magic Dragon," "The Muffin Man," "Barbara Allen," "The Impossible Dream."

When she graduated from high school, April decided to attend the same university she'd grown up in. This was not because she liked the place, only because it was free; she could not justify her parents' shelling out money to finance an education that was going to be basically worthless, she said—a supposition on her part to which Nat responded with bitter invective, and Louise with a slight shrug of the shoulders, a chastising "Oh, now, April." Danny remembered moving April to her freshman dorm; it was about two minutes from their house. Still, April insisted on packing everything she owned, all her clothes, her records, her books and stuffed animals, lugging them out to the car, driving them down and unloading them in the little cinder-block room she was to share with one Vilma H. Pampas of Los

Angeles. Her freshman year, when Danny was nine, she joined a hunger strike on the lawn of the president's house, which was across the street. Nat became incensed. Louise, worried about malnutrition, filled the kitchen with bottles of orange juice and vitamin C, thus turning it into a refueling station for starving students. Twice a day April brought groups of protesters by the house, and Louise fed them vitamins and orange juice, as well as an occasional, surreptitious apple slice. Danny hid in the laundry room off the kitchen, watching the pallid students down their pills. Why was it that they had to fast while he could eat? he asked April, who explained that she and her friends were protesting the firing of a popular professor who was being denied justice. Danny couldn't figure out the connection between these two conditions: Was he, in eating, aiding in the denial of justice? Must he fast as well? Worried, he wolfed down an entire package of Oreos while reading the backs of the empty orange juice containers. Fasting for a day was impossible for him to imagine.

It didn't stop there. All through Danny's childhood, it seemed, April was demanding that their family, for political reasons, not eat certain foods. Grapes, for instance. Louise would wheel her grocery cart down the supermarket aisle, and the little globes, piled in decadent bunches, would seem to Danny so sweet, so good in their beady greenness that he'd break down and beg his mother for some, ashamed at his own lack of resolve. Still, Louise was firm. "Do you know how much the men and women who pick these grapes are paid?" she'd say. "April told me, it's something like forty-two cents an hour. We're talking about children, Danny, children your age, sweating in the fields. They sleep in dirty shacks, without blankets, without toilets. How would you feel if you had to sleep in a dirty shack, with no room of your own, just so some other little boy could eat grapes?" But then, passing the fruit section and the mountains of grapes a second time, she'd let him pick a few on the sly and eat them right there in the store.

In Danny's elementary school civics class, he debated Roger Krauss on the grape-boycotting issue. Roger Krauss's father was the president of the local chapter of the National Rifle Association. "Would you like to sleep in a dirty shack?" Danny argued, but because Roger Krauss was more popular, the decision, by vote, went to him. It enraged Danny, already, the way that politics worked.

Afterwards, at lunch period, Roger Krauss and his friends would torment Danny—dangling the little bunches of grapes over their faces, eating them as seductively as women in Maxfield Parrish posters.

Shortly after all this happened Salvador Allende was assassinated in Chile.

Danny remembered April crying hysterically at the kitchen table. "It was the fucking CIA!" she shouted.

"Come on, April," Nat said. "The CIA! Really! You kids, with your conspiracy theories. What does the CIA have to do with Chile?"

"I wouldn't be surprised," Louise said. She was doing dishes, her hands deep in sudsy water. "Mark my words, Nat," she said. "I would not be a bit surprised."

"Ha!" Nat said. "Ha-ha!" He considered the possibility so absurd that when the weekend news marked Louise's words, he had to retreat to his toolshop in the garage for the rest of the afternoon. Louise walked around the house looking shell-shocked. To her own surprise, she was surprised. "Surprise," she later wrote, in a speech to be delivered to the Mothers Against the Draft, "was perhaps the single most important factor in awakening a backwards, middle-aged housewife like me to the problems in the world I lived in."

Sometimes, when Danny was in his late teens—all this years after April had dropped out of college, changed her name, and begun touring the country with her songs—Louise would have the Mothers Against the Draft over to the house for coffee and cake, the way she used to have the faculty wives. Nat, back early from his computers, slunk into the kitchen, alarmed by the collection of station wagons crammed into the driveway, and there he'd find Danny drinking Tab and suffering through an internal debate as to whether or not he too should register for the draft when the time came. Louise, oddly enough, felt that he should in order to protect his status as a conscientious objector; Nat, who took the whole thing far less seriously, disagreed.

"Are those women here?" he'd ask Danny.

"Yup."

"How long?"

"An hour or so."

Then Nat would open the refrigerator, take a spoonful of jam from a jar on one of the shelves, and sit down at the kitchen table to eat it. Eventually, when it became clear the meeting was going to last a long time, he'd put the spoon in the sink and retreat, via the back porch, to his bedroom, where Danny would often find him a few hours later, half asleep, watching *Mutual of Omaha's Wild Kingdom* with one open eye.

———

APRIL MADE HER DEBUT as a singer in the fall of her junior year, at an on-campus coffeehouse called Harriet Tubman's. At that time she was billing herself as lead female vocalist for Conway's Garage, the group led by her boyfriend, Joey Conway. Joey rode a motorcycle and had a thick, soft brown beard Danny longed to touch. He and April lived together in a big room in an off-campus house dedicated to nonviolent change, but sometimes, when Nat and Louise were away, they'd come over and sleep in their giant hotel-sized bed, and Danny would listen to them moaning through the thin wall that divided him from them. In the morning once, after April had rushed off to a meeting, he crept into his parents' room and stared at April's diaphragm and the big, half-squeezed-out tube of Ortho-Gynol jelly sitting on Louise's night table. He had never seen a diaphragm before, and he fingered the slippery rubber rim curiously, trying to figure out how the thing worked. Then the bathroom door opened, and Joey walked out, naked from the shower. Danny couldn't keep from looking at his penis, which was hanging down out of what seemed to him an astounding quantity of pubic hair.

"So you found that stuff, hey, kid?" Joey said as he pulled on his underwear. He smiled. "How old are you?"

"Almost twelve," Danny said.

"You know what it's for?" He came close, put his hand on Danny's thin back. "Yeah, you'll know," he said. "You'll know all about that soon enough."

He turned from Danny and pulled a red T-shirt over his head. "Your sister," he said. "Your sister—has one fucking fantastic voice."

"I like to hear her sing too," Danny admitted.

"Yeah, well, she is good at a lot of things," Joey said, picking up the diaphragm. He smiled. "I'll bet you already can't wait to get laid," he said, "can you?"

Danny turned around, and Joey laughed.

After that Danny didn't like Joey, though he longed to see him naked again. This was an essential contradiction he was bound to come up against again and again throughout his life.

———————

IT WAS JOEY, not April, who concocted the interest scale. He complained that Danny talked too much, and it was true: Danny was given to repeating the plots of movies he'd seen, or books he'd read for school, or National Geographic specials about termite colonies.

April sat him down one day to discuss it. "All adults," she said, "before they say anything, think about the interest scale. They think to themselves, 'This thing I'm about to say, where does it rank on the interest scale? Is it a one? Is it a ten?' The rule is, Don't say anything under eight."

Danny took the interest scale seriously. He thought it was an essential fact of adulthood that one should have to measure oneself against some common rule. And yet he had questions: Were shy or silent people shy or silent because they had nothing worthwhile to say? Danny could think of plenty of adults (Joey Conway among them) who, in his opinion, neglected to consult the interest scale, as well as others who were quiet, but who he suspected would have had plenty to say if they'd wanted to.

He asked his sister about this. She said, "These questions rate about a three-point-four." It was a mean period in her life in which it seemed Danny couldn't win, couldn't say anything without her or Joey laughing and shaking their fingers at him like old-fashioned schoolteachers. "Now, Danny, remember the interest scale!" But the interest scale worked. In a matter of weeks Danny moved from excessive talkativeness into a state of almost painful shyness, in which he barely said anything at all. April didn't seem to notice. She still liked to have him around, sitting on the big beanbag chair in her room, like a kind of mascot. Her friends offered him pot and alcohol, both of which he steadfastly refused.

As for Joey, he remained in the picture, sleeping with April every night on the big mattress she had spread on the floor of her room, plucking his guitar while she practiced his songs. Sometimes he came by the house for dinner with Nat and Louise. While Louise cooked, he and Danny played long games of Spit, the cards slapping and flying in a frenzy of motion, all the while Danny imagining situations in which Joey once again took off his clothes.

THE FIRST SONGS Joey and April performed were written by Joey. They were by and large bad—angry anthems decrying the wrongs being perpetrated by the university's administration. At the coffeehouse debut, Danny sat in the front row with April's housemates, Paula and Phyllis, nice girls with vaguely leftist sympathies, while on the stage Joey did something called "Talking Blues." This meant that someone in the audience would shout out a topic, and Joey would sing about it. Usually the topics were political. "Governor Reagan!" someone shouted, and Joey strummed his guitar and sang:

> "Gonna sing you a song 'bout Gov'nor Ron,
> He's got ice cream in his head,
> He's got a wife named Nancy who dresses fancy,
> And he wears his cowboy hat to bed!"

The game thrilled Danny. Song, it seemed, could be born from anything, any topic, any word. All one had to do was speak it, and Joey, like an old-fashioned magic lantern, would grant the wish. "Turkey!" Danny shouted. "Pizza! Bowling!" By this time Joey was getting annoyed. "Whipped cream!" Danny said, and a mischievous look came over Joey's face.

> "I wonder what erotic dreams
> This young boy has about whipped cream!"

48

As intended, this shut Danny up for the rest of the evening. He cowered between Phyllis and Paula and tried to avoid looking at Joey, who was now singing some dreadful love song he'd written called "When You Lay Me, Baby." He hated Joey now, but he was determined to sit through his set, if only for April's sake.

And finally—remarkably, thrillingly late, it seemed (and yet his parents had given him permission, for the first time, to stay out as long as he wanted)—it was April's turn. She strode onto the stage with what would later be called by reviewers "her characteristic performing confidence." Danny was entranced. Here was his sister, with whom he had grown up sharing a bathroom, and she was on a stage, a famous singer. She had long blond hair brushed over her shoulders and was wearing a peasant skirt and an Indian blouse with dozens of little mirrors sewn into it. "Thanks," she said to the audience, taking the guitar in hand. "I'm real happy to be here tonight with Conway's Garage."

After finishing four or five of Joey's awful songs—but were they awful, Danny asked himself sometimes now, or had he simply allowed April's accounting of these events to influence his own memory?— April said, "And now I'd like to sing a song in sympathy with the people of Cambodia and Vietnam, which Joey and I wrote together. It's called 'No More Vietnams.' And if you please, I'd like everyone to join in on the chorus."

She picked up her guitar; the lights faded to a crescent, surrounding her in darkness. Conway's Garage disappeared; this was April's moment; no accompaniment but her own would be necessary.

She sang. It was the sort of song that protest singers dream of writing—so vivid in its compassion, so powerful in its fury, that hearing it, Danny wondered how people could not be moved to change their lives. The song called for change. "Change!" April sang.

> "Will we never learn?
> I am too young to watch young flesh being burned.
> Well, as long as I've a voice to sing, I'll cry out to the world,
> I want no more Vietnams!
> (Come on, everybody!)
> I want no more Vietnams!"

It seemed to Danny that night that hearing April sing, no human being could possibly keep from seeing the light of left-wing ideology.

Not even Roger Krauss. Not even Roger Krauss's father. Sitting there in the front row, he fantasized somehow sneaking April's song over the public-address system at the National Rifle Association. How, after hearing it, could those men not be compelled to lay down their guns and join in?

April finished with a triumphant bow. The audience was on its feet in seconds. And then, when the applause was at its peak, Danny noticed Joey standing in the background, on the little stage. He was smiling tightly, as if he were trying to keep from hiccuping. Danny could tell from his expression that April was simply being kind when she said Joey had cowritten that song with her, and this realization pleased him fiercely, because it meant that April was the special one, April the one who would go far. Not Joey. And yet Danny suspected April did not recognize what was special in herself. "I owe it all to Joey," she was now saying to the campus newspaper reporter who was interviewing her. "Joey Conway, my partner. Come on, Joey, come down."

Nervously he climbed down from the stage. Danny didn't know Joey very well, but he knew that he had visions of glory for himself and April, and in those visions it was always he who was asked for the interviews and April who waited patiently to climb down from the stage. Things did not look good for him right now, standing there, his face tight, as if he were confronting right then, for the first time, the terrible disparity that often falls between one person's desire and another's talent.

Still, she loved him. A few nights later, having climbed out of bed for a glass of milk, Danny heard her confiding to Louise across the kitchen table. "To be honest," she said, "I'm addicted to his cock."

"April!" Louise answered, and clamped her hand over her mouth. Tiny peals of laughter spilled through her fingers, like bubbles escaping a pot that was boiling over.

———

AFTER THAT, "No More Vietnams" became such a popular anthem that April and Joey were persuaded to copyright and, finally, record it. Unfortunately, on that early, 45 rpm record—now a collector's item, since April is still listed as April Cooper—she is accompanied by Joey, whose voice simply cannot stand up to hers. He realized this soon enough, and agreed simply to play while April sang, and, shortly after that, to abandon Conway's Garage. And then of course it was only a matter of weeks before the shouts of "Ap-ril" from big audiences transformed "Joey Conway and April Cooper" into "April Cooper with Joey Conway." Soon enough, in a fashionable gesture toward matriarchy (and because it sounded better, she later admitted), April Cooper took on Louise's maiden name; she became April Gold. SHOWER OF GOLD, reviewers headlined. Then underneath: NEW SINGER SHINES IN UNEVEN DUO. In his notebook of April's career Danny had an old, yellowed clipping from the University of Oregon paper—saved no doubt with vengeful zeal—in which April and Joey are called "the peace movement's Sonny and Cher; once again, a phenomenally talented woman singer has doomed herself to be paired with a partner who is both smugly unappealing and musically inept."

Of course they broke up; one day April arrived home from the apartment she'd been sharing with Joey in a station wagon filled to the brim with clothes and books and announced that she was never going to sing again. It was an old station wagon, the same one they'd used to move her into her freshman dorm. She wouldn't leave the house for days after that; she sat for hours around the kitchen table, watching game shows and cracking peanuts out of their shells—a habit picked up from Nat. She gained weight. She could not sing without him, she declared one night at dinner, then headed off to the bathroom to vomit.

Once, during those six months or so that April was living at home, she took out a personal ad in the *Bay Guardian*, which read: "Zaftig leftist woman, 23, seeks inspired and enlightened man with movement experience for friendship." Everyone in the family was surprised—it seemed a rather uncharacteristic gesture for April—but then again, no one dared object to something that might lead to her starting up her life again. For a while there were no respondents, and then one morning April made a show of inviting Danny to lunch at a huge, steam-filled Chinatown dim sum house. "I want to take you to lunch," she said. "Anywhere you like."

Danny liked the dim sum houses, where women in white uniforms rolled carts down the aisles between the tables, shouting out the names of various steamed and fried dumplings, thick rice soups, sweet buns. "You know why there are no windows in dim sum restaurants?" he asked as he caught the warm smell of steam from an approaching cart. "Because you pay by the plate. If there were windows, people would throw the plates out the windows to save money."

"Danny," April said, "this is the tenth time you've told me that story. Remember the interest scale." He looked away, bit into something ambrosial wrapped in rice noodle dough. A perfect afternoon, other than that remark, an afternoon of thanks and love and goodness, offered by his sister to him in repayment for . . . services rendered? And yet, as was usual with April, things were not as they seemed, which in no way meant her intentions were less than honorable, her love for him less than genuine, only that there was a small other matter, something she needed help with, and she had hoped he wouldn't mind. And presently a pale-skinned man in a pressed white shirt and tortoiseshell glasses ambled down the aisle and asked if she was April and, when she said she was, shook her hand and sat down. The man looked at Danny next, somewhat confusedly, until April said, "Uh, Jim, this is my brother, Danny. Danny, this is Jim . . . I'm sorry, what did you say your last name was?"

"Tully. Jim Tully."

"Yes, sorry."

"Hi," Danny said. He looked at April.

"Danny, remember that personal ad I took out? Well, Jim is the first person to answer." She laughed and looked at her date. "Jim, you don't mind my little brother tagging along, do you?"

"Oh no," Jim said. "That's just fine. I have a brother myself, just about his age. How old are you, Danny?"

"Fourteen."

"Well, my little brother—his name is Bill—he's sixteen. He plays basketball."

"That's great," Danny said.

"Jim's a lawyer," April said. "He works for the Post Office."

"In a consulting capacity."

A woman came by with a metal tea cart, shouting out names of delicacies in hoarse Cantonese, and Danny made a show of his expertise, gathering from the cart, among other things, a plate of small, noodle-wrapped bundles topped with hard-boiled quail eggs.

"This is the weirdest food I've ever seen," Jim said.

"What?" Danny said. "You've never eaten quail eggs?" Had he shaken his head in disgust? If he hadn't, he decided later, he should have.

"Thank God Danny came with me," April said later to Louise. They had just gotten back and were sitting in the warm kitchen, taking off their shoes. "This little guy positively saved my life."

She grabbed his head and started kissing him.

"April—"

"I'm sorry, I can't resist it, you're too cute. . . ."

"April!"

"Your voice just cracked! Did you hear that?"

"April, let me go."

"So you didn't like this guy?" Louise said from the sink, where she was doing dishes.

"Oh, he was nice enough. Just boring. I couldn't have stood having to be alone with him. As usual, my beloved brother came through for me. Ah, well." She lumbered off toward her room, singing in a clear soprano, "I will never sing again. . . ."

But of course, soon enough, she did.

Alone, she was more popular than ever.

As for Joey, to Danny's surprise, he reacted to April's return to the stage with neither violence nor jealousy. He resigned himself to his failure; he returned to school. When Danny went riding his bicycle, he would see Joey on the campus sometimes, looking more quiet and bookish than usual. They never spoke; usually Danny rode away as fast as he could.

And soon enough there was another boyfriend, this time named Karl Mathias, and another manager, a professional with offices in a skyscraper in San Francisco. The manager was named Tina Tompkins, and under her tutelage April got gigs at big music festivals, sharing stages with Joan Baez and Bob Dylan. She traveled to Indochina on tour. The family could hardly keep up with her successes. Still, her attempts to get a contract with a major recording company persistently failed. *No More Vietnams*, her first album, was finally released by a near-bankrupt independent studio that operated out of someone's garage. Louise and Nat had to lend money to the producers to pay the final bills. For months that year Louise had to park her car on the street because their own garage was filled with boxes and boxes of the album; Danny would walk up and down the streets of the neighborhood, selling it door to door to neighbors, ex-teachers, April's friends from high school. It was a shoddy-looking thing, with a badly angled black-and-white photograph of April on the cover, but even Aunt Eleanor said the songs were wonderful.

Danny was, by this time, becoming more and more involved in April's career, skipping school (to his parents' chagrin) so that he might attend her concerts. Often he'd help out backstage, and late at night, at parties, smoke marijuana with April and her ever-increasing retinue of musicians, technicians, boyfriends, and of course women friends who worshiped her, who wanted more than anything to be like her. Another album—*Freedom*—was released, and this time it easily earned its keep; with great ceremony, April presented Nat and Louise with a check reimbursing her old debt from *No More Vietnams*. She was at her peak.

And yet, somehow, she was also too late. Danny thought, in retrospect, that they all suspected this, at those late-night parties after the concerts. It was by now 1977; the war was finally over—Danny remembered Louise crying over the baby lifts—and with its ungraceful conclusion, the spirit, the energy seemed somehow to have been sucked out of the protest movement. Had she begun two or three years earlier, perhaps, April could have been a mainstream star on a par with Joan Baez, say, or Joni Mitchell. But she was born late for that; her committed audience, even in 1977, was beginning to abandon her, retreating to business schools and law schools and medical schools. Finally she was left with a following that was loyal but terribly small— the fierce, diminishing nucleus of revolution, the truly committed few who had long before pledged themselves to the hard work of keeping up the light through the dark period many were already predicting ahead. The vision of these people was essentially fatalistic; revolution for them was hard work against terrible odds; there was nothing fun about it. Real revolution, they believed, occurred underground, in corners, during the dark night of oppression.

So, with the end of the war and the days of Berkeley glory, these hardy souls returned to the woodwork within which they had always functioned best, and were in truth probably relieved to do so. They specialized not in promoting mass revolution, but in small-scale advocacy of social change. This was April's audience, and as a rule it was not a very glamorous bunch: sallow-faced men with black-framed glasses and long, thin ponytails the color of wine falling down their backs; and their women—hale, wiry-haired, with scarves tied around their heads like Bulgarian peasants. They had babies with names like Justin or Molly, not Rainbow or God, and they carried them in slings worn over their breasts, and breast-fed them till they were six. They were not particularly interested in music as art, only as propaganda, only as an instrument of social change. The wild parties that had always followed April's concerts gave way to quiet potluck dinners in bleached, under-decorated houses, after which bald Buddhist poets would give readings from their work. April sometimes brought Danny, who was now in high school; they'd sit at the table together, listening politely and moving the soybean casserole around on their plates, both of them secretly dying for a cheeseburger, both of them secretly bored out of their heads.

It was around this time that April first sang with Margy McLaughlin. Margy, who was also managed by Tina Tompkins, was a committed lesbian who performed only with other women and whose songs were explicit and defiant. She was a beautiful, hollow-cheeked woman, with neatly crew-cut chestnut-colored hair, and she dressed in loose-fitting pale linen pants and shirts that gave her the look of a spiritually advanced being—an alien or a monk. Even before they met, they fascinated each other; they sought each other out, asking mutual friends, "Does she have a lover?" or "Is she gay?" nurturing crushes on album cover photographs so acute that by the time they did meet they had, in their own minds, courted, married, separated, and reunited a hundred times. (Or so April said when she told the story during the long bus trips between concerts.) They knew each other's songs by heart. When April was visiting her parents' house, she'd play Margy's album *Woman-Loving-Woman* over and over again on the old record player Nat had built from a kit.

They were lovers, April liked to say later, from the moment they met, the moment their hands first touched in greeting and they looked at each other and smiled.

April first brought Margy home for dinner on a March night during Danny's senior year at high school. She was the kind of dinner guest Louise adored—she insisted on setting the table and drying the dishes—and she asked Nat a lot of questions about his work. She had grown up on a farm in Iowa, but when she was sixteen, she had somehow made her way to Paris, and it was there, she said, that she did her real growing up. Danny kept staring at her, through the dinner, trying to determine if anything in her appearance gave away what had made her a lesbian. He had once heard Roger Krauss say that girls became dykes when they were too fat or ugly for boys to go for them, and yet Margy McLaughlin was neither fat nor ugly; rather, she had the slender body of a beauty queen. What impressed him most was how comfortable she seemed with her lesbianism—comfortable enough to have declared it to the world in a whole album of songs. Such an action must have taken inestimable bravery, he thought, much as he had thought fasting must take inestimable bravery when he was younger. By the end of dinner he adored her; he thought she was lovely and spare and smooth, as if she had been carved from a piece of soap. He believed he was in love with her, wanted to make love to her.

But when he looked at April and noticed that she was staring at Margy with eyes so much more urgent in their questioning than his own, he realized what he felt was not desire; it was nothing close to desire.

After that, April started to write songs with Margy, to perform with her, finally to record with her. Nothing was ever said to the direct effect that they were lovers, but Danny knew his parents suspected; they had started to have long discussions late at night from which he was barred. And finally the expected news arrived: April was giving up her apartment; she had decided to move into Margy's house in Berkeley. Danny volunteered to help. It was a small, stuccoed house with geraniums in the front yard. Inside the rounded entry was a succession of rooms with golden floors and cool white walls and vague pieces of furniture uphol-stered in pastel cottons—sofas that seemed to double as beds, beds piled with huge pillows. Danny had wondered nervously if April was going to have her own room, but life here seemed to defy such easy division; no room was discrete from any other.

Afterwards Margy burned incense, and they ate a meal of chicken cooked in a peanut sauce that went down smooth and sweet, like caramel, then burst with sourness, then burned. April explained how joyous she was to have finally discovered her own lesbianism, how glad that she would now be recording music only with women. "Yes," Danny said, forgetting, for the moment, that his own maleness might exclude him. "Yes." He often forgot, in April's company, that he was a man at all.

Louise grilled him when he got home. "What's the place like?" she asked. "Does April have her own room?"

"Sort of," Danny said.

"Sort of! What do you mean, 'sort of'?"

"Well—there are a lot of rooms. But the whole place is very open. I wish our house was like that."

Louise shook her head, closed her eyes. She lit a cigarette. "Well, it's her life," she said finally, and Danny went to bed.

Later, when everything was out in the open, and April had signed her first contract with Lesbia Records, the people she'd once worked with started to say she'd sold out. Women's music was suddenly a lively enterprise after all; Margy McLaughlin's concerts attracted crowds, which, if not quite as huge as the ones that had thronged to April's early concerts, nevertheless seemed rife with energy, with desire, with commitment and passion. Perhaps that was why April's old friends and cronies and ex-boyfriends chose to accuse her of opportunism, of trumping up a change of sexual identity in order to gain allegiance with a more profitable cause. Jokes started to circulate about her; men called her the "bushdiver." Out of work (for she was performing only with women now), furious with the world, April's male ex-accompanists gathered in the coffeehouses, now dark and dead, where they had once known glory, and mocked her. Oh, certainly her music had had feminist overtones, even in the earliest days, but these songs the men had treated lightly, as a whim of hers to be indulged. No, it was when she sang "Allende" that they cheered; when she sang "Out of Work"; when she sang "Why Get Married?" And now she was singing "Discovery," she was pairing up with Margy McLaughlin for duets of "Lover Woman of Mine." And worse, she had taken those early love songs, the ones that had made her boyfriends melt, and regenderized them, so that now the protagonists were clearly, blatantly pairs of women lovers. Even "Out of Work," which was about a woman whose husband has lost his job, became lesbian. "She's a damn good business—businessperson," the men would scoff, and laugh, and drink more beer.

And the men were not the only ones who looked on April's transformation with suspicion. Other lesbian singers who for years had been struggling to establish reputations watched distrustfully as she went onstage with her new Dutch-boy haircut and eclipsed them all. They too suspected opportunism; they too suspected that this was a straight woman in drag, out to steal the glory they'd been faithfully nurturing for years. And perhaps they were right. Perhaps April had shrewdly recognized in the women's music movement a potential arena for her impassioned voice, her angry and seductive songwriting. For April needed to write songs that bristled with commitment, with passion; the pulpy stuff women sang on mainstream stations bored her. She got on the stage now and soared where those other women had done nothing but crudely flap their wings; she was twice the musician, twice the singer, twice the songwriter that any of them, with the possible exception of Margy McLaughlin, had ever been, and they knew it.

Around this time Danny met Joey Conway again. It was the summer after his freshman year in college, and he was traveling around the state with April, helping out backstage at her concerts. Joey was sitting in a health food restaurant in Santa Cruz where Danny happened to be eating some dinner with a couple of the women from April's band, and he came over and said hello. He was dressed in a tight white T-shirt, and even though he'd shaved off his beard, he still looked thrillingly virile.

They went to the bar to talk. Joey was living in Santa Cruz now, he explained, with his wife, Diane. Both of them were graduate students in the History of Consciousness. "That's great," Danny said. "What a subject."

"Yes," he said. "It's very exciting." He paused, cleared his throat. "So how is April?"

"She's great. You know, I guess, that she's going to be performing tonight."

"Yeah, I'd really love to go. But damn it, I have this study group tonight; it's one of those things that's been planned for months. You think she'll understand?"

"Sure."

"I guess she's still living with Margy McLaughlin. At least that's what I've heard through the grapevine."

"It's true," Danny said.

Joey took another swig from his beer mug. "You know," he said, "I've got to hand it to April. She knew when to jump off a sinking ship. I mean, protest music's going nowhere. But this women's music. I guess it's real popular."

"Well," Danny said, "April's life changed, and her music changed too." (He was terribly self-righteous in those days.)

"Okay," Joey said. "I can buy that. But listen, Danny—I want you to ask her one thing for me. I want you to ask her, did she really have to rewrite 'Between Me and My Man' and make it 'Between Me and My Woman'? I mean, okay, rewriting a song like 'Out of Work' and making it lesbian, that's one thing. But she wrote 'Between Me and My Man' for me." He looked down into his beer.

"I can ask her," Danny said.

"I'd appreciate that," he said. "And listen. Tell her to write me, okay?"

"Of course."

Later he brought Joey's message to April in the dressing room where she and Margy were getting ready to go onstage. "Joey," Margy said. "How I long to meet him."

"How does he look?" April asked.

"Good," Danny said. He wondered if it was possible that she could still be attracted to him, or if she ever had been attracted to him at all, or if homosexuality was a one-way street, a choice you made and couldn't go back on.

"He asked if you'd write to him," he said.

"Sure," April said. "I'll write to him."

———

FOUR YEARS of his life Danny more or less gave April. Sometimes, of course, he was in school; then, from the little apartment he rented on Durant Avenue, he was her social secretary, answering her letters, negotiating her complicated phone calls, passing some people on and putting other people off. She was at Margy's house, in Berkeley, working, or she and Margy were on a farm somewhere near Salinas and couldn't be disturbed, or she and Margy were performing at a women's festival in Minnesota. "It's incredible," she told him over the phone. "Two thousand women, and all of them naked. I had no idea there were so many different kinds of breasts." This was the sort of remark she could make only to him. And then it was no longer April and Margy; they had "reached an impasse" but were still friends. Anyhow, no matter how Margy might have thought it, it was really April all those people were coming to listen to anyway.

And when he wasn't in Berkeley, he was with her, on tour. His parents were perplexed but resigned. "Well, at least you kids seem to be having a good time," Nat told them over the phone, and they agreed— "Oh, yes, Dad"—whether they were freezing at a pay phone at a gas station in Nevada or sitting in leather chairs in the stage manager's office at some impressively grand university concert hall. Danny drove. Danny totaled up the bills and tried to keep the books balanced, even though April, who had no head for money, seemed always to be losing the checks she was handed after the concerts. Then Danny had to call up whoever had issued the check, arrange for its cancellation and replacement. He sieved through her fan mail. He washed her underwear. Four years, and somehow, that whole time, he never questioned any of it, never doubted that it was anything less than his duty to take care of her this way.

And yet sometimes it got to him; sometimes, after the concerts, when the women sat in a circle at April's feet, passing joints and laughing at whatever stories she had to tell, he'd lift the tiny nub of ash and flame to his lips and recognize in a new way that he might disappear from this room right now and no one would even notice—not until morning, when she needed him to get gas, or make a call, or bring her coffee. He smoked the joint down to a nugget, then flicked it away into the long gray-streaked hair of a woman in front of him, who jumped slightly, instinctively touched her hand to her hair, brushed at it. And then, suddenly, a strange sensation: April was looking at him. April had seen what he had done. Across the crowded room a look of frustration, of older sister's annoyance with baby brother, which he met challengingly, sitting up straight, crossing his arms. She turned away from him, went on with what she was saying. Perhaps she recognized, even more than he did himself, how close he was to leaving her, how he was just waiting for the right excuse.

Sometimes he mattered to her; sometimes she came up from behind him and terrified him with an unexpected hug. "Powderfoot," she'd say, "I don't know what I'd do without you. I don't know what any of us would do without you. Remind me to buy you a present." He didn't remind her, and she didn't buy him a present, but occasionally, during a concert, she'd pick up her guitar and say, "This next one is for my brother, Danny," and sing "Family Heirlooms." It got to the point, toward the end of the four years, where he'd have to leave the room while she sang that song, just in order to preserve his resentment. It seemed unjust to him that she should be graced with such gifts, not because he envied her the gifts themselves but because somehow the beauty of her singing allowed her to get away with so much else that was so unbeautiful. She understood too well: All she had to do was open her mouth to sing, and the world forgave her everything.

NINE MYSTERIOUS and crucial years separated April's birth from Danny's. This meant that when Danny was nine, his sister was eighteen and had lived twice as long in the world as he had. The difference never seemed so vast, so insurmountable, as it did that magical year, for as they got older, nine years became less of a gulf and more of a bridge. Danny met and befriended people older than April all the time now, as peers, a fact the nine-year-old baby brother in him still couldn't help but marvel at; when he was a child, she and her friends had seemed so immutably older than he was. Now people April's age worked under him. He paid them. He could have them fired.

But the year April was eighteen, the year when nine years seemed an insurmountable eternity, it was a different story. That was the year April went into therapy. The university health services psychiatrist, Dr. Groening, told her that Danny probably envied her the time she had had alone with their parents, before his birth, and she was quick to pass on the news. Was it true? he wondered. Did he envy her those years? Bewilderment seemed a more appropriate word, or simply detachment. After all, April and his parents had been a family long before he came along; they shared with each other elaborate and entrenched rituals, masses of common history, so much that in his early childhood he was always having to ask questions: Where did the piñata above my bed come from? The trip to Mexico we took when your sister was five. What is the house in this picture? Our old house, where we lived in Boston, when April was born. Who are these women holding babies? That is your grandmother, who you never knew, holding your cousin Joanne. And that is your aunt Eleanor, holding your cousin Markie. And that is your mommy, holding your sister. He studied the photographs, memorizing the faces he would never see in real life, because the people they belonged to were dead or had aged beyond the point of recognition. It was like homework, like memorizing the parts of the body or the capitals. But the pictures he paid closest attention to were the ones his parents had had taken when April was a baby. There were hundreds of them—ten or twenty taken on a single day, sometimes, marked and dated and captioned, as if Louise and Nat had been under some sort of picture-taking enchantment, brought on by the miracle of first birth. "11/22/52: Mommy giving April her bottle." "11/23/52: Daddy puts April in her bath." Danny didn't know this energetic young couple, busily engaged in the rituals of baby care, and yet there were his father's ringed eyes and sharp nose on the face of that skinny boy; there was his mother's slightly upturned lip, her blazing dark eyes. What surprised him most was a sequence of pictures taken on the beach, in which their bodies were exposed: Nat stood paunchless and tanned in a bathing suit with a drawstring; Louise, next to him, knelt on the sand in an early two-piece suit that must have been terribly risqué, with pointy, conical breastpieces. Her abdomen—now crisscrossed with a variety of scars—was flawless, smooth. The color in these pictures had faded, and so the beach had a bleached, white aspect, the bright flowers on Louise's breasts fading, as if at the end of their season.

And as April grew, as her unspecified baby face took on the familiar features of his sister, the gaps between when the pictures were taken grew as well, until instead of every day, it was every six months, and then every year, at her birthday party. Then there were no dates. Then there were no more binders, just an old shoebox filled with snapshots. Very few pictures existed of Danny's own babyhood, and when he once asked his mother why, she looked at him strangely and put her hand on her forehead. "Oh, Danny," she said, laughing a little. "I'm sorry." He hadn't, until that moment, thought of it as anything to apologize for.

When Danny was growing up, he had a red rubber ball he liked to bounce. After school, in the afternoon, he'd walk for hours along the perimeter of the swimming pool, bouncing this ball, spinning out in his head the plots of imaginary movies and television shows, and later, when April started singing, making up songs. She had told him that if he wrote a song good enough, she would sing it. But somehow it was always someone else's tune he came up with during those predusk hours he spent outdoors, bouncing, bouncing. When he started at Berkeley, that familiar, thunking beat was what Louise said she missed most; she couldn't stand the silence, she told Danny, and joked about paying a neighborhood child to play handball against her garage. And later, when he was living in the East and went home for visits, he'd find the red ball waiting for him on his bed, and sometimes, when he had something to think through, he'd take it up and bounce it, though it was soft where once it had been tight, and riddled with tiny, unsealable holes. Louise, doing the dishes or ironing, felt a rare peacefulness come over her as she listened to that familiar thumping of her son and his ball outside.

Danny told Walter about the red ball. After that, whenever he seemed lost, distant, in his own world, Walter would say to him, "Bouncing your ball again?" and Danny would laugh and insist he wasn't. Still, he remembered those hours circling the pool as ones of supreme contentment and security. He had a vision, sometimes, of Wall Street at rush hour, men in business suits, women in pastel-colored tennis shoes, but not hurrying as usual toward the subway; instead, they are just shuffling along, bouncing, and in the world there is a sound like thunder as a thousand balls hit the pavement at once, fly again into the air, at once.

———

THE SUMMER JUST BEFORE April broke up with Joey, Nat and Louise rented a house on the beach for the family to spend a weekend. April and Joey were very excited about a game they'd learned and wanted to play after dinner. "April, you know how I feel about games," Louise said, but April insisted. "It's a very special game," she said. "You'll like it."

"How do you play?" Louise asked. "Is it tricky?" She had a native distrust of things that were tricky.

"It's easy. On the way down Joey and I made up a story about each of you, and now all you have to do, each of you, is ask yes-or-no questions. Then we answer them and that way you try to guess the story."

"That sounds fun," Danny said.

But Nat shook his head. "Not me," he said. "You're not roping me into this."

"Danny can go first," April said.

"Does this story take place in my house?" he asked.

"No," April and Joey answered in unison.

"Does it take place in California?"

"No."

"Does it take place on the East Coast?"

"Yes."

"Does it have to do with my telling a story?"

"Sort of—sort of."

"Does it have to do with my telling a poem?"

"Yes!"

As the game continued, the story came into focus: Danny was riding in a boat with April off the coast of New York, reading a poem aloud, and April got bored because it was a boring poem and pushed him off the boat into the harbor.

"April," Louise said, "that's a terrible story to tell about your brother!"

April and Joey laughed into their hands, and April said, "Now it's your turn, Ma! Your turn next!"

"Does this story take place in my house?"

"No!"

"Does this story take place when I'm out?"

"Yes!"

"Does this story take place in the supermarket?"

"Yes!"

"I don't know about this," Louise said. "Do I get sick in this story?"

"Sort of!"

Here is the story: Louise was shopping at the supermarket and got diarrhea. She couldn't find a toilet anywhere. Eventually she had diarrhea in the store. By the time they reached the conclusion, everyone was for some reason laughing hysterically, wildly. Danny especially; he was on the floor, heaving and flopping like a fish just pulled out of the sea.

"All right, I think it's time to fess up to what's going on here," Nat said.

"What do you mean, Dad?" April asked, all innocence, between laughs like hiccups.

"I'm a scientist. I can recognize systems. Tell them, April, or I will."

"All right, all right." But April couldn't stop laughing. "You tell them, Joey."

"Well," Joey said, "the truth is, Mrs. Cooper, we didn't make up any stories. We just answered no to every question that ended with a vowel, and yes to every question that ended with a consonant—"

"And if it ended with *y*, we said, 'Sort of,' " April added, still laughing.

"Unless of course the question was so good we couldn't resist saying yes," Joey said.

"So you see," April said—and finally, now, she was calming down— "those were your stories. You made up your own stories."

Everyone had a good laugh then. "Imagine," Louise said, grim-faced but smiling. "Well, I don't know what Dr. Freud would have to say about my story."

Of course, it was never played again. The game was in that category of phenomena that by their very natures can happen only once.

But the stories, oddly enough, lived on in Danny's memory, as vivid as dreams. He remembered the way the boat rocked in the noisy harbor, how April's hands pushed, and how the dark water seemed to swallow him. He remembered as if he were there—a mute witness, a child alongside the cart: the panic in the aisles of the supermarket, the women raising their hands to their noses. The bottles and boxes and pieces of fruit fly from Louise's overturned cart, rolling along the floor. And in the midst of it all, Louise herself, as she saw herself: befouled, degraded, humiliated beyond measure.

This was, Danny knew, what she was always afraid of happening, what she was convinced would happen if even for a second she let down her guard. "Her precious guard," April called it. Now that was a title for a song.

It seemed sometimes to Danny that the family could not get together for a birthday or holiday without April being compelled to air a grievance, vent an irritation, or ask an indelicate question. Psychological stillness seemed to her by necessity a sign of stagnation; it was as if she felt periodically obliged to stir up the dust of the time they had all lived together in the same house, a time which each year they seemed to have less of a grasp on, which each year seemed more and more a part of their history.

Here they are, then, a few nights before Christmas 1982, having just finished a dinner of lasagne and a cake April has made. (She reverts to old habits when she is home, dispenses with her celebrity, bakes from mixes, in Bundt pans, recipes from Betty Crocker Bake-Off cookbooks.) "Mom, there's something I've been wanting to ask you," she says in a tone the solemnity of which everyone has come to associate with trouble.

Louise puts down her cake fork and looks at Nat.

"I know there have been a lot of secrets in this family," April says, "things you assumed we didn't know. But there are things I've learned recently—I'd prefer not to say how."

"What?" Louise says, still looking at Nat.

"I know," April says, "that you were married to someone else before Daddy."

Louise throws down her fork; it jangles, reverberates against the table. "Oh, Christ," she says. "Did your father tell you that? Nat, did you tell her?"

He looks away. He doesn't say anything.

"Or was it Eleanor?" she says.

"It doesn't matter who," April says. "What's important is it's been told, and I'm glad to know. I want to know."

"It wasn't Eleanor," Nat says.

Louise turns away from Nat. She turns away from April. "I don't see why you're making such a big deal out of it," she says. "It was nothing. It just embarrasses me, that's all. It's like a big messy BM you had once. It's not something you like to talk about."

Everyone is quiet. Louise's eyes move from one face to the next. "All right," she says. "It's true. There, that's done. Now I don't want to talk about it ever again. Understand?"

April opens her mouth to question further.

"Sentence. Paragraph," Louise says.

She gets up from the table, gets up to do the dishes. Stretches tight rubber gloves over her hands. Fills the sink with suds. There are always dishes to be done, always some activity for her hands. Louise has beautiful hands, very dark and smooth, with whorled, soft skin over the knuckles. When Danny was growing up, she played the piano two or three hours in the late afternoon. Whatever piece she was learning, its stops and starts, its tricky phrases kept him from sleeping for nights afterwards, as if those awkward repetitions of practice were in themselves a kind of harmony, superimposed over the actual music. She knit so well she could read while she did it, cracking the spine of the book so that it would lie flat on her lap. Her fingers crossed the knitting needles, her eyes moved back and forth along the page. Most of the books in the house had been ruined that way, their backs broken in sacrifice to her ruthless industry.

Now Nat gets up from the table, approaches her from behind. "Honey," he says, "I didn't mean to upset you. But I was telling April about our youth, she was asking, and—it just slipped out. I was feeling nostalgic, and it slipped out. Anyway, why does it matter that the kids know? Really, it's not that big a deal—"

"That's for me to decide," Louise says hotly. The steam rises in her face. Nat puts his hands on her shoulders, and her shoulders thrust them away.

"Just leave me alone," she says.

"Okay, whatever you say." He walks to the refrigerator, takes out a jar of jam.

"Why don't you shut up?" she says softly.

Nat takes a spoonful of the jam and carries it out of the room with him. Louise's shoulders rise and sink. Her hands slow, still. Her head falls toward the suds. "Why does everyone in this family expect me to clean up their goddamned messes and jam jars and dirty spoons?" she says.

"Jam jars!" April says. "Jesus, Mother, I don't see why we have to pretend so much! Jam jars has nothing to do with it! It's like you've expected us to bury everything just because you have."

"You always have to have center stage, don't you?" Louise says. "No one else in the world is allowed to suffer except you."

April stands then. Danny stands. It is almost rehearsable, this scene, the variations from Christmas to Christmas are so slight. Danny walks out of the room, into his parents' bedroom, where Nat has already turned the TV on loud enough to drown out the noise of Louise and April fighting.

"Are they at it again?" Nat asks.

"Yes," Danny says.

"Okay," Nat says. "Looks like we're in for a long night." He holds the remote control on his lap. He flips from channel to channel, bringing on a barrage of contradictory images: children holding toothpaste tubes, the moving mouths of newsmen, the famous wheel of fortune spinning, spinning, landing on bankrupt.

There is a hangman puzzle on the television, the letters slowly filling in.

"So are you surprised?" Nat asks.

Danny shrugs. "I guess it's just hard to think of your mother as a sexual being—that is, sexual with someone else besides your father."

"I know," Nat says. "I had the same problem with my mother."

"I'm not going to ask for any details, even though I'm tempted."

"Someday I'll tell you the whole story. Christ, I knew your mother would react this way."

"Then why'd you say anything to April? You know she's a time bomb."

"I suppose," Nat says, "that I knew April would tell Louisy. I suppose I finally wanted to get things out in the open."

"You're asking for trouble."

Nat continues looking at the TV.

"Sabotage," he says.

"What?"

"Sabotage."

Confused, Danny looks again at the hangman puzzle. But the answer is becoming clear, and it isn't sabotage.

"A PIECE OF THE ACTION," Nat says, guessing just before the contestant on the television. Danny looks at him. His lips are tight, his brow wrinkled.

———

WHATEVER FIGHT HAPPENED happened in silence. Nat and Louise muffled themselves when Danny and April were home, locked themselves in the bedroom and had it out in fierce whispers—not for the children's sake but for their own. Both of them carried around a tenacious belief in keeping things private, an assumption that the witnessing of their battles would bring down on them the greatest shame possible. The door to the bedroom stayed closed for hours, a silent, aching abscess at the heart of the house, and of course Danny knew better than to knock.

Around ten o'clock April took her car and left; "to visit a friend," she said. Danny was sitting at the kitchen table, watching a rerun of *Saturday Night Live:* Gilda Radner as the pathetic, palsied child visiting a child psychiatrist. "Which one of these toys is Mommy?" the psychiatrist asks, and the child chooses the Barbie doll. "And which is Daddy?" the psychiatrist asks, and the child chooses the Ken doll. "And which is you?" the psychiatrist asks, and the child picks up a package of scotch tape.

"That Gilda Radner's funny," Louise said. Danny hadn't heard her come in. Her voice was a little hoarse, and she was wearing her pink bathrobe and slippers.

"Yes," he said. "She is funny."

She went over to her desk. There was a tub of clear, hot wax there into which she twice a day dunked her arthritic hands. From where Danny sat he watched the familiar submersion, the swift pulling out. She held her hands dripping over the tub until the wax hardened, then wrapped them in towels and sat down at the kitchen table. Bolts of soft cloth emerged from her pink bathrobe sleeves, and Danny remembered how the milky, opaque wax took the shape of her hands exactly—every vein, every nail.

"Is Daddy asleep?" Danny asked.

"Yes."

"Are you okay?"

She shrugged her shoulders. "I'm not in the mood to talk, Danny." He thought of asking more, but on the TV Gilda Radner was back again, this time as Rosanne Rosanna-Danna, describing tiny things, tiny news of the body, which both of them found difficult to ignore.

After that there was a commercial. She unwrapped her hands, peeled the white wax from her skin. It formed a soft, pale ball in her palm. She dropped it into the tub to melt again. Her hands glistened and gave off the faint, sweet aroma of paraffin.

"I'm not going to ask you any questions," Danny said. "I don't want to make you feel bad. But I think I should tell you—it really doesn't bother me. I mean, when April made her little announcement, my first thought was relief. I thought, Is that all?"

Louise laughed and lifted her eyes to the ceiling. "Thanks, honey," she said. "I just feel as if I've been paying long enough. Really, how long can you be expected to keep paying?"

"Paying who?"

She was looking toward the window, shiny as patent leather tonight as it reflected the bright kitchen lights.

"Good question," she said. "Well, I should go to bed. Good night."

———————

SO THERE WAS A wildness. A wildness in her youth.

Then, as far as Danny could tell, she had done a kind of penance for that wildness, she had willed a purgatory to grow up around her, and there, in this landscape of her own invention, she had endured for years the slow paying off of a slow-burning debt of guilt. No one had demanded this penance of her; it was entirely her own choice.

Of course there had always been hints. "Every married person cheats," she said to him once. "I just want you to know so you won't be hurt. There's no such thing as marital loyalty." He must have been five or six at the time. What could have prompted her to say such a thing, he wondered sometimes now, especially to a tiny child, for whom such advice could not possibly have done any good? But of course it was naive to assume his good was really at the heart of her words, as she insisted. Really it must have been a slip, like whispering, "I hate you, I want you to die," to your lover while he lies sleeping next to you: a test, a fantasy. Danny had done that to Walter once. Probably she never imagined he'd hear or remember those words. He was a child. It was like talking to the air.

But what could have been so shameful, so terrible that she felt this strong obligation to secrecy? A marriage in her youth? That was nothing. That was almost charming. And yet he had to remember that she was the daughter of a different generation, a different coast, a different idea of sin. It had become a crutch for her, that difference. She leaned on it when she didn't want to accept things as they were; when Danny first told her he was gay, she picked the crutch up and hit him with it. For a long time he believed it was merely an excuse for not changing, an excuse for resisting the disparity between how things were and how she had expected them to be, but now he wondered. He tried to hear the voices of his mother's mother and aunts, telling her what a bad girl she is, how she will never be anything but bad, how she doesn't deserve such a nice boy as that Nat Cooper. The voices, playing over and over in her head, joined, perhaps, by Nat's voice? Had he at some point reached a limit with her wildness? Were there flirtations, threatened (and perhaps real) adulteries?

"Sabotage," he said that night at Christmastime. But that was a long time ago. And after that, it seemed, the family was never together all at once: April was touring at Christmas; Danny developed a convenient and paralyzing fear of planes.

Sometimes it seemed as if Louise had changed. As if her self-imposed term of punishment had finally come to an end and she had paid in full. As if guilt and sin were a kind of mortgage, slowly, slowly winding down to nothing.

Walter and Danny were living in Manhattan the year after that particular Christmas. Danny hadn't asked, Louise hadn't told him anything. She called him up, and there was a new kind of lightness in her voice, a throwaway humor he barely recognized. She told him that Mr. Mulligan, the family accountant, had disappeared on vacation in Mexico. "They were in Guadalajara. According to his wife, he just stepped out to get cigarettes, and that's the last they've seen of him for a week. It's funny. I keep envisioning old Mr. Mulligan wandering around the Mexican desert in his suspenders. Because, you see, at first everyone assumed he was dead, but now the consensus seems to be that he was running away from everything. From his life. Just dropping it all." She laughed. "It's a shame. You know how much he charged to do our taxes? Fifty dollars. I challenge you to find another accountant in America who'll do a tax return for fifty dollars."

"Times change" was all Danny could think of saying.

"I'm thinking of going back to work, by the way. Do you know anyone who needs someone to sit in a dark office on a high stool, adding up numbers by candlelight? You know, like what's-his-name. The one who works for Scrooge."

"Cratchit."

"Cratchit, yes. That's the kind of job I'd like."

"I can't think of anyone offhand."

He could hear her rapping her fingers against the white formica of the kitchen counter.

"Maybe I'll apply at World Savings," she said.

BUT THERE WAS no high stool; there was no job. Instead, there was a new lump one morning (the body's old nocturnal betrayal) and a new regimen of chemotherapy. "The side effects aren't too bad," Louise told Danny over the phone. "I just feel a little nauseous sometimes. Anyway, this chlorambucil's working like a charm. Dr. Sonnenberg says he's very impressed; he may even stop the treatments earlier than he'd planned."

"That's great, Mom."

"Your father is taking me out for sushi for our anniversary. You know how I love sushi."

"I wish I could be there."

"Well, why don't you fly out for the weekend? No, don't worry, I'm kidding. I understand about your busy life."

"Come here and I'll buy you the best sushi you've ever had. There's a place on Third Avenue that has the most incredible sushi—"

"I know, I know, everything's always better on the East Coast, right, honey? New York sushi must be better than California sushi. Well, I'll have you know I'm perfectly delighted with our local Fuki-Sushi. It's just fine with me." She laughed. "You're like a broken record, you know that? And what you sing is 'New York's better, New York's better.'"

"Mom!" Danny said. "I do not!"

"Have you heard from your sister lately?"

"Yes. She's passing through here in a couple of weeks."

"Well, that's good. At least you two will be together. I was hoping to have her home for our anniversary. But I understand, she's busy too, with her tours and what have you. The other day a woman came up to me in the supermarket and said, 'Excuse me, but I've been given to understand you're April Gold's mother, and I just want to let you know how wonderful your daughter is and how very proud you should be and how great her songs are, especially "Marriage" and "Mother, Mother" and "Family Heirlooms," you really should be proud of those songs, she's such a sensitive writer.'"

"What'd you say?" Danny asked.

"Oh, I didn't say anything. But I should have told her about my plan."

"Your plan?"

"My song I'm going to write about the mother whose daughter is always writing songs about her, and what it feels like to listen to them. I think I'll call it 'I Am the Mothers.' You like that title?"

"I think it's a great title."

"Good. And I'll have you know I am also working on another idea: a hit squad composed entirely of terminally ill people. Isn't that great? They have nothing to lose, so they might as well take a few Latin American dictators along with them."

"You have wonderful ideas."

They agreed to talk again on the weekend.

But after she hung up, there was a strange, low buzz in the atmosphere, somehow, as if some machine, some essential, irreplaceable machine, were working just beyond Danny's sight. Like a broken-down boiler, patched in places, and all of them just waiting for it to give out. The space her voice had filled billowed out, a vast gasp reminding him, suddenly, of how high the stakes were. She would lose her life, and he would lose her, and at that selfish moment he simply could not determine which of them would register the greater loss.

———

WALTER OFTEN HAD TO work late; it was not uncommon, on a workday evening, for him to remain at his office until one or two in the morning. So when he felt he couldn't go home, felt he couldn't face Danny, he had an excuse. On those nights that he stayed in the city under false pretenses, he didn't go to bars and pick up hustlers, he didn't meet law clerks for illicit rendezvous in midtown hotel rooms. Instead, he sat in his dark office in one of the World Trade Center towers; smoked; stared out at the bluish night skyline of Wall Street, looking across the way at the other World Trade Center tower, the sporadic glowing squares which punctuated that dark mosaic, and beyond them more bright squares, miles of them, as if people were holding candles up to windows in memory of the lost and missing. He smoked low-nicotine cigarettes; he thought of Danny, alone in his own office a few blocks north, or in the living room in Gresham, the light from the TV casting shadows on his face. Their suburban life, the life he had urged Danny into, seemed absurd to him sometimes, even as he cherished its rituals. What right did they have to such a life? he asked himself. As if two men could be married, like anyone else! How the neighbors must snicker behind their backs! But really what kept him in the office—what kept him from going home—was the fear that he had swindled Danny, that he had betrayed him, and that soon—oh, the final act of betrayal, the final act of abandonment!—that soon he would have to leave him.

It was not that he didn't love him; no, he adored Danny! He loved him the way most people love only those lovers they invent in their dreams. For when they had met, Danny *was* Walter's dream. He was freedom itself. And Walter—well, Walter had tied himself for ten years to the stake of the law, he had learned discipline, he had taken steps to assure himself a moneyed safety for the rest of his life. Danny traveled around the country with his sister; he had gone to cities no business would ever bring Walter to, had stayed in communal houses instead of motel rooms. Walter loved the slightly flaky exoticism of that picaresque existence, and the curious, bewildered look that seemed to go with it, the unashamed voice, the eagerness for sex.

Danny held nothing back with Walter—no fantasy, no wish, no expression of pleasure. Other lovers Walter had had in college imposed strict rules—sex, yes, kissing, no—or they insisted on silence, there was a football player asleep across the thin wall; or they would call a passing stranger "That faggot!" almost as if the man were a different species. ("Well," this particular young man had said, when Walter called him on it, "you and me, we're different; we're not like them. We're normal guys who happen to like to have sex with other normal guys.") That tempting armature of deception Walter had managed, after some struggle, to slash down with the machete of his will. When he met Danny, he determined to say anything he wanted, do anything he wanted; but he had to train himself; he had to practice, mouthing forbidden sex words in front of the mirror. Danny was alarmingly unreserved, which Walter attributed to his growing up in that state of grace, California. He cried out, kissed passionately, as if no one had ever taught him these things were shameful, these things were forbidden. As they walked along the streets together, gangs of tough New Haven boys called out, "Fucking queers." Danny wouldn't hear. And it was not as if he blocked it out but rather, as if he were a little deaf, as if he lacked the capacity to pick up the coarser, the uglier frequencies. His freedom, his easy, generous lust (not unbridled, for there had never been any bridling; Walter's lust was unbridled)—these qualities had often moved Walter to tears in those early days. Hadn't he imagined, after all, when they first met at that lesbian bar, that Danny had been sent by some guardian angel, sent to save him, to carry him away from the law library in his gypsy caravan? Instead the caravan left—that collapsing van—and Danny stayed; rather than take Walter away, he had asked Walter to take him in like a foundling, fold him into his own ordered plans. And now, standing alone in his office, staring out at the lonely skyline of Wall Street at night, Walter wondered once again how it had come to happen that way, with him leading and Danny following and all the time Walter secretly wishing he were somewhere else, someone else.

Since their meeting in New Haven they had swum around in a series of fishtank apartments, and now they owned a fishtank of a house in the town where Walter had grown up. In the mornings they shaved together at twin sinks in the bathroom; they changed side by side into their gray suits and rode the commuter railway into Manhattan. On the train they sat opposite each other and read the newspaper. (Each had his own copy; they had reached that point in their relationship where it had become worth the extra thirty cents a day not to have to fight over the metropolitan section.) Just two ordinary suburban husbands, on their way to work, not particularly distinguishable from the hundreds of others who shared the train with them. Unless of course someone noticed the discreet good-bye kiss at the World Trade Center; but by then they were in the city, where such things were commonplace.

Each day they worked industriously, advancing, advancing, making more money. Hundreds of pressed white shirts later, hundreds of suits later, still swimming around. How wrong it all was! Walter sometimes thought. Danny should have been on some communal farm in California, he should have been playing Go at a health food restaurant, and when he wasn't there, he should have been traveling, seeing the world with April! (Where had her last tour taken her? India? Beijing? Romania?) Or perhaps it was Walter who should have been traveling around, who should have been seeing the world. His favorite movie was *The Razor's Edge;* he fancied himself Tyrone Power, seeking some large-capitaled truth in Paris, in the Himalayas, waving his arms, and speaking earnestly about the inarticulatable. Sometimes he suspected Danny liked this life they were leading more than he did, that he belonged here, in Walter's hometown, in his business suit, more than Walter did himself. But he never asked Danny if that might be true. Such fundamental matter was the marrow of their lives; it was too tender to bear conversation.

Walter hadn't told anyone yet, but he was preparing to quit his job. Quietly, quietly he was readying things for a departure on March Seventh—not a randomly chosen date, for on March Seventh, it would be exactly five years since the day Walter had joined the firm he was now associated with. And what would he do then? He hardly knew. But he would sell that fishtank of a house in Gresham; he would go somewhere, somewhere else. And he would find someone else—someone fresh and young, as Danny had once been, and, as Danny had not once been, willing to take Walter away, to Europe or the Himalayas or San Francisco. Another nice young man.

Was it his fault that Danny had asked Walter to keep him? Was it his fault that Danny seemed so much more comfortable in their comfortable house, so much more acclimated to this life they had chosen to lead, so much more contented? And yet, Walter reminded himself, if they hadn't met that night, Danny probably wouldn't have become a lawyer at all, he wouldn't have become anything close to the person he was now. Whereas Walter, without Danny—he had to admit—would have been exactly who and what he was with Danny: the same firm, the same house, the same life. Only the lover would have been different, or (more likely) there would have been no lover at all.

He put the cigarette out. (He must stop smoking for his new life.) He sat down at his computer terminal, pressed some buttons, typed some codes. And now, in the dark office, messages came to him through the glowing diodes, greetings, welcomes:

> Hot Leather: Rehi, Hunky Lawyer!
> Teen Slave Master: Hey Hunky Lawyer!
> don, 17: What's hanging, teen slave master?
> Bulging Strap: Did you hear Cary Grant died?
> Teen Slave Master: You, 17, once i get you in my cellar.
> NY Jock: Hunky lawyer!!!!!!!!!! How are those briefs??????

This endless conversation, to which he might always gain access, was the closest Walter came these days to actually cheating on Danny. He'd join in the dialogue, the circle of talk, and sometimes a message would appear, "Please talk with NY JOCK. To do so, enter /TALK 125." Once it had gotten so frantic they had switched to the phone. Their voices caressed each other; they pretended their own hands were each other's hands. Afterwards, half naked, spent, Walter slumped in his chair, looking out the window at the skyline, the neat squares of intermittent light. His shirt was unbuttoned; a distant neon sign pulsed in reflection on his chest. He didn't give out his own number or his last name. What drew him to this game was the very fact of its anonymity, the fact that no one could pin him down, that he could say whatever he felt like saying, asking questions he'd never dare ask with his voice, and hear them answered. He had a strangely intimate rapport with these men whose faces he had never seen, whose voices he had never heard; he thought of them fondly during the day, hoped they'd be there when he turned on the computer in much the same way he'd gone to the local gay bar in college hoping one or another boy he liked would be there, drinking in the corner. Now, however, he didn't want more than the screen's veiled intimacy.

He was on a private channel now. A flow of letters announced the intimate presence of one "Sweatpants."

>Hi
<hi
>What's up tonight, sweatpants?
<Not much u?
>The same. Where are you?
<NYC but I come from Shreveport, La.
<U?
>NYC
>A Southern Boy, huh?
<Yup
>So—you wearing sweatpants?
<(grin)
<Yep
>And under that?
<a sweaty jock. i just came from the gym
>Sounds hot.
<You like jockstraps?
>oh yeah . . .
<What do u look like?
>6'4, blond, blue eyes, 165 lbs. swimmer's build 7", cut
<6'1, dark hair, mustache, 160 lbs. here. 8½. tight hairy balls.
<How old?
>22
<20 here.

And on it would go into the night, sometimes for hours, this describing and assessing, this ferreting out of fetishes, this mutual indulgence and regard. So much of it was lies.

(There was nothing blond about Walter. He had dark, curly hair. His body was slack from lack of exercise; he was turning into his father.)

For diversion he typed:

>What's ur name?
<Ford urs?
>Cal
<shit . . . i can't do this shit anymore
>What?
<i am sick of this stupid crap . . . i need THE REAL THING!!!
>That's cool
<fucking machine . . . i sit here all night typing this shit
>My name's not really Cal. It's Walter.
<Why'd you change it?
>Sexier. And I am really 5'9, 150 lbs., 33, in a black suit.
<sounds hot to me . . . i love a man in uniform . . . where are u
  walt?

Again the question he didn't want to answer. He said good-bye ("huggers" was the compu-term), logged off quickly, leaving Ford alone, despondent, before his own terminal, before one of the hundreds of lit windows glowing all over town tonight. He put on his jacket, walked out into the hall. A black man was maneuvering a vast polisher over the marble floor near the elevator bank. Down and down, the whoosh of the elevator, which even now, after so many years, made his ears pop. It was a windy night; in the unnaturally illuminated plaza that separated the towers pieces of newspaper blew into the air, garbage hurried along the cement pathways as if on urgent errands, as if there were a whole life of objects, a life of old cookie fortunes and paper bags, inspirited by the wind with a sense of destiny or occupation.

He rode the PATH train to Hoboken, the mostly empty local through the string of suburbs to his own small station and the small, chilly car he had left there that morning. Down quiet streets he drove to this house that was his only according to some logic he failed to understand, this house he never would have noticed, never would have recognized, had it not been where he slept, where he ate, where on weekends he tended the garden.

Danny was in bed, reading, when Walter came in. Their dog, Betty, lay curled up next to him, but as soon as she heard the door, she jumped up to investigate. She really was Danny's dog; she had no loyalty to Walter. She exploded into life as soon as he entered, bounded upon him, but it was only because he was a distraction, a new smell. Soon enough she was back in bed.

And a few moments later Walter was lying in bed himself, Danny across from him, breathing, breathing. New flannel sheets patterned with lambs. The house vacuumed, pristine, the dishwasher humming. Danny had aged better than Walter. He was still slim, his body had retained its natural boyish musculature. Whereas Walter was getting fat, had a lawyer's paunch, cut himself while shaving. Sometimes at night like this he could look across the bed and see in Danny the same earnest-faced boy whose frank, unwavering smile had so entranced him that night, almost eight years ago, at that women's bar. The magic, the perversity of that meeting thrilled him still on occasion, though they rarely talked about it.

"What did you do today?" Walter asked quietly.

"Got home from work about six. Chatted with your mother."

"Anything else?"

"The dog groomer called again. He wants to have an affair with me."

"Should I be worried?"

"I don't think so."

They lay there, unmoving. "I can't sleep," Danny said. "This stupid song keeps running through my head."

"What song?"

" 'I gave my love a cherry that had no stone . . .' "

"Oh, that song . . ."

" 'I gave my love a chicken that had no bone . . .' "

"I remember that song. I always thought it was so strange—a chicken that had no bone. Like a monstrosity born after an atomic bomb."

"But what comes next?" Danny said. "Da-da-da-da-da-da-da? What's the next line?"

Walter was silent for a moment. "I gave my love a cornbread that had no pone."

Danny let out a snort of laughter.

"I gave my love a test tube that had no clone."

"Sorry—I gave my love a *Castro* that had no clone."

"I gave my love a problem that had no known."

"I gave my love a brass band with no trombone."

"I gave my love a heating that had no zone."

Their laughter rising up like bubbles in a fishtank.

T HE FIRST TIME Walter and Danny saw a pornographic
movie was in New Haven, a few weeks after their first meeting.
It was called—after Jerry Lewis, Danny supposed—*Sinderfella*, and it was awful, forgettable, nothing like the sleek videotaped
productions of their present lives. Even so they had walked, giddy and
thrilled, through the ruined streets of New Haven, grateful to be able
to indulge such a forbidden curiosity with each other rather than alone.
The shoulders of their coats brushed against one another; every few
steps Danny slipped on the ice, and Walter caught him before he fell.
The theater was called the New Regency, and its elaborate marquee
and foyer suggested it had seen better days. The old-fashioned ticket
booth in front was boarded up and empty. Inside, an Indian woman
with a black dot on her forehead collected the money at what must have
been once the candy counter. Then they went through another door;
they stumbled blindly for seats; they sat there in the dark and watched
it. Danny didn't remember much about the film itself, except that it
was done in a cheap and grainy eight millimeter that gave the bodies of
the young men in it a strange, whitish cast, as if they were composed
not of flesh but of light itself. The evil stepmother and the fairy
godfather were both played by a shrill-voiced, bald, fat man in a muu-
muu, and in the end, when the prince went off to find Sinderfella, he
knew which one he was because, of all the young men in the town, only

Sinderfella could take the prince's "gargantuan manhood." It was the sort of movie where people used phrases like "gargantuan manhood." The heads of the few other patrons sporadically punctuated the vast glimmer of the theater, as did the shadowy figures of men moving about the perimeter. Danny and Walter held hands, grateful for love and each other in such a strange, cold place.

It was February—and yet that might be wrong; Danny tended to remember his years in New Haven as a perpetual drizzling February, though he knew there had to have been glorious spring mornings as well, and stifling August afternoons—"February in New Haven," Walter used to say, "when the city's boring, your classes are boring, but most of all, you're boring." They were still new to each other then; everything that was stale and depressing for each of them alone seemed to be, for the two of them together, a discovery, a journey, a revelation.

Now they lived through machines, they were addicted to machines. They owned two nineteen-inch color television sets; two wireless remote-control VCRs; a Japanese stereo system with separate graphic equalizer and compact disc player; many compact discs (luminous arcs that still amazed Danny to look at); two sleek computers, each with a modem and printer; many kinds of software; a telephone that answered itself and redirected calls to other numbers; three air conditioners; a Cuisinart; a microwave oven; a can opener hinged to the bottom of the cabinet; a fancy German toaster; a coffeemaker that knew how to turn itself on at a prearranged time; a water pick; a garage door opener. And in the basement, in the backs of cabinets, rarely in use, other things, mostly gifts from Walter's father or mother: a machine on which hot dogs might be impaled and electrocuted; a yogurt maker; several kinds of ice-cream makers; a hamburger cooker for griddling a single patty at a time; a candlemaker; a plastic bag sealer; an electric toothbrush; a pasta roller; a gun that punctured red tape with capital letters; a card shuffler; a fondue melter; three hot pots; an electric knife; a pressure cooker.

There were not enough plugs. The outlets were stuffed with extenders; the extenders were stuffed with extension cords; wires tangled like matted hair under desks, cabinets, beneath the sofa. Electricity hummed through the house even when everything was turned off, wires connected to other wires, other machines, and on and on across the dark landscape of middle-of-the-night Gresham, New Jersey.

They had a piece of furniture—it was just invented, it didn't have a name yet—to house their collection of videotapes. Walter was an expert, a collector. He had mostly thirties comedies and pornography. One of each was usually the order of the night, like some peculiar rehashing of the old double-bill tradition. He had friends with whom he talked about the pornographic tapes the way other men talked about bottles of wine or racing cars. Gone were the days when pornography was something secret, something to be ashamed of; those funny black boxes with their spools of shiny celluloid were just part of the furniture now, as respectable as classical music. Walter even knew people who knew some of the greater stars of that strange pornographic universe. They were proud of what they did these days, his friend Dennis said; they even had their own little Academy Awards ceremony every year, with prizes given for acting, directing, costumes. ("Costumes?" Danny asked.) The stars wore jockstraps. Medals closely resembling those given at the Olympics were hung round their necks. And after that, presumably, more filming at poolside locales in Southern California. The voices of these films were background music to Walter and Danny's lives, a barely intelligible dialogue, dismembered by Valley Boy accents.

As for regret, it was—it is—chronically postorgasmic. The VCR clunked and rewound, and Walter, his pants around his ankles, invariably found himself overcome with sadness, as he stared at the expansive living room of his perfectly nice house, the living room that might have been lifted whole from the window at Conran's. As the film rewound, he rewound; he thought of Paris, he saw himself, suddenly, vagrant, in a dirty rooming house in Paris. Danny claimed it was generational, the children of the divorced or unhappy households of the seventies seeking to re-create in adulthood the stable family home they never had, but hoped for, all through their growing up. They do not run away; they do not go to ashrams or to visit the Great Wall. They stay home. They open Insured Market Rate Accounts.

At least as far as Walter was concerned, Danny had a point in pointing all this out. His own growing up, after all, had been less than secure. His father, Morry, had left home when Walter was twelve, and in the intervening years Walter had seen him only in restaurants— expensive, loud restaurants filled with the tumultuous machinery of giant organs; restaurants on the edges of highways that served things like buffalo chicken wings and fried potato skins; restaurants in the city with waiters and sous-chefs and porcini mushrooms; suburban Mafia dens with gold flatware, buffets, platters of jumbo shrimp, heaping bowls of chocolate mousse. Oh, his father had a house, not that far away, which he shared with a woman named Leonie. But somehow he never had occasion to ask Walter to visit that house, and Walter had never had occasion to press the issue. As for Iris, his mother, she was quiet and frugal, a schoolteacher, recently retired. After the divorce she had of course had to move out of the big family ranch house, which was quickly sold at immense profit. Years of solitude and suffering had led her to a sort of peace with herself. She lived in a condominium complex for singles, in an apartment rich with maroon carpeting, and she had a boyfriend, a retired elementary school principal named Hal. She remained a diligent mother. Often, when Walter got home from work, he'd find packages of home-baked bread waiting on his kitchen counter or a pot of soup simmering on the stove. The sink shone; there was a package of colored sponges sitting on the table with a note that said, "Remember—green for dishes, yellow for counters." Iris and Hal had subscriptions to the state opera and symphony, and sat in on a music history course at a local community college. In the summer they went on tours. In buses, with guides, they walked Rome, the Greek islands, and a good portion of the Great Wall of China; they saw Cairo and Istanbul; they "did" Moscow, where, under the watchful eye of the KGB, Iris delivered a letter from the children of their synagogue to the children of some refuseniks and openly, daringly took pictures of forbidden things. "The guard just looked at me," she explained, "and I looked at him, real tough. You think he'd take on an American lady who's likely to scream bloody murder? No way." And she laughed, passing around blurry snapshots of smiling couples, and street carts, and large gray buildings—what was forbidden about all of this even Iris couldn't say.

Walter saw his mother almost every day; he saw his father exactly twelve times a year—the very same visitation agreement provisioned by the original divorce. After their monthly luncheons, the dates of which were emblazoned in Iris's memory, she always called on some pretext and after a few moments, inevitably, asked how things had gone, how Morry was. "Fine," Walter always said.

"And did he have his woman there?"

"No, Leonie stayed home."

"It figures. I guess he was ashamed to be seen with her in public."

That was his family.

Funny how much more stable his own life appeared, at least in the eyes of the world. His parents were the ones, after all, who had trusted in the god of stability.

And so, pulling up his pants, Walter thought, perhaps Danny was right. Perhaps he really had chosen this life. Although, he reflected, as the mouth of the VCR spit out the rewound tape like a black tongue, it was more comfortable to believe that it had been chosen for him, foisted upon him, that given the option, he would have been in Paris now, writing novels or painting pictures. Asking questions.

Danny was in the other room of course, busy with something. Talking to his mother, his sister, his father on the telephone.

L OUISE WAS WATCHING *Women in Love* on cable and doing her hands. She had turned it on in the middle, so she didn't know what was going on. Men and women in antiquated dress, running around in the British countryside. There seemed to be sexual tension. Her mind was wandering—she was worrying about a dentist's appointment on Friday, a follow-up to root canal work, as well as a peculiar rash on her feet which itched—when suddenly something came on the screen that dazzled, and she was lost. A dark, bearded man was making love to a woman in an elaborate Victorian dress; the woman lay back on the grass, her skirts hiked up, and he hovered over her, naked, his hips bucking and thrusting. Louise caught back her breath and put her hand to her mouth, but of course for the moment she didn't have a hand. Nonetheless she did not move her arm—not until the man had finished, shuddering upon the girl's layered gowns, and the bland, soft taste of warm terry cloth and fabric softener began to cloy against her teeth.

The scene ended. The film returned to its previous confusing plots. Soon the characters were in a snowy landscape, running around in furs. She switched off the TV with the blunt, feelingless end of the terry-cloth arm.

But as she unwrapped her hands and peeled the wax from them, she was amazed at how vividly Tommy Burns returned to her. She assumed she had lost him; assumed that the intervening years, with their hard work and hard duties, not only had deprived her of the opportunity to experience such intense moments as those she had lived with him but indeed had robbed her of memory itself, dulling forever the sharp edges of her experiences, so that she hardly believed they had taken place at all.

When she was a little girl, she had once woken up from a nightmare, and her mother had said to her, "Don't worry, darling, it was just a dream." "But how can I tell when it's a dream and when it's not?" Louise asked, and her mother balanced a finger against her lip and said, "Pinch yourself. If you don't feel it, it's a dream." This had consoled Louise for forty years; she had pinched herself through forty years of dream-filled nights.

So she believed her affair with Tommy Burns was, or was something like, a dream. She remembered him, remembered the passion with which they had burned together. But it was the numb giving of other flesh, not her own, that strange sensation of pinching and pinching, and feeling nothing.

She thought of the bearded man, his body fevered, the girl in the layered skirts, and she was returned to the smell of Tommy Burns's breath, clam bellies smothered in fat, as vividly as if that dented, spitting vat had materialized in her own kitchen, along with the tattooed man and the fryer basket shaking in the bubbles. This made her move toward the bedroom, where Nat lay snoring, with a renewed sense of pleasure. The springy give of the carpet felt good against her itchy feet, almost as good as it had felt when it was new, back in their past, when carpeting itself had seemed such an extravagant luxury. So perhaps the carpeting really was new, and it really was ten years earlier, the past rushing forward to reclaim her for youth.

She took off her robe, climbed into her half of the vast bed. It was bigger than king size, an ocean of a bed; the sheet and blanket rippled like waves as she pulled them over. She couldn't sleep, so she tried to imagine what her life would've been like if Eleanor hadn't gotten sick and Tommy Burns had asked her to marry him. Then she'd be living in Los Angeles, in a house on a cliff, a house with huge windows, maybe overlooking the ocean. She would have different children as well; she had invented them and named them: Brad, the son, a doctor, handsome as his father but given to bouts of depression; Susan, a daughter, a lawyer, pretty and professional with carefully manicured nails. She didn't particularly love these imagined offspring—ultimately the fantasy of them made her grateful for her own imperfect children—but at the same time she believed in them; she believed they were the children she and Tommy Burns would have had in that other life, that life in which she was a Hollywood wife—heavily made up, with thickly glossed nails and a string of pearls around her neck. As it was, she never wore makeup.

NAT WAS GONE when she woke up in the morning. He rose silently each day at the crack of dawn and disappeared. As he slept soundly, unmoving, his absence really felt no different from his presence.

It was the day of her appointment. At noon, at the hospital, the news was that one of the black mollies had given birth; the tiny fry swam round and round the little nursery tank that Dr. Golden had suspended onto the side of the big tank, like one of those backpacks young mothers carried their babies in. Eventually her name was called; she went into the examination room and soon was relieved to see Dr. Wolff, the good resident, coming through the door. One reason Dr. Wolff was the good resident was that she didn't keep Louise waiting. Dr. Tallcott, the bad resident, had once kept her waiting in the examination room for more than an hour. She despised Dr. Tallcott, his clumsy hands and stupid humor, but would do anything for Dr. Wolff, whose gentleness and normalness were such a relief in that frightening place that she was often moved to tears, to extravagant praise at dinner parties, monologues of adulation that left the other guests nodding and nervous, not sure what to say, grasping for new subjects—anything to avoid the awful mention of the disease's name. But Dr. Wolff was slightly grave today as she felt Louise's lymph nodes. "Just a long night last night," she said when Louise asked, and smiled. "Thanks for noticing." Louise might easily have called Dr. Wolff by her first name—Deborah— except that she enjoyed the fact that this splendid young woman was a doctor and wanted to give her every opportunity to exult in that achievement. So she was always calling her Dr. Wolff. Dr. Tallcott she avoided addressing.

At length Dr. Wolff said good-bye; Dorothy came in and took a sample of blood. "That's it, honey," she said as she removed the needle, daubed the wound with cotton, and put on a Band-Aid. "You're free."

"Thanks," Louise said, reaching behind to untie the starchy white gown. Temporary freedom wasn't an insult to her anymore, it was a gift.

She dressed quickly, hurried outside. On the lawn next to the parking lot, the usual bunch of right-to-lifers were marching their beleaguered-looking children in a perpetual, droopy circle, as if they had been condemned to play ring-around-the-rosy for eternity. There were only women this afternoon, pale-skinned and moon-faced and young, in pink and green down coats; they carried signs that read, PROTECT THE UNBORN and THIS HOSPITAL COMMITS MURDER. Louise always nodded her head crossly when she encountered them, turned the corner with aggression, thrust off their petitions with fists. It was a weak gesture compared with the inexhaustible determination of these pale-skinned enemies, but it was all she could muster. She lacked the stamina of belief. Most people she knew assumed that cancer had made her a cynic and an atheist, but in fact she had been that way since well before cancer; what had fueled her hard work for progressive causes all those years was not hope for the ideal of a perfect world— man, she believed, was brutal and stupid, utterly imperfectible—but the endless end-of-fall burning of the endless dry leaves of hopelessness. All you could do was do what you could, stave off the chaos, one day at a time.

Before cancer, she had had fighting spirit; she had believed she held the power to change minds. Back then, when the protests were fresh, she took part in counterdemonstrations, and the tired-looking young women, in response to the statistics on teenaged pregnancy fired out by Louise and her friends, fired out scriptural quotation with mechanistic devotion. It was like a game show she had once seen on CBN, or the Christian Bimbo Network, in which contestants vied to identify biblical phrases as quickly as possible: "Corinthians one: seventeen!" "Matthew thirty-four: twelve!" It became clear to her pretty quickly she wasn't getting through; she'd never get through this armature of belief.

She backed off. She hated the antiabortionists, but she was also cowed by the power of their belief. It was like nothing she herself had ever come close to feeling.

She was tired. She looked tired. Several years ago she had ceased to concern herself with vanity, as she put it; now she kept her hair cut short, no longer bothered to dye out the gray. Usually she dressed in big sweaters and denim skirts or jeans. Her skin was dark and carved with deep grooves, like the bark of a tree. "What do I need with fancy clothes?" she said, when her old friends Myra Eber and Joyce Rosen tried to get her to go out shopping with them. "I don't need to look nice anymore. I don't have time." She meant it. What good did it do to spend hundreds of dollars on dresses from Saks, to pay outlandish dues to the temple just so you could hear the rabbi paraphrase, in lieu of a sermon, the entire plot of some movie he'd seen on HBO the night before? ("But, Louise," Joyce implored, "that only happened once! Rabbi only did that once!" "Once was too much for me," Louise said.) Her friends bought sleek Norma Kamali gowns and wore them to Rosh Hashanah services. Louise stayed home. She had no need for services. She had no time. After years in which the time stretched out, a dull horizon calling to be filled, for the first time in her life her days were numbered, and she was not going to waste a second pretending to piety in that so-called sanctuary, that hive of expensive clothing and gossip about who was getting divorced, who was cheating on whom, who was dying. She craved more than that. She craved the very thing she didn't believe in, the very thing the temple (she felt) could give her none of: She craved belief itself.

She talked about this with no one. She had no reason to. Her agnostic mother had taught her that religious feeling, like sexual feeling, was something slightly embarrassing, something you dealt with quickly and privately, if you had to, and didn't talk about in public. And that had been fine. For the first thirty-five years of her life she'd had no reason to think about belief, she was so busily engaged in existence. Still, things had happened she hadn't been prepared for: cancer, for one, and no one in her childhood had warned her, in between all that talk of marriage and family, that sons sometimes preferred the company of sons, daughters the company of daughters. Well, she had coped with that. She had coped with all of it, coming through the hurdles splendidly, she believed, as a result of an uncommon combination of lust for life and unrelenting pessimism. Odd that those two opposed tendencies should go hand in hand, but they did, and indeed, their doing so seemed to Louise perfectly sensible; in that unlikely pairing it seemed to her was the germ of religious feeling.

For in spite of her difficult and simple life, Louise had a dream, a lust, a vision. It was unlikely, unimaginable, so much so that she spoke of it to no one. There stood near her house, between the looming architectures of two corporate presences, a small, white, stuccoed building where the windows were always closed. It was a cloistered convent; for twenty-five years the nuns had never emerged, and no one (except, presumably, new recruits) ever went in. Food and linens and other necessities were supplied by a kind of carrier nun, who passed them through a turnstile inside the front door. Sometimes Louise stopped her car in front of the convent and stared through the trees at the yellow-lit windows, and once she thought she saw a glimmer of a face, a fleeting old face, passing by, not stopping to look out.

This was her lust: She dreamed of being a nun. Not a crusading nun who offered immune, self-immolating sanctuary to refugees or risked her life nursing children in war-torn Central American countries; no, Louise wanted to be a cloistered nun, a nun who loved Jesus alone, a nun who swathed herself in white cotton, and slept in a cold, still room, and pushed linens through old-fashioned roller washers. A silent nun, who had sworn never to speak, never even to mumble, not even in her sleep, not even when no one could hear. It was that cold, clear, silent life, and that life alone, which tempted her, that life so far from her own, with its frantic demands and waverings and deathly fears.

There was a legend about Louise in her family. Her own mother, Anna, told how once she had taken Louise—six years old—on a bus and sat her down opposite a pair of nuns. "Mommy," Louise had said, "why are those ladies dressed so funny?" Anna had laughed nervously and, clenching her teeth, given her daughter a look to suggest what terrible punishments would result from an inappropriate remark, before answering in a clear, dental voice, "Because they're nuns, dear." To which Louise responded, with a small but bewitching smile, "But aren't they beautiful?"

Louise loved this story, though she could not remember the incident happening. Her mother loved it too; she told it for forty years, sitting around the table after dinner or with her friends at the Chiffon Beauty Shoppe in Malden. And always it was Louise's wit that was praised, her know-how, her sensitivity to unspoken threats. "She knew what to say, I'll tell you," Anna told her laughing friends, assuming all the while that Louise's feeling about the nuns, even at ten, was the same as her mother's: bemusement and bafflement. Contempt. That old-world disdain. What surprised Louise was that no one had considered the possibility that she might have really thought the nuns were beautiful.

Louise, in her car, at stoplights, on long, luminous, empty avenues. Always when driving, from her house to the hospital or to the grocery store, she was nurturing this fantasy: the dream of a clean and clear life in which belief translated exactly into strength. A life in which she would rise early and go to bed early and never feel tired (as she always did now). A life in which all the photographic borders would crystallize and come into a sharper focus, and she would know, moment to moment, how it was she was meant to live, and why.

But of course this was just a wish, an idle fancy. She was a cynic and an atheist. She was a foe of the antiabortionists, doubted she would ever forgive the pope his audience with Kurt Waldheim. In her actual life, her nondream life, pragmatism prevailed. She was addicted to nasal sprays, could not sleep or breathe without them. Every morning and every evening she guiltily snorted from small bottles, imagining that this fear of not being able to breathe must be what was at the heart of being an alcoholic, a junkie. Garbage cans overturned, yogurt spilled in shopping bags, there were always forgotten places filling with dust. Some futile urge to order the world kept her moving, but the forces of chaos in her life were stronger than that other urge by far. Like Penelope she knit—sweaters, mittens, sometimes skirts and dresses. Unlike Penelope she put her knitting aside at night and slept, though fitfully. And what foiled her in her knitting was nothing more than the ordinary tangles of misread instructions.

"She's just bitter and dry and angry," she imagined people saying in private, when her name came up, and she approved. She liked the idea of being thought of as bitter and dry and angry. Anything but "Poor Louise Cooper. You know her husband has a lover, and she has cancer, and both—both!—her children are homosexuals. Isn't that terrible? Poor woman. If I were in her shoes—"

WHEN SHE GOT HOME, Nat was back already, cracking peanuts in the kitchen. He was often home early these days; he had little
work to do, little to occupy himself with. His research was at a standstill, his teaching a matter of prepared lectures he could give by rote.

"How did it go today?" he asked her when she walked in the
door.

"Fine," she said, searching his eyes for anything suspicious. There,
in his eyes, lay the clues to her other darknesses—his still-not-admitted
adulteries. Well, she didn't care about who he did it to, didn't care as
long as it was a prostitute in Thailand, a girl picked up in a bar in Los
Angeles, paid with dinner and a movie and the pretense of tenderness.
Even when it came to Lillian Two-Names, she didn't care if he was
fucking her; that in and of itself didn't bother her. She had had her own
moments after all, had her memories of Tommy Burns and Xavier and
Mike Spivack. Who cared if Nat had fuel to burn? No, what hurt—
what sliced like a knife through her heart—was this scene she often
imagined: Lillian Two-Names sitting across a table from some woman,
maybe a secretary from Nat's department, drinking coffee, weeping,
confiding. And the words Lillian says, in this reverie, cut sharp: "A
good man like that! Why does he stay with her? Pity, that's all, pity
because she's got cancer. If she didn't have cancer, he'd leave her, I know
he would."

The nameless second woman nods sympathetically. She is no one;
she is a nod, that's all.

"I just have to be patient," Lillian says. "I just have to wait."

The scene played in Louise's head. It expanded. It lit a flame.

"Remember we have that dinner at the Rosens' tomorrow," she
reminded Nat.

"Don't embarrass me with any political arguments this time, will
you?" he said, referring to the last dinner party they'd gone to, where
she'd challenged the dean of sciences on Reagan's foreign policy. (Nat
hated how she sometimes flared like that in public, then just went on,
saying what she had to say, indifferent to the comfort of the other
guests, who had to sit silently by, chewing on toothpicks. Indif-

ferent, finally, to his own comfort. He failed to see what good it did to stir up bad feelings or make unnecessary enemies.)

"Great," she said hotly, irritated to be reminded of this old indiscretion. In truth she felt guilty about it and was planning to make an effort at Joyce Rosen's party not to argue with anyone, but now Nat had put her on the defensive. So she said, "If that's the way you feel, I won't go. I'll stay home."

"Louise—"

"Never mind. You don't want me, I'm not going. That's it."

"That's ridiculous, Louise. She's your friend. Anyway, you're the one who accepted. If anyone isn't going, it's me."

"Why," Louise said, "do you always have to squelch me, to shut me up, as if my opinion's worthless? It just isn't fair, Nat. You're so damned determined to keep the peace, to keep everything nice and calm. But I'm not just going to sit by like some stupid wife while some big-bellied man holds forth about the glories of Ronald Reagan. I am just not. I have my integrity."

"I have my reputation," Nat said.

"I have *my* reputation," Louise said.

"You have *a* reputation," Nat said, "and if you'll pardon my saying so, it's not a very good one."

That stung her. She looked at him, and her first impulse was to say, Really? Is it true? Do people talk about me? She feared and despised the idea of people talking about her. But no, it was just a tactic, an attempt at intimidation.

"Shut up," she said challengingly.

"Why should I? You never do. You talk and talk, and it ruins the dinner party for everyone else."

Rage left her speechless. She wanted to throw something. There was nothing to throw.

"I wish you would just go to hell," she said, turning from him.

Nat walked out of the room.

"That's right, just storm away, you bastard!" And when there was no answer, she said it again: "You bastard! You bastard!" Her voice high-pitched, the words echoing across the house. A door, loudly slammed, was the only answer.

Then there was a moment's silence, before the crying started. He came back into the kitchen. Very efficiently he put on his jacket; he said, "I don't have to take this crap from you." She buried her face in her hands.

"Don't go," she said softly.

"Can't hear you," he said. "All that yelling has wrecked my eardrums."

A last surge of rage rose in her. "You bastard!" she shouted again, but it only gave him a good reason to slam the door.

She stood. She opened the window. "Nat!" she called. "Wait! Wait! I'm sorry, Nat, I'm sorry." But he was in the car already. She opened the back door, flew out after him. "I'm sorry," she said again, "I'm sorry." He was pulling out, turning away.

"Nat!" she called. Ridiculous, barefoot, in the street.

Immediately she ran back inside, grabbed her purse and car keys, ran out again, got into her own car, pulled out after him. He was turning left at the stop sign. She approached him from behind. He drove through, made a surprising, sudden right turn without signaling. The dusty rubber of the accelerator pedal was warm against her bare foot.

Three more stop signs. He was off his route, ashamed, or angry, or both, about where he was going. Finally: a red light on a country highway, no traffic, no cars. She pulled up her emergency brake and ran out, paying no attention to the street gravel, which was cutting her bare feet bloody. "Nat," she said, trying to sound calm, normal, "Nat, I'm sorry."

His electric window closed on her face.

"Nat," she said.

"Leave me alone, for Christ's sake," he said, his voice barely audible through the closed window.

"Nat, no!" She rapped on the window. Then the light changed, and he was off, leaving her there, barefoot in the intersection.

There was a sudden quietness in the aftermath of his parting in which she could actually hear the chirping of birds and the breeze moving the leaves. A child in a Hugga Bunch T-shirt stood across the road, her legs stretched over her bicycle seat, taut as a dancer on point. The child's bicycle had a white wicker basket attached to the front, and Louise found herself trying to remember the color of the wicker basket on her own childhood bicycle, in Little Nahant. A car approached from behind, slowed down in puzzlement at the sight of Louise's car, apparently parked there, in the middle of the road, and Louise, shaken, suddenly, from her rapt contemplation of the bicycle basket, shrugged her shoulders, smiled at the driver of the car, mouthed the word "stalled," got back in, and floored the gas pedal. In the rearview mirror she could see the driver of the other car shaking his head, and the child, like someone wakened from a trance, pedaling away in the opposite direction.

Back at her own house, she sat at the kitchen table. There, in the center, as always, were the salt and pepper shakers, a vase of flowers, the ceramic sugar bowl with its cracking moon and stars. As usual, she found herself retracing the torrid plot of the argument, trying to gauge her rectitudes as well as her missteps, squinting at those foibles she saw clearly. She couldn't help any of this. The old-news argument with the dean of sciences several weeks back kept replaying in her head, until she had herself convinced it was all ultimately the dean of sciences' fault, the world's fault. After all, if he hadn't started *that* argument, there would've been no subject for this one. Had it been wrong of her to challenge the dean? Should she have just sat by? All those blustery Ph.D.ed men, holding forth as if they owned the world, and she, powerless, without even a college degree. (A fact that Nat never mentioned to anyone, but which she knew was often a foremost embarrassment in his thoughts; she had gone to nursing school and dropped out at the beginning of the war.) Oh, Nat! (And now she addressed him with all the secret, unleashed eloquence she could somehow never muster in his presence.) Oh, Nat, don't you understand that what little pride I can gather these days depends upon my proving to the dean of sciences that I am his equal, his contender, and will not, like so many others, let his noxious opinions pass unremarked? But of course you only understand diplomacy, keeping the peace, making no enemies. As my mother used to say, "A person with no enemies is friends with a bunch of snakes." And in this new argument, this fantasy argument, she turns away triumphantly, leaving him speechless, without recourse, stunned by the rightness of her point of view, savaged, changed. "Louise!" he says. "You're right! From now on, no more diplomacy! Life is an adventure! And I don't give a damn what your reputation is! Anyone puts you down to me, honey, you can bet I'll tell him where to stuff it!" Yes, Nat! Right, Nat! As if a reputation for having a hotheaded wife were really such a terrible thing! True, if she had a reputation for having affairs, or lying, or poisoning cats! But really, in the scheme of things, was it so terrible to be a hotheaded wife? He should be grateful, she said to herself. Other men would've been grateful.

So, a voice said, why don't you leave him?

Forget it, forget it. Fear. Such unbelievable, all-consuming fear.

She got up, walked a hesitant circle of the house, and sat down on the yellow sofa in the family room, determined not to pace anymore; took out her knitting; put it down again. If, in the big, just world, she was right, didn't that make some difference, hold some influence, in the little world of her little life? Or was he judge, jury, and executioner? Marriage as dictatorship, not democracy; she'd suspected it all along. And even if she won on facts, what did facts matter? She'd never wanted it that way, she'd never asked for it, but there it was: As far as her well-being was concerned, his opinion was the only one that counted.

She got up, went back into the kitchen. The sun was beginning to set. The momentary sense of triumph brought on by her earlier raging had long since left her; she felt no pleasure, only sorrow that her anger had again won her nothing. What were facts? What did the dean of sciences matter; what did hotheadedness, her desire to prove her worth, matter? The truth was that Nat encouraged these fights because they gave him an excuse to leave.

She felt as if she had miscarried. Her stomach was raw. So she turned on every light; she turned on every television. She paced the bright arena of the many-windowed house, chewing on a cigarette-shaped pacifier, a plastic toy from when she'd quit smoking, wondering if this last fight might be the one too many, the straw that broke the camel's back. Driving after him like that! Why hadn't she just let him alone, let him stew it out alone, maybe feel a little guilty? Nat had endured so much with her, after all, in her own lapsing days; he had been patient, stoic; he'd never yelled. She owed him her loyalty for not leaving her when he really had a reason to, when it would have been so easy. Back then—had it really been thirty years?—his reasoning had been simple: He loved her, he said. More than anyone he could imagine. And she— oh, how she regretted it now!—she had said, "You make it seem so damn simple! Love for me isn't like that, it isn't simple. I have different kinds of feelings—sometimes they're very complicated." How she wished she herself had been simple then, as he had been, for by now he had taken her words to heart, and she dreaded the inevitable day when he'd quote them back at her.

He would be back by ten the next morning. He always was. Slipping in the kitchen door, slightly sheepish, his rage for the moment quelled. But never, never forgiving.

Quietly, patiently, she began to plan her apology: how she would kiss him and lay her head on his resisting or giving shoulder. How he would sigh, look away. How, if worse came to worst, if he said, "We can't go on like this," she would say what she was saving to say at that inevitable moment: "You cannot leave me. I can't live without you, and I can't die without you either." Those words that she had never spoken, but which reverberated through the house, provisional, assumed. All she had to do was say them, she knew, and their power would bloom like the power of a magic spell. Lillian Two-Names might call it blackmail, and maybe it was. But her pride—once such a strong shield—was by now so damaged it hardly existed at all. So she took comfort in those words and in the knowledge that in the final confrontation, she could save herself by using them, and keep him.

At about this moment Louise understood Nat's car to be pulling into Lillian's driveway. She had timed the trip. She imagined she could hear the wheels against the tiny bits of gravel in Lillian's driveway. Every nuance of that tiny crunching reverberated in her ears.

———

AS FOR NAT, by the time he got to Lillian's house he was close to shaking. For more than half an hour he'd been driving in meaningless circles, through unfamiliar suburban neighborhoods, down and around the circular ends of cul-de-sacs where the sidewalks sloped to the street. The houses he passed were series-uniform even in color—pink, mauve, lime, pink, mauve, lime—and brought back Carrollton to him, that perfect town of the future, built on garbage, where he had idealistically settled his family upon arriving in California. A sadness and a regret—he had invested in such suburban projects, back in the fifties, his own utopian urges, and now they had fallen to wear and tear and ruin, or, worse, the ravages of renovation, which individualized and wrecked what beauty they had, the beauty of one house the same after another. That mathematician's beauty, that city planner's beauty. Now he was on Ruthelma Drive, named, he suspected, for the wives of the builders. Ruthelma Drive, Tedlee Way. Louise had hated all that, had had no patience for it. And of course, all this time, as he drove aimlessly through the landscape of his past loves, he was convinced Louise was still following him, cursing Ted and Lee and Ruth and Thelma as much as she was cursing him. Where, in all of this, was Danapril Street? Natlou Street? Lillnat Street?

He pulled up along the curb of a closed shoe store. Waited. She didn't approach. Well, he had finally shaken her. And now he began to worry about consequences: What if she gets into a car accident? What if I drive her over the edge and she does something impulsive, something terrible? Turning off the ignition, he got out of his car and walked to an open pizza parlor, dug through the rows of sticky, dark tables and red-net candles to the phone booth, dialed his own number, then hung up before there were any rings. He couldn't bear to hear her voice. Oh, what should he do? He was tempted to go home again, except that the thought of her in the bed next to him in her lace nightgown, curled into herself like a nut, was almost too much for him. Going back would mean having to listen to her recriminations and resentments and unhappinesses all night. Whereas what he wanted now—what he needed—was something positive, some good light, some pleasure in his life. Louise took advantage of him, he told himself now. He was her dishrag, her handkerchief. When she hurt, or when she was scared about the cancer, or when she just felt her life was shitty, it was Nat she took it out on. Why the hell can't you clean up after yourself? Well, then, what *did* you do with it? I do everything for you, and you don't lift a finger for me. No, don't touch me. No, don't talk to me. Just leave me the hell alone. And underneath that, and oddly at the same moment: Touch me. Hold me. Help me.

He dug his way back out of the cavernous pizza parlor, drove to Lillian's. She was at the door, waiting for him, by the time he made it out of his car, slowed to hesitation by fantasies of Louise with a gun, hiding in the bushes. She had her hair pulled back in a bun, and wore a beige chiffon bathrobe, and smelled of face cream. "Nat, you look like you just got run over on the highway," she said, and taking his hand, ushered him quickly through the door. Her living room was bright, cleaning-lady clean, with Beethoven on the stereo, pictures of her clean-cut (heterosexual) children, smiling, above the dining room table.

As soon as he was in the door and it was locked, he fell into the sofa and sat there, slumped, while she fetched him coffee. "And I have that chocolate hazelnut torte you love so much from O'Hanlon's," she called from the kitchen. "I'll cut you a piece."

He smiled, unable to move, and waited for her to bring him the coffee and cake and sit down next to him.

"How was your day?" he asked.

"Crazy. That goddamned Krautheimmer is going to drive me insane, trying to plan this conference around all his agendas. But I don't want to talk about me! Natty, what happened?"

He shrugged. "Nothing unusual. A fight." And suddenly, to his own surprise, he was weeping.

"Natty," Lillian said. "Oh, Natty." And putting down her mug and cake plate, she enfolded him in her chiffon-enfolded arms.

"Jesus, Lil, I don't think I can take another day of it," Nat was muttering. "I just don't think I can take another day of it. She's crazy, Lil. No, no, she's not crazy. She's just so unhappy she does crazy things."

"She needs help," Lillian said quietly, strumming his hair with her long fingers.

"Coming to you like this, it's my salvation," Nat said. "But as soon as I'm here, I start thinking, Why does it have to end in the morning? God, why do I have to go back, why do I have to go back? God help me, I wish she would die. I can't believe it, I wish she would die."

"It's okay," Lillian said. "It's okay."

"But, Lil, I'm so scared when I think that. I hate myself for thinking that. I mean, it's all my fault."

"What's your fault?"

"Everything. The cancer, everything. Her whole life is my fault."

"No," Lillian said, and pushed his head away. "Now look at me, Nat. She may be miserable and she may have cancer and you may have done some shitty things to her, but her life is not your fault. No one's life is anyone's fault. God knows, it took me long enough to learn it, but I did. We make our own choices, all of us, Louise as much as anyone else."

"I guess, Lil." He sniffled and, taking a kleenex from a box on the coffee table, blew his nose.

"Nat, I've told you before—"

He shook his head.

"Nat, it could be the best thing you could do. For her as well as yourself. It could be just what it takes to force her to take her life into her own hands."

"She can't live without me," Nat said quietly.

"Don't be so sure," Lillian said. "Women have made remarkable recoveries, they've come to life in ways you wouldn't believe, and I think Louise could too." And then, suddenly, she laughed. "Me, the great feminist," she said. "The other woman. I mean, looking at it objectively, it's Louise I'm interested in, Louise I want to help. But I don't suppose she'd accept my help. Oh, well. The great, selfless Lillian Rubenstein-Kraft deludes herself again. Thinking I want you to leave her for *her* sake."

Thus admitting for the first time that evening her own unhappiness with the situation, Lillian turned away.

Nat laughed a little at that as, standing from the sofa, Lillian drew the living room blinds.

The phone rang. Immediately they both turned to look at it and, like people willed into enchantment or hypnosis, froze.

"I'm not going to get it," Lillian said.

"Don't get it," Nat said.

"I'm not going to get it."

They kept standing there, and as the phone kept ringing, they looked intently into each other's eyes across the room. Counting. Finally, when it was silent, they breathed and moved to each other in the center. Their hands intertwined.

"It *is* okay," Lillian said. "Remember, what we have is okay. We have rich, full lives. We'll take what we can get for the moment, and in the future?" She shrugged. "Who knows what'll happen? Right?"

Nat smiled. "Right," he said. "God, I wonder if that was her calling."

"It doesn't matter," Lillian said. "For the moment it really doesn't matter. It could have been my kids, but they'll call back. You know anyone can call back."

"Yes," he said. "You're right. But you know—oh, I don't know, maybe I should go home tonight. I mean, she was so upset, out there on the street, barefoot. I don't trust her. It's come far before; it's never come this far. Could it go farther? I mean, we are on the very horizon of finally saying the truth to each other, and yet somehow we hold back before saying it—you know, 'I'm in love with Lillian,' 'You can't leave me until I'm dead, I won't let you,' 'I can't live with you,' 'I can't live without you.' All of it. So we keep going in circles, and I think sometimes maybe the anxiety is giving her the cancer, or making it worse—I've read that could happen—and I think—God forgive me— sometimes I think I'm glad, I think I want her to get sicker so I can get on with my life, but then other times I'm just flooded with memories, flooded with memories of the children, us as a family, and I look at her and try to imagine not looking at her—I mean, her not being there to look at, you know? Her not being there to make a fuss or object or yell. You fill the dishwasher the wrong way and instead of a lecture— nothing. Because she's gone. And I think of turning on the dishwasher and the dishwasher starting and her being gone and, Lil, something caves in—it's like I'm gone too. I just can't stand the thought of losing her, I guess is what I'm trying to say. Which is maybe also why I can't leave—not just for her sake. I mean, Lil, forty years! Jesus God, forty years!"

For a moment they were both silent. Lillian looked away.

"Well," he said. "Well. What to do now?"

"I feel like a criminal," Lillian said quietly. "You know, for my own sake, I'm encouraging you to do things I'm not sure I really, objectively believe you should do, not in my heart."

"Everyone deserves some happiness, Lil," Nat said. "But you can only obligate others to your own happiness so long—up to a certain limit, that is. So the question is, When do you reach the limit? I mean, is marriage like sharecropping or something? Is it perpetual debt?" He shook his head crossly. "I refuse that model. I've given Louise enough to satisfy my own—moral code. Now I have to think of myself."

"And not leave her," Lillian said.

They were silent for a few breaths.

"And not leave her," Nat said.

―――――――

LATER THAT NIGHT Louise, who was in truth far too fearful of Lillian's voice even to consider phoning there, heard her own phone ring. She was sitting in the living room in her bathrobe, the knitting needles knocking gently, one against the other, the television talking in the background. When she heard the phone, she stood slowly, wondering if it might be Nat. She thought she should let it ring a few times, then changed her mind and lifted the receiver to her ear.

"Mom, it's me," Danny said.

"Oh, Danny, hi!"

"How are you?"

"Oh, you know. Okay. How are you?"

"I'm fine. I was wondering if I could talk to Dad, I have a money question—"

"Well, actually, Danny, he's not home." She paused to come up with an excuse for him, then decided he didn't deserve one. "He's visiting a friend," she said.

There was a moment of silence during which Danny apparently decided not to pick up on her cue. "It's nothing urgent," he said. "Can he call me tomorrow?"

"Sure he can."

"Good. Anyway, anything important up?"

"Not much," Louise said. "I'm thinking of becoming a Catholic."

There was another brief silence. "Excuse me?" Danny said.

"I just said I was thinking of becoming a Catholic."

"A Catholic. Why?"

"I think Catholicism offers a lot to people who have to be alone." (In fact, this idea hadn't occurred to her until that moment, but it seemed true as she said it.)

"Well," Danny said, flustered, "I don't know much about Catholicism. Forgive me, Mom, if I sound surprised, but I never thought you were a religious person."

"I haven't been up until now. But my life is changing, Danny. I need to do something—because of my life." Suddenly she felt herself on the verge of crying, talking about her life like that. Already she had gone too far; she didn't want him to know she was crying. So she covered the mouthpiece with her hand and struggled to control her breath.

"I think it's great that you want to change your life, Mom, but—well, what about getting a job? Wouldn't that be a good idea? You were talking about that last week!"

"Danny!" she said. "Who would hire me?"

"Lots of people! Anyway, I thought you were going to apply at World Savings."

She laughed. "Don't be silly. A dumb old lady who doesn't have a college degree—what would they want with me at World Savings?"

"Mom, you're not dumb or old. You're very smart."

"Well, that's very sweet of you, son, to say so."

"I mean it."

"Thank you. It's always nice to know you can depend on your children for flattery, even when you're an old rotten hag."

"Mom, for Christ's sake!"

"Listen, Danny," she said, "I have to go—something's in the oven."

"Mom, I—"

"I'll talk to you soon, honey. Don't worry about me, I'm fine."

"Mom—" He sighed, whether with relief or frustration she couldn't tell. "Okay, then. Bye."

She hung up quickly, blew her nose. Instinctively she moved to the kitchen, as if there really were something in the oven. But of course there wasn't. She turned it on to clean itself.

But as she walked back to the living room, the vision returned to her: the vision of the stone cell, the white robe, the gentle relinquishing as the scissors snipped away and the hair fell in locks to the floor. It stunned her, this vision; she suddenly had no strength, and she crouched where she stood, in the middle of the dining room, almost in a position of prayer. With her hands she pressed shut her eyelids, as if by pressing she could really block out the vision encroaching upon her. "Dear Lord," she said. "Dear God. Dear Lord."

So she remained, on her knees, in the dining room, for what seemed like several hours. She was trying not to think of her husband and his two-named lover, but instead to feel the ecstatic release as those inevitable shears—cutting, cutting—removed from her the burdens of her life.

Eventually she stood up. One of her feet had fallen asleep, and the buzzing was like a cry uttered by her body, a cry for life anyway.

She hobbled toward the bedroom. It was well past two. One more day of life, one more day in the world, she thought, and tried to remember—as she got into the bed, penitent, purified, and vowed to eternal silence—that this in itself was something to be happy for.

FROM THEIR FIRST MEETING Walter had felt a curious affinity for Louise. Some quality of unadmitted hesitancy, in eyes that would have looked, to most people, steadfast and determined, came through to him as he shook her hand at the San Francisco airport. It was the end of the first semester of his second year at law school, and even though they'd known each other only a month and a half, Danny was bringing Walter home for Christmas. ("But isn't it a little premature for that?" Walter had asked. "No, no," Danny said, "it's right, it feels right to me.") Once Walter agreed, Danny lied over the phone, telling his mother they'd known each other nearly six months. Apparently his need to show Walter to his family was so urgent that he felt no qualms about stretching their brief courtship out like that, and not only to Louise; soon he was telling everyone they'd known each other six months; he even had himself convinced they'd known each other six months. (Six months! It had seemed an inconceivably long time then, since it was nearly six times as long as they had, in fact, been together. Now six months passed in a breath, an instant, and each day that point at which their time together would be doubled receded further and further into the future.)

Louise and Nat stood in the crowd of airport welcomers, not really that different from their photographs, nervous but smiling. In theory they had already evolved into the kind of parents who, without reservation, make up the double bed in the guest room for their son and his "friend," but they hadn't yet had to put the theory into practice. Even so, what strain Louise was feeling, as she shook Walter's hand, she covered brilliantly; only someone with equal skill at subterfuge would have been able to see through the cracks in her makeup. She had met her match in Walter, who noticed in her face that afternoon all sorts of things she would have preferred no one notice, chief among them an expression—how could he put it right? Wildness, yes, but tamed, or long suppressed. Whatever it was, it was vivid to him in her eyes, which looked quickly away, and in her mouth, which held fast and stayed closed, and when he heard the stories about her, the impression only became stronger: There was the history of desires felt, indulged, deemed improper by mysterious authority, then relegated to some back attic of the mind, not to be thought about again; and there was the wear of years spent nose to the grindstone of a life she imagined to be more suitable than the sort of life her nature made her lean toward.

How strong she was! How much stronger than Walter, who, a coward in both directions, had neither truly indulged nor fully rejected his urges toward what he imagined to be the unsuitable. He was too undisciplined, he had realized early on, to shake his homosexuality altogether, or hide it in the corners of an otherwise heterosexual life, yet at the same time he contemplated the late-night, cigarette-reeking prowl of the city with both distaste and apprehension. And so he had determined to do something quietly revolutionary: to incorporate his sexual nature into a life of suburban domesticity, uproot the seed of homosexuality from its natural urban soil and replant it in the pure earth of his green garden. It had, by and large, worked, and yet he realized he'd made a singular mistake. For it wasn't just the love of a man he'd been drawn to in his early days in the city; it was the rank garden of the city itself, with its brief yet intense gratifications, its dangers and easy disappointments. In contrast, Louise apparently had had her share of wildness. Under different circumstances, she might have been reckless; Walter could imagine her spilling champagne, at dawn, into the Grand Canal or sleeping on donkey back. But she was stubborn and afraid, and had settled instead for a house, where what satisfactions there were derived from order and clarity, warmth, early bedtimes. She did crossword puzzles in her bathrobe till nine. At eleven she watched the news, soaking her hands in wax while the violent upheavals of the world splattered like gore itself against the inner side of the glass screen. To Danny and April she was a muddle, all rage and inexplicable longing; they were afflicted with the egotism of children looking at mothers, they saw her mind as a series of puffed layers, each concealing a slightly less soggy, slightly more essential truth; she was angry that the dishes weren't done; no, she was angry that no one helped her; no, she was angry that her husband took her for granted, and she had given him everything, everything. And that was it, as far as they were concerned; they returned to this model of layers every time she called, or came up in conversation, until that model seemed to Walter as much of an evasion, a layering, as anything they could accuse Louise of.

His own version of Louise was simpler: He saw her as a woman of guileless passion who, for one reason or another, had suppressed that passion and instead steadied her gaze on the dependable horizon of the domestic sphere. Of course he had heard about the early marriage, and Tommy Burns, not to mention all the mysterious gaps in her history. And unlike April and Danny, who shrugged their shoulders in mock bewilderment at the question of Louise's youth—she was their mother, they seemed to be saying, how could she even have existed before us?— Walter had no doubt what filled those gaps in: men, most of them handsome and untrustworthy; men who thrilled, gratified, and ultimately abandoned her, proving again and again the truthfulness of her own mother's warnings—he's no good; there's no future there; stay away from him, Louise. When, at twenty, she settled instead with cautious Nat, perhaps she was imagining that in the utopia of California, in that city of the future he was insisting they would soon live in, she would be able to satisfy the urges that had, up until now, pulled her away from Nat and toward a more disreputable, to her more natural kind of life. These days, in the landscape of Louise's face, there was defiance just barely cracked by the beginnings of hesitancy, as if after forty years of telling herself not to look back, forty years arguing to herself the rightness of her life (and by that time what choice was there?), she was finally feeling the twitching in her neck, the urge to turn and ask the question to which the answer seemed so inevitable, so stupidly obvious: You shouldn't have married him.

EQUAL AFFECTIONS

———————

IT WAS EARLY March, the first day the thermometer by the window had crept past sixty, and the sun was too bright to stare into. In the morning Walter woke up looking—not happier exactly, but there was in his face a kind of zest for occupation, like the dog, Betty, when after much barking a ball was thrown for her, or Danny's mother when she first touched her sharp pencil to a new crossword. At ten he went to the nursery and at eleven came back with an assortment of tiny buds sprouting in green boxes, and envelopes on which were printed photographs of luminous lettuces, polished-looking cucumbers, fat tomatoes piled in baskets. For Danny, who had grown up in that part of the world where the shifting of seasons is something you have to look for to notice, there was something mythic and tender about this first defiant spring day and its attendant rituals. For months now Walter had spent his weekend mornings buried in bed, but today, at the sight of the new brightness through their bedroom curtains, he had bounded up, pulled on his shorts, and run outside into the yard. In the young sunlight, his legs were white as the paste in elementary school, white as something newborn—a larva bursting from its shell, the black hairs writhing like antennae. He knelt in the dirt, almost in a position of prayer, busying himself with the simple rituals of spades and shovels and soil. The T-shirt he wore rode up his back as he worked, revealing the white, vulnerable indentation just above his buttocks. Soon that spot would be brown, browner than the rest of him.

Danny was happy for Walter, and relieved. Living with someone who is depressed is hard work, and for a long time now Walter had been sullen and ignoring, preferring the mute company of his computer to Danny's fleshly companionship. Just last night, for instance, all night, the TV had been on; they had watched *20/20*, and then a pornographic tape, and then Walter had stood in front of the mirror, naked, his belly jutting out, and said, "Behold man." Danny beheld. He still thought Walter quite handsome, though really he had gained a lot of weight. Still, he wanted Walter to know he loved him, so he embraced him from behind, wrapping his arms tight around his diaphragm. Walter continued to stare into the mirror, but it wasn't, Danny sensed, because he was so fascinated by what he saw there. Rather, his eyes seemed to have gone out of focus; he was gazing at a blur, a mass of unspecified flesh breaking up into planes before him. "We should go to bed," Danny said, and Walter blinked and sighed at the newly reconstituted sight of himself. He had some sort of date to converse with a man in Memphis, so Danny went alone to bed, while across the house keyboard buttons clicked, conveying messages of lust and virility.

And now, in the garden—sunlight, like a miracle. Walter, sweaty and dirty and smiling, is holding in his cupped palms a pile of earth out of which a small shoot of parsley blooms. "Remember the parsley we planted last year?" he says. "This is it. It survived the winter. Isn't that wonderful?"

He pulls a dirty sprig off the little plant and with his fingers tucks it between Danny's teeth. The taste is sweet and gritty, and Danny smiles back.

"Of course I'll plant more. Parsley, basil, mint, sage, chervil. I bought them all! Think of the cooking we can do!"

Danny nods. "I can't wait, Walt," he says sincerely. As if in eagerness to make the day come faster, Walter bends down, preparing to reroot the little parsley. But Danny, going back into the kitchen, is hesitant to be too grateful; what if, tomorrow, the weather is cloudy? What if, as so often seems to happen here on the East Coast, it turns out that spring has had a false start and they will have to endure another brief season of snowstorms before the real rebirth of May? In that case, will Walter return to bed, return to the winter ritual of television, computer conversation, videos? Danny hopes not.

The phone rings. Outside, Walter stops, turns to listen as Danny answers.

"April Gold, please." The voice is a woman's, brusque, and apparently already annoyed at what she assumes will be unconscionable delays.

"Um, she's not here," Danny says. "I'm not expecting her until next week."

Walter puts his spade down. He gets up on his knees, which are black with mud, puts his hands on his hips.

"I was given this number," the voice says.

"I'm sorry. I really don't know what to tell you."

"Who is this, please?"

"Her brother," Danny says, more sharply than he probably ought to.

"Jesus," the woman murmurs, thinking her whisper inaudible.

"No, the name is Cooper."

"There's no need to be rude. Look, just tell her Irene Gould called. That's Gould, with a *u*. It's most urgent that I speak to her."

Danny hangs up before the woman says anything else.

"What was that?" Walter asks.

"A bitch."

"Calling for April?"

"I don't know what the hell April thinks she's doing, giving these people my number when she's not supposed to be coming for a week."

"Maybe she's going to be early."

"I mean, she treats me like her fucking answering service. She's done this before, and I've warned her."

The phone rings again. Alice Klippen, for April. "She's not here," Danny says.

"You can give her this number," Alice Klippen says, "but she'll only be able to reach me there between seven and nine-thirty. Before seven I'm at my office—I think she's got that one already—and after nine-thirty I'll be at a party with my friend Roz, but wait—no, first we're going out to dinner, and then to a party, so maybe she should call me at Roz's place. Oh, but damn, I don't have the number, and it's not listed. Okay, listen—have her call Sydney Green on West Twenty-fifth Street—have you got a pencil?"

"I'm taking it all down," Danny says.

"So have her call Sydney Green, who is listed, and ask for Roz Steele's number, and there'll be a message from me on Roz's answering machine telling her where she can reach me. Alice Klippen."

"Okay."

"You got that all?"

"I got it."

"Great. Thanks. Bye."

He hangs up louder than he should.

"You haven't written anything down," Walter says.

"What can I do? I didn't have a pencil."

"Maybe you should let me answer it next time," Walter says, and strides into the kitchen. "Gosh, wouldn't it be great if April really is arriving today?"

"Great," Danny says.

"Aren't you excited? I mean, she's your only sister. Aren't you glad she's coming?"

"Well," Danny says. "I suppose." He leans against the refrigerator, crosses his arms. He is remembering other times when she arrived on short notice, showing up at his and Walter's apartment just as they were about to go to bed. No call, just the buzzer ringing, her voice: "Hi, it's me—"

"April."

"I'm early."

Or she had been late. She had stood him up, keeping him hours at airports or restaurants, then calling at four in the morning. "Powderfoot, I'm so sorry, I just couldn't get away—"

"What do you mean 'I suppose'? You are glad she's coming, aren't you?"

Danny stretches his arms behind his head. "Of course I'm glad," he says. "Of course."

"Well, I'm going to take a shower," Walter says, abandoning, at least for the moment, his half-planted buds. Left alone in the kitchen, Danny scowls at the phone, daring it to ring again and be for her. An old, blistering anger, an old argument ricocheting again through his memory: "I'm not your goddamned answering machine, April!"

"Danny, where else can I have people call?"

"I don't know, but it's not fair to me. And on top of it, they're rude."

"You know I'd do the same for you, Powderfoot."

"Don't call me that when we're having a fight."

That memory, and others: the van stopped outside a filling station in Nebraska, the wind strong: Danny has been driving for five hours. "But, Powderfoot," April says, "we have to work out these arrangements before Omaha. You're the only one who's expendable." And months later, New Haven: Danny tells her he is leaving the tour, and she smiles. She seems delighted. As if she can get along without me, he thinks. As if what I've given her—all the time I've devoted, the shitwork I've done—amounts to nothing.

The phone rings again, and he answers it challengingly. "Who is it?" he demands.

"Just me," Iris says. "I wanted to let you boys know, there's a great special on chicken breasts at King's, so I bought you four or five packages. It's good to freeze them, and who knows, I mean, when in the last five years have chicken breasts been under two dollars a pound? Perdue too?"

"Thanks, Iris," Danny says. "That was really thoughtful of you." It occurs to him, at this moment, what an immense virtue thoughtfulness is. Anyway, he is relieved to be talking about chicken breasts, relieved to be reminded of his own detailed life, most facets of which have nothing to do with April. She has not even arrived yet, but since the phone call it has felt to Danny as if an enormous balloon were expanding inside his house, pushing him into an ever-narrowing crevice between balloon wall and house wall. And that crevice is where he must live while April is there, that tiny crevice between her ever-expanding ego and all the rest of his life.

"It was crazy at the store today. A real madhouse. I remember when this was a small town."

"Well, Iris, I could have warned you. King's on a Saturday."

"You have to eat!" Iris says, then sighs. "Oh, well."

She hangs up just as Walter is coming out of the bathroom. "Has April called yet?" he asks brightly.

"No!" Danny shouts, slamming down the phone.

"I was just asking, you don't have to get mad!" Walter shakes his head as he towels off, then cheerily hops off to the bedroom to put on clean clothes. Apparently the prospect of April's arrival has added considerably to his already improved mood. He takes mute pleasure in the way she and her coterie can transform the place into a hive of counterculture exoticism: incense burning in a guest room; pot brownies baking in the oven; women curled together in sleeping bags on the living room floor. New people! Conversation! Company! Apparently Danny's own relentlessly cheerful presence is just not enough for Walter. From the computer, it seems, he will move on to April. All of which makes Danny angry, as does the knowledge that Walter will treat April reverentially, indulgently when she arrives. Danny has privately been hoping to teach April a lesson over the course of this visit, but now he fears that Walter will undermine whatever position of strength he attempts to take. He can just see Walter making her bed, doing her laundry, even winking at her across the room—sheets and underwear in hand—as Danny sternly tells her she has to do these things herself this time. She will always find someone; if not him, someone else.

Soon enough the phone rings again. "I'll get it," they both say, but Walter's hand is quicker. "Hello?" he says. There is a pause, and he smiles and laughs. "Where are you? Really? They're at Friendly's," he reports to Danny, cupping his hand over the mouthpiece. "They're having Peanut Butter Cup sundaes."

"Goodie," Danny says.

Again Walter laughs. "They want to know what to do now," he says.

"Well, tell them to get the hell over here," Danny snorts. And to his own chagrin feels excitement, giddiness, delight.

"Danny says get the hell over here," Walter dutifully reports. "What? Oh. Okay. She wants to talk to you." He hands Danny the phone.

"We're early," April says.

"I know."

"Want to know why?"

"Why?"

"A cancellation in Rhinebeck."

"Ah."

"Right now we're at Friendly's. I love Friendly's. I wish Friendly's was in California."

Danny can see her, standing at the pay phone in the back of the big, barnlike Friendly's. Undoubtedly the old ladies who frequent the place are staring in earnest at her band of oddly dressed accomplices.

"Well, you know how to get here from Friendly's," Danny says.

"We'll be there in twenty minutes."

"Okay. See you then."

"Bye, Powderfoot."

"Twenty minutes," Danny says to Walter. But Walter is gone. Already he is making up beds.

It is still March. Just a few weeks before the month begins during which the whole world will fill with her name.

———

"G O D," April says, stretching her head back so that the sun will touch her face, "it's good to be out of that goddamned van."

An electric churning noise issues from the kitchen, where Walter is preparing daiquiris. April, dressed in blue jeans and a white blouse embroidered with tiny blue flowers, lies back on one of last summer's battered chaises, dragged from the garage just a few minutes before her arrival. She is pale and seems to have gained some weight.

Three are with her: Mikel, the guitarist, a short, pretty, well-muscled woman in running shorts; Leela, the new drummer, a woman older than most of April's ever-changing band members, tall and reedy and with something of the look of a mild kindergarten teacher; and Paul, the pianist, a man (in and of itself extraordinary, a sign of changing times), indeed, an extraordinarily handsome man, darkly tanned and muscular and shirtless. His body gives off a strong smell as he lifts suitcases from the van, Walter in his shorts running up alongside, offering to help.

"Powderfoot, honey, do you have any Tab?"

"You're early," Danny says. "I haven't had a chance to shop. Just Diet Coke."

"You know I cannot stand Diet Coke," April says. "I have a reaction. Just water then."

Although the implications are teeming in his head, Danny fixes her a glass of water, with ice and even a slice of lemon, and brings it to her on the porch. Leela is explaining to Walter that she and Mikel won't be staying with them; they will be taking the van to visit friends in Bucks County. As for Paul, he's heading by train to New York, to meet his lover, Barney, for a rendezvous. Paul smiles, and Walter looks nervous.

"But," April says, "you're going to have me to yourselves for an entire blissful, restful week before the New York concert. A brief vacation." And Walter, cheered by this news, smiles again.

"Thank you, darling," April says as she takes her glass of water. Like a queen, Danny thinks, lying on her chaise lounge. She has always taken it for granted that he will do her favors, as if asking them really is the prerogative of the older sibling.

"Ah," she says. "I can't tell you how glad I am to be here, Powder-foot. Really glad, no fooling. I am beat. And just think what fun we'll have this week. We'll go shopping at the grocery store, and I'll make cakes and brownies, and we'll watch TV and eat popcorn."

"April," Danny reminds her, "both Walter and I work."

"I could take some time off," Walter volunteers. "Leave early, that sort of thing."

"Well, we'll have fun at night then. During the day I'll work, too. You don't know how long I've been waiting for a stretch of time longer than two days in one place. I have this idea for some new songs I've been dying to get started on, and I just haven't had a minute, what with the concerts and all. But now. Yes. Now I'll have some time." And she lies back in the sun, smiling slightly, and closes her eyes.

Leela and Mikel are finishing packing up the van. "So where do you hail from?" Walter asks them.

"Oregon," Mikel says.

"Oakland," says Leela.

"And what about you, Paul?"

Paul is lifting a huge amplifier out of the van and onto their lawn, and Danny thinks he really should ask him whether April is expecting to use their house as a warehouse as well as a hotel.

He remembers the interest scale.

"St. Louis."

"Well, we're off," Leela says, climbing into the passenger seat of the van. "We'll see you in a week, I guess. Take care."

"Aren't you going to say good-bye to April?" Walter asks.

"Wouldn't want to wake her."

And indeed, turning, Walter and Danny are astonished to see that April has fallen asleep. Her head tilted to one side, one hand drooping over the edge of the yellow plastic chaise. She is snoring very quietly.

D ANNY HAD A COLD, and his mother had taken him to the doctor's office. All around him, children were shuffling, sneezing, snorting, their mothers leafing through out-of-date copies of *House & Garden* or *Family Circle*. He had just finished reading *Highlights for Children*, finished comparing the meticulous behavior of that wonderful boy Gallant with the oafishness of his hideous alter ego, Goofus, when he noticed lying among the magazines a pair of big, bright children's books with glossy covers, one called *Bible Stories* and the other *Tales for Tots*. He picked up the second one; on the cover a red-cheeked, red-haired little girl was feeding an apple to a pony while her freckled brother chased around a puppy with a bright nub of a tongue. The book had a lot of pictures, most in color, which reminded Danny of *My Weekly Reader*. As he thumbed through it, one of them in particular caught his eye: It was of the freckle-faced little boy on the cover, only now he was lying in a hospital bed with casts on both his arms and one of his legs, and bandages wrapped around his head. Just above his nose the bandages were blotched red. The boy, according to the story, was Timmy, who had been hit by a car. His friend Jimmy comes to visit him, and when he asks how Timmy is, Timmy looks up at him and says, "It's okay, Jimmy, don't be frightened, for I know I am loved by the Lord Jesus." The next picture was of the same hospital bed, only this time empty, the sheets and the pillow slightly rumpled. Jimmy was standing by the bed, looking up at the ceiling and smiling, a large peach-colored hand resting on his shoulder. "Timmy's body died," the story concluded, "but his soul went up to Jesus."

Danny closed the book. He did not cry. The death of children, at that point, was in and of itself not enough to frighten him; Kenny Schiff, after all, had shot himself while playing with his father's gun, and Andy Conklin's brother had died on his bike, and Marisa Wu had gotten leukemia. No, what disturbed him about *Tales for Tots* was how pretty it made death, how cozy and red-cheeked and freckle-faced. He was only a child himself, and probably he was more shaken than he knew, but reading the story, he felt welling up in himself not fear so much as outrage, that such things should be left around in pediatric waiting rooms, where other children, more vulnerable than he, might read them.

He tapped Louise's shoulder. "Mom," he said.

"What?"

"Look." He handed her the book, watched her eyes move back and forth as she skimmed the story, then widen when she reached the end. She slapped the book shut so loudly that a few women glanced up from their magazines. Then she stood, holding the book in the air, and Danny became worried that she was going to lose her temper and make a scene, or take out her rage on the wrong, undeserving person. She had done these things before.

"Mom," he said, "what are you going to do?"

"Take care of this once and for all."

"Mom—"

But already she had marched up to the nursing station. Peggy Thaxter, the nurse, whom she knew and liked, smiled up at her and said, "Can I help you with something, Louise?"

"I'd like to know who's responsible for this—this garbage being left here for little children to read."

She slammed the book down on the counter of the nurse's station, and Peggy Thaxter stepped back.

"Garbage?" Peggy Thaxter said. Louise opened the book to the story of little Timmy. "My God," Peggy said as she read it. "I had no idea. They just leave them, you know, those Seventh-Day Adventists, they come by when no one's looking and leave them so people will buy them. See, there's a little order form in the back. I never paid much attention to them until now, figured they were harmless, but now that I see, well,

Louise, thank you, thank you, thank you for bringing this to our attention; I'll most certainly make sure Dr. Kerr sees this, and I'm sure he'll agree, these stories have no place here."

She took the book from Louise and deposited it on a shelf behind her desk.

Louise nodded and sat down again. "Did they get rid of it?" Danny asked.

"Probably it'll go right back out as soon as we leave," Louise said. "You can't trust these people."

"Not even Mrs. Thaxter? I'm sure we can trust Mrs. Thaxter."

Louise looked at him, opened her mouth as if to say something, then shut it again. "Did that story scare you?" she asked instead.

"No, but it might scare some other little kid, littler than me."

"Not anymore it won't, if I have anything to do with it."

How strong she could be, when she needed to.

Strong and frightening.

———————

DANNY WAS SITTING in his office when the phone rang. "Hi, it's your father," Nat said. "Don't worry, everything's okay."

"Good," Danny said. Nat prefaced all his calls with such reassurances, as if he felt obliged to dispel from the start any possibility of bad news.

"Things are going along just fine here, but I did think you ought to know, your mother's been having some—well, sort of rash, on her stomach and feet. I'm sure it's nothing. At first we thought it was poison oak, but it doesn't seem to be that. Anyway, it's just a rash, nothing serious, only Louise is kind of uncomfortable. Has to take a lot of special baths."

"That's too bad," Danny said. "I hope they figure out what's causing it."

"Oh, I'm sure they will. Anyway, just wanted to let you know. Has April arrived at your place yet, by the way?"

"Last night. You can call her at the house."

"Good. I may do that if I have a chance. But you'll fill her in, won't you? I just wanted to make sure I knew where I could reach you. And everything is going well with your job and all, I suppose?"

"Fine."

"Your house okay?"

"Fine."

"How's Walter?"

"He's just fine."

"Good. Well, I really ought to run. I'm at the office too. Give him my best. I'll talk to you soon."

"Okay. Bye, Dad."

"Bye." He hung up. Nat's phone calls rarely went beyond such simple goals as determining that Danny was fine, that he knew where he could reach him *in case*. This giving and receiving of reassurance was a business motivated not so much by love as by anxiety, for Nat had the soul of the caretaker, who checks one house after another and, finding things are as they should be, moves on. It reminded Danny of the way his father used to kick the twenty-year-old cat Elvira when she was asleep, just to make sure she was still alive. This need for reassurance has nothing to do with love. Oh, love strengthens, and purifies, and colors it, but in essence it is virtueless, an addiction. He did what he had to: made the phone call; established that everything was in its proper place and just fine. A matter of clearing the conscience, which, in Nat's case, seemed to be something like clearing the throat.

Danny was about to get back to work when the phone rang again.

"Danny, it's your mother."

"Mom! Dad just called. How are you?"

"Well, I've been better," she said, in her mock-weary voice. "Just tired. This damned thing keeps me up all night, in and out of the bath-tub, otherwise I just can't sleep at all. And don't suggest Benadryl—I'm so doped up on Benadryl I feel like I might keel over. But listen, I called to ask you to do me a favor. What I said to you the other night, about wanting to become a Catholic—just forget it, forget I said anything."

"Mom—that's easier said than done."

"Okay, okay. Then just promise me something, will you, honey? Promise me you won't say anything to April or to your father. Please."

"Are you giving up the idea?" he asked hopefully.

"I consider that nobody's business but my own," she said. "And I want you to help me keep it that way, okay? I shouldn't have said anything to you. Some things are private."

"Well, of course, Mom. If that's what you want."

She sounded relieved. "Oh, thank you," she said. "Thank you, Danny, I knew I could count on you." And suddenly she laughed. "You know what I was remembering this afternoon?"

"What?"

"How once when I was a little girl—seven or eight maybe—it was my mother's birthday, and I'd been saving and saving to buy her this little blue ceramic pillbox I'd seen at the five-and-ten. It was very pretty, with white ribbons that weren't really ribbons—they were molded out of the ceramic, which at that point I thought was the height of elegance. Anyway, this was the first time in my life I'd ever bought anything at a store, and the lady took my money—it must have been pennies mostly—and counted it, and handed me the pillbox in a little bag. I was so excited I started skipping. And then, about halfway home, I dropped the bag on the sidewalk. Now the box itself, it was all right. But the top—the top was completely smashed. I almost started to cry right then. All those weeks I'd saved to buy something pretty for my mother. And, you know, she always said I couldn't do anything properly. So I went back to the store—I was terrified, shaking all over—and I stood by the table where the pillboxes were, and when no one was looking, I grabbed another top. I just grabbed it and ran. I ran all the way home, and when I got there, I hid under the bed for an hour. I was convinced the police were chasing me and were going to drag me feetfirst from under the bed. But no police came. Finally I got out from under my bed and took the pillbox out of the bag to wrap it. And wouldn't you know it—it was a blue pillbox, and I'd grabbed a pink top."

They were both quiet for a moment.

"That's a terrible story, Mom," Danny said.

"I don't know why I remembered it just now. Funny, the way things come back to you. And at the oddest times. I guess it's just part of being old."

"Mom, you're not—"

"Thank you again," she said, "for your confidence."

"Of course—"

"Son," she added, as an afterthought.

APRIL WAS ASLEEP on the living room sofa when Danny got home, surrounded by scattered sheets of music and magazines, her guitar upright against the wall. A sweating tumbler of partly melted ice and Tab was slowly soaking ruin into the mahogany coffee table. Gingerly Danny picked it up and carried it to the kitchen, trying not to look back at the perfect circle of discoloration it had left in its wake.

"April," he said quietly when he walked back into the room.

"What?" she shouted, and bolted up from where she lay on the sofa, all waving arms and flying blond hair. "Who's there?" She looked up at him in confusion. "Danny," she said.

"I'm sorry I woke you."

"What time is it?" Shifting onto her side, she peered intently at her watch, as if struggling to remember how to tell time. "Six-fifteen! Jesus, it was four o'clock a minute ago." And brushing her hair from her eyes, she looked up at him and smiled coyly.

Danny smiled back. "You deserve the rest."

"Yeah, I guess I was more bushed than I realized. I mean, this concert life can really get to be exhausting. But you know that." Pulling her legs in front of her, she maneuvered into a sitting position, buried her elbows between her knees, and yawned into her hands. "I'm sorry if I scared you," she said. "I don't know why, I always panic when someone wakes me up. Wonder what nether region of my psyche that comes from. Anyway—oh, shit!" she said when she saw Danny was unloading groceries from a paper bag. "I was going to surprise you! I was going to go to the store and have dinner and my special Bundt cake waiting for you when you got home! Shit. I'm sorry."

"April, you don't have to cook for us."

"But I want to. You know I love your kitchen, it reminds me of Mom's kitchen."

"So you can stand around and think wistful thoughts. You don't have to cook."

"Excuse me a second." Pulling herself onto her feet, she stumbled into the bathroom and locked the door. When she emerged into the kitchen a few minutes later, she looked considerably more herself: hair brushed, face washed, the smell of cologne emanating from her neck. She was wearing her usual jeans and rumpled blouse. "Can I help?" she asked.

"I'm just unloading groceries," Danny said.

"A hausfrau, as always. Grandma would laugh." She took an apple out of a bowl, bit into it, and threw it away. "Who'd have guessed it'd be me, the girl, traveling around all the time, while my little baby brother becomes the hausfrau?"

"You sound envious."

"Maybe," she said. "Part of me longs for a kitchen like this, all the time. Going to the store, and baking cookies, and watching soap operas all day."

"You wouldn't last a month," Danny said.

"Do you have any gum?"

He shook his head.

"Then maybe I'll make brownies," said April, suddenly excited by the prospect of a project. "Do you have any brownie mix? Flour? Sugar? Chocolate?"

"Probably I have everything except one essential ingredient," Danny said.

"I'll check," April said, bounding up with renewed energy. She rummaged through the pantry, filled her arms with canisters, jars, and bottles, then lined them up on the kitchen counter. "No chocolate," she said. "Damn. Well, I could run out and get some. Only I don't really feel up to it." Suddenly she put her hand on her stomach. "On second thought, maybe I don't feel up to making brownies." And she collapsed into one of the kitchen chairs. "I get nauseous so easily these days."

Danny started to put back the various canisters, jars, and bottles April had taken out of the pantry.

"Powderfoot," she said, "what would you consider the most surprising news I could tell you right now?"

"Oh, let's see. That you're marrying Oliver North? That you're giving up your singing to work for the Nicaraguan freedom fighters?"

"Well, not quite. But I do have some surprising news."

"Oh?" Danny said from the pantry. "What?"

April audibly shifted in her chair. "Well," she said. "Okay. How to say it? Oh, hell, I guess I just have to say it."

"Don't tell me," Danny said from the pantry. "You're a lesbian. Oh, my God!"

"Better than that. I'm . . . pregnant."

Danny turned to face her. April shrugged her shoulders and smiled.

"How the hell did that happen?" Danny said.

"Not in the usual way," April said, and looked at her brother as if trying to read his face. "Oh, don't worry, no penis has come near my body in at least ten years. No, it was more complicated than that. But before I get into the details, tell me what you're thinking. Are you happy for me?"

"Well, April, of course I'm happy for you. It's just a little bit of a surprise, that's all. I mean, I've read these stories in tabloids about sperm on toilet seats accidentally impregnating nine-year-old girls while they pee and everyone thinking it's immaculate conception, but to be truthful, I never believed such a thing could happen to my sister." He smiled oddly. "You're kidding me, aren't you? You're joking. You better tell me, April, if you're kidding, because you know I can never recognize obvious jokes, so taking advantage of me is kind of like taking advantage of a handicapped person."

"I don't make it a habit to sit on that sort of toilet seat," April said.

"You're not kidding."

She shook her head.

"Well, how did it happen?"

"It's a long story. You better sit down."

"I don't want to sit down."

"Suit yourself. You remember Tom Neibauer? Tall, good-looking, with a beard? He does computer music and has a deaf Chinese lover?"

"No."

"Of course you do, you met him lots of times; he was in that house with me senior year of college. Anyway, for the last couple of years Tom Neibauer's been suggesting to me that I have a baby with him. Fairly casually, at first, but then the more I saw him, the more serious he got. You see, it seems that for years he'd been looking for a gay woman to have a baby with, and he decided I'd be perfect. So he came over for coffee, and he said he wanted to prove that that homophobic notion that homosexuals can't procreate was bullshit, he wanted to prove that we could have children too, and be an example, a role model for other gay men and women. And he also said he'd be the primary caretaker and all that too, that he'd raise the baby and the baby would live with him if that's what I wanted, and I could see the baby when I was in town. He said all this at once. And of course at first I just laughed. I mean, I totally dismissed him. It's true, he's a very sincere, progressive, forward-thinking man, but what I basically decided was going through his head was, I want April Gold to have my baby, because in his crowd April Gold having your baby is something that would carry a lot of cachet. Or at least back then it would have carried a lot of cachet. Now I'm not so sure. But anyway, he kept calling and asking me to think about it, and I kept thinking about it, and as I thought about it, it occurred to me that, well, maybe it's not such a bad idea. I mean, I *have* had these sort of bizarre mothering instincts come over me a few times during my life. I'd thought about it too, but never really that seriously, because I have to travel all the time, and I wasn't sure I was ready for the responsibility of raising a child. But then I thought, if Tom takes primary responsibility, I'd have a baby, and Mom would finally get a grandchild, and there certainly would be a lot of songs to get out of it, though that really wasn't a primary consideration. And Tom, who is a very good salesman in his own way, I guess he sensed that I was getting close to saying yes, so he showed up at my house one day with these composite pictures he'd made up with a computer from a photograph of me and a photograph of him, and he said, 'This is how beautiful a baby we could make.' And right there, on the spot, I just decided, why not?" She laughed suddenly. "It's funny," she said, "I imagined the whole thing would be very scientific, very medical, with doctors and nurses and sterilized gloves. But what really happened was nothing like that at all. Whenever I was home in San Francisco, and I'd get my period, I'd call Tom, and he'd make some calculations, and on the appointed day he'd jerk off in a cup, I guess, and either he or Brett, his lover, would run over with this cup and a turkey baster. I said I didn't think that was very precise, but he insisted he'd consulted with a lot of people he knew, and that he didn't want to get involved with hospitals or doctors or anything like that. So he'd come over with his little cup of cum, and either Fran or Nina Klenck— you remember her, my old friend from college who's subletting my house? she married Jeff Bernstein last year, incidentally—one of them would be over as well, and we girls would go in the bedroom and basically do it with the turkey baster. Only I kept laughing, because I was thinking, how ridiculous to be lying here on my bed with no pants on and a turkey baster like Mom used at Christmas between my legs. So we'd fill up the turkey baster and empty it and fill it up and empty it, and when all the stuff was gone, we'd make pancakes. This was about three years ago, incidentally."

"How did Fran feel about all this?"

"Well, it was sort of interesting. Fran was all for the whole thing, even after we broke up. But the other lovers I've had since, most of them have gotten pretty nervous. The last one, Summer, said she couldn't handle it at all, it was just too heterosexual for her, and whenever Tom or Brett came over, she'd have to leave the house for the day. But to continue—it went on like this for three years, and nothing happened, and I figured after a while nothing was going to happen, not because there was anything wrong with me or Tom but because the whole thing was so haphazard—you know, the sperm could have died in the car or whatever. But Tom insisted he wanted to do it the natural way; he didn't want doctors involved except this holistic guy he sees who I can't stand anyway. I would have forgotten about the whole thing, except he was very persistent, very industrious, he kept calling to find out if I'd had my period and when I was going to be in town and all. And he kept showing up with his cup, and I kept doing the thing with the turkey baster and thinking, Really, this has got to stop. And then, lo and behold, here I am on tour, and I don't get my period. Very interesting. So I go out with Mikel from the band, and we buy one of those little home tester kits where you pee and if it turns blue you are and if it doesn't you're not. And it did. And I went to a doctor. And your sister is eight weeks pregnant. The end."

Danny sat down. "I can't believe this," he said.

"All true. Girl Scout's honor."

"So how do you feel?"

April shrugged. "Happy. A little scared. But happy. Actually, I'm totally confused." And she looked into the distance of the kitchen window, in which her own reflection hovered over Walter's newly planted vegetable garden.

"How long have you known?" Danny asked.

"Three days."

"Have you told Mom and Dad?"

"No, I wanted to tell you first."

"Well, you better tell them soon because if you don't, I'm just going to have to do it myself."

April's mouth opened in outrage. "What the hell does that—" It shut again. "I was planning to call them tonight," she said softly, looking away from her brother. "I haven't even informed the father yet."

Abruptly Danny stood, circled the kitchen table, then sat again, his forehead on his fist. "Look," Danny said, "let me just first say I think this is great. I do, I'm really happy I'm going to be an uncle. But there are a few things I've got to ask you about. First of all—well, I know this is a hard question and all, and that you trust your friend, but as he is a gay man—well, has he had an AIDS test?"

"Boy, you go right for the jugular, don't you?" April said, and laughed. "But don't worry. I freaked out about the same thing about a year and a half ago, and before I'd even mustered the courage to ask him, he called me up to tell me he'd gone to have the test, and he was negative. He's so responsible he even had the doctor send me a letter confirming the test results."

"Good," Danny said. "That's one worry out of the way. Now, my second question. Have you written up any sort of legal custody agreement?"

"Danny, I've only been pregnant three days! Anyway, Tom's going to take care of it."

"April, I know he's your friend, and you trust him, but as a lawyer I feel obligated to warn you, you really ought to make sure you're protected."

Suddenly April smiled big teeth at Danny. "As a lawyer," she said. "I can't believe it. My little brother. *As a lawyer.*"

"Look, if you don't want my advice, fine, I know plenty of people who'll give you exactly the same advice for five thousand dollars or so. Just spare me the insults." Dramatically he marched out of the kitchen.

"Oh, Danny," April said, following him into the living room, "I'm sorry. Please forgive me, I just lapse into this big-sister thing, I look at you and I think, is this big, handsome lawyer really my little squirt of a brother?"

"Think whatever you like about me, April. But I am really worried about the possibility of your getting shafted in this thing."

April sat down on the sofa. "I'm all ears," she said.

"All right," Danny said. "Well, first of all, this primary-caretaker stuff. I think it all has to be laid down in writing. If you want him to be the primary caretaker, I think you have to establish, from the outset, that if at any time you are not satisfied with his performance as primary caretaker, you can regain custody of your child. And I think you also have to establish that if you change your mind once the baby is born, you can nullify the agreement and raise the baby yourself. I mean, you're not that far from surrogate parenting here."

"Well, of course I see what you mean, Danny," April said, "but really, Tom's not like that. You talk as if we live in this vicious dog-eat-dog world and he and Brett are really just conspiring to use my womb and take my baby. But they're not. These are very progressive, enlightened leftists here, two men who basically think the American justice system is fucked. They side with the victims. They wouldn't set foot in a courtroom on principle, much less wage a lawsuit. The whole point is, I want to be the baby's mother, and Tom wants to be the baby's father. In fact, it's very sexist of *you* to assume that just because I've decided I want the baby to live with Tom, I somehow don't care about the baby or don't plan to see it or be part of its life, and it's unfair to assume Tom wants me out of the way. I will be very much an active participant in the raising of this child."

"That's fine. That's great. And that's why you've got to have a legal agreement assuring your continued involvement. Not to mention grandparents' rights, uncles' rights. Who's to say—I'm not saying it, but who's to say—that Tom might not decide he doesn't want your family involved with the baby? I just want to make sure that's covered in the legal agreement. Better you take care of these things before the baby's born and spare yourself a nationally televised trial."

"You have become so distrustful since you moved to New York," April said. "Really, such an easterner."

"It's my job to look out for you, April. I always have. And talk about sexist! This baby is yours more profoundly than it's Tom's. It's your body, remember. Don't let him treat you like you're carrying this precious thing of his, only to have him forget you once it's safely in his house."

"If you just knew Tom," April said, "if you met him once, you'd see how pointless all this is."

"I know from experience, no matter how well you think you know someone, you can never guess. You've got to protect yourself. Hell, if you're afraid he'll be insulted by a legal agreement, just bat your eyelashes and tell him your big bully lawyer of a brother is forcing you to do it all."

"*Little* bully lawyer of a brother," April said.

"You just have to get in a last dig, don't you? Big sister to the bitter end."

She stretched her arms luxuriously behind her head. "Oh, all this is too much," she said. "Here I am, all alone, with no one in the world. Me and my little baby." She spoke these words experimentally, as if trying them on for size, then laughed; they didn't fit.

A rattling at the door announced Walter's return. He was carrying two huge cardboard boxes, which covered his face, and when Betty, the dog, leaped to greet him, they nearly tumbled. "Betty, get off, for Christ's sake!" Walter called from behind his boxes. "Danny, can you help me with this stuff?"

Danny hurried to relieve him. "What is this?" he asked as he took one of the boxes.

"Mangoes," said Walter. "I bought them at the station at Hoboken."

"This is enough mangoes for about twenty years, Walt; they'll rot before we eat them."

"So I'll give some to my mother," Walter said. "Anyway, you just watch. They'll get eaten. Hi, April, how was your day?"

"Fine," April said. "How was yours, Walt?"

"Just fine."

For a second April and Danny looked at each other.

"April has some news," Danny said, and April turned the other way. "News?"

There was squealing at a significant enough distance away to suggest the mutilation of small dogs by the tires of a bus. "Goddammit," Walter said. "Betty must have slipped out the front door. I'd better get her." He went into the kitchen and returned holding the Dustbuster. "This will get her back, it always does." He pushed the button on the Dustbuster, and the little vacuum cleaner gave out its familiar suction roar. Betty barked more loudly, farther away. "See you soon!" Walter said gaily, and was off, calling, "Betty! Betty!" into the night.

April looked at Danny. "What's with the vacuum cleaner?" she asked.

"Betty and the Dustbuster have a love-hate relationship. She likes to fight with it and lick it. I think she thinks it's alive, since it's about the size of a little dog. And as we've learned from hard experience, it's the one object short of hamburger meat that will entice her back inside once she's escaped into the world."

"I see," April said. They walked out onto the front porch and surveyed the early-evening suburban panorama. Across the street a young man wearing cutoffs was watering his lawn, while next door three blond children chased each other in circles, calling, "You're it! You're it! You're it!" And in the middle of the street, like some absurd pied piper, was Walter, in his black lawyer's suit. He waved the Dustbuster over his head, offering its wail to the twilight air, and, in the warm, bark-filled night, waited.

ARCH SEVENTH came and went. Walter did not quit his job. At the office his secretary marked the advent of her fourth year in his employ with the gift of a carnation and a card which, when you opened it, sang out "Auld Lang Syne" in a tinny, computerized voice. Other than that, the only acknowledgments were a letter from a senior partner, congratulating Walter on work well done and expressing hope that his association with the firm would last another five years, and a piece of electronic mail, or e-mail, when he switched on the computer in his office early on the anniversary evening. It was from Bulstrode, one of his computer friends.

To: Hunky Lawyer
From: Bulstrode
Subject: Fifth Year Anniversary

Walter,

Congratulations! You have now passed the point of no return. You have resisted temptation, and great rewards are in store for you as a result. Welcome to the real world! Farewell, dreams of youthful wandering! Just wait till you turn forty!

Fondly,

Bullie

Walter smiled. It seemed ironic to him that of all the people in his life, only Bulstrode, who wasn't really in his life at all, had bothered to acknowledge the passing of this pretty significant day. Bulstrode was a banker in Louisville, Kentucky, and they had "met" (if "met" was the right word) one dreary winter Sunday when Walter was scanning the roster of names logged onto the gay channel in search of some sort of flirtation or dirty conversation. ("Interactive pornography" was how he described it to friends.) Among the Willing Slaves, Sweaty Jocks, Hung Studs, and Tight Ends who were jockeying for space and attention in that strange electronic gay bar of the mind, he had been amused to see for the first time his Louisville friend's aggressively offbeat handle, and since Bulstrode was one of his favorite characters in *Middlemarch*, one of his favorite books, he had dashed off a message, asking if indeed a literary allusion was intended. Bulstrode responded with a chat request; they retreated together to that little hypothetical private room, where Bulstrode acknowledged that Walter had guessed his source. He was Bulstrode because Bulstrode was, like him, a banker; also, he added, because the name had enough of a violent edge to interest the less literary. And who was this hunky lawyer, who recognized a name from *Middlemarch?* What was he doing in semiliterate compu-land? "Information," Bulstrode typed, "we want information!"

In his past computer-enhanced communications Walter had been reluctant about divulging any true history, but Bulstrode for some reason put him at ease. Walter admitted certain salient facts, being careful not to be too specific, then asked Bulstrode about himself, a subject on which he was less forthcoming not, Walter suspected, because he had anything to hide, but because the facts of his real life simply held no interest for him. "Bulstrode's" biography, which he gave pieces of, was not, it quickly became clear, a thing of the real world. When Walter asked how old he was, he answered, "Bulstrode is 32," which made him suspect the banker in Louisville to be significantly older. In the meantime, Bulstrode admitted to several other alter egos: In moments of high-campy imaginativeness he was "Rick-18," and in moments of extreme horniness he was "Rough Master." His real name was either George or Martin, depending on when you asked him. He said he was 6'2'' and weighed 175 pounds, had brown hair, blue eyes, a beard, a medium-hairy chest, and a seven-and-a-half-inch cock. All of this was probably a lie. Why not lie, after all, when there were so many barriers between you and the person you were speaking to? What harm could it do? And anyway, these particulars, once they were dispensed, never had much bearing on Walter and Bulstrode's conversations, even when those conversations took a decidedly sexual edge.

One cold Sunday evening Bulstrode asked Walter to call him. It seemed an inevitable progression, like sex on the third date. Walter was nervous and excited as he dialed the number, as if he were on the brink of doing something forbidden, but of course it was just ten digits, followed by a distant-sounding series of rings.

"Hello?"

"Bulstrode?" Walter asked.

"Walter? Hi!" And Bulstrode laughed. He had an appealing baritone with a slight, delicate southern lilt to it. "I'm glad to be talking to you!"

"Me too."

"You have a nice voice. Very masculine, very sexy."

"Thanks. So do you."

There were a few seconds of nervous breath, and then Bulstrode said, "I can't believe it. Finally I'm hearing your real voice. And you know what? You sound just like what I imagined you would."

Bulstrode was, it turned out, a veteran and an aficionado of the gay channel, the denizens of which he had maintained steady relations with for almost three years. "I've had quite my share of adventures as a result of it too," he told Walter. "For instance, have you noticed a guy who comes on occasionally, not too often, with the handle Barracuda?"

"I'm not sure," Walter admitted.

"Well, he's this kid up in Boston, a comp sci grad student at MIT. I had a pretty major love affair with him last year. We just broke it off a couple of months ago."

"Really?" Walter said. "Wow, I'm impressed. I guess I just never imagined people could really start relationships this way."

"I'd say this was just about the most serious gay relationship I've been in," Bulstrode said. "Jimmy—that was his real name—he and I were really in love. It was the best and the hardest thing I've ever been in."

"Long-distance relationships are tough," Walter said affably. "Did you usually go up there or did he come down to visit you?"

"Oh, we never met," Bulstrode said.

For the space of a beat, Walter was silent. "You never met?"

"Oh, no. We just talked on the phone."

"Oh."

"Yes. Every day, sometimes two or three times. And then one day I call him up and he says to me he can't take it anymore, it's getting too intense. Just like that, he breaks it off. Personally I think it was his dad. His dad was putting a lot of pressure on him, about being gay. The next thing I knew, he'd changed his phone number. I left him e-mail, but he just ignored it." Bulstrode sighed. "Too bad. I really went for him. And we were sexually in tune, you know? The way few people are in life. Jesus, I've never had sex like that."

"You mean phone sex," Walter said cautiously.

"Yes, of course. The most intense, incredible, horny, hot phone sex I have ever had. Sometimes we'd be on the phone five, six hours. He always came three or four times, but I held back. I wanted to wait until the very end and then really make it big."

"You always like to wait a long time before you come?"

"I sure do. How about you?"

Their conversation took a different direction. Afterwards, sweaty and spent, Walter crawled into bed next to Danny, who lay rigid, facing the wall.

"Have fun with your boys?" Danny said.

"Sure," Walter said. He tried to laugh at what had just happened to him, turn it into a joke, a light diversion, as Danny imagined it was, but all that night, Walter couldn't get Bulstrode out of his mind. There was something irresistible about him, about the very noncorporeality of him, as if he really were that imaginary friend most children invent at some moment or another. Before Bulstrode, Walter had been resolutely anonymous over the computer, but now something in that lilting voice persuaded him to tell all. How astonishing to live like that, without ever having to touch, without ever having to show your face! A life of that sort required no care, had no accountability!

At home, with Danny, Walter had been plagued by a numbness lately, a lack of sexual feeling toward his lover's body, which he could not fathom; here, after all, was the same flesh for which he had felt incomparable lust just months before, and it might as well have been a lump of raw bread dough, for all the arousal it now mustered in him. Was it time? he wondered. Did it happen to every couple eventually? Perhaps there is only so much lust a single body can inspire in another, perhaps only so many orgasms before the loved one's body simply becomes drained of that mysterious, pleasure-seeking juice of attraction. And yet Danny didn't seem to have the same problem. That night, after Walter had rolled away to face the wall and sleep, Danny was suddenly on him, taking Walter in his arms and reaching his hand down toward his belly, possessed, clearly, even now, of the same old desire that had started up so many years ago, in a dorm at Yale.

"Not now," Walter whispered. "I have to sleep."

"What's the matter?" Danny said. "Saving it for Hung Jock?" He laughed in what Walter thought was a sarcastic way and turned away from him.

"Bulstrode," Walter said, but it was without breath; no sound escaped his lips.

Across hundreds of miles of telephone wire, the next evening, Walter told Bulstrode about his father and mother, his sister, his dog. He confessed his increasing sexual ambivalence toward Danny. He admitted he was addicted to pornography. All this Bulstrode absorbed, an enormous crackling silence on the other end of the telephone line. He offered close to nothing in return because he had almost nothing to offer. From what Walter could tell, over several years Bulstrode had given more and more of himself to the computer until his outer life, his life in the world, eroded, broke off, a dry husk. As for the life of the channel, that was a different matter. Here he was full of stories, anecdotes, events. One evening a group of men in or near New York had been discussing the pleasures of sex in the aisles of the Adonis, a gay porno theater near Broadway. "I just love the Adonis," one of the men had written. "The atmosphere there positively emulates sex." Both Bulstrode and Walter had been on at the time, and later they laughed about it. "Can you believe it?" Walter said. "I was really tempted to type something mean, like 'Truer words have not been spoke.' But I didn't. Instead, I sent him a message, saying, in effect, 'I think you mean "emanate." ' Then he tells me to check my dictionary program! Jesus, these guys are so arrogant!"

Bulstrode was laughing, hard. "The thing you've got to realize," he said, "is that most of these guys, for all their computer wizardry, don't know very much about the English language. Some of them are positively subliterate. What I love is when words get reduced to letters—

you know, 'What are you up to?' with the 'are' and 'you' as letters and the 'to' as a number. That always gives me a chuckle." His voice suddenly grew pensive. "Did I ever tell you about Rudy?"

"Rudy? I don't think so."

"Well, Rudy was this really sweet working-class kid, eighteen or so. He used to spell like that, which is why I was reminded. Anyway, I got to know him pretty well on the channel. He was a nice kid, he liked older guys, he said. We had phone sex a few times, which was hot—he got off on me calling him son and him calling me Daddy—and sometimes afterwards we'd talk seriously. That was when I started to realize he was really in trouble—you know, out of work, the father's an alcoholic who beats him up, the mother's gone. No wonder he wants to call me Daddy. Anyway, one evening a bunch of us, maybe ten of us, were on, when Rudy logs on, and he says, 'I've just taken thirty-seven Valium.' Suddenly there's this incredible panic. Everyone's trying to keep him awake, you know, the way you're supposed to, to distract him, but pretty soon he just stops answering our messages. Of course we can't call him; the phone's hooked up to his computer, and he's still logged on. But we knew where he was from, and a couple of us had his phone number, so what we did was, this guy called Snapper, he called nine-one-one and got the emergency number for his area and told them what had happened and gave them the number. They had a book to get the address from the number, got over there, and sure enough, there he was, slumped over his desk with the machine on. A couple of weeks later he came on and told us we'd saved him. We'd saved his life."

"Jesus," Walter said.

Bulstrode was silent for a moment. "It was," he said, in his careful Kentucky accent, "one of the finest moments, one of the truly finest moments, of my life. I helped save someone from the jaws of death."

He laughed softly. "Walter," Bulstrode said, after a few seconds of silence. "Can I tell you something?"

"Sure," Walter said.

"I really like you."

"I like you too."

"No, I mean it. What I mean is, I—I love you."

"Ah—" Walter said.

"Are you upset to hear that?"

"No, not upset, just—"

"Just what?"

"Well—we've never met."

"I feel as if we have."

"It's just—I don't know, it seems weird to me. How can you love someone you've never seen?"

"I've seen you. In my imagination I've seen you. And isn't that better? That way nothing can spoil you for me. That way you'll always be perfect."

"But I'm not perfect," Walter said. "And that isn't love."

"Everyone has his own definition of love," Bulstrode said. "Anyway, don't get so uptight. I'm not demanding reciprocation or anything. I just wanted you to know—the level my feelings had elevated to."

Walter was quiet for a moment, grasping for something to say. "Well, I'm glad you told me," he said finally. "I am, uh, touched." He cleared his throat. "Listen, I think I'd better go now. I've got to get going."

"Aren't you horny?" Bulstrode asked.

"Not tonight, really. Maybe tomorrow—"

"What time?"

"I don't know—sevenish."

"Shall I call?"

"No, let's meet on the computer. Okay?"

"Okay."

Walter hung up. He felt suddenly ashamed, and frightened, as if he really had been having an affair and the affair had gotten out of hand. Of course that wasn't true. He could change his number, elect never to turn his computer on again, and Bulstrode would disappear from his life. There would be nothing to confess to Danny; Danny would laugh. Disappear! he would say. How could Bulstrode disappear? He hardly existed. Who he was, what he looked like, how old he was, even his name—all these things were mysterious. His house was mysterious; his clothes were mysterious. Yet he and Walter had had the conversations lovers have, had brought each other to orgasms as lovers do. Where are you? Bulstrode had asked. What are you wearing? Are you hard? Unzip your pants. Open your shirt. Imagine I'm kissing you, undressing you.

Imagine I'm loving you.

Bulstrode, it seemed, had ceased to believe in the barrier between imagination and act. And why not? What are we, after all, Walter wondered, but voices, synapses, electrical impulses? When one person's body touches another person's body, chemicals under the skin break down and recombine, setting off an electric spark that leaps, neuron to neuron, to the brain. Was that really all that different from what happened when fingers pushed down buttons on a keyboard that sent signals across a telephone wire to another keyboard, another set of fingers? Wasn't there, in all of that, something of a touch? All around him, Walter heard people complaining about how they wished they were different, wished they were bigger, smaller, smarter, sexier, thinner. Bulstrode had found a way around all that; he had found out how to become the self he imagined, the self his real life, apparently, constricted him from fully being.

And Walter understood. More than once he had stopped in front of the mirror in the lobby of the World Trade Center, stunned by the dark-suited, well-groomed man who faced him with such confidence and easy, necktied glamour, and wondered how that man could possibly be himself. Some people invented themselves. And yet there were others—Danny, his mother—who seemed to say, Who I am is who I was, where I come from, who my mother and my father were. The past forms me. The past owns me. The pit of family called endlessly for Walter, voices beseeched him to acknowledge his own inseparable link to all the hands and voices and smells, the dark nails and wet kisses, the bloody lipstick smears, while on the other side, there was Bulstrode, patently himself, declaring to Walter his strange, disembodied love. Did Bulstrode want Walter to leave Danny for him? And if so, where would he go? Would they live forever in the constricted little corridor of noncorporeality, an endless private chat? Would his world be a phone booth? Thinking all of this, he became frightened and longed, suddenly, to be touched.

He went to Danny. Calling his name, he tore across the house, to the bedroom, where Danny was watching TV, and threw himself on him, professing his love as loudly and suspiciously as a husband who has just come from a hooker. Danny laughed and pushed him away. "I can't breathe," he said. "You're choking me. Jesus." Walter rolled over, panting. "What's with you?" Danny said. "You're never like this." Walter panted. On the television white-coated doctors hurried through hallways, pushing fearful-eyed patients on stretchers.

He had known a deaf woman once. She had lived in the other half of the two-family house he and his mother shared right after his parents' divorce. Her name was Jeanette, and she sold hot pants door to door. Walter remembered his mother squeezed into the tight red shorts, her legs wobbling like Jell-O as she turned in front of the mirror, murmuring, "I just don't know." The deaf woman was talkative, and had a vague, throaty, approximate voice that he loved to listen to. What amazed him was that even though she had never heard a single sound, she was nonetheless pushing forward the muscles of her throat, trusting that whatever communications resulted would come to life in that world which existed for her only as an act of faith. And wasn't love always like that, in the end, a mere gesture made across unknowable miles? If that was true, then Bulstrode, in his isolation, his reaching across the continent, was merely, consummately human.

Still, Walter couldn't bear the thought of hearing his voice again. Instead he clung to Danny; he spent every moment he could hugging or kissing Danny. A week or so later, when he finally logged on again, he was surprised to find no messages, no e-mail from Bulstrode. He wasn't sure why, and he also wasn't sure if he was glad. Perhaps Bulstrode was ashamed to have been rebuffed at that tenderest moment; perhaps, in his narrow world, he could not bear the sound of Walter's voice anymore, or even the sight of his name, now that Walter had received and ridiculed his most intimate offering. But Walter thought it was more likely that he had simply found someone else out there among the Hunky Dudes and Top Guns, another distant friend with whom to talk and laugh and confide across all the miles, and pass the loneliest of hours.

T HE RASH, whatever it was, brought Nat back to her. It was almost like a manifestation of his guilt, like stigmata, and indeed, her palms and feet were red, parched, and could be scratched bloody. He came back to her in sorrow, as he always did when she became sick, and for a week he was there every night. No fighting. He endured her crying, her middle-of-the-night terrors, her insistence she couldn't take another day of it. He accompanied her to the doctors—the dermatologist, who shrugged his shoulders; the allergist, who shrugged his shoulders; the second dermatologist, who ordered tests and mentioned dental trauma—supportive, unwavering, as he always managed to be under such circumstances. If she hadn't been so uncomfortable, she would've felt gratified, loved, except she knew it was not out of love that he was comforting her, merely out of guilt and fear. (He did fear losing her.) And to his credit, he took care of her very well, very convincingly. Still, if she hadn't been suffering, he wouldn't have been home—this was the equation their lives had come down to—and so she wondered if perhaps her subconscious really *had* willed the rash into being, as a way of keeping him there. No, she had lived enough through pain and its ravages to know her subconscious would never have been so stupid as to bring physical grief upon the body just to satisfy the thin needs of the soul. Pain was worse than sadness; there were moments when, waking up in the middle of the night, raw and itching, she would have gladly divorced Nat if in return she could have been divorced from her own skin.

Baths helped her. Also, she had checked out from the library some works of Catholic theology, most of which she found dull and hard to concentrate on. It didn't matter. Faith, she understood, didn't have to be a matter of intellect. She had only to watch Clara, who cleaned her house, maneuvering her way through the rooms with an earphone plugged into her ear, sermons every second of the day, to understand that faith didn't have to be a matter of intellect. Faith—if not blind, then mindless—had accompanied Clara through all the thousands of miles of vacuuming that had been her life these last twenty years. It accompanied her through quick lunches of canned olives dumped in a bowl, through the drive back and forth from the small stuccoed house she shared with a hazy collection of fellow churchwomen, children, new arrivals from the islands. Faith, Louise was coming to understand, was not an argument in a book; faith was a little radio, cheaply made, a wire crawling up a white uniform and creeping, like an earwig, into the ear. Something you listened to every moment of the day. She knew what Clara would have thought of it all. What was an itch, what was cancer, compared with the ravages suffered by Christ? Live chastely, Louise had heard her mutter more than once. Tithe gratefully.

———————

IN ANY CASE she should have known better than to confide in her sister. Every time in her life she'd confided in anyone, especially her sister, it had turned out dreadfully. But Eleanor had a way of coaxing things out of her.

For one thing, she always came unexpectedly, and never without substantial gifts of food—cakes, pies, casseroles, pâtés, sometimes a whole turkey or roast beef. This gave her a reason to stay awhile, whereas if Louise had had her way, she would've invented excuses, put Eleanor's visits off, one after the other. Her little sister, whom everyone assumed to be her older sister—Eleanor was fatter, her hair grayer, her eyes more worn, not to mention the brace and the cane—was mostly an annoyance to Louise, a source of guilt, frustration. Why did she live the way she did? Why would anyone choose to live that way? She had married Sid Friedman, after all, supposedly a psychologist, in Louise's opinion a rogue, and passed thirty years with him on the constant brink of bankruptcy; they were always putting money into talentless songwriters, or "prime land" that turned out to be tumbleweed-strewn desert, or dubious kitchen gadgets that sat unused in Eleanor's drawers for years. More than once the meandering small talk of Eleanor's food-bearing visits had led to requests for loans or tales of no-risk schemes, airplanes and pyramids, in which it would be a crime for Louise and Nat not to invest. Louise, who had never borrowed a dime in her life, wondered, Does she have no shame? She wondered this even as she wrote the check. And Eleanor was "litigious," a crossword puzzle word, meaning she sued people—contractors; plumbers; drivers whose cars scraped the paint off her fender; people from whom she had bought dogs, garage door openers, motorbikes, washing machines. Her motivation was not so much justice, or even revenge, as it was a sportsmanlike determination to get the most she could out of her small misfortunes. "I take an optimist's view of the hazards of daily life," she liked to say. "Everything's an opportunity, if you look at it the right way." Louise studied her coffee.

For three years now Sid and Eleanor had been living a town away from Louise and Nat. Before that, for two decades, it was Los Angeles—an easier distance for Louise, since it meant having to see her sister only once or twice a year, on holidays. In those days, when Eleanor flew up, Louise invariably dragged Danny to the airport to pick her up, only to find she was not among the passengers disembarking from the plane. Then Louise would hear herself paged—always a terrifying experience, her own name booming through the loudspeakers—and at the white courtesy telephone listen as Eleanor promised to be on the very next flight, an hour from now. Often, by the time Eleanor actually got off the plane, Louise and Danny had been waiting three or four hours. Still, finally, there she was, stumbling down the long airport corridor with her children (still children then), her messy hair flying, waving her cane, and saying in a mock child's voice, "Oh, gee, Mommy, is Auntie Louise mad at us? Won't Auntie Louise forgive us for being a teeny-weeny bit late?"

"Three hours is not a teeny-weeny bit late, Eleanor."

"But we're so sorry, Auntie Louise, and we couldn't help it, the traffic was so terrible! Oh, dear, what can we do to make Auntie Louise love us again?"

This was Eleanor at her worst.

Eleanor at her best was the morning her oven exploded. Louise stood with her in her kitchen, examining the charred interior. She was still in her pink bathrobe and furry slippers. "Ellie," Louise said, "I'm sorry. I know how important an oven is to you, and that this one was expensive. I'm sorry."

But Eleanor only shut the oven door and said, "Look." The glass had fractured without breaking and was run through with a network of intricate and tiny cracks.

"Oh, Ellie," Louise said.

"It's kind of pretty, isn't it?" Eleanor said, running her finger over the shattered glass. "I almost like it better this way." And smiled. She had managed to look beyond the destroyed oven, the son in Alaska, the daughter who would never have children, not to mention the unpaid mortgage and the upcoming court date and the ever-present threat of destitution and ruin. In the midst of a terrific fight with Louise once, screaming as they drove along a Boston highway to visit their senile mother, screaming as they got out of the car in the nursing home parking lot, screaming as they approached the electric doors, Eleanor had suddenly stopped and said, "Look at that flower, growing in the cement." And in a second she was on her knees examining the little flower that had struggled through the stone, so thoroughly delighted that Louise could only step back, silenced, impressed. Eleanor had forgotten her argument in the noisy cement parking lot; she had forgotten her sister and her mother and her children. She had forgotten them all.

As little girls they had sat together on a two-seat toilet, their underpants around their ankles, perched on the edges of the twin bowls that reached from the common tank like two fused cherries on a stem. They liked to sit for hours like that, and talk in quiet voices, as little girls do, close enough in age, back then, not to notice the difference. As they got older, it became clear that Eleanor would always be the uglier, the less intelligent, the less lucky of the two, yet also, in many ways, the more contented. She could sit, as a teenager, in the grass, her crutch by her side, and look in a way that Louise knew meant she was really seeing things, seeing them in a way Louise envied. She noticed grass, flowers, trees, stars, and remarked on them. "Look at the stars, Louise!" she might say, and Louise, to whom they were only stars, only nodded, ashamed at her lack of vision. In high school, in spite of the crutch, Eleanor met and fell in love with Sid Friedman and dated him happily, gratefully until their wedding, untroubled by his bad breath and awkward haircuts. What a pathetic choice, Louise had always thought, and yet she could not help but feel slightly disgusted, slightly surprised that Eleanor, four years younger, was married and settled first.

They grew up contentious, at odds. In adulthood Louise resented Eleanor, avoided her, considered herself—resolutely—the lucky one, without a cane, without a brace, with (relatively) normal, happy, healthy children. Eleanor never expressed even the slightest resentment of her sister; she was constantly, infuriatingly loving, no matter how cruel Louise might be. Her nonstop, smiling affection was a tactic, a weapon, Louise decided. Revenge came through the mail: obscure articles about sibling homosexuality, as well as alarmist tabloid clippings about AIDS, slow death, and postinfectious promiscuity, and photographs of gaunt, dying men clutching teddy bears. All, Louise reminded herself, because of her own tragic children. In person Eleanor was all smiles, always the bearer of gifts, and made no mention of the letters. She lived in one of a hundred identical houses built in the fifties, in cramped quarters, where the furniture was old and cat-scratched, the carpet stained. Only in the kitchen had no expense been spared, and yet even that room was constantly littered with empty boxes and cans and rotting vegetable rinds. Odd—Louise had always assumed that Eleanor must have hated having to live under such circumstances, must have grown hot with jealousy when she walked into Louise's clean-smelling, commodious kitchen, with its tile floor and window-ledge hummingbird feeders. And yet, she sometimes wondered now, children aside, was it right to assume that Eleanor longed for more than she had, longed for the stable bank account and big house her sister cherished and nurtured? Sometimes it seemed to Louise as if turmoil itself somehow powered Eleanor's life, as if she and Sid staved off settledness and certainty—those still pools—in favor of living always in the wave, the furious ocean, of going after things, of getting. Thus disaster—or at least the sensation of disaster—eluded Eleanor. She had said it herself: Everything's an opportunity, if you look at it the right way. If you thought about it, her life had unfolded as an endless chain of opportunity, possibility, while Louise sat in her perfect house, awaiting the mutiny of the cells. If you thought about it that way. But of course, Louise had to remind herself, few people would have thought about it that way, and fewer would have chosen Eleanor's life over her own.

What was indisputable—and indisputably annoying—was that Eleanor and Sid lived topsy-turvy in the messy bed of love, happy with each other as Louise and Nat—between clean sheets, in tight parallel—hadn't been for years. They were in love with each other in ways so obvious and absolute as to make irrelevant the fact that Louise could not imagine how anyone could fall in love with either one of them. They cared only what they looked like in each other's eyes—what did the world matter?—and it was this single-minded vision that rendered Eleanor's clippings obsolete, pointless. What use were they when she really had had the upper hand all along?

———

A CAR PULLING INTO the driveway, unexpected, was the sign. Fresh from the bathtub, relieved for the moment of the exasperating itch, Louise stood still in her bedroom, hoping it was someone turning around. The engine, however, turned off instead of turning over. She heard a car door open and slam, and then the familiar scraping of Eleanor's cane against the gravel.

"Hello, dear," Eleanor said as she made her noisy stumble through the kitchen door. "I brought a buckle and a slump." She hoisted a large paper sack onto the kitchen counter and fell into a chair. "I've been experimenting with old-fashioned American desserts all week," she said, pulling off her coat. "We ate the cobbler, and Joanne and Ed took the crumple. Here, hand me that bag." Louise did, and Eleanor pulled from it two tin pans, wrapped in wax paper and filled with incoherent splendors of fruit and cake. "No more aluminum pans in our house," Eleanor said. "It causes Alzheimer's."

"Glad to know it," Louise said. "One more deadly thing. Anyway, thanks, Eleanor, I'm sure Nat will enjoy these."

"They're not for Nat, they're for you," Eleanor said.

"I'm on a diet."

"Thin as a rail and on a diet! Me, I've been on every diet there is, it doesn't seem to do much good."

"A diet's why I'm thin as a rail."

"Oh, don't be ridiculous, you've always been skinny. Anyway, eat it if you want, and if you don't, give it to your friends. Everyone does what they can, and you know me. What I do is cook."

"Thank you, Eleanor."

"Anything, dear. I figured I might bring a little cheer, since you were uncomfortable with that rash of yours."

"I've felt better."

"Do you have any coffee?" But Louise was already pouring. She scrutinized her sister, who was, as usual, a mess, her hair unwashed and uncombed. She was wearing stretchy pink pants, a blouse with a hideous pattern of yellow flowers, blue sandals through the open ends of which two scratchy blue toenails peeked. They were the kind of sandals that jam the toes together, the kind their mother had worn. Eleanor had always favored unlikely colors.

"So this latest lawsuit is a real fiasco," she was saying, "thank you, half a cup is fine. Have I told you about it?"

"I have trouble keeping them all straight."

"Oh, I'm sure I told you about this one. A couple of months ago I was at the movies, seeing *Out of Africa*? Anyway, the movie was about to start, and this man in front of me was smoking, even though there's a no smoking rule. Well, you know how allergic I am to cigarettes! So I just tapped him on the shoulder and said, 'Sir, there's no smoking in this theater.' He ignored me. So I tapped him on the shoulder again and said, 'Sir, maybe you didn't hear me. There's no smoking in this theater,' and this time not only did he not say a word, he actually took another cigarette and lit it up. As a challenge. So finally I tapped him on the shoulder a third time, harder, and I said, 'Sir, if you don't put out that cigarette I'm going to have to get the management.' And you know what he did?"

"What?" Louise said.

"He turned around and said, 'Lady, if you don't shut the fuck up and let me watch the movie, I'm going to throw this fucking Coca-Cola I have here in your fucking face.' His exact words. Well, I wasn't going to take that for a second! So I stood up and got the manager, and of course when I came back, he wasn't smoking. They're tricky, that kind. 'This man abused me verbally because I asked him to quit smoking,' I said. 'I want him thrown out of this theater.' Well, the guy just looked up real innocent, but sure enough, everyone around confirmed he'd been smoking. Then the manager—he must have been on the take—he said there was nothing he could do about it except tell the guy not to smoke anymore. So he told the guy, who sort of shrugged, and went off and I sat down again and the guy lit up a cigarette, turned around, and blew the smoke in my face. That was when I slapped him."

"You slapped him!" Louise was interested in spite of herself.

"I was angry! And then he stood up and turned around and put his hands around my throat. I still have a mark, see? So I screamed, and then there was a real commotion, and the police came, and I had him arrested. Simple as that. I'm suing him for emotional distress and medical expenses. Seems pretty open-and-shut, right? Wrong! Guess what?"

"What?"

"On the advice of his lawyer, he's countersuing me for slapping him *and* for false arrest! Can you imagine? The whole thing has gotten so out of control we tried for an out-of-court settlement, but he wouldn't hear of it. Believe you me, this thing is costing us a pretty penny." She shook her head sadly. "Well, what can you say? What can you do? Someone makes trouble and they end up suing you. Part of me really wishes I'd never pressed charges. But then I remember, I really do have a case, you see. The usher's promised to testify on my behalf, and the other day a lady called me up who was in the theater, she saw the whole thing. And when I remember what he said to me! The nerve, to tell a woman of my distinction she has a fucking face." She laughed and blew her nose.

"I don't blame you," Louise said, and poured more coffee.

"Oh, well, enough about me and my boring lawsuits," Eleanor said. "So how are the kids?"

"Danny's fine. April's fine." She frowned for a moment and concluded, "The kids are fine."

"Both of them back east?"

Louise nodded.

"Are they going to get out West anytime soon?"

"I don't know. I suppose so."

"You'd think they'd care enough to come out and visit their parents now and then," Eleanor said. "How long has it been, three months now? I tell you, Louise, I count my blessings every day I've got my Joanne around the corner." Then she looked away, thinking, Louise supposed, DES. Was it possible for her ever to think of her daughter without those letters flashing through her brain?

"You know, Markie says he's moving to New York," Eleanor said, brightening suddenly. "Has some girlfriend there he met up in Alaska, or so he claims. Do you suppose he could call up Danny, or maybe stay with him at first?"

"You'd have to ask Danny."

"I know it's an imposition—let's face it, my Markie's an imposition—but I hate to think of him wandering around New York by himself. God knows what kind of trouble he'd get into. Still, he's saved a bundle of money up there in Alaska, and he says he wants to go to New York. I don't trust the whole thing, that's for sure." She sighed. "Well, maybe they could just have dinner—Markie and Danny. They are cousins, after all."

"I'm sure Danny would be happy to do that."

"Good!" Eleanor said. She noticed Louise's left hand moving unconsciously along her right arm. "Your rash?" she asked.

Louise looked at the table, nodded.

"Any better today?"

"It doesn't get better. It doesn't get worse. It just stays. Stays and stays." She stood, suddenly agitated.

"Poor baby," Eleanor said. "You've had too much pain to need this. Anyway, it's just a rash. It'll clear up."

"I suppose. But, Ellie," she said, suddenly turning, "I'm up all night with it. I take these baths, and then I'm okay for maybe forty-five minutes, and then it starts up again. I'm taking Benadryl too, that seems to help a little." She sat down again and took another sip of her coffee. "Right now, I feel fine. I probably have twenty, twenty-five more minutes of feeling fine. Before it starts up again."

"Have you seen a dermatologist?"

"The dermatologist doesn't know, the GP doesn't know. Dr. Stern thinks it's the result of dental trauma—you know, that root canal disaster last month? So I said, 'Dental trauma! Doctor, it's not my teeth that itch!' " She laughed. "Want more coffee?"

"No, thanks," Eleanor said. "How's Nat doing through all this?"

Louise stopped, sat still a moment before refilling her mug. "Fine," she said, knowing that moment of silence had told Eleanor everything she wanted to know.

"Louise," Eleanor said, putting a doughy white hand over her sister's parched red one, "you know if you need anything, you can always come to us. You know that. Sid and I are always here for you."

"Thanks," Louise said.

"You want some buckle or some slump?"

"Not right now."

Eleanor got up to clear the table. Louise watched her as she stumbled to the sink, washed the cups out, stacked them to dry. Sometimes, on mornings like this, when it was raining slightly and she was still in her bathrobe, an odd, ancient intimacy overcame Louise about her sister, and they were returned to two little girls sitting on the twin bowls of that miraculous double toilet. It was an intimacy Eleanor encouraged and Louise struggled to resist—she didn't want to be so close to anyone ever again—but somehow the old warmth, the easy familiarity, took her in every time. Even now it was happening; in spite of her annoyance, she felt herself becoming soft, tractable.

Eleanor sat down again. On the table was a small pile of library books, including several by Thomas Merton. "Thomas Merton!" she said. "Isn't he that theologian?" She took one of the books and examined it with a look of mock-seriousness. "Catholicism," she said, in a deep, television voice. "I remember the Catholics in our neighborhood, don't you? You remember that afternoon Mary O'Brady and her sister trapped us on the merry-go-round? She and her sisters kept spinning it and spinning it, even though we were crying to get off, and they shouted, 'You killed Christ, Louise Gold! You killed Christ, Eleanor Gold!' She shook her head. "Great people, the Catholics."

"Not all Catholics are ignorant ten-year-old girls," Louise said, taking the book back from her.

"Why are you reading this stuff? You've never been interested in religion."

Louise shrugged her shoulders. "I'm interested now," she said.

Eleanor looked at her suspiciously.

"Oh, Eleanor, it's nothing," Louise said, standing up and taking the books to the laundry room, where she deposited them next to the wax cauldron. "Really, just something I've been thinking about, toying with."

"Does this have to do with Nat?" Louise said. "Is this because of what's going on with Nat?"

"Nothing's going on," Louise said. She had thought she wanted to resist telling Eleanor, but suddenly she realized how much she longed to say it, to tell Eleanor all about it; she could barely hold back.

"I am just thinking about Catholicism—as an alternative," she said, sitting down again, and looked nervously at her sister across the table. She had not talked about it with anyone except Danny. She had not talked about anything important with anyone for years.

Eleanor stared at her rather blankly.

"An alternative?" she said.

"Well, if you must know, I'm thinking of possibly—changing my faith. I think Catholicism has a lot to offer people who have to be alone. So I've made an appointment to talk next week with Father Abernathy of the Most Holy Trinity Catholic Church on Coolidge Street."

"Oh, my God," Eleanor said, and suddenly she was shaking her head violently. "Oh, my God, what would Mama say? She would die, Louise, she'd die a second death in her grave."

"Come on, Eleanor! Mama was not a religious woman, and neither are you, for that matter. What do you care what I do?"

"Louise," Eleanor said, taking her hand, "think twice before you do this, sweetheart. Why Catholicism? We're Jews, Louise, one hundred percent. Maybe you should talk to Rabbi."

"The rabbi does not interest me," Louise said hotly, taking back her hand. "The rabbi is an egotistical, horny womanizer who, I don't have to remind you, left his own wife and three kids out in the cold not three years ago for, yes, a Catholic."

"Then another rabbi. Or a counselor. You know the Sisterhood does peer counseling. But a priest?" She shook her head. "It's just not normal, Louise. It's not healthy. Maybe you should see a psychiatrist."

Louise steadied her gaze against the window. "I shouldn't have said anything to you," she said. "I knew I shouldn't have."

"That's not true, Louise, it's good you've told me. I can help you now."

"I don't need your help," Louise said. "Don't you see? It's not a question of getting help. It's a question of—how I'm supposed to live my life, or what's left of it. Because none of *this* is any good anymore"— she gestured vaguely at the kitchen, the washing machine, the pictures of her children on the bulletin board—"all this talk by psychiatrists and rabbis isn't any good anymore. Nothing *helps* anymore. If Catholicism gives my life meaning, then what's wrong with it? No one cares about me; I'm not ruining anyone's existence; my kids are grown up, and God knows they've made their own decisions. And I feel something for it, Eleanor, I—oh, forget it, you won't understand." She ran her hands through her hair. "Look, just promise me you'll leave me alone to do what's best—what *I* feel is best for *me*. Okay?"

"Louise," Eleanor said, "I understand what you're saying. You're feeling low, and you need—"

"I'm not feeling low," Louise said. "There is a lower than low." And she looked shyly across the table, to see if those words had put pleasure in her sister's face.

Eleanor looked only grave.

"You're right to know to get help, sweetheart. But I wish you would think about the source you're trying."

"I have," Louise said. "And I'm not going for help, I told you. Help has nothing to do with it."

Her sister stood. "It's probably time for me to go now, isn't it?" she said. "Try to think about what I said."

"Think about what I said," Louise answered.

"I will if you will. Deal?"

Louise shrugged and looked away.

———

LATER THAT AFTERNOON, while she was doing a crossword puzzle, the phone rang. "Mrs. Cooper?" said a bright female voice.

"Yes."

"Hi, Mrs. Cooper, you don't know me. My name is Melanie Frankel, and I'm the new assistant rabbi at Temple B'nai Mitzvah?"

"Oh, for God's sake," Louise said. "Look, forget it. I know my sister told you to call, and now I'm telling you, forget it."

"Mrs. Cooper, I just want to talk to you for a moment. I understand you're having a very difficult time right now, and I want you to know I'm here if you need me. It's my job. You're disillusioned with your own faith—I understand that—but please, before you change your religion, let me make a case for it. You owe that to yourself, as a Jew and as a woman."

"This is none of my sister's business," Louise said quietly. "And it's none of yours. I haven't set foot in that temple for five years, and I've always paid my dues. I am my own person, and I will make my own choices."

"I just want you to think carefully, Mrs. Cooper. It's generally a bad idea to make major decisions at a time of crisis. Now I won't keep you on the phone anymore, but if you ever want to call me up or come by, I'm here to talk. Okay?"

"The only thing you can do for me is tell my sister to leave me the hell alone."

"She's only thinking of you—"

"I wish it were that simple."

"Well, she loves you very much. She's very concerned, Mrs. Cooper."

"You're a young woman," Louise said, "and you don't know me. And you're very naive." Then she hung up.

OF COURSE, part of her wanted to call back. Opening up to Eleanor had ripped something in her; suddenly, for the first time in years, comfort tempted. The young woman's voice, so calm, so urging—it would have been easy to fall into that voice, crying, to fall into what she imagined were that capable young woman's capable, strong arms. But she must not. She couldn't trust it. What was comfort, anyway? Just an anodyne, a painkiller, a false oblivion, probably addictive. For those purposes she had a cabinetful of lovingly prescribed bottles: Valium, Percodan, Halcion.

She stood from the sofa, throwing aside the crossword puzzle—a drug in its own right. The phone rang again.

"Louise, just listen to me for one second—"

"Leave me alone!" she said loudly into the phone, into her sister's ear, and hung up. The silence that followed was as palpable as the absence of someone who has just died. Eleanor muffled, for once. And suddenly Louise panicked, and wondered, Is this it? Is this the irrationality of the dying? Crisis, Rabbi Frankel had said. "I am in a time of crisis," Louise said aloud. "This is me, Louise, in a time of crisis." Yet as she said those words, it was as if someone else were speaking through her mouth.

Oh, she hated her sister now, hated her for turning the tables, for making her the sick, the weak, the needy one, herself the strong, healthy, rational being who must do what she can, even against Louise's wishes, to help her. How she must have wanted it, after all those years of weakness and failure, after polio and crippledness and her dreadful husband and dreadful children—to be, for once, strong and well, to feel she has everything and can therefore minister to the one who has nothing. How she must be gloating now! Louise thought. How she must be loving it! When the balance was different, Louise hadn't loved it, she hadn't wanted it. It was a wretched position into which fate had thrown her, sitting all those afternoons in their quarantined house, listening to Eleanor's faint breathing in the sickroom she was forbidden to enter, and thinking of Tommy Burns on the beach, in the blazing sun, the water, and the sand, and the sea gulls shrieking, and all the while, in the stifling house, her own tan peeling away, revealing pale winter skin too early. How she had longed to be back there, among the other swimmers, her friends! She had hated Eleanor that summer, though she kept her mouth shut, did everything she was told, helped in the kitchen and with boiling the sheets. And maybe she had wished Eleanor *would* die. Maybe she had wished more than anything that Eleanor would die, or disappear, or never have been born, just so that she could be free again, to run back out onto the beach and in the ecstatic sunlight call to Tommy Burns, "Tommy, it's me, Louise! I'm here! I'm back!"

Eleanor knew it. She knew it, and now she was exacting her revenge.

Louise looked at the clock. It was four o'clock. At five Nat would come home and take her to see another doctor. At once she understood that she would never call the rabbi back, though she failed to recognize exactly what it was that was going to intervene.

She took up her knitting and a book; both kept falling into her lap. The Benadryl had made her drowsy, too drowsy to move to the bed. All that hour she kept falling into something close to sleep, and then she was with Eleanor again, the killers of Christ, clutching hot metal as the merry-go-round whirled faster and faster, and the O'Brady sisters' arms went one over the other, one over the other, like something being braided. The world was a dizzy blaze of color then, their screams slurred by the rackety clanking, and it felt as if someone were trying to pull her by the ankles, though her feet held tight, and her mouth filled with wind, and she wanted it to go on, she wanted it to go on and on.

FOR SEVERAL DAYS April didn't call her mother to tell her she was pregnant. She didn't feel strong enough for censure or disapproval, she told Danny, and that was exactly what she was sure she would get from Louise. Danny disagreed. "This will be wonderful news for her," he insisted across the kitchen table. "Up until now she's all but given up hope for grandchildren. Think how happy, how surprised she'll be."

"I wish I could be so sure," April said. They were sitting together early one evening, finishing the last of some chicken soup Iris had dropped off that afternoon. "I don't think I need to remind you that Mom has never once publicly praised anything I've done to anyone, anywhere. Hell, usually it feels like she's doing the opposite—you know, playing down my singing career to her friends like it was just counterculture weirdness, some adolescent phase I'm going through." She laughed. "I can just imagine her casting her eyes heavenward and saying something like 'Jesus, April, what have you gotten yourself into now?' And that, my dear brother, I simply do not need."

"Look, April," Danny said, "you're right, she isn't very good at expressing praise. It's some tic from her upbringing; I'm sure it has to do with Grandma. But you must remember, in her own way, she's very proud of you, even if she can't say it. Remember the scrapbook, after all."

"The scrapbook," April said, as if it were a joke. Yet it was true. For years Louise had methodically cut and pasted the detritus of April's life into a brown leather album, every review and interview and advertisement and article and flyer and concert poster and even ticket stubs, when she could get them, always replacing the album afterwards on the piano, where it sat, never spoken of or called attention to, but available for all inquisitive visitors or curious cousins to peruse.

"Oh, all right," April said finally. "I'll call tonight."

"Why don't you call now?" Danny asked.

"Danny! I can't call now—"

"Sure you can. Why not? Why put it off?"

April looked frightened. Danny picked up the phone and handed it to her.

"Jesus," she said.

She had only to press one button—it was that sort of phone—and then there was Louise's familiar, oddly childlike hello, which always made strangers think she'd been crying.

"Hi, Mom," April said.

"Hi, honey," Louise said. "You at Danny's still?"

"Uh-huh."

"Having fun with your brother doing all those wonderful East Coast things we poor savages out West are deprived of?"

April laughed. "Well," she said, "it's true, you don't have Friendly's out there."

"What's Friendly's?"

"A restaurant." April cleared her throat. "Listen, Mom, what would you think would be the most surprising news I could give you right now?"

"Right now? That you're getting married."

"Well," April said, "I'm not getting married, but I am—pregnant."

"Pregnant," Louise said.

"Yes."

There was a sort of strangling sound, and then Louise was crying.

"Mom," April said. "Mom, why are you crying?"

"I'm sorry," Louise said. "I'm just—it's just—oh, God, I just never in a thousand years—pregnant! April, how?"

"It's a long story," April said. "Suffice it to say the father is a nice, responsible man who lives in San Francisco, and we won't be getting married. And it wasn't an accident, it was something we planned—"

"Planned? What do you mean, planned?"

"We just decided to have a child together," April said. "Artificial insemination."

"Jesus," Louise said. "Never in all my life—artificial insemination! April, why didn't you tell me you were doing this?"

"I didn't think it would work," April said. "I didn't want to get your hopes up."

"Hopes up!" Louise suddenly sounded angry. "Listen, you better not be expecting me to raise this baby for you, April—"

"What?"

"Because if that's what you're thinking, you can just forget that—"

"Mom, what are you talking about? I don't expect anything like that from you. I was just calling to tell you you're going to be a grandmother." She let out a frustrated sigh. "You know, I knew you'd react this way. Danny said, no, no, she'll be happy, but I knew you'd just use it as one more reason to get angry at me."

Louise was silent. "No one ever told me," she said, "I would have to deal with something like this."

"I'm sorry."

"You know, you've never thought responsibly about anything, April, you've always just gone ahead and made your decisions—"

"Mom, I do not need your responsibility lecture right now—"

"So how are you going to raise this baby, I'd like to know? Traveling all the time the way you do, what kind of life is that going to be for a baby? Did you think about that?"

"There's a father, Mom."

"What do you mean, you're leaving him with the father? Who is he? Who is this guy?"

"A very nice man. Very responsible. He'll take care of the baby when I'm traveling."

"What's his name? What does he do?"

April was quiet for a moment. "I'll tell you that later."

"Christ," Louise muttered. Then: "Oh, why, why you had to tell me this now—look, I want to forget we had this conversation. I just want to strike it from the record. You haven't told me anything, I don't know anything—"

"But, Mom."

"I'm sick, April!" And once again she was crying.

159

"Mom," April said in a shocked, silenced way. "I'm sorry, Mom."

"You don't know the half of it." She seemed to be blowing her nose. "Look," she said, "for now we haven't had this conversation. When I'm better, you can tell me again. Okay?"

"I don't know," April said. "Okay."

"Good. Listen, I have to go now, I need to take some medicine."

"Mom—"

"Good-bye!"

April put the phone down.

"April," Danny said.

"You were wrong."

"April, I'm sorry. But look, I'm sure she'll come around."

"She said she was sick," April said, twisting her hair around her pinkie.

"She had some sort of rash."

"It sounded terrible. It sounded really awful."

Danny put his hand on his sister's shoulder. "I wouldn't worry about *that*, April," he said. "It's just a rash, after all. Since when has a rash been such a big deal, especially compared to everything else Mom's gone through?"

April didn't answer.

"She'll be fine," Danny said. "Fine. And believe me, once she's feeling better, she'll be glad."

———

THEY DID NOT HEAR from Louise or Nat until later in the week. All that afternoon April tried to write songs; first about the scrapbook, but it sounded too much like an elegy, she complained, and her mother wasn't dead yet. Then a kind of feeding frenzy overtook her—she ate most of a box of Oreos—and then a frenzy to create, a furious, willed insistence to write one song, just one goddamned song, before dusk. She thrashed around the house, swinging her guitar into the air like a fencing sword, then swooping down onto any available bed or couch to resume her creative posture—half sitting, half lying, guitar in hand, music pad and pen at her side. By five she was desperate for ideas. "Ontogeny recapitulates phylogeny," she said to Danny. "Which means that as my baby develops, it goes through the entire process of evolution. Isn't that miraculous? Is there something there for a song?"

"I think that theory's been disproved," Danny said. "Or at least significantly abbreviated."

April tried a few experimental chords on her guitar. "First a fish— first a cell—first . . ." She raised her eyebrows, smiled, and imme- diately sang out, clear as day, "Is there a moment of conception, a moment when you began to be . . . Oh, shit," she said. "This is going to piss off the pro-choice people. I'd better start again."

And back to the notebook, her fingers rifling through her long hair, chasing after inspiration with hands like claws. The sun close to set- ting. "April," Danny said, "remember that afternoon you took me to dim sum and it turned out you had a blind date with that guy who had answered your ad?"

"Vaguely," April said, between chords. "It's not a period of my life I look on fondly, full as it was of penises."

"Well, I've been really pissed off about that for a long time now."

April looked at him. "Pissed off? Danny, it must have been fifteen years ago."

"Yes, it was, and, well, it seems to me you set me up. You told me you wanted to take me to lunch, and really you just wanted to use me as protection in case your blind date was a creep. Which, as I recall, he was."

"Danny," April said, putting down her pencil, "you are so full of crap I can't believe it. Yes, I did want you to protect me, but I asked you first, and you said sure, anything to get your beloved dim sum! I was straight with you from moment one! Jesus, you really must not think much of me if you've twisted things around that much."

"So it's my memory against yours?"

"Afraid so."

"And of course because you're the famous singer who can write a song about all of it, your word wins. Great." He stood up and marched into the kitchen.

"What are you getting so upset about?" April called after him. "We're talking fifteen years ago. Fifteen years! This is ancient history!"

"Thirteen," Danny said. "It was 'seventy-five."

"Forgive me," April said. "Look, I'm trying to write a song here, do you mind?"

Aside from "This is my house," which he didn't like the sound of, Danny could think of no response to a line like that. He went into the kitchen. There was nothing to do there, so he poured himself a cup of coffee and sat at the table. Outside, rain poured down steadily. The street was full of blurry yellow light, occasional streaks of red when a car went by. Even here, behind the swinging door, he could make out the clicking sound of Walter chatting away at his computer, as well as the muted chords of April's guitar, ambling toward creation. All in all, a peculiarly satisfying scene, though he wasn't in the mood to admit it: his house, on a rainy Sunday, full of the noise of other people's lives, and Danny, like his mother, just sitting in the kitchen, trying to take it all in, once again a child in the midst of his summer vacation who sits down and tries as hard as he can to appreciate the rapid passage of pleasure and to make of appreciation itself a pleasurable state. "I appreciate this moment," Danny said now, "I feel this moment," and was instantly sixteen again, sitting across from his mother at the Neiman-Marcus lunchroom, eating a sandwich called a Towering Pagoda. Of course, just as then, even as he said it, the moment was slipping away.

———

TOWARD SIX O'CLOCK April had her song. Walter and Danny sat down on the sofa to listen:

> "Oh, my baby, growing in me,
> You are the earth and you are the sea,
> You are every creature that ever came to be,
> Oh, baby, go to sleep. . . .
>
> You saw the earth as a primeval place,
> You watched the dinosaurs crawling its face,
> You swam the waters, and the vastness of space,
> Oh, baby, go to sleep. . . .

You are the fish and you are the fowl,
The ones that bray and the ones that howl,
You are the tiger and the wise hoot owl,
Oh, baby, go to sleep. . . .

You are the best and you are the worst,
You are the last and you are the first,"

The phone rang.

" 'You are the only one'—goddammit to hell!" April shouted, putting down her guitar. "The fucking phone always interrupts me the first time I play a song!"

"I'll get it," Danny said, and hurried into the kitchen to pick up.

"Danny, it's your father."

"Hi, Dad."

He waited for Nat to say everything was fine, but Nat didn't say anything, and then a few seconds passed, and still he didn't say anything.

PART TWO

THE LAST TIME Louise thought she was dying, she was dying. Refracted light, light coming from some mysterious source; there didn't seem to be any windows. And pain, somewhere, dwelling in, or on, her body. The only thing was, *she* didn't seem to be dwelling in or on her body. It was as if the pain had displaced her and she were floating somewhere in its perimeter, coming close, then floating away again. Occasionally she tried to get back in, to lift her eyelids like the garage door, and what she saw was machinery, something pumping, and heads in masks, and funny flowered hats. A pair of eyes under black-rimmed glasses stared down at her—Nat's, of course. "The way she feels now, it's like she's washed down ten Valium with twenty martinis," said a doctorish voice, and she wanted to laugh, because of course, it didn't feel that way at all—she didn't feel good, only removed, pushed back from herself and the pain that was herself, that seemed to have taken over. "Everything's going to be okay, Louise," Nat said, laying a rubberized hand over her own hand. "I know this seems pretty rough, I know, but we'll get through it. All the doctors are confident." He spoke as if she were terrified; she wasn't, though apparently, not so long ago, terror had been near. She remembered: an ambulance in the driveway, and the surprising, brilliant blue midday sunlight as they brought her out the kitchen door, still in her nightgown. Terror, yes, and sorrow. Feeling that way seemed to have happened years ago.

"The children are on their way," Nat said. "They'll be here in the morning."

So I must be dying, Louise thought. It's okay, she wanted to say, I'm not so afraid now, but something blocked her throat.

DANNY STOOD AT THE luggage carousel with April and Eleanor, watching a planeload of suitcases thunking down the conveyor belt. He was naming the colors to himself as they fell over the lip: blue, green, gray, yellow, gray, gray.

"You're staying at your house, April," Eleanor was saying. "That nice couple who are renting it said it would be fine, they'll turn down the couch."

"You mean we aren't going home?" April said. She had taken a Valium on the plane and was still woozy from it, running her fingers through her hair.

"Well, honey," Eleanor said, "they're moving your mom tomorrow morning to the burn unit in San Francisco. It's a long drive. We figured you'd want to be closer."

"The burn unit," April said.

"They've been talking about it since yesterday morning, sweetheart. Didn't your dad tell you?"

"Yes," Danny said.

"She's not burned. It was a rash," April said.

"I know, I know, she's *not* burned, but what's happened to her, they think they can treat it better at a burn unit, where they have special equipment and doctors for dealing with skin problems like that. And anyway, those nice friends of yours, Jeff and Tina, I called them and explained everything, and they said it would be fine for you to stay at your house."

"Jeff and Nina."

"Yes. Sorry. As for your dad, the hospital has some apartments across the street, so they're putting him up in one of those. And by the way, Joanne wanted me to tell you, anything she can do, she will. I know you two haven't gotten along that well, but cousins are cousins."

April put her hand on her forehead. "I can't believe this," she said. "I mean, we were just sitting in Danny's living room, in New Jersey, and I was singing, and everything was normal—"

"There's my bag!" Danny said, and ran for it.

―――――――

AFTER THEY'D COLLECTED the suitcases, Eleanor led them out onto the curb. "Sid should be pulling around any second with the car," she said. "You know it's impossible to park here these days, so he's been circling. What a day."

Danny looked up. The sun was high and yellow, the sky a nervous, bright shade of blue. He remembered he ought to take off his coat and sweater and roll up his sleeves.

"Are you hungry?" Eleanor said. "I thought you might be hungry, so I brought some cookies." She pulled a foil-wrapped package from her purse.

"No," April said. "Christ, no."

"Okay, okay," Eleanor said. Then a battered station wagon rounded the bend, and they saw Uncle Sid waving and honking the horn.

―――――――

SID DROVE THEM to April's house. Jeff and Nina, old friends of April's from college, greeted them with a wariness which, Danny suspected, was only partially the result of not knowing what to say. Looking around, he saw signs of sudden rearrangement—lines in the carpet suggesting a recent repositioning of the sofa, some concert posters hung askew—all evidence of a hasty attempt on their part to put things back in the order they'd been in when April had rented them the house six months before. The place was theirs, legally, for another year, but even so, April marched through the door with territorial fervor. "Why isn't there any Tab?" she asked, after opening the refrigerator.

"Well, we don't drink it," Jeff said.

"But I'll get it next time we go to the store," Nina said.

April sat down at the kitchen table.

"Seltzer?" Jeff offered. She nodded.

"We're so glad to see you," Nina said, reaching for a glass.

"Only sorry it had to be under circumstances like this," Jeff added.

The sofa bed was pulled out and neatly made, and noticing Danny notice it, Nina said, "We thought one of you could stay here."

"And the other in the study. We put the kids together."

"That's fine," April said absently, sipping from the glass of seltzer. "Fine."

There was a pop of relief, as if a blister had been punctured.

Jeff and Nina were responsible leftist ex-hippies in their mid-thirties, both social workers, so no one would have suspected anything dishonorable of them. Hidden under their bed were the shards of a Mexican vase that their three-year-old, Esther, had knocked over a few months before and which they'd decided not to mention unless April mentioned it first.

"It must feel funny, being a guest in your own house," Nina said now, mostly to make it clear April was the guest.

"I have to go to the bathroom," April said. She got up and stumbled to the bathroom.

From the backyard the three-year-old, Esther, came charging. She was dressed only in a diaper. "Break out of jail!" she screamed, and ran directly into Danny's legs.

"Hello, Esther," Danny said.

She looked up at him, shocked, he supposed, by his large and unexpected presence, and then there was that terrible openmouthed moment in which a child decides to cry. Esther twisted her face as if she were about to spit, put up her hands like a boxer, covered her eyes in sheer disgust and terror.

"Mama!" she screamed.

"Esther!" Nina said, gathering her up, and laughed. "What's wrong with you? It's Uncle Danny. You've met him before."

"Hi, Esther," Danny said.

Buried in her mother's sweater, Esther shot Danny a look so purely venomous he had to turn away.

"She's just scared," Nina said, laughing nervously. "Right, Essie? She ran into the kitchen and didn't have any idea Uncle Danny would be there, and she got scared, right?"

Esther sobbed. April emerged from the bathroom. For a moment her eyes met Danny's. Immediately they looked away from each other, both frightened, suddenly, by a prospective intimacy that seemed almost incestuous. In all the hundreds of scenarios of his mother's dying that Danny had invented over the years, he had never imagined anything quite like what he was confronting now: April's house occupied by strangers; a burn unit; a child covering her eyes with fists. He had envisioned, dreamed, acted out more likely prospects: slow declines, darkened rooms, last requests, the familiar hospital minutes from the house he'd grown up in. Instead here he was, in a different house, half April's, about to spend a night on a couch before confronting his mother in a hospital he'd never set foot in.

Was it true he owned a house, had a car, an office with his name on the door, all more than two thousand miles away? That old feeling stole into him, of the East Coast, and all that mattered to him there, becoming unreal. Fear of the planes going on strike, and being trapped.

He excused himself to call Walter. April's study was in a state somewhere halfway between its previous identity as a shrine and its current one as the bedroom of a child. There were some hand-scrawled drawings on the wall, scotch-taped among all the pictures of April with famous people. A menagerie of Sesame Street animals was piled in a corner.

"It's seventy degrees here," he said when Walter picked up. "What's it like there?"

"Probably forty-five or fifty."

"Remember in New Haven, how I used to call you when I went home, and there'd be a storm or something, and I'd make you put the phone out the window so I could hear the wind and the hail? I'd just be standing there, in the sun, in my mother's kitchen, missing you so much, and I wanted to hear the hail, I wanted to know New Haven still existed, and snow, and you."

"I remember," Walter said.

"I could see you then," Danny said, "holding the phone out the window, and the phone getting dusted with snow. I could see you."

"I know," Walter said. "I know you could."

Danny cried.

"If you want me," Walter said, "I'll be on the first plane. You know that, right?"

"The first plane," Danny said. "Okay."

———

THEY BORROWED Nina's car and drove to the hospital.

To get to the burn unit, you had to go up to the second floor, then cross a kind of corridor bridge that connected the new part of the hospital to the old one. There was a display of drawings done by burned children—red-scrawled figures, openmouthed, beating off the flames—then a dreary waiting room—three vinyl-covered sofas and a coffee-stained coffee table piled with old copies of *National Geographic* and *Boating News* and *Family Circle*. Nothing you would want to read in anything but a moment of desperation, during which, of course, you would want to read nothing else. The lighting was bare fluorescent strips, one of which, on its last legs, flickered a dull yellow. No effort had been made to make the place cheerier, probably on the theory that anyone sitting there was going to be beyond that point where decor could provide consolation.

Nat was lying on one of the sofas, a black visor over his eyes. He had Louise's blue bathrobe draped on his chest. "Dad," Danny said softly, and his father's hand reached to pull off the mask.

"Son, hello," he said to Danny, squinting into the bright light. "April." He stood and hugged them distractedly. "Just grabbing a few winks," he said. "Listen, Dr. Thayer wanted to talk to us as soon as you got here, so I'll just tell the receptionist, okay?"

"Where's Mom?" April asked.

Nat pointed toward a door that said: BURN UNIT—STERILE ENVI-RONMENT—PLEASE WEAR APPROPRIATE PROTECTIVE CLOTHING. He signaled to a woman seated at a desk across from the sofas, and she nodded and picked up a phone. Then she hung up the phone, looked at Nat, nodded again.

"Okay," Nat said. He led April and Danny through a swinging door into a tiny, windowless conference room. Dr. Thayer came in; he was a man in his sixties, with professorial glasses, graying hair, and a bow tie.

Danny and April shook the doctor's hand, said their names, and everyone sat down.

"Well, I've got to say this for your mom," Dr. Thayer said, "she is one strong lady. Tough as an ox. You take a woman in her sixties, immunocompromised, and with all the shit she's been through, I wouldn't have put money on her getting this far."

No one said anything.

"Her heart is good and strong, that's why," Dr. Thayer said. "And she's skinny."

"All these years Louise swam every day and kept to her diet," Nat said. "She always said it would be worth it, I should do it too. I didn't listen."

"What's happened to her?" April asked.

"Have you ever heard the term 'chemical burn'?" Dr. Thayer asked.

"No."

"Well, basically what's happened to your mom is that—something very, very rare, but which happens sometimes to immunocompromised people. There's a reaction—it could've been that drug she was being given, the chlorambucil, or maybe the dental trauma when she had that crown put in—but whatever it is, there's a reaction in the skin, like an allergy, only much, much worse. It starts off looking just like a rash, and that's why it's so hard to recognize. Then it turns into a burn. The skin is the body's most sensitive organ, and once it's damaged, anything can happen. You become susceptible to all sorts of viruses and bacteria, and even more so if your immune system's shot to begin with. And that's what's happened to your mom. Her skin has been damaged, and as a result, a number of secondary infections have come in. Pneumonia, for one, and blood septicity, which is what used to be called blood poisoning. Plus there's some kidney trouble, and a few secondary bacterial infections that wouldn't in and of themselves be anything to worry about but with insult added to injury are causing her some serious problems." He coughed. "We've got her on every antibiotic you can name, and she's starting to respond, but I have to be frank with you. I don't know for sure if she's going to make it."

Danny felt a palpable retreat, a giving way, inside himself.

"I've had twelve cases like this," Dr. Thayer said, "and I've lost eleven of them." He adjusted his glasses. "Still, your mom is strong. She's an ox. We're fighting for her, and she's fighting with us. We're doing everything there is to be done—treating her skin, putting her through the baths, the whole shebang. It hurts like hell, but she's taking it. And by the way, the one nice thing about a chemical burn, it doesn't leave scars. Your mom pulls through, she'll look great, like she's had a face-lift."

"You know, I told her that," Nat said, "and she gave me this look, this classic Louise look, as if to say, 'Great, all this for a face-lift.'" He laughed. "A sense of humor's a good sign, I think, don't you?"

"Absolutely," Dr. Thayer said. "A great sign. So now the job is, get her skin on its way to healing, then deal with everything else. As it stands, we may have to put her on the respirator if the pneumonia kicks up again, but that's not so bad, really; at least she's breathing that way. And we may have to hook up dialysis if her kidneys don't get going. But as I said, we're waiting before we decide. She's being monitored sixty minutes an hour twenty-four hours a day in what I can guarantee to you is the best-run burn unit on the West Coast and maybe in the country."

"Can we see her?" Danny asked, hoping Dr. Thayer would say no. But Dr. Thayer said, "Sure. I think it would be great for her to see you all."

"When?"

"Right now, if you like."

"Wait," April said. "Wait. I don't know if I should go in there—I'm pregnant." She looked around, as if she expected someone to laugh or accuse her of lying.

"No problem there. It's a sterile environment to protect the patients from you, not the other way around. As long as you wear protective clothing and don't stay too long at any one time, there's no risk to your baby's health."

April rubbed her nose and looked at the floor.

"Oh, and congratulations, by the by. I'm sure knowing a grandchild's on the way is one thing that will give Louise real fighting spirit. This the first?"

"Yes," Nat said.

"Have six myself," Dr. Thayer said. "The oldest is seventeen. The youngest is six months."

———

OUTSIDE THE DOOR to the burn unit, they slipped paper sacks over their shoes and put on white gowns.

"Did she tell you?" April asked Nat when Dr. Thayer had turned away to talk with a nurse.

"What? Oh, yes," Nat said, rather distractedly. "She told me right after you told her. I would have called, but then things started getting bad."

"Are you happy?" April asked.

"April, it's not a good moment for you to ask me that—"

"Come on, Dad. Just answer that one simple question, and then I won't bother you about it anymore."

"Look, we can talk about this more once your mother is out of the woods."

"Fine. Yes. Just tell me if you're happy."

Nat paused for a moment as he slipped his arms inside the wide sleeves of the white gown. "Yes, I suppose," he said. "I suppose I'm happy. Do me up, will you?"

He turned around, and April tightened the gown over his tweed jacket.

———

"NOW I HOPE you're prepared for what you're going to see," Dr. Thayer said as he led them along the curving corridor that surrounded the burn unit. "She looks like shit. She looks trashed. I don't want you to be shocked."

They pushed through a swinging door into a room full of noisy machinery. Danny smelled burning rubber. A number of nurses and doctors, all dressed, like Danny and April and Nat, in white robes, were doing a number of things—operating the machines, writing notes on big medical charts. One woman was telling another a joke about Jim and Tammy Bakker. In the background someone sang about Luckenbach, Texas.

"Welcome to command central," Dr. Thayer said. "The patients are all around us, behind the glass partitions, so we can get to them fast."

Like a tourist, Danny looked around at the windowed rooms, most of which had their curtains drawn. In one corner were some large stainless-steel tubs that reminded him of the tubs used in college dining halls to make soup.

Behind one of the glass partitions the curtains were not drawn. Some more figures, dressed like the rest of them but also in hats and masks, stood huddled over a bed set up in the center of the small room like the bed of a queen. It was in this direction that Dr. Thayer motioned.

"It's hot in here," April said.

"The burn unit's kept at a high temperature and humidity level because it helps the skin to heal faster. We even have our own generator, in case of a hospital blackout. Now, put these on and we'll go in to see your mom."

They put on rubber gloves, paper masks, and paper hats patterned with pink and purple flowers.

"These hats remind me of Aunt Eleanor's blouses," April said.

"Okay," Dr. Thayer said when they were all done up. He looked them over like a father about to send his kids trick-or-treating. "In we go."

Danny thought, It's Halloween, and we're all dressed as Aunt Eleanor. They walked through a swinging door into the glassed-off queen's room, and the phalanx of masked and hatted technicians dispersed. More humming machines, connected to Louise by rubber hoses and thin plastic tubes that intertwined under and around the bed, a nest as confusing as any in the house in Gresham.

After examining the red numbers on one of the machines, Dr. Thayer said, "I'll leave you alone for a few minutes," and headed back out the swinging door.

There was Louise. Her body was wrapped neck to toe in gauze, like a mummy's. Someone had greased her hair, and pushed it roughly back behind her head. On her face—the only part of her not covered by the white gauze—red sores and blisters had erupted. Her whole face was red, but not the red Danny thought of when he thought of sores and blisters. This was red as in roses, or fire engines.

They forced themselves not to look away, even though it was worse than they'd imagined, even though nothing, Danny thought, could have prepared them for what he was seeing. It was as if her body had undergone some magical transmutation or were in the throes of possession. The horror of it was that even like this, she was still, defiantly, herself.

April's eyes, above the mask, were wide; she was standing with her back straight and not flinching. Following her example, Danny pulled himself up tall. (Louise had often complained about his posture.) This is me, he thought, and that is her, and we are in this room. Look at her.

He looked.

Louise's eyes were swollen, bloodshot, and barely open. She started shaking, violently, spasmodically, as if an electric current were seething through her. "I forgot to tell you about that," Nat said. "Her fever spikes every afternoon, and she gets these uncontrollable shakes. But it passes, it passes." He moved closer.

"Hi, honey," he said.

"Nat," she said. "Nat. I—"

"I know, I know," Nat said, "these shakes are rough."

Her teeth were chattering violently. "I want—I want—don't—"

"The kids are here, Louise, April and Danny, see?"

She lifted her neck slightly, and her head bobbed like the head of the toy basset hound Aunt Eleanor used to have behind the backseat of her car.

"Hi, Mom," Danny said.

"Hi, Mom," April said.

She smiled vaguely. "Hi—hi—Dan—" Through all the chattering Danny could hear her striving for a certain jokey intonation she had often used when she was sick—her voice rising into the high-pitched vibrato of the guilt-inducing Jewish mother: "Oh, I'm fine. Your poor old mother is just fine." It was funny; she could barely get out two syllables, could barely speak at all, and yet the old singsongy rhythm of that punishing, familiar voice remained within her grasp. Even in such dire straits as these, it seemed, she was determined to try for dignity.

"How are you feeling?" Danny asked.

Louise managed to shrug a little and say something that sounded like "Eh."

And Danny and April laughed. They laughed and laughed.

"Good old Mom, still has her sense of humor," April said.

But she wasn't paying attention to them anymore. Again she turned to Nat and said, "I want—I want—" and pointed at the table.

"What?" Nat said. "What do you want?"

"Klee—klee—"

"Kleenex?" Nat said. "You want a box of kleenex? Here's kleenex." He handed her the box.

"No!" she said, and her face screwed up in irritation. "No, Nat!" A familiar tone of anger. "My—my—"

"Oh!" Nat said. "I remember now! She hates the hospital kleenex," he explained to Danny and April. "She wants her own box, from home. Right?"

Weakly Louise nodded, and her head fell back on the pillow. The shaking seemed to subside slightly.

"Danny, why don't you ask the nurse if we could bring Louise her own kleenex, okay?"

"Sure," Danny said. He turned and pushed through the swinging door, back into the room Dr. Thayer had referred to as command central, where he pulled off the hat and mask and deposited them in the bins marked for that purpose.

"You're not going to believe this," he said to a freckle-faced nurse who was making notes on a big chart and humming along with the Judds. "She says she doesn't like the hospital kleenex and wants the real thing."

"I've heard stranger," the nurse said. "But you can get them for her if that's what she really wants."

"Thanks," Danny said. He put on another hat, another mask, another pair of gloves. April and Nat had pulled up chairs and were sitting next to Louise's bed.

"A little more than ten weeks now," April was saying. "I hope it's a girl so I can name her after you."

Louise lay blessedly still, for once, giving out, with each breath, a soft wheezing.

WHAT DANNY THOUGHT OF, while he was standing there, standing over his mother's bed, was a photograph Nat had saved from the war, when she was working as a welder at a shipyard. She had been asked to model ladies' welding uniforms for a catalogue, and in the picture she stood proudly against a cardboard backdrop in a jumpsuit of leather and metal, holding a blowtorch to one side. The suit was cut to the shape of what in those days was called a figure—something Louise had in spades—and now, as he looked down at her body in its tight white wrapping, what was surprising to Danny was that it looked young; it was the body of a sleek, athletic girl, with strong legs, flat hips, wide shoulders. It had never occurred to him that his mother might be in such good shape, since for years she had worn only the loosest, most matronly clothes, and for a moment Danny wondered if, in the brutal light of the burn unit, she'd been somehow brought back past modesty and wifeliness to the rebellious girl who in 1944 had held up a blowtorch in the name of liberty and America.

A brown liquid flowed to her body through one tube; a yellow liquid flowed from it through another. Danny observed this flowing, and then the door opened and Dr. Thayer came in again, carrying a wet cloth in a stainless-steel pan. "Hello, Louise," he said, leaning over her. "I brought something for you." Cautiously he dabbed the cloth over her swollen and blistered eyes, and her face inclined toward his in pleasure. "Yes," he said, "that feels good, doesn't it?" slowly running the cloth down her cheeks, toward her lips. It was the sort of intimate moment which, had she had been in better shape, she would have forbidden her children to witness, but now she seemed oblivious to everything but the cool cloth. "Yes," Dr. Thayer said. "Yes. Feels good." Her mouth opened and closed, making over and over again, in that still and humid room, the gesture of a kiss.

NAT WANTED TO SIT with her alone for a few minutes, so April and Danny took a long, last look before moving out the swinging door. They were both worried that she might be dead before they got back, but even in circumstances like that you can only look so long. Masks came off, gloves, flowered hats. Then the long corridor. The bags on their shoes came off; the robes came off. They crossed the corridor bridge to the modern, efficient, new part of the hospital. Things were almost cheerful here; women were walking up and down hallways, leading their IV poles like elderly grandmothers. All the ordinary calamities, broken legs and babies and cancers. April and Danny went down the elevator and out the sliding glass doors.

On the steps of the hospital, in bright sunlight, April heaved breath like someone who has just emerged from a fire. Danny touched her arm. She heaved. He put his arms around her. The cotton of her blouse was soaked through with sweat.

She pulled him down onto the cement steps and started to cry. Her head fell onto his chest; she was crying wildly, oblivious to the fact that strangers surrounded them. Her hair was in his mouth, the long strands soft and faintly sweet-tasting, and he was crying too.

But how long can you cry? They couldn't cry forever. They had no burns; their bodies felt good to them.

Finally April extricated herself from Danny. She wiped her nose with her left arm. Her skin was pale and freckled, and looked astonishingly innocent. "I have to go to the bathroom," she said, and blew her nose.

They got up from where they were sitting on the steps and stumbled back into the hospital lobby, where Danny, at a pay phone, dialed Walter's number.

"Walt," he said.

"What? Danny, what's happened?"

"I need you to come out," Danny said, closing his eyes. "I need you here."

After Walter had agreed, Danny hung up and leaned against the wall. Soon April was back, her face wet and shiny.

"I suppose we should go back up," she said.

"No, not quite yet. Let's rest a minute. Or maybe take a walk."

"Okay," April said.

But they didn't move.

THERE WAS, in the burn unit, a kind of perpetual arrhythmia, as in a fun house. Nothing ever happened when or how it would have anywhere else. Work went on in the middle of the night, dinners were eaten at dawn. The only event of any regularity was bath hour, every afternoon at one, during which the patients were maneuvered into big steel tubs, soaked in some stinging yet miraculous broth, scrubbed and debrided. The baths were unspeakably painful, and as a result bath hour was the one period each day when visitors weren't allowed in the unit, so when one o'clock came around, Danny and April and Nat usually put on their jackets and lumbered outside to have lunch. The brilliant sunshine made them squint and stumble, and seemed intended for other creatures than themselves. Whatever was fiery drew them: fierce Thai curries, Korean vegetables pickled with red peppers, sushi smeared with wasabi. When Walter arrived, he went along, but like a mute witness, an observer from the world outside. "Listen," Danny said to him, "April wants to go to this Japanese place that has these big bowls of noodles, but I'm in the mood for Chinese. What do you think?"

"Whatever," Walter said, "whatever," not quite believing Danny cared so much about lunch at a time like this, but at the same time not wanting to make trouble; what did he know of it, after all?

All the rest of the day the life of the burn unit took them over. Things were serious enough here that vague or contemplative questions took on a harsh edge of answerability. How long can you cry? Danny had wondered that first day, when he and April sat gushing on the hospital steps. Well, there was an eight-year-old boy in the room across from Louise's who had been crying for thirty-six hours. The noise he made was rageless—a low, hoarse, grieving lament that sometimes pitched and sometimes faded, but never ceased, and finally blended with the other noises of the burn unit, the humming, pumping, and churning of the various cruel and life-sustaining machines, and the country and western music from the tape deck, and the hushed joke-telling of the nurses gathered at command central. It seemed that there was nothing you could not get used to.

The boy was named Jaime Delgado. Around the time April and Danny were getting off their plane from New York he had been applying a lit match to a gasoline canister. His parents, Jesús and Dorell, themselves never wept, though they smoked and chewed their nails. Jesús was a biker, not quite a Hell's Angel; he was of a type familiar to April, who in earlier days had sometimes accepted the protection of bikers during potentially violent concerts. Nat had never met a biker in his life, much less straddled or even imagined straddling the warm leather seat of some mufflerless machine, but it didn't matter here. In the burn unit old distinctions—age, wealth, religion—ceased to have any meaning. Here was the perfect democracy; suffering, the great equalizer. Gallows humor, yes, but also gallows compassion, gallows clearheadedness.

Jaime Delgado had third-degree burns over most of his body, and Nat was full of questions and concern for his recovery; at the same time Dorell—a woman who seemed to be all elongations, long black hair, spindly legs and fingers, predatory red nails—couldn't seem to get enough information about Louise's situation. She nodded earnestly as she absorbed everything Nat was only too glad to tell her. One symptom of the waiting room was not being able to stop talking; "How's your wife doing?" was a risky question, bound to trap the unexpecting querier in a good half hour of conversation, so the nurses and receptionists and social workers deftly avoided small talk on their way to and from lunch. Fortunately Nat and Dorell seemed to be able to draw relief from each other, or at least distraction. They leaned close together, and spoke so softly that usually all anyone else in the waiting room made out of their conversation were matchbook strikings of tongue against palate, and slow givings out of breath, and expelled grunts of disbelief mixed with horror.

Jesús Delgado was less inclined to discuss his son's condition, but he liked to talk. He told Nat about the three times he'd crossed the country by motorcycle. "That's my idea of an education, Professor." (He and Dorell called Nat Professor, which was more than he could say for his students.) "Seeing the world, the wind at your back and all that. Going real fast, watching everything pass by. It's a big country. Now I don't pretend to know nothing like you must know, but I know how big things are."

"I wish I knew that," Nat said.

"But maybe you can tell me something else, Professor. Maybe you can tell me why us instead of anyone else, any of those other people, have to be sitting here tonight, instead of at home eating dinner? And don't say God, I stopped believing when I was twelve."

He looked across the waiting room at his ancient mother, Aurora, who, dressed in black, was crocheting roses onto a pink background and murmuring novenas to herself. "Lucky she don't understand English too good," Jesús said, and, smiling at her, laughed. She raised her eyes and smiled back.

"So what's your answer?" Jesús said a moment later, and Nat pulled himself up, back straight.

"Well," he said, fumbling, "statistical probability suggests that bad things happen to everyone sometime. In other words, chance."

"The old wheel of fortune," said Jesús. "Spinning, spinning, spinning."

"Yup," Nat said. "But in real life, you can't put it on a gift certificate."

At that Dorell raised her eyes and laughed. "Oh, that's funny," she said. "You know, I tried out for that show last time I was in L.A. Made it to the final nine. Too bad, I would've loved a trip to the Bahamas, Puerto Rico. Someplace you could lay out in the sun and relax."

"Yup, that would be nice," Jesús said, stretching his arms behind his head, "laying on a beach right now."

His mother suddenly lifted her eyes, looked at them all, then returned to her crocheting.

IN THE WAITING ROOM, cigarette butts filled stained and weather-beaten plastic ashtrays; periodically someone sitting there got disgusted and emptied them into the wastebasket. As night wore into day—a single, timeless progression, marked only by the departure of the secretaries (there were no windows)—the one substandard fluorescent light tube flickered, dimmed, but never blew out. Sometime in the late evening a custodian passed through with a bucket of strong disinfectant and swabbed the linoleum floor until, for a few brief minutes, it actually shined.

DINNERTIME. Too many friends always had the good idea to bring food. Eleanor arrived with platters of turkey and roast beef, homemade mayonnaise, rye bread, and tomatoes; Danny went out for cartons of Chinese noodles, fried rice, chicken with Peking sauce; Jesús's Aunt María brought enchiladas, flautas, chiles rellenos. There was too much food, an overwhelming abundance of food; plates and trays covered the coffee table as well as a good portion of the floor. No one knew where to begin, except Eleanor, who loaded her plate with everything. "Oh, this is so delicious!" she said as she tasted the chiles rellenos Jesús's aunt had brought. "What is your recipe?"

She addressed this question to Jesús's mother, Aurora, who looked at her blankly and smiled. "You like?" she said.

"Oh, I like very much," Eleanor said. "I write a cooking column."

The old woman nodded.

"A cooking column—you know, in the newspaper—and I'd like to write one about you." Eleanor pointed at her and said, "You."

The old woman nodded some more.

"Yes," she said. "Mexican cooking very good."

INSIDE THE BURN UNIT was a life of perpetual battle, small headway against huge disaster.

Nat was always there already when April and Danny and Walter arrived in the morning; either he'd been there all night or he'd come before dawn from the dingy apartment he'd been given across the street. Around eight when they pulled in, smelling of wind and car exhaust, he'd fill them in on the night's activity, and then the four of them would meet with Dr. Thayer, usually in the waiting room, sometimes in the little conference room.

Good news was not plentiful, but it came sometimes. "She's looking good," Dr. Thayer said on Tuesday, "really rallying." By Wednesday the respirator was in place—no more talking—and her fever was up to 104°. Wednesday afternoon it was down again, and the antibiotics were taking hold. Early Wednesday evening her kidneys failed. The doctors and nurses huddled round to work on her; that was the phrase Kitty, the night nurse, used. "They've been working on her a couple hours now, trying to fix her up."

Inside Louise's room, machines with inscrutable dials and red-lit readouts spun lines of blue light that told her heart and breathing rates. The smell of burning rubber subsided, or seemed to—maybe they just adjusted to it. Even Louise herself looked more like herself, in spite of the tubes that snaked into her throat and nose and under bandages into both her arms, one leg, her right side. Her hands had been unwound; she was kept covered with a light blanket. But when she slept, her head fell to the side, her jaw hung loose and open. Danny watched her sometimes through the glass as she slept, while around her the machines continued to draw the progress of her life in their fine, glowing hands. There was something brutal about her having to lie there like that, alone among all that life-sustaining technology.

Thursday morning she was lucid and had things to say. Nat sat with her for three hours, engaged in a game of charades, Louise gesturing as best she could with her hands, Nat struggling to interpret the gestures. Mostly she wanted to tell him things he already knew. She couldn't breathe; she was afraid of suffocating; she wanted her own kleenex. Sometimes she tried to write. The sheets piled up, her illegible messages usually zigzagging off the page in a pencil-breaking scrawl of rage.

Outside Cousin Joanne had arrived for a visit. "Hello," she said to Dorell Delgado. "I know we haven't met. I'm Joanne Finkel, Louise's niece? And I heard about your son, I was so sorry but, um, I wanted to give him this."

She handed Dorell a Macy's bag inside which was a big box wrapped in Masters of the Universe gift paper.

"It's a Lego assortment," Joanne said. "You know, for building airplanes, houses, cars. The guy at the store says boys love it. And it should keep him busy, once he's feeling a little better." She smiled, looked away. "I don't know, I just thought he might like it. You can return it if you want."

"Thank you," Dorell said. "That was nice of you."

"Oh, good," Joanne said. She fell back against the wall, relieved, apparently, not to have the present thrown back in her face. "I do what I can," she said. "I'm like my mom that way, only not so good a cook. And I love kids. I don't have any of my own—yet." She looked up at the ceiling and said, "I guess what I'm trying to say is just, I don't know you, but I feel for you. Woman to woman. You know what I mean?"

"Listen, I'm sure Jaime will like this. He's probably gonna be here a long time; he needs toys like this to keep him busy. I'll show it to him today."

Joanne smiled, looked at the floor. "Great," she said. "Thanks. I mean, you're welcome. I mean, thanks." She laughed. "Thanks and you're welcome," she said. "Isn't that the right thing to say?"

———

IN THE LATE AFTERNOON Walter and Danny broke their vigil and walked the length of gridded streets, up and down steep hills, until the bay and the red-ribbed Golden Gate Bridge were staring at them. San Francisco may be the quietest city in the world, especially on a brisk, bright afternoon when the wind lurks and surprises, coming out of nowhere among the steeply staggered houses, then disappearing again into its hiding place. Chimes, somewhere. A dog scampering up a sidewalk, its own leash in its mouth.

They stood for a while, gazing at the panorama of boats and blue water.

"I think we should probably get back," Walter said after a few minutes.

"Oh, Walt. Do we have to? Couldn't we walk a little more?"

"I think your dad will be wanting us back."

So, regretfully, they headed back, stumbled down the same hills they'd marched up, across the parking lot and through the sliding doors and into the elevator. Here, on the elevator, Danny visibly tightened with fear. The doors finally opened, and in the main waiting room Walter took Danny's hand; he turned; they hugged. A middle-aged nurse, walking by, said, "Really, couldn't you be more discreet?"

Instantly they broke apart, pretended not to know each other.

After a few seconds they found each other again. "Let's go," Danny said, rather miserably, heading off toward the corridor bridge. But Walter said, "Hold it right there, ma'am. Ma'am, hold it right there." He followed the nurse down another hallway, calling, "Hold it right there, ma'am." His hand on her shoulder. Very loudly, so that people turned, he said, "I want to see your name. Jenkins. Mary Jenkins. Good, I'll remember that."

She looked up at him rather timidly.

"You're making a spectacle of yourself," she said.

"I'm making a spectacle of myself! No, I wouldn't say that. In fact, I'd say I'm making a spectacle of you."

The nurse's eyes darted, checking for witnesses. Then she came closer. "There are children around here," she whispered.

"Mary Jenkins. Yes, I'll remember that name," Walter said. He turned, started walking away, before announcing to the lobby at large, "Please be aware that Nurse Mary Jenkins is a bigot."

"You're just making a fool of yourself," Mary Jenkins said, rather uncertainly and loudly.

"We'll see who your superiors consider the fool."

He walked in one direction. Mary Jenkins walked in the other.

―――――――

WHEN THEY GOT BACK, Louise's fever was 105°. Kidney function was at a standstill. Skin healing nicely, Dr. Thayer added, as an afterthought. "Too bad, because now her skin is the least of her problems. Even with the antibiotics taking effect, we're not out of the woods."

How was this different from any other moment in the last twenty years, with death always in the vicinity? This was the difference: What had been vague was now palpable. That elderly aunt in the attic, who sat in on all their meals but did not pay any rent—they had hoped she'd disappear one day, look for other lodgings. Now, it seemed, they were having to realize what Louise, perhaps, had known all along. Her lease was infinitely renewable. She would always be the last to leave.

―――――――

THURSDAY NIGHT Louise's fever was down to 100°, and Dr. Thayer used the phrase "guarded optimism."

Danny and Walter agreed to stay late so that Nat could take a rest. They sat for hours doing crossword puzzles in the dim waiting room. Around midnight they were just about to eat some Chinese food they'd brought in when Kitty, the night nurse, came out for a break.

"Care for an egg roll?" Walter said.

"Thanks," Kitty said. "Boy, you guys sure have a lot of food out here all the time. It's like a twenty-four-hour picnic."

"It helps to pass the time," Walter said.

Kitty put the egg roll on top of a napkin and then, taking another napkin, drew off the excess grease.

"Your mom's fighting hard," she said as she took a bite. "They're working on her again now. Some problem with the dialysis, but nothing too serious. But, boy, I've got to hand it to her. She's got fight."

"You must see a lot of that around here," Walter said.

"That's for sure. Really, some of the bravest people ever. It breaks my heart, but it also makes me feel, like, the human race really is pretty amazing. You know, the guy I live with now, I met him when he was a patient on the unit."

"Really?" Danny and Walter said simultaneously.

"Yup. He was in real bad shape, but we talked a lot, and it started getting pretty serious. At first I thought it was unprofessional—I was married at the time, though my husband and I weren't living together—but then I asked my supervisor and she said, 'Go for it.' She understands that things like this are rare, you can't pass them up."

"What happened to him?" Danny asked.

"Well, he worked for the phone company, and he got electrocuted," Kitty said, popping the last bit of the egg roll into her mouth.

"Jesus," Walter said. "Is he okay now?"

"Oh, sure." Kitty wiped her fingers with the napkin. "He's paralyzed from the waist down, but other than that, he's fine. And he's about to get a big settlement, so we'll be able to take a nice vacation for once in our lives. I mean, you know what they say. There but for the grace of God. Here today—" And she knocked on the hollow-sounding sheetrock wall.

"Thanks for the egg roll," she said. "I've got to get back now."

"You're welcome," Walter and Danny said simultaneously.

———

AT TWO Kitty appeared at the door again. They were both asleep on one of the plastic sofas. Danny jumped awake, startled.

"I'm sorry to scare you," Kitty said, "but your mom's real lucid all of a sudden, and she says she wants to see you."

"Yes," Danny said, his hand on his forehead. "Okay. I'll be right there."

Her head slipped through the door, and Danny stumbled toward the box of robes. "Go back to sleep," he said to Walter, who muttered something unintelligible, then buried his head again in the crook of his arm.

Alone, Danny dressed himself in the now-familiar robe and paper shoes. "The burn unit," he imagined writing, "was ablaze with activity." Much of it came from Louise's room, where the lights were on bright. Nat had returned while they were sleeping; already masked and robed, he was leaning over the bed, from which Louise gestured manically.

Danny put on his hat, gloves, and mask, and went in.

"Hi, Mom," he said.

Her eyes were more open than he'd seen them in three days. She reached a hand out toward him, and he took it. He squeezed; she squeezed back, weakly, did not let go. Like children pretending to be boyfriend and girlfriend, they held hands.

It was an odd, unlikely gesture; they had always eschewed physical affection with each other. Now, it seemed, in the urgency of the moment, all the old rules had to be forgotten, and new ones learned.

With her free hand Louise pointed at her chest, then at him.

"What, Mom? What are you saying? I can't understand."

She clenched her eyes shut in frustration. Then she pulled her right hand free of Danny's and started drawing something on her own stomach. The hand moved in a relentless circle, and her face tightened with pain.

"*O?*" Danny asked. "The letter *O?*"

"*D?*" asked Nat. "*D* for Danny?"

Louise shook her head. She made another motion, this time toward the pad and pencil on the night table. Obediently Nat handed them to her.

Very slowly Louise grasped the pencil. It fell out of her fingers, and Nat picked it up for her. She could barely hold it and, with the bandages and tubes in her hand, could barely move it, but nonetheless, she managed to get something down on the pad of paper and push it back toward Nat.

Nat picked up the pad of paper and looked at it before handing it to Danny. The paper had her initials printed on the top, in lacy blue script—it had been a gift from Eleanor, for grocery lists—and on it she had drawn a jagged heart. One half was bloated, the other atrophied, barely there at all.

"A heart?" Danny said, and Louise smiled. She smiled and nodded. She pointed to herself, pointed to him, pointed to the heart.

"You love me," he said. And laughed. It had taken such a long time to get the message across! "Oh, Mommy, I love you too. I do." But her eyes were already closed.

"She seemed to feel it was urgent," Nat said afterwards, while they were taking their robes off. "I guess she just had to get it out."

"I guess," Danny said. He rubbed his eyes. "Listen, I think Walter and I are going to head back to April's now."

"You do that, son. I'll see you in the morning."

"Are you coming out?"

"No, I think I'm going to sit here with your mother a little while longer."

"Okay."

But as Danny stumbled back toward the waiting room, shedding paper clothes along the way, he thought only of the oddness of it, and how much it was like his mother: another message, the gist of which was, I am still myself.

"She's getting better," he whispered to Walter, who was sitting on the sofa now, his head in his hands. "I know it. Now let's go home."

"Okay."

They headed, arm in arm, across the corridor bridge. The windows were full of blackness and stars. And still Danny did not realize what his mother herself had realized, waking from sleep and pain just ten minutes before: This was the last moment for crossing over. From now on even the simplest of messages would be impossible to convey.

I JUST SAW YOUR MOM," Dr. Thayer said to Danny and April when he ran into them the next morning in the hallway. "I don't know, I don't like the looks of it."

"What?" Danny said. "What's wrong?"

"Well, her condition isn't significantly worse. It isn't significantly better, mind you, but it isn't worse. The thing is—she just doesn't seem to be fighting anymore. I look in her eyes, and I just don't see that *spark*." He shook his head. "Your dad's in with her now," he said. "She's in bad shape, I'm afraid."

"I don't understand," Danny said. "Last night, she was so—animated. She was really *there*."

"That's what Kitty told me too," Dr. Thayer said. "Well, I may be wrong. Let's hope so."

Saluting them, he continued toward the elevator.

———

SHE DID NOT wake up that morning, or in the afternoon. Several doctors, specialists in various things, came by to look in on her.

At about three Dr. Thayer took Nat into the conference room for half an hour. They came out together, and Dr. Thayer went into the men's room. Nat sat down in the waiting room with April, Danny, and Walter.

"Dr. Thayer wants to change the direction of your mother's treatment," Nat said. "He wants to shift the emphasis from trying to cure her just to making her comfortable. He thinks, basically, that unless something drastic happens, she'll probably die within the next three days, and we should focus, for that time, just on making her as comfortable as possible. Several other doctors have seen her, and they all agree."

He stared into his lap as he said this, and when he finished, he did not look up.

There was no sound for some time.

"You mean they're giving up?" Danny said. "How can they give up?"

"She's given up. She's not responding."

"He said she wasn't significantly worse."

"This morning. Since then everything has started to slip." Nat rubbed his eyes. "I think we should all start thinking about the serious probability that Louise is going to die. Soon."

Danny covered his eyes with his hands. "Yes," he said softly. "Okay." And very softly, April started weeping.

OUR GOD, *who art in Heaven, thy kingdom come, thy will be done.* What was that shape on the ceiling, like a water stain in her childhood bedroom, water leaking through from the roof? She and Eleanor made it into pictures, horses and cars and people having sex. How odd to see it now—if seeing was the right word, her eyes were so heavy to open, and it was blurry. If only she could open her eyes a little more—there, she did it. Ah, yes—her vision was brilliant, twenty-twenty again! What a relief to have it back, after so many days of barely seeing at all. And now of course she could *see*, it wasn't a water stain at all, it was someone—something—descending toward her from the ceiling. An angel? Angel of death, angel of mercy, angel of hope? She wanted to reach toward it. If only she could pull her arms loose from all those needles stuck in them! Just a good tug and pull them free! She curled her fists and tried, and to her surprise, they came loose, the tubes and needles fell away around her, dripping, clattering. What a relief, to stretch her arms up again toward the angel, the thing coming toward her from the ceiling! It seemed to be holding something out to her, holding something in both its hands. What was it? It looked like a tiny house—yes, a little house, like a dollhouse, with light coming from the windows. And then, suddenly, it was obvious. This was no angel descending. This was Tommy Burns. Blond, muscled Tommy Burns, naked as the day he was born, his penis hard, with his smell of grease and deodorant. "I'm gonna make love to you, Louise." "Tommy!" she wanted to call, and reached her arms toward him, to touch him, to take him in. There was sand in her skirt and underwear, and it itched, and he was close, close enough; her hands touched him, and red blushes rose on his heated, pale skin. "Tommy," she said, "Tommy." His body falling over her like a blanket. The moon high. "I'm glad you're back." Gratefully she closed her eyes—under her, the cold hardness of sand in the small of her back. The white door in the tiny house in his hands opened.

———

THAT EVENING Eleanor was dispatched to fetch a portable tape player and some of Louise's favorite music: the Brahms Requiem, Beethoven's Sixth Symphony, a pair of Edith Piaf tapes. Next to the recorder one of the nurses affixed a sign that read: HELLO MY NAME IS LOUISE. PLEASE TURN MY TAPE OVER WHEN YOU COME IN. THANX.

So there was always music. She lay swathed in music.

"She looks almost happy," April said. She and Danny were watching her through the glass, in that brutality of exhaustion, her head fallen to the side. Was it wrong to imagine she was turning toward the music?

April was almost right. There was, on her face, a look—no, not of happiness. But perhaps of peace.

Later Danny went into the room and sat by the bed, holding her hand in his. "Mama," he said, "can you hear me?"

He felt a faint pressure from her fingers, like the grazing of an insect's wings.

————

FOR HOURS Nat sat alone with her among the music, holding her hand. Edith Piaf, the little songbird—wasn't that what they called her? She was always Louise's favorite. Before, when the songs came on, Louise had sat back and closed her eyes, and Nat knew she was imagining herself away from their house, imagining herself in Paris, perhaps, or Berlin, some city with an edge. A black strapless dress, a martini glass. Was she there now? She wasn't here, that was certain. The respirator breathed; all the little dials and digital displays read out the progress of her slow retreat. How strange, he thought, that she was about to die; even with all the illness, all the morbid doctorly predictions, Nat had somehow secretly assumed she would outlive him, she was so much more ferocious about it all than he was. A heart attack, quite sudden, perhaps, on a plane, was how he imagined he would go. Nonetheless, here he was, alive, holding her hand, nursing her through these final hours. When they had gone to see the therapist, she had complained that he became loving and responsible only when she was sick, never when she was well, and he hadn't been able to answer her except to wonder, Was that *why* she was sick? Did she do it to make him love her? It had always *felt* to him as if some remote capacity for control and care started up in him when she went into the hospital. He knew what to do, understood the ropes, could reason with the nurses and interns. But when they were at home and she was well, he lost touch with all those generosities, they eluded him, his old restlessness started up again. She was irritable, and he was too, and he found himself looking, always, out the window. Then sickness again, and she needed him and him alone. The children would not do, her friends would not do. He accepted this; no one else knew how to take responsibility. During one of those first hospitalizations, either the lump in the breast or the gallbladder, April had arrived barefoot, she was actually bare-foot, and perched herself in a corner and started eating the candies someone had brought Louise. It was almost too much. "Being a mother is a one-way street," Louise had told the therapist. "I accept that. I accept the loss of my children." Still, Nat wouldn't forget that first afternoon Danny was gone, when she was unpacking the groceries and saw she had bought his favorite cereal, the kind only he ate, automat-ically, she was so used to getting that kind. She had sat down at the kitchen table and stared at the box, just stared at it, for what seemed like hours.

There was an electrical shifting somewhere, like a car changing gears. One of the machines righting itself in some way. Nat pulled himself up in his chair, looked down at her face. Her head fallen to the side, her mouth and nose, stuffed with tubes, lay open in the uncon-sciousness of sleep. Just a few days before, when the itch was getting really bad, they had gone together to the new Neiman-Marcus store at the mall. She was in a pretty good mood that day, he wasn't sure why. Maybe it was just the brightness of the store, that smell of new things, and the room where they had cookies and coffee while you filled out your charge account application. There was a magnificent food hall, where Louise was happy to find Port Salut, a cheese she had loved once and hadn't had in years. And at the perfume counter they had Sor-tilège, her favorite, which was rare and impossible to get in the States, and in this case too expensive; she would have Joyce Rosen buy it when she took that trip next month to the château country. Upstairs, past the waterfall and the jewelry displayed in a magnificent tank of tropical fish, she found a matching pants and top, made out of a soft yellow chamois, which felt so good on her reddened skin he couldn't have been happier to buy it for her. For two or three days after that, getting worse, she wore that outfit; it was the only one her skin could bear. Then the fever set in.

Now the pants and top hung in her closet, among all her other clothes. Sorting through them was something he'd never imagined hav-ing to do, he had taken it so for granted that he'd go first. Well, April would help him. But what would they do with all the clothes? April would never wear them, goodness knows; they were too small and certainly not her style. They would fit Lillian. A terrible thought. Throw it out. Yet Lillian—he closed his eyes, made a small fist. A bud of happiness, a tiny marble of happiness he could roll in his palm, and no one would know. What a terror, and what a delight, that no one knew what he was thinking. And lucky. Would Danny understand? Would Eleanor? Would Joyce Rosen, or even Stan Rosen? How could he explain to any of them the secret, wide-eyed joy that had, at this moment, stolen into him; how could he explain it, or make them understand that it in no way mitigated his grief, his terror at the prospect of losing Louise? They would say, "You're a shit, Nat. You're a self-deluding, lying shit." But he knew. And as quickly as it had come, the seizure of joy passed. He slumped back in his chair, watched his wife.

Would he know when she died? Would the machine tell him? Perhaps she was dead now. He ran his fingers over her bandaged palm, the lines there so familiar to him, after more than forty years. The skin is what you get to know best; even damaged, he recognized the little lump below the knuckle of her forefinger, and the slightly discolored band where she'd worn her wedding ring all these years. The wedding ring, on the bedside table now; it had gotten too uncomfortable to keep on.

She shifted slightly, moved her head. Eyes fluttering, then settling back. "Louisy?" he said, suddenly hopeful. "Louisy?" but he already knew it was just her body, already knew she wasn't coming back. He ran the fingers of his right hand up her bandaged, needled arm, and in the meantime his left hand, dropped below the bed now, rolled the secret marble back and forth, back and forth.

"A SLOW, SLOW winding down," Dr. Thayer said. "Each breath just a little less powerful than the one before."

He was standing with Nat, Danny, and April around Louise's bed. All of them were waiting for her to die, now that it was clearly a matter of minutes—at most, hours.

"I think she expected a lingering death," April said. "Wasting away and all. She hated that idea so much too."

"She was never fond of attention," Danny said, "particularly when she was weak. She got embarrassed easily. She wanted to be left alone."

"Once, she told me she'd kill herself before having to have her friends parading before her, saying good-bye," Nat said. "With pills, of course. Well, she didn't need to, as it turned out."

"Perhaps it's better this way," Danny said. "I mean, if this hadn't happened—well, a lingering death from cancer would have been what she'd have had to face, wouldn't it?"

"And yet," April said, "I can't help but wonder if she longed for a slow death this last week—all that time to get used to it, to make bequests, tie up loose ends. There really just wasn't enough time for her, or for any of us. She must have had to deal with so much so quickly."

"There really is no moment of death in cases like these," Dr. Thayer said. "It's like Zeno's paradox. She's half alive, then a quarter alive, then an eighth alive, then a sixteenth alive. At some point you just have to decide. And"—here Dr. Thayer turned his head to examine the blue lines on the machine next to the bed—"I think we are well past the one-sixteenth point now." He coughed, looked at his watch, and turned to Nat.

"So," he said. "It's now two twenty-four. For the death certificate, shall we make it, say, two twenty-five? That's—forty-two seconds from now."

Nat nodded.

"All right," Dr. Thayer said. He kept his eyes on his watch. Next to the bed the respirator breathed.

"Ten seconds—five—two twenty-five." He put his wrist down, looked at Nat, and said, "That's it."

Danny blinked. He stepped back and stared down at his mother, but she looked the same now, dead, as she had a second ago, alive.

Wasn't death supposed to be final, recognizable? A hand closing the eyes, a face going white, a sheet pulled over the head?

None of these things had happened. There was no high-pitched scream from the machine, no shift in its charting of her body's decay. Dr. Thayer was moving toward the door; Nat had a hand on April's back, he was talking cremation, he was talking effects and insurance.

"Wait," Danny called.

They turned and looked at him.

"What is it?" Dr. Thayer said.

"Yes, what is it, Danny?"

He opened his mouth to speak. How could he explain that he wanted back that wink of an eye, that instant? If only Dr. Thayer could turn back the hands of his watch, then, perhaps, he could not blink and would witness the precise instant she crossed over.

"Never mind," Danny said. "Sorry."

"Well, I'll leave you alone for a few minutes," Dr. Thayer said, and went out.

Nat was standing by the bed. On the night table was the misshapen heart from the night before. He picked it up. He took off his glasses. He put two fingers on the bridge of his nose.

"Daddy," April said. She put an arm around his arm and led him toward the door. Danny looked once more at his mother—his mother's body, now. And suddenly he imagined her somewhere else, perhaps trapped, like Charlie Chaplin, between the moving hands of Dr. Thayer's watch as it decided the moment of her death.

"Well, I guess there's no point in waiting around here anymore, is there?" Nat said. He shook his head. "I guess not."

He headed out of the room then, so that only Danny was left, April holding the door. Danny turned one last time to look at his mother. "Well, good-bye," he said, as if he were speaking to her by telephone. "Talk to you soon. Or not. I guess not." He breathed once, deeply, and said, "Good-bye, Mama." Then he pulled off, for the last time, the hideous flowered cap, and even though he knew he would never, ever see her again, he didn't turn around.

THERE WAS NO funeral. "Louise wouldn't have wanted it,"
Nat said as they got into the car. "She never did have any
patience for ceremony."

"How quickly we've slipped into talking this way," April said. "As if
she's been gone a hundred years, and everything difficult, everything
that was messy and hard to interpret about her, we can just wrap up in
little packages. 'She never did like ceremony.' 'She always was partial to
a clean kitchen.' I assumed that at least it would take a couple of months,
at least some time would pass before we started talking that way."

"Well," Nat said, and coughed. "Anyway, I *was* thinking of maybe a
party tomorrow, a sort of paying-respects party, you might say. Nothing formal. So that Louise's friends can—what was the word that social
worker used, Danny?"

"Seal."

"Yes. So her friends can seal. A sealing party. I like the sound of that.
With coffee, maybe cookies and cake. No speeches, like I said, nothing
formal. Does that sound okay with you?"

April and Danny nodded. Each of them was holding a small plastic
bag inside of which was a single object—Danny had Louise's eyeglasses, April her toothbrush, Nat her wedding ring—and as they got
into the car, they clutched these bags to their laps like children with
favors from a birthday party. Walter had Nat's suitcase. She had been

dead—Danny checked his watch—forty-seven minutes: half an hour to settle the bill, another ten minutes waiting for the effects to be sterilized and brought out from the burn unit, plus good-byes. Everyone—Dr. Thayer, the nurses, Jesús and Dorell—had taken a long time saying good-bye.

Now that they were all seat-belted, Nat turned the key in the ignition, and for the last time they coasted out of the hospital parking lot and onto the freeway. It was a beautiful day. The city dissipated, fragmented, until the occasional clumps of green hillside interrupting the houses became countryside, and it was the clumps of houses that were the interruption. April had opened her window and, like a child, was extending her hand, feeling for the round ball of the wind.

"Music?" Nat said.

"Sure," said Danny.

Nat pushed a cassette of *Man of La Mancha*—it was the only one he owned—into the mouth of the tape deck.

> I was spawned in a ditch by a mother who left me there,
> Naked and cold and too hungry to cry.
> I never knew her, I'm sure she left hoping
> That I'd have the good sense to die. . . .

"And by the way," Nat said, "about the food, I don't think there should be anything too fancy. Cookies, coffee cake. That's all."

"Fine," April said. The capacious highway glided between the humps of mountains. Then they were all silent, listening carefully to Aldonza's lament, and April faintly humming along.

————

AT HOME, lights snapped on, televisions. Clara had come twice during the week, so the rooms felt vast and cool—an enormous relief after the cramped corridors of the hospital. As soon as they were inside, April immediately set herself to baking. There was a banging of pots and pans in the kitchen; sugar and flour canisters were taken out of the pantry and opened. The weatherman on the local news was describing

the progress of a hurricane that was in the process of devastating South
Carolina; it was called, by some astonishing coincidence, Louise. "Not
only is there fear of serious property damage to the Carolina coastal
region, there's even some suspicion that Louise might hit the New York
City area or Long Island." An image came on the screen of torrential
rains, half-drowned houses, children maneuvering through suburban
neighborhoods in rowboats.

"I can't believe it," Danny said. "I can't believe what I'm hearing."

"Change the channel," April said. "*People's Court* should be on."
Obediently Danny switched. A woman claimed her neighbor's dog
had killed two rabbits plus a chicken; she pushed her child forward to
describe the rabbits' remains, while the neighbor, stoic, stroked repeat-
edly the smooth brown head of the dog in question, a nervous-looking
spaniel that at one point barked unexpectedly, much to the amusement
of the courtroom audience. "How would you feel about tollhouse
cookies?" April asked Danny, who was sitting at Louise's desk. "Or
maybe that really rich chocolate peanut butter cake I made last summer. We're having a party tomorrow, after all; we need food."

"Dad said nothing too fancy," Danny reminded her.

"What's fancy about chocolate peanut butter cake? Now a proper
gâteau with butter cream and maybe ground walnuts and meringue—
that's fancy."

"I guess," Danny said. Cautiously he surveyed the kitchen. What
they had been afraid of most—finding things—was already happening:
a shopping list on the table, for instance—bran, chicken parts, skim
milk, margarine—not to mention last week's *Times* crossword puzzle,
lying on the shelf by the living room sofa. It was only half finished, the
handwriting faint and slightly jagged, as if she had had trouble holding
the pencil. Right now the house was clogged with Louise, bits of hair in
the shower and on the roller head of the deodorant canister, fragments
of skin and dried blood, but these things would break apart, disinte-
grate, just as her smell would fade from the closet. No, what lasted was
handwriting, it was the only preservable thing that is unique to each of
us, and so Danny wondered if he should save the shopping list, save the
crossword puzzle, those shadowy aspects of herself his mother had
sloughed off before the ambulance took the rest of her away.

In the kitchen Danny studied the crossword puzzle. No one in the
family except Louise had ever gone in much for puzzles, probably

because each of them was in his own way afraid of challenging her assumed superior skill at them; puzzles were the one thing in the world she felt she truly did best. Danny wasn't sure if he was as inept at puzzles as he pretended to be, or simply afraid to intrude upon this area in which his mother felt so proud. When Sunday had rolled around, and that magically thick paper from the other, better coast arrived on the doorstep, it was understood that you were to leave the magazine section for Louise. Once April asked if she might give the puzzle a try and then erase her answers, but only once.

And so sometime in those last days or hours, Louise had sat down, as always, to do the puzzle. Perhaps this was out of stoic devotion to her routines, a stubborn refusal to give in to illness. Or perhaps she had steadied her gaze on the cool black-and-white grid in the hope that it would distract her from fear, or pain, or both. It didn't matter, because at some point she had had to throw the puzzle aside, at some point the pain or the fear got too bad for ordinary antidotes. It would have to have been a severe circumstance; she had never not finished a crossword puzzle in her life.

On the television, Judge Wapner delivered his grave and sensible verdict. Danny took a sharpened pencil from the ceramic blue jar on his mother's desk and pulled himself upright in his chair. "Twenty-seven down: The muse of history," he read aloud. "April, who was the muse of history?"

"Beats me," April said.

"Clio," Danny said. "I think it was Clio. Yes, that fits. Now—thirty-two across: Tone, combinative form. Oh, what the hell is 'combinative form' anyway? You know, I meant to ask Mom. For years I meant to call her up and ask her what the hell 'combinative form' was anyway."

"I think it just means the form you use when you put a word together with another word," April said.

"Combinative form," Danny muttered. He sat back, trying to remember, but was distracted by the familiar array of objects on his mother's desk, each shivering with significance and melancholy: the ragged, paper-clipped stack of coupons, added to and subtracted from since Danny's infancy; the white cube with its cargo of stamps; the calendar filled with appointments—mostly doctors' and dentists' appointments—stretching out into the next month; the pile of un-opened mail. There was a pad of paper hand-stamped with her name by Cousin Markie in his junior high school printshop; a magnetized paper clip holder April had given as a birthday present years ago; a ceramic pillbox Nat bought her once, with the words "Within you see what pleases me" laced around the edge. When you opened it, there was a mirror. Even the mail had a timeless feel: bills, bills, flyers from department stores, get-well cards in thick ivory envelopes embossed with the never-changing names of her friends: Jack and Myra Eber, Sherrye's Hair Design Studio, Joyce P. Rosen.

The house was quiet, except for the sound of beaters, as April whipped egg whites into a froth. From Nat's bedroom, the faint voice of a television. (April had shut *The People's Court* off.) Then Walter calling: "Danny."

April turned the beaters off, held them in midair, dripping foam. "What is it, Walt?"

"Could you come here? To the living room?"

"Okay!" Danny got up, and April, wiping flour onto the thighs of her jeans, followed him. Walter was sitting on the living room sofa, Louise's knitting bag between his knees.

"Walt, what's wrong?" Danny asked.

"I'm sorry," Walter said. "I know I shouldn't have been snooping in your mother's knitting bag, and there's no excuse for it, but I found something I thought you'd want to see."

"What?"

He reached into the bag and pulled from it a yellow baby bootie patterned with ducks. "I guess she hadn't finished them, because—here's the other one." He fished out a second bootie, still intricately webbed to the needles, like an embryo born before its time.

"Let me see it," April said impatiently, and Walter handed her the finished bootie.

Nat came in, buttoning his pants. "What's wrong?" he asked. "Is something wrong?"

"We found this in Mama's knitting bag," Danny said, handing the half-finished bootie to Nat.

"Oh," Nat said. "Oh."

"Do you know who she was making them for?" April asked.

Nat shook his head.

"Well, could it be possible they were for me? I mean, don't you think that's possible?"

"Yes," he said. "I think probably she was."

April scrutinized the half-finished bootie, then handed it back to Danny, who put it on the table. No one seemed to be able to hold it for very long.

"She was always knitting things for people," Nat said. "So many sweaters. You know, she gave Rose Henninger a cardigan in exchange for piano lessons. She was always making bargains like that. I can bet you, half the people tomorrow will be wearing something Louisy knit for them."

"I left mine in New Jersey," Walter said, blowing his nose.

"I'd like to finish it," April said. "The bootie, I mean."

"You don't knit, April," said Danny.

"Then I'll learn," April said.

———

THAT NIGHT there was more news of Hurricane Louise. The threat to the East Coast was becoming more serious. Danny and Walter sat at the foot of Nat's bed, watching as, on the screen, a computer image of the storm menacingly stalked the sleeping heart of Manhattan.

"I hope our house will be okay," Danny said.

"Don't worry," Walter said, "my mother will batten down the hatches if she has to. Anyway, it's only supposed to graze New Jersey in the coastal areas, and even if it does pass over New York, it'll be pretty much weakened by then. Just a storm."

"So why is everyone making such a big deal out of it?"

"Because it was a huge hurricane. Hurricanes almost never get that far north in any version."

"The word in New York now is this," the weatherman said. "Louise is coming and she's mad as hell. Over to you, Chuck."

Nat, who was lying sprawled over his half of the big bed, in boxer shorts, aimed his remote control at the television and switched the channel. On the screen now, the drones of a termite colony marched silently to satisfy their enormous, pregnant queen; then *Wheel of Fortune* came on; then a talk show, on which a woman with streaked red hair was crying; then *The Flintstones*. "Not much to choose from," Nat said, returning to the termite colony, and Danny and Walter settled, stretched, getting comfortable as Danny and April had gotten comfortable all through their childhoods, to watch the meticulous activity of the insect world.

But in the kitchen April stirred and mixed and beat. Bowls dripped batter onto the countertops, spatulas and whisks filled the sink, flour dusted the stove and floor. Any minute Louise might have come through the door from the grocery store, crossed her arms over her chest, and asked April just what on earth she thought she was doing, but she did not; neither did she pull rubber gloves onto her hands and start filling the sink with water, or go into the bedroom to ride the exercycle, or settle down on the living room sofa with a book and her knitting. She did not answer the phone, and she did not vacuum the rug. She did not dunk her hands in wax. She did not watch the news.

Sitting there in front of the television, Danny closed his eyes and for a moment saw his mother standing in a room somewhere high in the celestial spheres. Apparently she had wriggled through the machinery of Dr. Thayer's watch and, upon emerging, found herself in an afterlife not unlike a mental hospital. She wore a white hospital gown, and her arms were held back by angels dressed as psychiatric orderlies, standing on either side of her as she looked down at the doings of the earth. She seemed to want to say she saw it all: She saw April dirtying three pans where one would do; she saw Nat eating jam with a spoon, then leaving the spoon on the counter. She was cursing, pulling to free herself from the tight grip of the angels, but they only smiled. They held fast with infinite patience, infinite sympathy. They had all the time in the world.

In the laundry room someone had unplugged the vat of wax; its contents was hard as candles. When, later, Danny ran a fingernail over the cloudy surface, lines appeared like those a skater leaves on an iced-over pond.

———

IN THE MORNING Eleanor arrived early to set up for the party. She had put herself together, for once, put on lipstick and had her hair done. With the help of Sid and Joanne she carried into the kitchen six platters of cookies, four elaborately decorated cakes, two roast turkeys, and ten loaves of rye bread. "I thought I told you, Eleanor, nothing fancy," Nat said when he saw Sid bringing in the last of the food. "Just cookies, coffee cake. For God's sake, this isn't a Christmas party."

"Oh, pish," Eleanor said. Putting her crutch aside, she eased herself into one of the chairs at the kitchen table. "None of this is that fancy, Nat, and anyway, you're going to have a lot of mouths to feed. As my dear ma used to say, nothing makes people hungrier than a funeral."

Nat looked away. "Why everything in this family has to be food, food, food, I have never understood."

"Oh, Natty," Eleanor said, reaching out her hand toward him, "I'm sorry if I overdid it. But you know me. Everyone does what they can; what I do—"

"Is cook. I know."

"Anyway, think of it this way: You all are not going to be in any mood to make dinner for the next couple of days, and this way you'll have all the leftovers—if there are any leftovers, that is."

"I just didn't envision it this way," Nat said. "I wanted something simple."

"It *will* be simple. Don't worry so much."

Across the kitchen Joanne was unloading cookies; in a drill sergeant voice, Eleanor instructed her which of Louise's platters would be best for which cake, and how to garnish the turkeys. April came in and upon request from Eleanor unveiled the chocolate peanut butter cake, lemon torte, Black Forest cake, tollhouse cookies, and walnut balls she had made the night before. "April, you're turning into a first-class baker," Eleanor said. "I'm proud."

"It doesn't matter, does it, April?" Nat said. He was skulking in a corner, near the washing machine.

"What, Dad?"

"That I said simple. Nothing too fancy. No, you just go right ahead and do what you want."

"But, Dad—"

"Forget it, just forget it. Tell me if you need me to do anything, will you?"

"Dad!"

But he had retreated to his bedroom and turned on the television. Soon he was staring at a soap opera in Japanese.

"Do you know what this show is about?" Danny asked when he passed by later.

"No," Nat said.

"Well, that must be sort of fun," Danny said. "Guessing every-thing from intonation. I'll bet that old lady is the mother of the younger one, and they're fighting about—maybe her marriage to that other guy?"

Nat kept his eyes on the television, his hand on the remote control.

"What do you think?" Danny said. "Am I right?"

"I don't know, it's in Japanese," Nat said. "How the hell am I supposed to know?"

"I was just asking," Danny said. He considered saying more, then changed his mind and headed into the kitchen, where Clara, bedecked in black polyester, was unwrapping the same loaf of dense, inedible fruit bread she had given the Coopers every Easter and Christmas since 1966.

"Isn't that nice," Eleanor was saying. "Clara brought something as well. Certainly won't be any food shortage today, will there?"

Clara smiled, pulled on rubber gloves, and was about to start hand washing when she noticed Joanne putting an expensive glass bowl in the dishwasher. "Mrs. Cooper says never put that one in the machine," she cried, grabbing the bowl away from Joanne, who immediately looked to her mother for guidance.

"Oh, I've washed many a bowl in my day, Clara," Eleanor said. "Believe me, it can go in."

Clara looked distraught. "Mrs. Cooper always said no."

"But, Clara, I'm a professional cook, and I'm sure that bowl can go in the dishwasher."

Clara shrugged then, and Eleanor shrugged, in a way that made Danny suspect both of them of having, for a long time, nurtured dreams of control in this kitchen.

"Well, if you insist," Eleanor said. "I don't care really, just wash it by hand."

"No, no," Clara said, "I'm sure you're right, Mrs. Friedman. The dishwasher it is. Mrs. Cooper always was peculiar about things."

They smiled at each other, and Joanne put the bowl in the dish-washer.

PEOPLE STARTED TO ARRIVE around eleven: colleagues of Nat's, women from the Mothers Against the Draft, nurses who had remained close to Louise after her various hospital stays. Danny remembered his mother saying, once, that she had no friends, that they were all really Nat's friends, but he saw today that it wasn't true: People had loved her. He greeted half-remembered wives of half-remembered retired physics professors, and couples whose children had been in his class in high school, and elderly women who approached him, open-armed, crying, "Danny, little Danny, how you've grown!" in hoarse voices. Soft, spotted hands touched him, arms draped in dark silks. "I remember you, darling, but I'm sure you don't remember me!"

"I'm afraid not."

"Ah, the young people! You don't remember your old friend Goldie Silvers, who made you that pudding cake you liked so much when you were a little boy!"

"Ah, of course! Mrs. Silvers! But your hair's shorter."

"Twenty years under the hair dryer next to your mama, you can bet it's shorter! It all fell out! Why, I remember you when you were just a baby, it was yesterday, and now look at you. What do you do?"

"I'm a lawyer."

"A lawyer! I knew it before, I just forgot. Your mama was so proud of you, she talked all the time!" Then, in a lower, more somber tone: "Danny, it's a terrible thing, her being gone, but you know she had a lot of suffering, and there was only more suffering in store. So maybe it's not the worst tragedy, is it?" Nodding.

"No," Danny said. "Maybe not. No." Nodding together.

"You're a good boy," Goldie Silvers said. "A real special one. And I still make that pudding cake, if you ever want one!"

"Thanks," Danny said. They parted. The doorbell rang and rang.

Nat, as always, answered it, greeting now a woman named Dixie Watkins, who, like Goldie, had for years sat next to Louise at the hairdresser's. She worked at the House of Humor, selling whoopee cushions and glasses with pictures of women who undressed as you drank. Her husband, Benny, had caused a scandal years before by arriving at a New Year's Eve party in a Nixon mask; Oscar Lowell, the provost of the time, had walked out in a huff. Now Benny shook Nat's hand somberly while Dixie looked on, dabbing a purplish smear from under her eye. Altogether Louise's most unsuitable, most tacky friends, but among the ones Danny liked best. Dressed in tiger stripes, her eyeliner running, Dixie kissed Danny on the cheek and in her brassy Texas accent asked, "Is there anything I can do for you, honey?" almost like a generous-hearted madam.

"Thanks, Dixie, but no," Danny said. "We're okay."

Over her shoulder he saw another familiar-looking woman approaching him, one whose name he couldn't recall, a woman with white hair and a powdered, teacherly face. "Danny," the woman said, "hello, dear," and shook his hand.

"Hello," he said. "How are you?"

"Oh, I'm fine, I'm fine, never mind about me. How are you all doing?"

"We're okay, thanks." He remembered a trick of his mother's for correcting just such a social embarrassment. "Ah, this is my mother's friend Dixie Watkins."

"I'm Nancy Needham," said the powder-faced woman, shaking Dixie's hand. "I was this boy's librarian in elementary school, though I'll bet he doesn't remember."

"Doesn't remember!" Danny said. "Mrs. Needham, of course I remember!" And laughed perhaps too loudly. Her husband had once been a colleague of Nat's.

More commiserations were exchanged. Dixie Watkins asked what Danny was doing with himself lately and nodded favorably when he told her. Then Nancy Needham asked if he might have any advice for her son Nicky, who was applying to law school. "Tell him he's going to have to absorb so much useless information he'll think his head's going to fall off," Danny said, and she laughed. "That's not so different from being a librarian, is it?"

"Honey, I couldn't do it, my mind's a sieve," Dixie said. "In one ear, out the other with me. I can barely pass the driving test. Oh, gee, I'm just going to say a word to Nat over there."

"Is he free?" asked Nancy Needham. And leaving Danny for the moment, the two women headed off toward where Nat stood, momentarily free of company. Danny looked around. The crowd had grown enormous and was squeezing out the two doorways of the dining room. So many faces! Young people had grown old, old people (seemingly) had grown young. Oscar Lowell, after a heart attack, had lost seventy pounds and now ran ten miles a day. He was by the fireplace in a red sweat suit. As for Francine Cantor, who was having radiation, she stood gauntly in the corner, a lopsided wig teetering on her hairless head. Her wrists—impossibly thin—were covered with spots; each finger supported a heavy ring; she wore thick bracelets of ivory and cut glass. Danny wondered that her matchstick arms didn't break from the weight of such accoutrements, remembering a time not so many years before when she'd come over to swim in the pool with her then-husband, Bruce, and offered lessons in lifesaving. Francine had been a young, energetic woman then, and had dragged Danny across the pool by the hair. Like many of Louise's acquaintances, she was the ex-wife of one of Nat's colleagues; across the house somewhere, Danny knew, Bruce Cantor stood with his new wife, a blond girl in her twenties whose name no one could remember. Now Francine was old, alone, dying, lighting a cigarette.

He turned away just as she was about to see him, just as she was about to offer an acknowledging, conversation-requiring smile. He was facing Sarah Goldberg, who in elementary school had been fat and asthmatic and had worn octagonal wire-rimmed glasses. She had asked for, and was given, a water bed for her bat mitzvah. Today she stood with her mother, Linda, against the dining room wall. They weren't talking, just standing together, looking out on the crowd, each with a cup of coffee in her hand. Sarah was less fat than Danny remembered her, a big girl neatly dressed in a denim skirt and cream-colored blouse. Her hair was long, luxuriously thick and long. Did she still carry a little can of breathing medicine in her purse? He hadn't seen her for twelve years. And again, just in time to avoid a meeting of eyes, he backed away. There, cutting cake, were the Eadys from across the street and their daughter, Jennifer. And across from them, Millie Bartell—wife of the dean—eating cookies off a little plate. Some faces had changed, but some, like Millie Bartell's, seemed not to have changed, not even remotely. Had Millie Bartell's life been as unvaried as her face? Danny wondered. Had it been an unending, placid succession of days spent cleaning, shopping, occasionally substitute teaching at the high school? Or were appearances, in this case, deceiving? Not too far from Millie, in the same room, stood Bill and Janet Hartpence, whose daughter Julia had set off a car bomb in 1968 and was just this year becoming eligible for parole. Upheavals of various sorts had ravaged their faces; they looked old and tired. What a far cry from Millie Bartell, for whom things had gone so smoothly, for whom the weather had been so balmy. Cancer, heart attacks, deaths, children in prison—these storms had passed her by. And so she came to funerals, or sealing parties, or whatever one chose to call them, and ate cookies, and kept quiet. How did it feel to be so lucky? Danny wanted to ask her, but then, realizing she was about to see him looking at her, changed his mind, turned around, was confronted with another familiar face, another hand waving, another voice calling, "Hi, Danny!" The party was a pinball machine, and he a steel ball being ricocheted from one unwanted encounter to another. Jennifer Eady this time. He waved to her and moved across the room.

In the kitchen, meanwhile, April had taken out the electric mixer and was making a last-minute icing for one of her cakes. Myra Eber, who had just put her coat away, touched her shoulder, and April screamed.

"Oh, I didn't mean to scare you!" Myra said.

"Mrs. Eber!" April said. "I'm sorry, I guess I'm just jumpy."

"Don't apologize, dear," Myra Eber said, smoothing her jacket down with her palms. "So how are you? You all surviving?"

"I guess so."

"Well, I just wanted to make sure you knew, Jack and I, our thoughts are with you, and—"

April turned the mixer on high, and Myra, her mouth still open, stopped in mid-sentence.

"Go on," April shouted over the high wail of the mixer. "I can hear you. Go on."

Bewildered, Myra looked behind herself, to see if anyone was listening. "I just wanted to say," she shouted above the mixer, "anything we can do to help we'd be happy to—"

April shut the mixer off.

"We'd be happy to do," Myra said, more softly.

"That's nice of you," April said.

———

IN HER HEAVENLY PRISON it seemed Louise had finally stopped fighting the archangel orderlies, though for good measure they still held her arms. Even so, their grip was not so tight. With their other hands they stroked her back in sympathy, having once been alive too. One of the stories she used to torment Danny with was about how, on the morning of her ninth birthday, she had put a spider down Aunt Eleanor's skirt, and in punishment her mother had locked her in her bedroom for the duration of her own birthday party. She had lain on her neatly made child's bed then, determined not to cry, plotting unimaginable vengeances and rebellions, while downstairs children laughed and danced and ate, their voices booming up through the floorboards even when she covered her ears, even when she buried her head in the pillow. What about the presents? "She saved them for me to open later," Louise sometimes said, but other times she claimed her mother had given them all to Eleanor, "to make up for the spider." In both versions of the story, after the party a piece of the cake was brought back up to her, with a rose, and part of her name, LOUI, in icing, and grim-faced in the silent aftermath, her eyes red from crying, she would not touch, would not even look at it.

———

DANNY WAS STANDING near the fireplace in the living room when Walter found him.

"Hi," Walter said.

"Hi. Where were you?"

"Talking to Margy McLaughlin. We were in April's room. Are you okay?"

"Sure. It's nearly two. People are starting to leave, so the torture will be over soon anyway."

Nat cruised through the living room, waved at them. "Isn't someone going to say something?" Walter asked.

"What do you mean, say something?"

"You know. Just a few words of remembrance. Or maybe April could sing."

"You heard my father in the car. My mother would hate that, people getting up all teary-eyed to talk about how wonderful she was. She'd be embarrassed."

"I think your father's the one who'd be embarrassed," Walter said. "Forgive me if it's none of my business, but it seems to me he's using this whole supposed dislike of ceremony on your mother's part to justify his own dislike of ceremony, his own embarrassment."

"It's out of my hands," Danny said. "And anyway, what right do I have to tell him how to bury his wife—or not bury her, as the case may be?"

Walter was about to say more when a low, gruff voice called out, "Danny boy!" from the horde of well-wishers. Two elderly, fat men in nearly identical beige suits were waving in greeting from the door. "Hi!" Danny called, waving back. "That's Sy and Herb," he added in a low voice, to Walter. "They were my grandfather's oldest and youngest brothers. The other two died in the war. What were the names? Herbert, Sydney, Milton, Seymour. You know, all the time I was growing up I thought those were the most ordinary Jewish first names, until someone pointed out to me that they were British last names. I guess to my great-grandparents those names must have sounded so modern, so sophisticated, so—non–Eastern European. And now they're just Uncle Miltie, Uncle Sy, Uncle Herb. Do other people have Uncle Donne and Uncle Wordsworth?"

"Probably somewhere," Walter said. In truth, it was hard to connect those poets and gentry with their namesakes, Danny's cigar-smoking uncles, slouching up to him now from the door. They were in their middle seventies, fat, with hair in their nostrils, and for thirty-two years they had not spoken to each other. Herb still owned the family's struggling seltzer business, while Sy—cut out of the company forty years before by his brother—had had his vengeance at last, making millions in the bottling trade. They lived in Southern California, only a few miles apart, in similarly locked and sentineled retirement communities, and had flown up on the same plane, in different rows. Thirty-two years of mutually inflicted noncommunication between brothers sounded terrible to those who didn't know them, but in fact Sy and Herb had spent so much of their lives not speaking that when they stood together at family functions, there was no edge left to their silence; it was just habit. They talked around each other, through other people. They almost seemed like friends.

"Danny, you're looking good," Sy said now. "How's the legal profession going?"

"Fine, Uncle Sy."

"And you still like living in that, excuse me, stinking hellhole New York?" Herb asked. "No, sorry, New York, New York, it's a wonderful town. Excuse me, Danny. I love New York."

"Uncle Herb, we've been living out in Jersey the past couple of years. Didn't Mom tell you?"

"No memory here," Sy said. "It's going, going, gone. Still, always nice to have a place to get away. Minna and I, we were in Brookline forty-two years, and there wasn't a day I wasn't glad for a little green to come back to, instead of some cramped apartment. We're really a country family, you know, back in Europe. According to my grandfather, it was a hundred miles to the nearest train."

Aunt Eleanor, coming over on her crutch, joined her uncles to form a circle around Danny and Walter. "Uncle Herb and Uncle Sy want to take the family out for Chinese food," she said. "After the party. And Nat says it's okay with him if it's okay with you and April, and April says it's okay with her if it's okay with you. So it's up to you."

"It's okay with me," Danny said.

"Good. Then I'll make a reservation at Ming's."

She moved away, and Danny and Walter, excusing themselves, pushed their way back through the crowd of hungry mourners into the kitchen. For the moment April was alone in there, by the oven, struggling with the baby bootie on its needles.

"Quiet!" Danny said. "What a relief."

"Teaching yourself to knit?" Walter asked.

"Trying," April said.

"Shouldn't you use a book or something? What you're doing, it looks a little catch-as-catch-can."

"Well, I've almost got the hang of it," April said. "It's not that hard to figure out. I just followed the path of the yarn, you know, through the stitches Mom had already done, and now I'm trying to copy it."

The buzzer on the oven went off, and April screamed. "Sorry," she said, resting a hand over her heart, and switched it off. She opened the oven door, where another golden cake bubbled in its pan, and, with potholder mitts on her hands, drew it out.

A girl with stringy brown hair, a burlap satchel on her shoulder, and a guitar case peered in through the kitchen door. She knocked. Again April jumped.

"April?" she said.

"Yes?" April said, turning around.

"Hi. I'm Sally Degner," the girl said, creeping into the kitchen. "My sister Jenny was in your class in high school?"

"Oh, sure, I remember," April said. "How is Jenny?"

"Oh, she's fine. She's living up in Oregon now. She said to say hi to you. We met a couple of times back then, you probably don't remember, I was just a little kid. I came today with my mom—she was in the Mothers Against the Draft with your mom—and I just wanted to say, I'm really sorry about your mom, it's really terrible."

"Thanks," April said. "Uh, this is my brother, Danny, and his friend Walter."

"Hi," the girl said, not looking at them, then turned once again toward April. "I just wanted to tell you, I think you're really great, you're my very favorite singer, and all my friends in school like you as well. We listen to your albums all the time."

"That's nice to hear," April said. "Where do you go to school?"

"Oberlin," Sally said. "I'm a sophomore. Right now I'm out on spring break. I'm actually kind of a singer myself, and I write songs too."

"That's nice," April said.

"Thanks. Anyway, I know it's presumptuous, but—how would you feel about listening to some of them? I mean, I know things must be sort of hectic and all, but I thought if you had any free time—"

April closed her eyes. "Things are a little crazy around here," she said.

"Oh, I understand," Sally answered. "God, it must be terrible. I mean, I'd heard your mom had been sick a long time, but—oh, God, if I lost my mother, I just—I don't know, I can't imagine it. I'm really sorry."

April smiled tightly and nodded. "It's okay," she said.

"Well, maybe instead—well, maybe I could leave some of them with you—you know, just to look over and stuff—and tomorrow maybe I could call, and if you liked them, maybe we could get together later. Would that be okay?"

April smiled tightly again. "Sure."

"Oh, great," the girl said. She opened her satchel and pulled out a thick booklet of sheet music. "I can't tell you how much I appreciate this," she said, handing April the booklet. "You know, you're my very favorite singer."

"Thanks," April said.

"So I'll call tomorrow," the girl said.

"Yes."

"Okay, great. And thanks again in advance for looking at my songs."

"Thank you," April said. "I mean—you're welcome."

The girl slipped back out of the kitchen, once again leaving April alone with Danny and Walter.

"I cannot believe this just happened," Walter said. "I absolutely cannot believe someone would be so insensitive, so completely self-serving as to—"

"Oh, she's just an ambitious little singer," Danny said. "April gets stuff like this all the time, don't you, April?"

April sat down at the table. "I didn't know what to say to her," she said. "When she said she was sorry, I mean. I really wasn't sure what to say."

"You should burn those songs," Walter said. "The nerve of that girl."

"Should I have said, 'It's okay'? 'Don't worry'? 'It's not your fault'? I mean, what do you say when someone says, 'I'm sorry your mother died'?"

"Don't worry about it, April," Walter said. "Just put it out of your mind."

"I'm not used to being at a loss for words," April said. "Well, I guess I can look at her songs. It won't take me too long. And who knows, maybe she's great."

Walter looked to Danny helplessly. "Am I hearing what I'm hearing? What's going on here?"

"Well, I really don't see how it can hurt," Danny said. "Look, April, if you have time, do. If you don't, don't."

"I feel like I'm missing something," Walter said. "Your mother died yesterday, didn't she? Your mother died yesterday and this twitty girl is giving you deadlines to look at her stupid songs?"

Both Danny and April glanced up at him blankly and a little foolishly, like schoolchildren who have failed to understand a lesson.

———

LATER CLARA WAS loading the dishes into the dishwasher when she suddenly stooped, bent over double, closed her eyes, and let out a low, sustained wail. Uncle Sy, who was sitting at the kitchen table, shuffling and reshuffling a deck of cards, stopped for a moment and looked at her. Then she pulled herself back up onto her feet, took a handkerchief from a pocket in her dress, blew her nose, and returned to loading the dishwasher. She continued to cry, softly yet unceasingly, as she loaded the dishes, and periodically stopped to wipe her eyes or blow her nose.

Nat, coming into the kitchen, found her this way. He approached her the way he had always approached Louise, from behind, putting his hands on her hot shoulders.

"You know, Clara," he said, "you'll always have a job with me. Don't you worry about that."

"Mrs. Cooper's with God," Clara said, reaching back and putting her own hand over Nat's. "I know. She told me she saw the light, and now she's with God."

"Yes," Nat said. "Maybe she is."

———

AT SEVEN everyone who was still left loaded into three cars and headed off to Ming's, a big, fancy Chinese place by the freeway. That afternoon the university's annual football reunion had kicked off, so the restaurant was full of huge men in rented tuxedos, drinking shots of brandy and recalling magnificent plays.

"Order anything you want," Uncle Herb said. "It's on me."

"Yup," Uncle Sy said. "It's on me."

No one was interested in ordering except Danny and April. They had always been rather aggressive at Chinese restaurants, and tonight, almost in tribute to their lost mother, they took the huge menu between them and fought it out, haggling and bargaining to orchestrate a perfect balance among all the particular tastes assembled tonight, not to mention Joanne's vegetarianism, Uncle Herb's low-salt diet, and the aversion of half the table to anything "too hot." The only thing they did not argue over was sweet and sour shrimp, though both of them despised it. It had been their mother's favorite.

They ordered a vast quantity of food, so much that Uncle Herb looked a little blanched, even though he kept saying, "Anything, anything. It's on me." Soon the dishes began to arrive. The sweet and sour shrimp glistened like neon in their thick red syrup. Platters filled up the lazy Susan at the center of the table and were taken away, only to be replaced by other platters. Across from Danny, Nat was nodding wearily at Aunt Eleanor, who was telling him about the terrible experience she'd just had with her home computer. "I'd just finished putting every recipe I have into that thing," she was saying, "and then, the next day, I stick the disk into the slot—whammo, it's empty. Every recipe I ever had, gone."

"Didn't you have a backup?" Nat asked.

"No, I didn't know I needed one."

"Well, you must have the hard copy."

"Hard copy?"

"Paper. You must still have the recipes on paper."

"Oh, no. I'd burned them all the night before. Burned my bridges, you might say. I thought, This is the age of the computer, Eleanor, why keep your drawers stuffed with all those ratty notebooks?" She sighed. "There must have been about a thousand recipes, some dating back to my grandmother, and all of them now, just gone. When I think of the hours I spent!"

"That's terrible, Eleanor. I'm sorry."

"Eh, you live and learn. So here's my question: What do you think I can get in court?"

"In court?"

"From the company. You know, for loss of income, loss of documents crucial to my career, emotional distress."

Nat put a hand on his forehead. "Eleanor," he said, "if you didn't make a backup copy—"

"So what? I still bet I'd have a case."

Nat buried his face in his hands, then unburied it and tried to explain to Eleanor why it would be unfair and unethical for her to bring the computer company to court when she hadn't made a backup, and everyone knows—it was the first rule of computers—that you should always make a backup.

"Backup, shmackup, how was it my fault? To this day I don't know how it happened. I put the disk in, I took the disk out, I put the disk in again and it's 'unreadable.' How is that my fault, I'd like to know?"

"I'm not saying it's your fault. The disk got dusty, or something glitched. These things happen sometimes. Who knows? The point is, you should have made a backup, so even if you do get money out of the computer company or the disk company, it won't be fair."

"Well," Eleanor said. "From now on, I guess I always will make a backup. Listen, if it comes to trial, can I call you as an expert witness?"

Nat looked grimly at the table.

"That was a joke, Natty," Eleanor said. "Ha-ha."

"Ha," Nat said.

"Anyway, I'm not really serious about suing. Ah, look!" A waiter was arriving with yet another platter. "Good old shrimp with lobster sauce. Remember that place in Boston we used to go, Natty? You and me and Louisy and Sid? With the shrimp with black beans. We were so young. I tell you, it really makes you feel old to lose a sister. All my life I know I'll have certain things, but never again in my life will I have a sister."

She took the napkin from her lap, touched it to her eyes. Nat didn't say anything.

"Look, let's be honest for once," Eleanor said. "I know Louisy didn't like me too much all the time. I don't blame her, I was a pain in the neck. But I loved her. I really did. You think she knew that?"

"Yes," Nat said. "Oh, Eleanor, of course she knew that."

"I felt sorry for her all these years. Being sick like that. I really did feel for her. It just seemed every time I tried to show it she pushed me away—"

Nat wriggled uncomfortably. "Eleanor, Louise really loved you too. You just irritated each other. That's common with sisters. Anyway, she pushed a lot of people away. She wasn't very good at accepting sympathy, she always assumed it was pity."

"We used to sit together on that little twin toilet," Eleanor said, and took a deep breath. "Well, enough of this. I'll just pull myself back together here." She sat up straight.

"Danny," she said, "would you please pass the beef?"

"I think it's pork, Aunt Eleanor."

"It doesn't matter," Eleanor said. "Pass it anyway."

———

I T W A S on his way from the bathroom, which was full of vomiting football players, that Danny once again had the vision of his mother: She was looking hungrily down as usual, an angel on each side, only this time—he saw it distinctly—there was a bandage over her mouth. A single square of white gauze. Why a bandage? He tried to hear her voice in his head, and suddenly it was gone. Sentences she had often used spoke out of his mind, but in vague, uncharacterized intonations. Her voice, which Danny had heard a thousand, a hundred thousand times, which was as inescapably her own as a set of fingerprints, or handwriting—how could memory lose something so precious as that? He tried to recall if there was anywhere a tape recording, or a super-eight movie—something on which there might be preserved the minutest reminding fraction of how his mother spoke—but from heaven, Louise, her mouth a square of light, looked down at him and shook her head: no.

Across the room some of the football players had cleared away the tables, linked arms, and formed a chorus line. "We're gonna beat the fuck out of those Oregon ducks," they were singing as they kicked out their legs in haphazard synchrony. Danny sat down. Fortune cookies went round. There was a cracking sound as all around the table the little crescents of stale dough were broken open, the slips of paper extracted and read. "I got two," Uncle Sy announced. "What does that mean?"

"Double good luck, Uncle Sy," Cousin Joanne said.

"Or else they cancel each other out," Eleanor added. "No one knows the answer to this mystery."

"Well, I hope Joanne's right," Sy said. "Because they're both goodies."

He looked hopefully round the table, but no one asked him to read his fortunes aloud.

————

"WHAT A STUPID DINNER," Nat said in the car, on the way home. "And by the way, who can I thank for sitting me down next to Eleanor? That woman is the biggest pain in the ass I have ever known in my life, and I can tell you now, I didn't appreciate it. Boring me to death all evening with her ridiculous lawsuits and recipes and computer problems."

"I don't know how it happened," Danny said.

"Why do you have to imply that everything is someone's fault?" said April. "Jesus, there weren't place cards, Daddy; people sat where they sat."

"Yeah, well, someone could have done me the favor of taking the place next to Eleanor instead of just leaving the space open for whoever happened to be stupid enough at that moment to go to the bathroom. Tonight, of all nights, someone could have been thoughtful enough to consider in advance what might be nice to do for me." He shook his head. "Whoever had this idea of going to a restaurant in the first place was an idiot. No one wanted to be in a stupid restaurant. And all that food! It was gross, positively gross. People in mourning shouldn't eat like pigs."

Danny looked in shame at the floor of the car.

"I think," Walter said cautiously, "that Herb and Sy just needed to do something—you know, to give something."

"Sure," Nat said. "They meant well. But, Jesus, after what I've just been through—what we've just been through—it was the last thing I needed. All of this, this whole day—it was all too much. I wanted something quiet, something respectful. Other people had to make it a fucking bar mitzvah."

"You know, Dad," April said, "if you want to accuse me of something, I wish you'd just come out and do it. I wish you'd just say what you're thinking: You just wanted a nice little party, but uh-oh, here comes your crass, vulgar daughter, who bakes a zillion cakes and insists everyone go out for dinner and doesn't even sit down next to Aunt Eleanor for Daddy's sake, like a good little girl would."

"April—"

"Fuck the truth. Fuck the fact that she was my mother, not just your wife, and you didn't lift a goddamned finger all day. Who cares if Eleanor made ten times as much food as I did, or that Uncle Sy had the idea for the dinner? If it's convenient, just yell at me, blame me—"

"April, would you just stop it? A fight is the last thing I need right now."

"No, I won't! You act like you're the only person in the world who's ever felt anything, like no one loved Mom but you. Everything has to be your way, no speeches, Mom wouldn't have liked it, no songs, Mom wouldn't have liked it, nothing too fancy, Mom wouldn't have approved, and now, no fight, I'm not up to it, I have to be protected. Well, that's bullshit, Dad. You're not the only one who gets to make decisions, or vent their feelings, or—or anything—"

"Will you be quiet?" Nat shouted. "Will you just please stop yelling, April?"

"We're all a little overexcited here," Walter said. "Why don't we try to calm down?"

They were pulling into the driveway. Almost immediately Nat switched off the ignition, moved to open his door.

"You act like you loved her so much," April said. "That's what I can't believe. That's what absolutely kills me."

"And just what do you mean by that?" Nat said, turning to face her. "Are you saying I didn't love your mother? Then I would like to ask you, April, what the hell gives you the right to judge whether or not I loved your mother?"

"Because if you loved her, you wouldn't have been fucking someone else," April said.

There was a sudden silence.

"Don't act so surprised," April said. "It didn't take a genius to figure it out."

Slowly Nat removed his hand from the door latch and leaned his head against the steering wheel. "Oh, God," he said quietly. "Oh, Jesus." And he started to cry.

"Yeah, you cry," April said. "You cry." She got out of the car and, running into the driveway, started spinning herself in a mad circle, her arms in the air, the way she often had as a little girl, whirling and whirling until it seemed to be the world that was whirling. In the midst of it all she jumped up once, heaved her arm into the sky, as if the moon were a ball she wanted to catch, and, flailing suddenly, landed hard on her behind.

"Shit!" she said. Walter jumped out of the car after her, shouting her name.

"I'm okay!" she said with some annoyance. "Just leave me alone!" She was sitting with her legs spread in front of her on the asphalt, her hands between her knees, and Walter stood back from her. "I'm okay," she said again. "I just need to sit here a minute and I'll be okay." And she bent over double, gasping.

Then it was as if the world had turned upside down, and nothing would ever feel quite the way it had before, nothing would ever be good again. It was like Louise had died. April had her head between her knees, she was moaning loudly, and already Nat was out of the car, pulling her away from herself and, with Walter's help, easing her up. Danny ran inside to call the emergency room and tell them they were coming, and even though April protested that it wasn't necessary, she gave in to the arms loading her into the backseat, her father's urgings to lie still, the familiar atmosphere of terror and emergency. Nat was behind the wheel again, starting the ignition, and as they pulled out, April was conscious not just of hurting but of a peculiar sense of relief, as if they were finally heading the way they should have been all along, away from comfort and toward the depths of grief.

FOR A LONG TIME afterwards Danny couldn't help but wonder if April had meant to hurt herself. Even after it became clear that everything was going to be fine, that she wasn't going to lose the baby, he still couldn't help but wonder, and not because he imagined April might secretly want to get out of the pregnancy everyone seemed so convinced she'd entered upon unwisely. No, his suspicion was rooted in a belief about his sister that was both simpler and more sinister than that. For April (as he knew better than anyone) had always been a scene stealer, from the moment she'd first strode onto that coffeehouse stage to sing "No More Vietnams," to her famous eclipsing of Margy McLaughlin in concert, to the afternoon she'd gone to Louise's hospital room barefoot and eaten all that candy. She had even stolen the scene from Danny the one moment in his life he'd made any real trouble, the night he told his parents he was gay, by airing, in the middle of it all, an unrelated but pressing grievance: She was tired of being treated like a scapegoat whenever Louise was in the hospital, she said; yes, she'd come barefoot, yes, she'd eaten the candy, but her father behaved inconsistently, one minute telling her it was her duty to take care of her mother, the next ordering her out of the room. April, Nat had said, that's all very well, but is this the time? It most certainly is the time, she had answered. And even though Danny was in a certain way relieved—the pressure, after all, was now off him—he still resented her timing. It seemed she couldn't bear anyone taking away her starring role on the stage of family crisis.

When they arrived at the emergency room that night, April couldn't stand up. Hunched over, she leaned up against the receiving desk, her hands on her stomach, and gave her name. A Jamaican nurse then put her arms around April's middle and maneuvered her, cranelike, through a set of swinging doors, murmuring, "You'll feel just fine in a minute, honey, just fine. We'll let you know how she is," she added to Nat as the doors swung shut.

"Okay," Nat said. He looked at Danny and smiled oddly. "Well," he said, "here we are again. Guess we just couldn't stay away, could we?" He laughed. Across the room an elderly man in a dinner jacket was pacing a small stretch of linoleum near which a black teenager lay spread across a few plastic chairs.

"I guess we ought to get comfortable," Walter said. "We might be here awhile."

They staked out their territory with the expertise of natives; almost immediately Nat had procured coffee, Walter magazines, Danny was taking off his shoes. And why not? For over a week now, a fluorescent-lit limbo very much like this one had been their home. Their eyes had long ago adjusted to its brutish yellow light.

Nat was just stretching out on one of the vinyl couches by the back wall when a doctor issued from between the swinging doors and called out, "Mr. Cooper, please."

Immediately all three of them were on their feet.

"I'm Dr. Carpenter," said the doctor, a hesitant-looking young man with freckles. His eyes were fixed on Nat, for reasons of seniority, Danny suspected. "I just wanted to let you know your daughter is fine, and so's her baby. Tight as a drum in there, really. Usually a fall like that does more damage to the mom. Anyway, she does have some bumps and bruises—nothing serious, but we'd like to keep her here overnight, for observation, just to make sure there aren't any problems. She asked me to tell you folks not to worry."

"Thank God," Nat said. He put a protective arm around Danny's shoulder. "You know, it's funny for us being back in a hospital right now, because my wife died just yesterday, up at the St. Francis burn unit. I think the last thing any of us expected was to be at the hospital again tonight."

"Dad—" Danny said.

"Oh, I see my son thinks it's a little strange for me to tell you all this, given that I've just met you and all. But you're a doctor. You see people die every day."

"Well," Dr. Carpenter said, and cleared his throat. "Even so, I am sorry to hear about it. In any case, she's being moved to a room right now. It's a little late for visiting hours, but if you want, you can pop in, just for a second, to say good-bye."

"Great," Nat said. "Which way?"

"Room four-eight-two. Fourth floor. Oh, and by the way," Dr. Carpenter said, smiling white teeth at Danny and Walter, "which one of you is the lucky dad?"

They looked nervously around the room for whoever it was he was speaking to before realizing it was them.

"Actually, I'm her brother," Danny said.

Dr. Carpenter looked expectantly at Walter. "I'm with him," said Walter.

"Oh," said Dr. Carpenter. He coughed again. "Well. She's going to be in room four-eight-two, on the fourth floor. You can take the elevator over there. And take care."

After Dr. Carpenter had shaken all their hands, they put their shoes back on, cleaned up their campsite, and rode the elevator to the fourth floor. There was a long, empty corridor, a series of closed doors. Down the hall a charwoman was swabbing the floor with ammonia.

"You must be the Coopers," a nurse said as they approached a bank of rooms. "It's past visiting hours, so you'll have to make it quick. You can come back tomorrow morning at ten."

She led them through the door marked "482" into a dark room with a curtain down the middle. On the other side of the curtain, closer to the window, light was pouring from an elevated television, even though the sound was off.

"You'll have to whisper," the nurse said. "Mrs. Ellingboe is asleep."

Nat assured her that they would. In the bed closer to the door was April. She wore a green hospital gown; her hands were crossed over her pale, slightly freckled chest.

"Hi," she said in a soft voice. "I'm a little woozy; they gave me something to make me sleep."

"Hi," Danny said.

"The baby's going to be fine," April said. "The doctor checked, and he says there's no problem."

"I'm glad," Danny said. "So is Walter."

"Is Daddy here?"

"I'm here," Nat said.

"I'm sorry we had a fight."

"Well, um—I am too."

"Good." April stretched her arms behind her head. "Here we are, back in the hospital, only now it's me in the bed instead of Mom. Funny, huh?"

"Funny," Danny said.

"Guess they just can't get rid of us so easily."

"Nope."

"Too bad it's not the same hospital. I liked that hospital better than this one."

The nurse raised her eyebrows, then mouthed that it was time to go.

"April," Danny said. "We have to go now. We'll be back in the morning."

"Oh, that's fine," April said. "Whatever they gave me, I'll sleep like a baby. It's better than Valium."

Once again the nurse made a gesture of departure.

"Bye," they all whispered, this time in unison. By then she was out cold. The nurse stealthily tiptoed across the room and switched off the television before following them out the door.

———

"YOU KNOW," Nat said in the car on the way home, "there's really no reason for you two to stick around here anymore. You might as well head back to New York."

Danny hadn't allowed the thought of going back to enter his head for several days, but now that Nat mentioned it, he remembered his house, his dog, his job; he remembered the way time normally moves.

"I do need to get back," Walter said quietly.

"But what about the clothes?" Danny asked. "What about sorting through Mom's clothes?"

"I can take care of that. Well, actually, I was sort of assuming April would help me, but now I'm not so sure I can ask her."

"Not so sure!" Danny said. "Why?"

"I just don't know if she'll want to, that's all."

"Oh, Dad, you know April gets over her temper tantrums in about two seconds."

"April can always get over April's temper tantrums. The problem is, it can be a lot harder for the rest of us." He laughed. "Jesus, she just has to put herself in the center of everything. Louise dies, so April has to almost have a miscarriage."

"It's not like she planned it that way," Danny said, even though he was wondering if she had. "She was very upset. We all were."

"It's embarrassing to me, the whole thing," Nat said. "I mean, God, the whole thing was so stupid. You know, I was afraid they were going to think I beat her up or something, even if she told them the truth, that she fell. Isn't that what beaten wives and children are supposed to say, after all? They fell? They walked into the refrigerator? I was having fantasies of going to jail, and every time April said, 'Really, I fell,' the nurses and social workers saying, 'Sure, honey, sure,' and thinking, It was her goddamned father. I guess April just doesn't look the victim type."

"Dad, she did fall."

"Do you know what time it is?" Nat said. "Three thirty-eight A.M. Funny, I'm not a bit tired."

"Neither am I."

"Neither am I," Walter echoed.

They turned into the garage, where Nat switched off the ignition and leaned over into the backseat, close to Danny's face.

"What April said," he said.

"Dad, we don't have to—"

"What April said—I know you're probably curious whether it's true or not and what the story is. Well, I'm prepared to tell you, but I have to ask that you give me some time. I'm not quite ready—for anything yet. You see, I had no idea April knew. I had no idea anyone knew, except your mother."

Danny made a noise of protest, then was silent.

"Give me a little time on this one, okay?" Nat said. "I just need a little time to figure things."

"Sure, Dad," Danny said. "As much time as you need."

———————

HE LEFT HOME. He left home and he went home. In Gresham there was soup on the stove, stew in the freezer. Iris had left a sympathy card perched against a vase of flowers on the shiny kitchen table. "Your loss has touched our hearts, and we feel it with you," the card read. "Lots of love, Iris and Hal."

"She sent one to my father too," Danny said to Walter, who was sorting through the mail. "Nice of her, considering they've never met."

"My mother is like that," Walter said.

He went to pick up the dog, and Danny unpacked. The only thing he had brought back with him that he hadn't originally left with was the picture of his mother in the leather-and-metal welding suit, and he put it on the refrigerator. "People used to tell me I looked like Gene Tierney," Danny remembered her saying once, when she was showing him this picture. "She went mad, you know."

"She was beautiful," Danny had said.

"Yes, she was," Louise had said, gazing at the photograph of herself. "Too bad she went nuts."

———————

AS FOR Hurricane Louise, she came and went; like Louise herself, in anger, the storm lost steam quickly; its entrance was less dramatic than the threats with which it preceded itself. A few telephone poles fell, here and there a tree, and then Hurricane Louise swept out to sea.

Even so, Danny couldn't help thinking how much his mother would have enjoyed it all. She had been born, after all, on the anniversary of the Great San Francisco Earthquake and never failed to mention the coincidence. Now, just a few days after her exit, her slow brownout, it seemed that Hurricane Louise had determined to rise from her birthplace in the Atlantic and at least threaten that famous coast from the loins of which Louise Gold had been ejected, which she had fled, which had stolen back her son. It was as if Danny's mother were coming back in some harsher, more elemental form; as if she were declaring her refusal to leave this world quietly, with only a sealing party to see her go; as if she were insisting that for one trembling moment of silence, they all stand up and recognize the force of her departure.

S AN FRANCISCO is a city of edges and fear. There are streets so steep the sidewalks have steps. Cars park sideways, so that the upward-facing door you can barely open at all. When you open the downward-facing door, it falls so swiftly forward it can knock you over.

It is usually while waiting for the light to change at the top of a hill like that, when you are wondering how, in that split second allotted you, you'll be able to get from neutral to first before your car rolls back and smashes the one behind it, that you begin to recognize the precarious, tilted balance of this city, how everything is stacked in trembling perfection, like a house of cards, waiting for the inevitable, always threatened rumble underfoot. Here is where the body snatchers landed, after all, to replace the self with its nonself replica, burgeoning from a pod; and here is where the streets so often fill with candles and silence, in memory of those lost to more insidious invasions; and here is where a madman murdered the mayor and a supervisor, and was forgiven, and where nuns with beards ride motorcycles down crowded streets, and where people meet nightly in groups to talk out their terror of the quakes. Fear is in the fog, in the silence of streets so unbearably beautiful and still, late at night, they seem paralyzed. By the water, whole neighborhoods of houses shine white as teeth.

It was into this high-strung and glittering city, this infectious and absorbing city, this city of tall spires and bridges like arteries, carrying golden corpuscles to and from an irradiated heart, that April disappeared, as she so often had before, upon her release from the hospital. On doctor's orders she had stranded her unfortunate band somewhere back east and left it to her manager to deal with the roadmapful of canceled concerts. Her house was still sublet, and not unusually, she was having money problems, so she fled from her father into the welcoming network of the earnest left, the small cells of sixties fervor that still smoldered in the city's outer reaches, knowing her friends there would be sure to take care of her. First she was with Summer, the on-again, off-again lover who had so disapproved of her having a child, and then she was staying with a group of women in a house in Bernal Heights, and then she was with Tom Neibauer, the father of her child, and his deaf lover, Brett Wu. Their house was on one of the streets with sidewalked steps; it made her uncomfortable, she told Danny, the way she had to sit almost totally sideways in the passenger seat while Tom or Brett struggled to pull the huge door closed. "I keep thinking, here I am, round and pregnant, and I'm just going to roll out the door and right to the bottom of the hill." Tom was taking wonderful care of her, though. His house was at the top of a forty-six-step outdoor stairway, and every time they went out he carried her up and down the stairway, like a bridegroom with his bride. During the day, while Tom and Brett were at their jobs, she drank fortified milk shakes he had blended for her the night before, and watched soap operas. Sometimes she baked whole wheat muffins and fruit breads, using apple juice instead of sugar. (Tom didn't eat sugar.) Pregnancy, she declared, was proving so far to be a thoroughly agreeable state.

"Are you showing yet?" Danny asked her. It was the middle of June, and he was calling her from work, in New York.

"A little," she said. "I'm starting to swell, I guess is how I'd put it. You can't really tell in my clothes so much as when I'm naked. It's interesting, I've always had a big stomach, but this is different. It's tight, sort of. And sometimes I feel the baby inside, moving around, which is an incredible feeling. The best part is, being pregnant has made me more creative than I've ever been. My breasts pour out milk, my guitar pours out notes. I'm writing like a maniac, song after song, and Margy thinks it's the best work I've done in years."

"And your fans?"

"What about them?"

He affected an interviewer's voice, a high falsetto he had heard on a Lily Tomlin album once. "How does the feminist community feel about this revolutionary step you're taking, Ms. Gold?"

"Well, it certainly is the talk of the town," April said. "Especially Tom's involvement—a few of them don't approve of that, but most do. As for the having-a-baby thing, it's no big news anymore. I'm hardly the first to have succumbed to the invading pleasures of a turkey baster." She laughed. "I like to think," she said, in a more serious tone, "that Tom and I are serving as role models."

"Role models, yes," Danny said. "You always have wanted to be that." He paused a moment. "Dad called me last night, by the way. You know he's going to that computer expo in Montreal tomorrow? So he said, 'I just want you to know where we'll be staying.' Slipped in the 'we'll,' like I wouldn't even notice it."

"True to form," April said. "It doesn't surprise me."

"I tried to change the subject, and then he said, 'You know, Lillian used to be up at McGill; she's got lots of friends in Montreal.' Just like that. That night you fell, on the way back from the hospital, he promised he'd tell me everything, explain everything, as soon as he was ready. But he never did. Then he calls me up and tells me Lillian's going with him to Montreal as if I've known all along who Lillian is, what her name is, as if we've had a hundred big conversations about it, when the fact is, everything I know about Lillian I know from you. Something's missing here, some conversation's been skipped."

"He knows you know and you know he knows you know, so therefore he doesn't have to ever actually tell you," April said. "It's called blanketing the posterior. Covering your ass. This way, if you object or make a fuss, you'll be the one who sounds hysterical, and he'll be all innocence; he can just accuse you of overreacting and chalk it off as more craziness from his children. I know the tactic. I've called him on it."

"It was my fault, too, I guess. I guess I really didn't *want* to know all these months—"

"What did you say when he told you?"

"I just said I hoped he'd have a good time. It's none of my business anyway." He was quiet a moment. "Have you spoken to him lately?"

"Oh, he called the other night, to ask which of Mom's jewels I wanted. I said I'd come down next week to go through them—provided he promised he wouldn't be around. He was certainly happy to agree to that." She laughed unpleasantly, then said, "I hope you don't think I'm still mad at him just because of what happened after the party, Danny. I'm over that. The problem is, that's just the tip of the iceberg."

"Oh?"

"Well, among other things, his way of informing me about this Lillian Rubenstein-Kraft or Kraft-Rubenstein or whatever her name is—let's just say it wasn't too sensitive. First he tried on me what he tried on you. For a week last month he kept calling me up and saying things like 'Lillian and I are going to the faculty senate dinner next week.' 'I thought I'd take Lillian to the Ebers' party.' I knew what it was all building up to, and sure enough, before I knew it—the clincher. 'April, Lillian and I would like you to come down and have lunch with us next week.' " April mimicked this final request in a high, singsong voice.

"Ah," Danny said. "Well—did you?"

"Are you kidding? I said, 'Dad, I can't believe you're actually asking me to dignify this affair of yours. And while we're at it,' I said, 'I really wish you'd have enough respect for my mother's memory to wait a little while before you start parading Lillian around in public.' " She paused. "You know what he said to that?"

"What?"

"He said, 'April, it's none of your goddamned business,' and hung up. Except for the call about the jewels, that's the last time I spoke to him."

"Oh."

"I wasn't surprised. I know what he's up to. He knows it's lousy of him to be out in public with this woman just—what?—two months after his wife's death, he knows everybody thinks it's lousy, including me, so what he does is, he projects all his guilt onto his convenient guilt-absorbing daughter. It's a very old pattern, taking out his anger on me for what he's done wrong; believe me, it's happened plenty before. But the difference is, this time I'm not going to let it get to me. He can think whatever he wants, I'm not playing his game. I'm not sixteen anymore; I'm a grown-up woman with a life of my own. Fuck him, as far as I'm concerned."

"Well, April," Danny said, "he is our father. And if he's going to be with Lillian, then we have to deal with it."

"Why do we have to deal with it? Why do we have to have a relationship with him?"

"Because," Danny said. "Because he's our father."

"Plenty of people I know don't speak to their fathers. I'm sure plenty of people you know don't speak to their fathers either."

"Yes—and I never wanted to be one of them. Frankly, I'm surprised you're treating this so lightly."

"I'm not treating it lightly," April said. "I am not treating it at all lightly. Look, he has just walked all over me, and walked all over Mom, long enough. It's time I stood up for myself. It doesn't mean we'll never reconcile; it just means for once in his life he's got to make the first step. I'm tired of always being the one to make the first step, Danny; I'm sick of being the peacemaker, the one who forgives, the one who comes back and in effect admits yes, April's crazy, April acted crazy, and now she's coming back begging, she's not saying it, but look, she's back. That's what he thinks, and I'm tired of letting him think that. I'm not going to do it anymore. He has to call me this time. And if he doesn't—well, I don't need him. I honestly don't need him."

Danny was silent.

"By the way, I'm almost done with that bootie," April said. "Did I neglect to tell you, in my new maternal mode, I'm becoming an ace knitter? I sit in front of the television with my feet in furry slippers, and while I watch whatever shenanigans are going on on *Santa Barbara*, I knit. Every Sunday I do the crossword puzzle too."

"That's great," Danny said.

"Ah, well, enough about me. What do you think of my songs?"

Danny was silent.

"That was a joke," April said. "Ha-ha."

"I got it," Danny said.

"Oh, we're Mr. Serious today, aren't we?" April said. "Mr. No-Sense-of-Humor."

"April!"

"How's Walter?"

"He's fine. We're taking our vacation next month. We're going to rent a house out on Long Island, by the beach. You should come visit. Lie in the sun, get more pregnant."

"Maybe I will," April said. "Maybe I just will."

"I hope you do, April. I have this incredible desire to see what you look like pregnant. Frankly, I can't quite imagine it."

"Fat," April said. "Mostly I look fat."

————————

LATER THAT AFTERNOON Danny called his father.

"I understand you and April had another little fight," he said.

"April had the fight," said Nat. "Not me."

"Well—what's going to happen?"

"What's going to happen," Nat said wearily. "As far as I'm concerned, what's going to happen is, I'm going to go ahead and lead my life the way I see fit, not the way my daughter sees fit. The rest is up to her."

"Funny," Danny said. "She thinks the rest is up to you."

"I'm not surprised," Nat said. "All her life April has managed to shove the responsibility for her own problems onto other people."

After a strangled second or two Danny said, "I wanted to ask you— how serious is this thing with you and Lillian?"

Nat was silent for a moment. "Serious," he said. "Well, that's hard to say. Pretty serious, I guess. Yes."

"I was just curious."

"You've met Lillian."

"Of course. She's very nice."

"Oh, I'm glad you think so. I remember you saying her son Steven was in your class in high school? Well, he's married now. He lives up in Sun Valley, Idaho. We may be going next weekend to visit him. First time in my life I'll have been skiing."

"That would be fun to watch," Danny said.

"Very funny," Nat said. "Anyway, I'll just be on the kiddie slopes. Starting to ski, at my age!" He sounded, for a moment, wistful.

"Do you disapprove of what I'm doing, son?" he asked.

"Dad—" Danny said, "I don't know. I mean, it really isn't any of my business."

"I'm glad to hear you feel that way. Now I only wish your sister would come round to the same conclusion. She seems to have it in her head that she has to protect your mother's memory, or that I never loved Louise, or some nonsense like that."

"She's upset, Dad. Mom hasn't been gone that long."

"But what she doesn't realize—and this is what your mother, more than anyone else, realized—is that once someone is gone, they're gone. Life is for the living. Danny, I loved your mother. I know that and Louise knew that. I don't have to prove it by going through some ritualistic period of mourning, especially to April. I'm going to be sixty-four next month, you know."

"Yes, I know."

"And there just isn't enough time. I hope you can persuade your sister of all this, because she won't listen to a word from me."

"Well—I'll try."

"Thank you, son," Nat said. "By the way, for whatever it's worth, the results of the autopsy came in. They showed Louise had a tumor in her lungs. A big one."

"Oh," Danny said.

"The doctor had been worried about that. Louisy didn't want me to tell you. It means that even if she'd survived the burn unit, she probably wouldn't have lived a year."

"Oh," Danny said again.

"I thought you might find that comforting. I thought you might find it made the suddenness of her death a little easier to bear. Does it?"

Danny thought about it for a moment and said, "Not really."

"No," Nat said rather miserably. "It doesn't make a shit's worth of difference to me either."

INSIDE WALTER'S COMPUTER, meanwhile, the erotic masque continued unabated. So many newcomers were logging on that the channel was often packed, particularly on Friday nights. You could try to get through for hours and receive nothing but a busy signal, a situation that enraged the old-timers; Bulstrode was constantly collecting signatures on electronic petitions, or sending angry e-mail to the administrative offices of the service, which were located in Duluth. Other than that, things went on as usual; every time he logged on, Walter was happy to see a few familiar names embedded in the pornographic cast list. Lies continued to be told and tolerated. What did it matter? It was not as if any of them would ever actually meet. Two of the regulars, Mastermind and PandaBear, had met, and it had been a disaster; they had arranged a secret rendezvous in a Washington, D.C., hotel, yet when the momentous weekend finally arrived, no sooner were they checked into their room than they had logged back onto the computer, under the joint handle "Master/Panda." All Friday evening they were there, and Saturday as well. What had gone wrong? Walter wondered. Had the sight of the other's physical body been more than each of them could bear? Or had each merely been so disappointed at the unmasked reality of the other that in order to salvage what they could of their fantasies, they had elected to return to the electronic medium where their courtship had begun? The problem with real intimacy, Walter had long ago learned, is that you cannot just shut it off. Real people have a way of banging against the doors you've closed; they know your name, your phone number. They live with you. And that, he decided, was not altogether bad. What the computer had offered was the safety of isolation, the safety of control. Voices, words, telephone numbers came through the circuits, but you could always hang up, you could always log off. There was nothing to risk, nothing to lose, even with Bulstrode. And even so, from those heights of safety, those heights of self-protection and anonymity, Walter longed for nothing more than the rich landscape of the dangerous human earth. It was funny—for most of his life he had kept his eyes focused straight ahead, on the law, or else on some fantasy of escape, to Europe, to Asia; he had assumed that by looking only forward, he could eventually lose the sadness and dissatisfactions of his childhood. But the further he went, the more Walter realized that, like it or not, he was inextricably bound with the people who had mattered to him and who mattered to him now, the people whose loves defined him, whose deaths would devastate him. He would never, could never be Bulstrode, self-invented, untouchable, a journeyer among the keys. And for this he was glad.

When they were at the hospital, when Louise was dying, Walter had stood for hours just outside the glass partition of her room. Inside, beyond the glass, Danny and April and Nat wept and raged and struggled through Louise's death, Louise struggled through Louise's death. All that separated him from the spectacle of them was a piece of glass. It could have been a television, or a window, or a mirror, but in fact it was a door, and every hour or so someone came out, usually crying. What right did he have to complain? He was just there for Danny; it wasn't his mother. Yet there was a door. And someday, probably not too long from now, he was going to have to walk through that door; he was going to have to confront himself what was waiting for him on the other side of that door.

The computer was not a door.

He shut off his computer. Somewhere across the house was Danny. What to do? What to say to him? He started walking, then, for a moment, hesitated. Don't be an idiot, he chided himself. Go to him.

Danny was sitting at the kitchen table, reading the newspaper. Approaching him from behind, Walter was suddenly flushed with affection for his clean-shaven neck, his comfortable, round head. "Danny—" he said.

"Yes?"

"Danny, I—" He faltered. Danny put down the paper, swiveled the chair around to face him.

"What is it, Walt?"

"I missed you," Walter said.

Danny looked up at him. Walter had his arms folded behind his back and his head bent forward, like that of a penitent child.

"But I haven't gone anywhere," Danny said quietly.

"I have."

Danny reached up a hand, lightly brushed it over Walter's cheek. "And are you back?" he said.

"I'm back," Walter said. "I'm back."

F OR TWO WEEKS that July Danny and Walter rented a little
cottage on the beach in eastern Long Island. A few days after
they'd arrived, April came to visit. They met her at the airport.
For some reason Danny was worried he wouldn't recognize her, worried that pregnancy would have changed her appearance in a substantial and unpredictable way, but when she got off the plane, she was,
quite simply, herself, April, at her most beautiful. All through her life
Danny had watched his sister alternate between periods when she
looked overweight and drab and other periods in which a splendid,
unexpected beauty bloomed in her, and now it seemed she had made
the crossover once again. Her hair, sun-baked, glowed at the tips; her
once-pasty skin had a deep golden cast. Indeed, as she waved and
smiled from the crowd of emerging passengers, Danny couldn't help
but remember that time when her career was at its peak and each night
she stepped from backstage into an onslaught of flowers.

She was definitely pregnant, he saw from where he stood amid a
gaggle of other welcomers, her belly humping up beneath her dress in a
way that reminded him of Flemish Madonnas. But she also looked—
and this surprised him—thin and fit, as if she'd just emerged from one
of the rigorous tuna and tofu diets she sometimes subjected herself to,
rather than weeks of soap operas and milk shakes. Her dress was sewn
from a rich, burnished orange fabric and, like the dresses she'd worn as

a teenager, had little mirrors embroidered into it. She had her hair tied in a braid that coiled over her shoulder like the tail of a neck-riding pet mink, and her ears were studded with various tiny and delicate earrings—stars, moons, and planets—from the midsts of which two low-hanging pendants of beaten silver drooped.

"I am so glad to be off that plane, Powderfoot!" she said as she kissed him among the other little reunions. "When are we going to the beach? Now?"

"Of course. We drove in from there."

"And Walter?"

"He's waiting in the car."

"Goody! I can't wait to hit the sand! I even brought one of those special maternity swimsuits. You should see it, I look ridiculous."

They gathered her luggage from the carousel and headed outside. It was a hot, muggy New York summer day; outside the airport, cars and taxis fought for the few free inches of curb Walter had managed to monopolize. In sunglasses and a Bermuda shirt, he kissed and hugged April and hoisted her luggage into the trunk. "Thank God for air-conditioning," April said as she struggled to pull the seat belt over her distending belly. "I forgot how humid New York gets in the summer."

"Well, you won't have to think about it anymore," Walter said, "because we are hitting the beach!" And with a few sharp honks of his horn, he cleared the snarl of the arrivals curb, taking them out onto the highway.

On the way April told them about her summer. She hadn't lasted too long with Tom and Brett, she explained. "It was way too confining, and Tom was really being a pain in the ass with this whole healthful-pregnancy thing of his. I mean, I'd take a Tab from the refrigerator, and he'd say, 'Are you sure you need that, April? It could be bad for the baby.' It got to where I had to hoard my Tabs in my room and drink them secretly at night. Anyway, finally we both agreed it would be better if I moved out. His heart's in the right place, and he's going to be a great father, but in the end I just couldn't take his watching me like a hawk all the time. So I decided to go to Margy's—she's been living the last couple of months in this house up in Muir Woods, and since her lover just left to take a job with the Foreign Service, she said she'd be glad for the company. It's a beautiful place, and—guess what?—next door there's a couple of women—Jane and Melinda are their names—who have two children by artificial insemination, a boy and a girl. I got to talking to them, and they turned out to be just great. They told me about the problems their kids were having in school, and what they did to help them, and how they'd explained to them who their fathers were. Neither of them knows who the fathers are, incidentally, it was all kept secret, so in a lot of ways my situation is going to be totally different. But it was a great education anyway. I'm sticking to your car." She lifted her thighs from the vinyl car seat and pulled her dress down back down under them. "So how's your stay been so far, boys?"

"Fine," Danny said.

"Quiet," Walter added.

"Although we certainly have been enjoying the beach house."

"How long have you been out?"

"Just five days now."

"Nine to go."

"It feels like we've been there forever, and just a few seconds, both at the same time," Walter said. "I think next summer we're going to rent the place for longer and go on weekends."

"And when's Dad coming?"

"Saturday. You'll stay, won't you?"

"Oh, sure," April said. "Dad and I get along great now. Ever since I made him go to that shrink with me, he's been a pussycat."

"What happened with the shrink exactly?"

"Well, she was just so eminently reasonable and sincere that Daddy had to agree with her, even if he didn't with me—you know, that it wouldn't be such a big sacrifice to take it easy with Lillian, especially if I agreed not to guilt-trip him. Ever since then we're best buddies."

Danny couldn't tell if she was speaking sarcastically. Nat's version of the reconciliation had been—to say the least—more subdued.

"He *is* coming alone, isn't he?" April asked.

"Of course."

"I'm just asking because he didn't tell me one way or another, and you know that's one of his favorite tricks—to not say anything and then—surprise—bring her along. He did that last week. Made a big deal about wanting to have a reconciliatory dinner with me. I get to the restaurant, and there she is."

"And how was that?"

"Well, it was funny. I'd decided in advance that whenever the inevitable meeting happened, I was probably going to have a tantrum or something as soon as I got to the restaurant, and that maybe that wasn't such a bad thing, maybe it was actually necessary, you know, to clear the air and all. But then I got there—remember, I wasn't expecting her—and I was totally taken aback. I mean, here she was, this perfectly nice, politically enlightened, feminist woman, really. Very pleasant, very bright. Couldn't be more different from our mother."

"How?"

"Confident. Self-assured. Not a vulnerable bone in her body, as far as I could tell—at least that's the impression she wants to give."

"Well, I don't think he's bringing her this time," Danny said. "I mean, on a big trip like this, where he's staying with us, I think he'd have had to say something—don't you?"

"I'm sure he's not bringing her, Danny," Walter said.

"Not that I'd mind so much if he did; it's just that we really don't have room. The cottage has only two bedrooms plus a pullout couch."

They were well away from the airport now. Outside, the city smog began to dissipate, letting in squares of sunlight. In spite of the air-conditioning, April opened the window, as she was so fond of doing, and let her hand drag with the wind. "Oh, I almost forgot," she said suddenly, pulling it back in, "I brought something for you." She rummaged through her purse, fishing out at last a cassette tape, which she handed to Danny. "A present."

"Really? What is it?"

"Just some early recording I've been doing for my next album. I was hoping you'd play it."

"Great!" Walter said. "Put it on."

"Now?" Danny asked.

"Sure, why not? We've got at least another forty-five minutes to the beach."

Danny took the cassette out of its case and fed it into the tape player. "One-two-three," a woman's voice said. Then guitars, drums, and April, singing the lullaby she'd started to compose at their house, just before Louise got sick. It seemed to have happened years ago.

"It sounds good," she said. "It sounds better than it did before."

"Yes, it does."

"It's great."

Then April began to sing along with herself in a loud, sure voice.

————

WHEN THEY ARRIVED, Danny and April took a walk on the beach. It had gotten suddenly, surprisingly chilly, chilly enough so that April—to her disappointment—had to forgo her maternity bathing suit. Now she walked barefoot along the tide line, hitching up her dress with her hands to keep the ends from getting wet. She had very fat, very white feet, with thick toes and bluntly cut, yellowing nails. Whenever they stopped a few seconds in one place, the sand swept up and buried April's feet. She seemed fascinated by this phenomenon and stood observing it until the sand was up to her ankles. "It's like quicksand," she said to Danny. "When I was a kid, on TV and in movies, people were always falling into the quicksand. I used to have nightmares about it. Now you don't see quicksand so much anymore." She shook her head, feeling, apparently, old, and swiftly pulled her feet out of the sandy muck.

They moved up the beach. "There's this guy who usually sits right over there," Danny said, pointing at a small hillock dotted with sea grass, "who I was really hoping to show you. He sits there all day in this tight little swimsuit with this positively huge erection, and everyone who walks by does a double take. It's like *Candid Camera*. The other day Walter and I sat here for hours, just watching different people's reactions—an old lady with a dog, a young mother, a couple of real tough-looking local boys. No one, and I mean no one, can miss it. They look, they kind of go into a spasm, sometimes they turn around to take another look, and this guy, he just smiles at them. He wears these terrifying reflective sunglasses that blast your own face back at you. And he must be incredibly turned on by showing himself off like that, because it never goes away—the erection, that is." Danny sighed audibly. "Too bad he isn't here. He'll probably be back tomorrow."

"You boys certainly do find novel ways of keeping yourselves entertained," April said.

"Well." Danny blushed. "Even *you* would notice this one, April."

"One of those *horrid* things, and huge to boot? Yes, I'd probably notice it. I'd probably notice it and run screaming in the other direction. 'Penis alert! Penis alert!' " She laughed. "That was an old joke of Fran's, probably the only funny thing she ever said in her life, the bitch." She looked suddenly bitter, remembering her ex-lover, and put a piece of sea grass she'd picked up into her mouth.

They sat down. Danny uprooted several pieces of grass and formed them into a tic-tac-toe board, the squares of which he filled with *X*'s and *O*'s dragged into the sand with a stick, while April gazed intently into the surf.

"April," Danny said.

"Yes?"

"Do you ever—you know—miss it?"

"Miss what?"

Danny looked away. "Sleeping with men."

"Oh, that. Why do you ask?"

"Well, you know, Mama never really believed you when you came out to her. She told me once, just last year. She said, 'I know how that girl thought about boys, and it's just impossible for me to believe she was faking the whole time. I think she's faking now.' "

"Mama, like many women of her generation, believed what she wanted to believe. I mean, certainly, I *thought* I was attracted to men back then, I *thought* I liked sex with them."

"So you're saying that was all a societal delusion? That you were somehow being tricked?"

"Well, not exactly. It's just—sure, I liked having sex with men, but it wasn't as *important* to me as sex with women. It didn't mean as much."

"So answer my question. Do you miss it?"

April shot him an older-sister glance. "Since when," she asked, "have you been given permission to ask me questions of a personal nature?"

"Come on."

April smiled. "Okay. The answer is no, I haven't missed it— because—" She straightened out her legs, pulling her dress over her knees. "Now, Danny, can I trust you to keep this secret? Not a word of this must be breathed to anyone, not even Walter."

"Swear to God and hope to die, stick a needle in my eye," Danny said.

"Okay. Well. The answer is no, I haven't missed it because I have done it a few times—a *few*, mind you—over the last several years."

"You mean you've had sex with men?" Danny sat up, smiling.

"Don't sound so gleeful about it! Jesus. But yes."

"How many?"

"A few."

"How many is a few?"

"Three, all right?" She laughed at his indignation. "It doesn't mean I'm not gay, it doesn't mean I'm any less committed to lesbian causes, it just means I—transgressed, I guess is the word, a few times. The 'thrust,' Fran used to call it. She always talked about missing the 'thrust.' Well, I never missed the thrust so much, but I've always believed in doing what you want, sexually; I think it's important for women not to be enslaved by notions of what they should or shouldn't do—and I don't care if those notions come from their mothers or uptight orthodox lesbians who think dildos are signs of male oppression. It was for variety's sake, if nothing else. Anyway, I liked them fine—the men, that is—although frankly, all this fuss about penises I don't understand. They strike me as basically ugly."

"Ugly is in the eye of the beholder."

She looked at him impishly. "You like them, I imagine."

"Oh, yes."

"You like them big?"

Danny's face turned bright red. "April!"

"I answered your question, now you answer mine. You like them big?"

He stammered. "Well—sure—I guess—"

"Is Walter's big?"

"April, I refuse—"

"Come on."

"I don't know, size isn't that important—"

"So it's small."

"No!"

"Then it *is* big!" She slapped her knee. "I knew it. They say you can tell from the way a man walks, though I've never been sure if that meant his attitude or, literally, how he walked—"

"Well, it's not *huge*, April—"

"How big?"

Danny made an approximation with his hands.

"Is that as big as the guy who lies on the beach?"

"No," Danny said. "But it's—big enough." He fell back on the sand, grinning with embarrassment. A light wind blew by, bringing up prickles of coolness on his skin, and then for a few brief seconds the sun emerged from between some clouds. "Ah, that feels nice," April said. She lay on her back, pointing her full stomach toward the intermittent sun, and hitched her dress up over her legs, her underpants, the rounding soccer ball of her stomach. There, in shocking contrast with her face and legs, the skin was the color of Cream of Wheat.

"If my baby's a boy," she said, "and he's gay, like his father and his uncle and his mother, then I want you and Walter to take extra-special care of him, to see he turns out all right. Tom's loving, but he's not exactly worldly—I mean, I don't want my son growing up to be a herbalist."

Danny laughed. "What makes you think it's going to be a boy? You didn't have that test, did you?"

April shook her head. "It's just that I have a feeling. Call it woman's intuition."

The sun disappeared again, and she pulled her dress down.

"I've been trying to come up with names. What do you think of Bartholomew?"

"Bartholomew," Danny said. "I like it. And he could be Bart for short."

"At school."

"But what would his last name be? Bartholomew Gold? Bartholomew Cooper? Bartholomew Neibauer? Or are you thinking of hyphenating? Bartholomew Gold-Neibauer. That's an awful lot of syllables for a little baby."

"You know, I hadn't thought to discuss that with Tom," April said. "I assume, however, his name will be Bartholomew Gold."

"And if it's a girl?"

April lifted her head and looked crossly at her brother.

"Oh, of course." Ashamed, Danny peered through squinting eyes at the disappearing sun.

"Louise," he said.

April put her head back, closed her eyes. "Louise," he said again. It pleased him and surprised him, the sound of her name in his mouth, and he realized he hadn't spoken it in many weeks. "Louise," he said. "Louise. Louise."

N O ONE LIVED in the cottage during the year; it was rented and occupied only for summers, and as a result its rooms had a transient, restless feel about them, as if a lot had happened there but none of it had been allowed to settle in. The living room had bleached white floors and was furnished with a hodgepodge of elderly sofas and armchairs, each of which gave off the scent of rot and long, unheated winters. But Nat liked it. "It reminds me of Little Nahant," he said, pushing open the doors onto the terrace. There, in the distance, were dunes, ocean, sky. "That smell of salt and fish in the wind. Makes me remember how I used to bicycle to see your mother that summer I was seventeen." He was quiet for a moment, his eyes following the vapor trail of an airplane writing a message in the sky. Then he turned to face his family.

"So here we are," he said. "All together again."

"That's right," April said. She stood against a wall, guitar in hand, fingering the strings in a way that suggested restlessness for an audience. "All together again," she more or less sang, plucking with her index finger. Walter picked up a dust bunny and three pennies that had dropped on the floor, while Danny, in the kitchen, did dishes; he had been doing dishes all week. The first time these four people had been together since Louise's death three months earlier. Was it wrong that they should be gathered here, of all places, in an anonymous rented cottage thousands of miles from the house and kitchen table which, like it or not, was the natural locus of at least three of their lives? And yet perhaps there was something to be said for reconvening on neutral ground, far away from everything familiar, and the ghost, even now pulling on rubber gloves to wash dishes in that other, faraway sink.

Nat looked thinner than before, tanned, well rested. He was doing some renovating, he announced to his children. The burnished orange shag carpeting they had put in when Danny was a teenager had been torn away, replaced by industrial gray. Ditto the yellowing white wallpaper with its pattern of black flowers—flowers from Hades, Louise had called them; the walls were white now. "My aim is to streamline," Nat said, and Danny could tell how relieved he was to be finally stripping away the layers of old wallpaper, returning the house to its elemental forms—plywood and pine and oak, plaster and sheetrock. Perhaps, when it was over, it would become a place he could go on in.

Walter had bought swordfish steaks for dinner. "We were going to go out," Danny told his father, "but the restaurants around here are overcrowded and overpriced and just not very good, especially this time of year. Last time Walt and I had to wait an hour for a table."

"Well, it's a good thing then, because you know how your mother feels about waiting," Nat said.

"Feels?" April said, lifting her head from a magazine, and Nat closed his eyes.

"Correction. How your mother *felt* about waiting." He laughed nervously. "Funny, isn't it? Even now sometimes I forget. She wouldn't wait in line for anything, your mother. Plus she was always getting in fights with waitresses, or sending things back, or complaining about the service. She'd say something was undercooked and then, when it came back, that it was overcooked. Sometimes I think pieces of meat got cold in the middle just in terror of her inspecting them." He laughed at his own joke—his children laughed too, out of respect—and then he smiled and pulled his hands behind his head. "You know, I just remembered something. Once we were in a restaurant, your mother and I, and she asked to have some kind of fish broiled instead of sautéed, and when the waiter said he wasn't sure the chef would do that—it wasn't a bad restaurant, it just was some sort of fish you're *supposed* to eat sautéed—she looked at him and she said, 'Young man, in

France there is a man who every several years goes to the very finest, the most expensive restaurants and orders a boiled egg. And if the restaurant is really fine, he is brought a boiled egg, and it is the most delicious boiled egg he's ever had. But if the restaurant is not fine, if the waiter harasses him, if the cook makes the egg badly, this man, who happens to represent France's most illustrious restaurant guide, takes away one of the restaurant's stars. Some of the finest chefs in France have killed themselves over a boiled egg.' Well, needless to say, I couldn't believe it. God knows where she heard that story. But there it was. So then the waiter disappears, and we're sitting there, Louise drumming her nails against the table because she's hungry, goddammit, and all of a sudden there's some sort of commotion at the front of the restaurant. Who should it be but the chef himself coming out of the kitchen in his big hat, holding a huge silver tray with a top on it that was big enough for a roast suckling pig. He starts marching very solemnly down the center of the restaurant, coming closer and closer, and I can tell your mother's getting nervous. The next thing we know, he's there, at our table. He puts this huge tray down in front of Louise—I swear, the thing takes up the whole table—and at this point your mother looks up at him, kind of scared, like maybe she's gotten in over her head. 'Madame,' he says, 'your dinner.' And very timidly, like she's afraid a snake's going to jump out, she lifts up the top."

"What's there?"

"I don't dare guess."

"You got it," Nat said. "One egg, boiled, in a silver eggcup." He laughed and clapped his hands together once. "At first she looked all upset, like she was about to cry. But then the chef started laughing, and patted her on the back, and the waiters laughed, and soon everyone in the restaurant was laughing and applauding, though none of them knew exactly why. And sure enough, they took away the tray and presented her with whatever fish it was she ordered—broiled." He was smiling broadly. "I always loved that story, but your mother, she made me promise I'd never tell it."

"Why?" April asked.

"She said it embarrassed her. You know how she was, she got embarrassed easily. In fact, as I recall, that evening she was so upset she couldn't even eat the fish."

"Speaking of fish, dinner's just about ready," Walter called from the deck, where he was grilling.

"Goody," April said. "I'm starved."

They sat down at the table, where Walter distributed the swordfish steaks, each striped with light crustings of charcoal. A familiar conversation ensued, one the family had had many times, only this time Walter played Louise's role.

"Is it moist enough? I hope I didn't dry it out."

"It's perfect."

"It's not undercooked, is it? Because if it is, I can put it back."

"No, it's perfect."

"Mine's perfect too."

"By the way, does anyone want some salad? There's salad."

Plates were handed out for salad. How comfortable they were already, how inured to this new configuration! It was as if subtle shifts had been made in the apparatus of the family that compensated for the vast throwing off, the lightening, which the loss of Louise had caused. A new balance settled, neither unpleasant nor strange; indeed, life without Louise altogether was turning out to be neither unpleasant nor strange, but rather pretty much what each of them expected. It was easier. No fights, no sudden refusals, no admonitions to clean up the kitchen, goddammit. They could go to restaurants and wait hours for a table now. They could do the crossword puzzle when Sunday came. None of which meant each of them wouldn't have given up almost anything to have her back, even for an instant, even for the space of a breath.

And of course, because it was a family dinner, April had a question. "You know, Daddy," she said, "I've been waiting for the right time to ask you something."

"Oh?"

"I've been waiting to ask you what the real story was about Mama's first marriage—you know, what she wouldn't let you tell us that Christmas."

"Is that all?" He laughed with relief. In the new order of things this once-dangerous question was almost quaint, it was to be welcomed, particularly considering the other things April could have brought up.

"Well, it's not really much of a story," Nat said. "A couple of summers before we got married, your mother went off to spend August in

Provincetown. She told us she was working as a maid at a hotel, but it turned out she was really working as a barmaid in a honky-tonk. So her father sends Uncle Sid and me up to rescue her, only when we arrive, it turns out she has no intention of being rescued. She was living in a room behind the bar, and at night she'd get woken up by the sound of the bouncer throwing drunks against the wall. She was having the time of her life. And as you all know, once your mother got her mind set on something, there was no way of talking her out of it. So she stuck out the summer, and then—for reasons that to this day elude me—she decided to do something very bizarre. She decided to enroll at the University of Alabama."

"The University of Alabama!" Danny and April said in unison.

"Now remember," Nat said, "this was 1943. If you were Louise Gold from Malden, Massachusetts, it simply wasn't an ordinary thing to enroll at the University of Alabama. But she was no ordinary girl, and I guess she thought maybe she could have some more adventures down there. Anyway, there was only one Jewish boy on the whole campus, one other Jew besides her, and he was this Orthodox fellow named Solomon Bloch. They met, and she married him, right there in Alabama. She must have been nineteen, twenty at the most. Apparently, as soon as she did it, she regretted it and ran back to Boston, and then the next thing we knew she was getting on the train to Reno for a divorce. That same train Norma Shearer takes in *The Women*, remember that movie, April?" April nodded. "And she stayed on one of those funny dude ranches for divorcing ladies, just like in the movie, for—six weeks, I guess it was—until she was free of Solly Bloch, at which point she came back to Boston and she and I started up again. We got married just a few months later, in a civil ceremony with no one but her parents and my parents and Eleanor and Sid.

"I thought that was the last of Solomon Bloch, until one afternoon, just before you were born, April, we were in Filene's basement, and suddenly Louise turned white and ran away to the ladies' room. Didn't say a word, just turned and ran. Naturally I was surprised. So I looked around to see what had upset her, and what should I see but a fellow in a black hat with a beard, going through this big bin of underwear. Now nature doesn't offer you opportunities like that every day, so I sort of sauntered by where he was standing. He was actually quite handsome, when I think about it. He had a wife—a pretty wife—and two little boys. When Louise finally came out of the ladies' room, I suggested we say hello, but she wouldn't hear of it. She said if we didn't leave right then, she'd throw up. It was that afternoon she made me swear never to tell anyone about it. She was very ashamed."

He looked down at his lap; for a few seconds all of them looked down at their laps.

"So what happened after you got married?" April asked. "Was that when she went to work as a welder?"

"Oh, I guess. The war was on. I was in the Navy and working on my degree, and she was working at the shipyard. She certainly was the prettiest one in the factory, so pretty that Ma—she was the fore-woman—Ma wanted Louisy to come work for her in a whorehouse she ran on the side."

"Ma," Danny said, and remembered his mother making a tuna fish sandwich for him to take to school. "That Ma," she had said, "she used to bring these wonderful sandwiches to work—meatballs and sausages in hot sauce—and I'd bring tuna fish. Well, Ma thought tuna sand-wiches were the most delicate, ladylike things in the world, and she wanted to trade. I think I got the best end of that deal."

"She told me about Ma," Danny said.

"Then," Nat said, "there was your mother's friend Lena."

"Lena?"

"Lena lived with her three children at the dump, and when she decided to get married, she came to your mother to ask her if she should wear white. People came to your mother a lot for advice in those days."

"What did she tell her?" April asked.

"Yes, I suppose," Nat said. "She was partial to the affirmative. You know, she didn't get paid as much as the men, which made her mad. But what could she do? A war was on." He took a swallow of coffee. "There were a lot of guys at that shipyard who really liked Louise. Jerry Stern, Mike Spivack. You know, we met Mike Spivack a long time later, in Mississippi, of all places, when I was doing a seminar down there. That was when your mother was asked to be one of the judges for the Miss Mississippi contest. She and Mike spent the whole weekend dancing and dancing. I had work to do, of course." The shadow of a faded, ancient anger passed over Nat's face. "After that, Mike ended up marrying one of the girls from the contest. Betty Ann, her name was. They're up in Chicago now." He shook his head. "Mike

Spivack," he said. "Oh, you were a wild one, Louise Gold! Boy, it was hard to catch you. It was just like those *Road Runner* cartoons, and she was the roadrunner, and I was that stupid coyote, and every time I'd have her, the next thing I'd know, she'd just slipped away. You know what they called that in my day? Moxie."

"Moxie," April said.

Outside, the sun had finally gone down, the crickets had started up in the trees. They were shrieking wildly. No one had noticed them; no one had even noticed the advent of dusk.

"Those crickets," Nat said. "Why, just yesterday, before I left, the damned robins were screaming in the pyracantha bush. Remember how the robins get drunk on pyracantha berries out in the yard, April? Louisy hated it, she used to go out in the yard and shake her fists at them and say, 'The drunks!' So now, when I hear the crickets, that's what I think of. The robins, and the pyracantha, and Louisy saying, 'The drunks!' You didn't know that, did you, Danny?"

He shook his head.

"You live with someone your whole life and you think you know them. But there are always secrets, aren't there? So many things you don't know about Louise, so many things Louise and I don't know about you. Things no one knows. Finally you're alone. That always used to frighten me, but I'll tell you kids, the older I get, knowing I'm alone is more and more a relief." He smiled. "Why, I remember that day Eleanor told me Louise had gone off to Alabama, I thought I'd go crazy. I loved her so much I thought I'd die from missing her. And now, looking at how things turned out, I can't help but laugh at how I behaved, thinking I couldn't make it without her. I used to call her the Ice Princess, because of a movie we saw together. And when she went off to Alabama, I called her there, I called her and said, 'Louisy, whenever you come back, I'll be waiting for you.' You know what her answer was? She said, 'Nat, don't wait for me because I'm never coming back.' Well, she came back, just like her mother predicted, with her tail between her legs, she came back so scared I wouldn't want her anymore, she was shaking when she asked me. But I did, and the next thing I knew, she was smothering me with kisses and telling me it was only me she'd ever loved, and would I forgive her, and life wasn't worth it without me. And we got married. And the thing was, it wasn't magic. It was just life. It was just our lives." He shook his head sadly. "Later, after you were born, Danny, things changed."

"How?" April asked.

"I don't know, quite. All I can tell you is, after Danny was born—well, nothing was ever good enough for Louise anymore. I mean, things go badly for everyone sometimes, and in a marriage each person is bound to do something sometimes that hurts the other or upsets the other person. But it seems to me at some point your mother just stopped seeing the good altogether; she started only seeing the bad, and pitying herself. She never wanted to go out for dinner or movies. It seemed like the slightest little thing could tick her off. You know, I have a friend who thinks that some people are just genetically more inclined to be optimistic, to look on the bright side. If I say so myself, I think I'm one of those people. But your mother—sometimes I think she was just born to be unhappy, no matter what the circumstances."

He looked at his plate, at the fish skin and char, the squeezed-out slice of lemon. April had already sucked the juice from her own slice, was gnawing away the zest.

"That's called blaming the victim," she said now, softly.

"What?"

"I said, that's called blaming the victim."

"Your mother was not always a victim, April," Nat said. "Believe me, there were plenty of times when she was decidedly not the victim. And later—well, frankly, it was a role she liked to play. It became a crutch for her, a way to avoid taking responsibility for her own behavior, for changing it. Anyway, I'm not blaming her for anything, I'm just explaining something about her—character."

"I love," April said, "the way you are suddenly such an expert on her character. It's like your saying it doesn't matter what the circumstances of her life were, it doesn't matter that you were trying to stay away from her as much as you could, or that she had cancer. No, Mom wasn't unhappy because of the circumstances of her life, she was unhappy because of some genetic tendency." She put her lemon slice down. "If you ask me, that's just an excuse to convince yourself you're not responsible so you don't have to feel guilty. I mean"—and here her tone softened—"I'm not saying there isn't any truth to what you're saying, I'm not saying she *wasn't* in certain ways—depressive. But the fact was,

things changed *between* you, not just *in* her. No one person is responsible. You two were fighting all the time."

"This really isn't the right time to talk about this, April—"

"When is the right time?"

"When we get home, I will be more than happy to make an appointment with Dr. Hirschman and the three of us can talk this thing out in
the proper environment. But in the meantime, I think it's time for me to
call it a night." He stood up, stretching his arms so that his shirt pulled
loose from his pants. "So if you all will excuse me—"

"You don't want some more coffee?" Danny said.

"No, thanks."

"Do you have enough towels?"

"Plenty."

"Okay, then. Good night."

"Good night."

"Good night."

Only April hadn't said good night. As Nat moved toward the bedroom, he stopped to hover over the place where she was sitting. Very
tentatively he placed his hand over her hair, as if he were thinking of
running his fingers through it; she pulled back; lifting his hand, he
patted her on the shoulder.

"April, honey," he said, "please believe me. I'm not trying to shirk off
responsibility for anything or anything like that, I'm just trying to tell
the story—the way it felt to me. I thought you wanted to know how it
felt to me. That's all."

"Good night," April said.

Nat sighed and coughed. "Good night." Then he went into the
hallway and closed the guest room door behind him.

They all got up. April immediately opened the patio doors, went
outside, and stood in the wind. "Guess I ought to do the dishes,"
Danny said, starting to collect plates, but Walter said, "Whoa, boy,
hold on. I'll do them tonight. You keep April company."

"Thanks, Walt," Danny said. He followed his sister out onto the
patio. The heavy moon had cast a roadway of light across the water.
Had their mother walked that roadway, out past the horizon, to the
place where hurricanes swell into being and are born?

April had her hands on the railing of the porch. When Danny put his
hands on her shoulders, her fingers curled more tightly around the

spokes. His presence was light as mosquitoes on her neck, his breath warm.

The ocean in all its furious glory reminded them both of nothing more than a sinkful of suds.

"Do you think she had a terrible life, our mother?" Danny asked.

April looked intently at the moon for a moment, as if she were mulling his question over, and then she said, "Yes."

AND YET Danny could not leave it at that—could not let April's grim summation, stated with such an air of resignation and finality, stand as the final fact, the last word on his mother's life. Even if he had set her up with his question, taking advantage of her fondness for the dramatic in order to assure it was she, not he, who said the words both of them had been thinking for days, for months, he could not let it stand. You shake a life out, you turn it over and see what falls to the ground. What do you find? A piece of cake with a flower and the letters LOUI written on it. A half-finished baby bootie. Two pillboxes—one blue with a pink top, one mirrored inside and laced with the words "Within you see what pleases me."

He sees his mother in her lacy pink bathrobe on a warm spring morning, sitting down at the little kitchen desk to pay a few bills. There is the pillbox, sitting just where it has sat for—how long? Twenty years? She picks it up. It is egg-colored, painted with tiny ribbons and flowers, as well as the famous inscription, which she reads again. And though she has done it a thousand times before, though of course it no longer holds any hope or surprise for her, she lifts off the top. Her face looks up at her, or part of her face, haggard, maybe fearful, and like a girl, she smiles, grateful to know that in that tiny stadium at least she will never not be loved.

PART THREE

IT IS A SUNNY, cool spring morning. Louise is sitting at the kitchen table in her best gray tweed suit and pearls, drinking a cup of coffee and inspecting the crossword puzzle she finished the night before. Periodically she looks up at the clock, hoping it will tell her the time has arrived when she can reasonably leave. To make the minutes go by faster, she has been trying to remember the other occasions in her life when she wore a formal suit: the afternoon she accompanied Eleanor to court, she supposes, and a few of those faculty wives' luncheons, and several of the early doctor visits, when she was called in to hear the bad news. She was scared of the doctors then, humbled; she felt she had to dress up for them. Those days have passed. Now when she goes, she wears jeans, loose sweaters, whatever she happens to have slipped over her neck. Today she has been dressed—dressed up—since seven.

When it is finally a reasonable time to leave, she gets up, goes out the door into the chilly midmorning, astonished, suddenly, by the colors of the world: the red of a hummingbird sitting on her feeder, the brilliant purple of the lilies Nat planted in neat rows. She gets into her car, heads out the driveway and into town. She has sprayed perfume on her neck and breasts, as if she were on her way to have an affair, which, in a sense, she supposes she is. On the radio, men with nasal voices describe traffic disasters that cannot touch her. She is driving down affluent tree-lined avenues where people are polite, looking for a street name she double-checked on the map the night before. It finds her easily, she turns a corner, and then, just a few minutes early, she is there. It is a surprisingly modern building, low, the color of soap. A long corridor lined with spade-shaped windows connects the church with a solid, houselike building she supposes must be the rectory. Alongside it stretches a neatly pared lawn.

She gets out of her car. The doors to the building are heavy and dark, but they glide open easily when she presses her hands against them. Inside, a woman at a desk looks up at her. She says who she is and is told to sit down. She waits in a dark, cool antechamber, twisting her gloves in her hands, and then the woman at the desk appears and informs her that Father Abernathy is indeed expecting her and is ready to see her. She stands, her chest suddenly heaving with anxiety, and follows the woman into an uncluttered office.

Father Abernathy is a man in his sixties, slightly paunchy, with white hair. When he stands to shake her hand, she notices that his skin, like hers, is mottled with pale pink blotches.

"Won't you sit down," he says.

"Thank you," she says. She sits down.

"So, Mrs. Cooper, what can I do for you?"

She is quiet for a moment, and then she says, "Father, I wish to convert. I wish to become a Catholic."

He drums his fingers against his desk. "What is your present religious situation?" he asks.

"I'm Jewish by birth," she says. "Really, I'm nothing. I've never practiced."

"And what is it about the Catholic faith that has drawn you?"

She looks at the floor. "It's strong," she says. "I need something strong."

"Is there a particular reason you're thinking you'd like to convert right now?"

She closes her eyes and says, "My husband is in love with another woman. I have cancer of the lymphatic system."

Father Abernathy's eyebrows just barely twitch. He is used, she knows, to the safe distance of the confessional.

"So you feel," he says, "that the Church can offer you solace."

"I feel the Church offers many things to those who have to be alone," she says. She looks away from him, out the window at the vast lawn and her car beyond it. She feels, suddenly, impatient, longs to taste the host, to feel its subtle pressure on her palate, like a tongue depressor. She leans forward in her chair.

"Mrs. Cooper," Father Abernathy says, taking off his glasses, "think about this for a while. If you're going to join our church, you have to really want to. You are wounded, and Christ heals our wounds, but that in and of itself isn't reason enough to do something as drastic as change one's faith." He leans closer across the desk. "Have you thought about counseling?"

Her eyes open wide, and she sits back.

"Yes," she says. "I have. I have thought about it."

He takes a piece of paper and a pencil from a drawer inside his desk. "I'm writing down for you the name of a friend of mine at Family Therapy Resources, on Claremont Avenue. Go and talk to her. Also, perhaps, talk to the rabbi at your synagogue, if you have one. Then, after that, if you still feel the Church is what you seek, come back and we'll talk some more."

He hands her the slip of paper. She stands. "Thank you, Father," she says, slipping it into her purse and reaching for his hand. "Thank you." Tears bud in her eyes. Perhaps he cannot understand, will never understand what she is feeling right now, perhaps no one ever will, and yet it won't matter, because she does. She understands. Failure, yes. Embarrassment, yes. And pride. The things she has so rarely spoken of seem to fly about the room now; they are out of her; they can't hurt her. She will visit the counselor or not; she will come back to Father Abernathy or not. It doesn't matter. She decides. She, and no one else.

"It was like pulling thorns," she says.

"Excuse me?" Father Abernathy says.

"I just meant—at first I was so embarrassed. I felt like I'd wasted your time and made a fool of myself. But I realize now you've helped me more than you can know. Thank you."

He blushes. "That's what I'm here for," he says. "Listen, let me walk you to your car." And taking her arm, he leads her out of the dark rectory, out onto the sidewalk. The sun is high and glorious, and she has to shield her eyes with her hands.

Through the car window Father Abernathy says, "God does hear us. Things will be okay."

"Thank you," Louise says.

Then he steps back, and she turns the key in the ignition and heads out onto the street. From the sidewalk, in his black suit, he waves. Why didn't she realize it was so simple? Faith, that cheap radio, that wire creeping into the ear. Already she owns everything she needs. She waves back, pulling away from the green lawn and into that most glorious of skies, her sense of harmony nagged only by the itching starting up again under her clothes.

This was in late March, a week before she went into the hospital. She never told anyone except Clara.

ABOUT THE AUTHOR

DAVID LEAVITT is the author of a collection of stories, *Family Dancing*, and a novel, *The Lost Language of Cranes*. His fiction and articles have appeared in *The New Yorker*, *The New York Times Book Review*, *Harper's*, and *Esquire*, among other journals.

Mr. Leavitt grew up in Northern California and was graduated from Yale University. He lives in East Hampton, New York.